Entwined
With The
Dead

To my dad who wanted to read my book and
insisted he was an adult and could handle a spicy monster romance
and then came back with the comment—

"If he is undead, how does he get an erection?"

Thank you. I am now scarred for life.

HECTOR'S JOURNAL

March 3rd, 2037

It's been a few days since the explosion in the genetic splicing research lab.

I couldn't stop them. The other scientists mutated into monsters just as I have. They seemed to be cognitively intact, but this mutation seems to have brought out their strongest desires. Doctor Liatris has bitten several of the survivors and has moved on to the surrounding villages outside of Chernobyl.

I have a hypothesis that we have mutated to have a poison gland that allows the transmission of this mutation.

I have noticed the ones he attacked and turned are not like him. Suspect this mutation is acting like a virus.

Victoria seems to have some heightened sexual desire. Her mutations are milder, and she is targeting attractive young men to turn.

I am starving, yet I have no desire to hurt anyone. Why?

Chapter 1

Lisa put her hand on Hector's shoulder.

He jolted and spun on his metal stool. Small vials of pink liquid rattled. His elongated fingers swung towards her, before realization set in. What started as a feral attack ended in him putting his large hand on her shoulder and letting out a long breath.

"You startled me."

"No surprise. You were concentrating hard." Lisa didn't even flinch, as she was completely confident that he would never hurt her, despite what he was.

Hector was a First Turned, also called a Lord, and was one of the scientists of the Chernobyl lab that started the apocalypse that ended the world. Ever since she met him, he had been solely focused on finding some sort of cure.

Their RV had been stripped and rebuilt, something she had done three years ago, a short time after he rescued her. Solar panels on the roof charged a battery bank that powered the small computer and lab equipment in front of Hector. She'd torn out the dining area that was built into the slider to make a lab space.

Both front seats reclined and could be used as beds, there was a couch right behind them, and they tore out the queen bed in back and built bunk beds. It was far from the normal life she once had in Colorado, but it was much more luxurious than what many had.

The carpet in the RV was badly stained with blood when they found it. Over time Lisa had acquired carpet tiles and, although patchwork in appearance, recarpeted the whole vehicle. There were no more TV channels, digital streaming, or radio, but they did have a small TV and a game system that still worked.

The whole place smelled like the linen scented spray that Bruno found at the gas station they raided recently for supplies. It was intense for the first few days, but now the smell reminded her of home.

Lisa had grown up in Colorado and worked in interior construction, specifically for new builds. She had inherited a home in the mountains when her father passed away, where she had lived on the weekends when she wasn't renting at cheap hotels through the workweek.

She was lucky enough to be in the mountains when the horde hit Denver. The attempt to keep them out with a blockade failed quickly.

When Hector found her, she'd already survived seven years alone in the mountains. It took five years for the horde to hit the US. The Denver blockade held them off another three years. Then it was all over.

Her father, before he passed, loved to hunt big game, and she often went with him. She did well physically at the cabin, fending for herself, but mentally the loneliness and thoughts of being the last person alive almost killed her.

Lisa reached for Hector's shoulder again. He had half stood up, but still dwarfed her. Mutations were evident across his body from his ashen gray skin and noseless face to his elongated fingers and backwards knees. He was a visage of nightmares, and yet the kindest person she knew, with endless depths of guilt and sadness.

"Get some rest," she said. "It's been quiet for the last three nights and there's been no sign of Servants in this area."

Servants were the second turned. For some reason photosensitivity was a developed trait that worsened as these creatures mutated. That typically only left the Lords and Servants out in the daylight. The rest would hide somewhere out of the sun. It made the light of day their only solace.

Hector rubbed both hands over his face. "Maybe I do need a little rest."

Mariah came up from the back bunks and crossed her arms. She had her blonde hair pulled back today and wore a stained white apron that accentuated her larger upper curvature. "You both need some rest. Night shift is over."

Lisa smiled. Night was over, but she had some projects she wanted to get done. She ran the night shift with Hector and Flint, while Mariah, Bruno, and Spot ran the day shift. Looking around the RV she didn't see Spot or Bruno. Flint was at the wheel.

"Where are the others?" Lisa asked.

Mariah pointed a thumb over her shoulder back at the bunks. "Still sleeping. I'll wake them up in a minute." She raised a hand to her mouth and yelled up front. "You good for a little bit longer while I make breakfast?"

"Sure thing, Mama M. I'll stay up the rest of my life for your cooking."

"That settles it. Hector, go take a rest dear and stop worrying so much. Lisa, if you want to stay up a speck longer, I'll have breakfast made."

Lisa smiled. "Sounds good. I'm going to work on a couple of things around the RV."

Hector looked over to Lisa. He wore a brimmed hat and goggles, so his features were hard to make out, but he still appeared sad.

Lisa's heart melted. She grabbed his hand and pulled him back towards the bunks. In the tight space, she had to slip sideways to get past Mariah.

"What are you doing?" asked Hector. He stuttered slightly revealing a mix of what sounded to be confusion and apprehension.

"Making sure you get to sleep."

"You don't have to do this."

"Like it or not, it's happening." She pulled him into the cramped back room with thin bunk beds on either side and just enough room to squeeze between. Lisa stood on her tip toes and snatched his hat from him.

"Don't—"

She cut him off. They'd done the same song and dance before, and she knew where he was going. "You saved me, now let me help by taking care of you." She slipped a finger under the strap of his goggles and pulled them off. The gaze of his almost solid black eyes instantly went to the floor.

She placed a hand on his cheek and tried to encourage his gaze back to hers. "You know I don't care how you look."

A slight smile pulled at his thin lips as he nodded.

"Now, let's get you tucked in." She motioned to the top bunk.

Hector was too tall and lanky to stretch out, but he was able to curl up. Lisa grabbed a blanket and pulled it over him. Pausing a moment, she glanced behind her. Bruno was still passed out on the bottom bunk with Spot sound asleep on his chest. Smiling, Lisa reached under the pillow of the top bunk above Hector and pulled out a small teddy bear.

"I know you might think you're all too old and too busy, but I picked this up a couple towns back for you."

Hector eyed the small brown furry thing for a moment.

"It's just something to cuddle with so you never feel alone." Uttering those words made her own chest ache, but she hid her reaction from him.

His shoulders relaxed and he seemed to melt into the bed. He took the bear, pinching it between two long fingers, and then he tucked it close to his chest. "I don't understand why you care so much about me."

"Because you're a good man." She emphasized man. Even though he had mutated into what he is now, his mind and heart remained the same. He wanted nothing more than to reverse or cure the mutating infection that he didn't even cause. She had a feeling he'd never be able to do it, but she'd never discourage him. It seemed finding this cure was all he lived for. "Rest well," she whispered.

Turning in the tight space, she kicked Bruno's bunk. "Hey, wake up."

Bruno sat up, throwing Spot from his chest. "Zombies are coming!"

"No, they're not. It's breakfast you nut."

He threw his blanket back and somehow popped up from bed in the tiny space between Lisa and the back wall. "Most important meal of the day," he shouted, raising a finger.

Spot nudged her legs, awkwardly trying to move past. She shooed the mutant dog out into the open room. Hector found Spot several years ago. It wasn't common to find an animal that had been turned since, according to Hector, the virus didn't spread to animals well. He had done some testing to see if he could turn Spot back to a normal dog. Results? She suspected the dog was stupid to start with.

She'd watched that dog try to understand what his tail was for a whole day, before he lost half his tail and an ear to a zombie. On top of that, the creature seemed to now be immortal and immune to being turned or infected by others.

Spot and Bruno had a close relationship. Something akin to a lonely boy and his dog kind of thing. Everyone here had their ways of dealing. This was better than what Bruno used to do to deal.

Bruno rummaged for something in his bunk, turned, locked wide eyes on her and yelped.

Lisa grabbed him by his green poncho and yanked him from the bunk room. "Shut up. Hector is trying to sleep."

"I'm sorry," he whispered. "You startled me."

Lisa rolled her eyes. The space was crammed with Bruno in front of the bunk area. She was standing blocking the bathroom door. Spot was prancing along the floor, crashing his chonky back end into the cupboards. Then there was Mariah, trying to prepare breakfast and getting very crammed.

6

"Okay, everyone, out of the way," said Lisa, waving her hands.

Mariah pushed herself against the counter where she was prepping some veggies at the sink. Spot bounded to the front of the RV. Lisa moved aside into Hector's lab space, which made enough room for Bruno to move up front.

There were two seats in the cab. Flint was driving, so Bruno took the passenger seat, reclined it a few inches, and let out a long sigh. They were moving slow, maybe thirty to forty miles per hour. It was the safest pace as abandoned cars and bodies still littered the roads.

"Hey, we got a car cluster up here," Flint yelled back to them.

"I'm coming," Hector's muffled voice came from the back.

Lisa pushed back past Mariah to the bunk room. "Oh no you don't." She caught Hector half out of bed. "You need rest and that's not up for debate."

"It's dangerous out there."

She crouched down and grabbed his shoulder. She knew he had incredible strength, but his bony figure made him seem frailer than he was. "It always is. Let us take care of this. There hasn't been anything of concern in days out there. I doubt it will start now."

He let out a long breath, his face tilted towards the RV floor. "I suppose."

She gave him a gentle push back into bed, which he didn't fight.

With weighted emotions she left him to join the others. Flint had stopped the RV and was now twisted in his seat, his gaze on her.

"We ready to sail, Mistress?"

"Don't call me that," Lisa snapped. She slid past Mariah again with Spot hopping at her feet. Bruno seemed to be asleep, so she kicked the back of his seat.

Bruno snorted. "Huh. What?"

Flint slapped Bruno's knee. "Wake up man. We got some scavenging to do." He hopped from his seat, strapping a machete to his hip as he moved.

Bruno stumbled after him. They piled behind Lisa at the door. She had remade the RV door to be heavier, reinforced, and open towards the front of the bus. She undid the heavy latch and the door creaked open.

The beaming sunlight of midday washed in.

Bruno raised his hands to his face. "Oh! It's so bright. Do we have to?"

Flint slapped a hand at him again, just missing as Bruno swayed back. "Where's your sense of adventure? It's been ages since I got a little action."

"Hey!" Lisa snapped. "Don't even think that way. Action is the last thing we need." Just as she went to step out, Spot bolted and knocked his bulky bulldog body into her knee. She grabbed at the doorframe to keep standing and had almost regained her balance when Flint shoved his way through.

Lisa gritted her teeth. They all handled this world differently. Mariah cooked, Bruno slept, and Flint looked for trouble. Always trouble. As she cast a glance at Bruno, he shrugged.

Leaving Mariah to cook and Hector to sleep, the rest of them left the RV. They were on a two-lane highway in the middle of long neglected fields that had been overgrown with small trees and grass almost as tall as she was.

A cold shiver traveled down her spine. It would be easy for something to sneak up on them, but not very likely with the sun being so bright. Anything out there at dawn would have been scrambling for darkness, which was scarce..

The road was blocked by two small cars rearended together, a truck with its nose in the ditch, and a white cargo van on its side. The had solid metal panels in the back making it a probable zombie hiding spot and would also be difficult to navigate around.

Spot had run over to the grass to poop. For an undead animal, he still pooped a lot. Mostly in shoes. Flint was ransacking the nearest car like a child would rummage through a school bag. Trash and other bobbles were flying out the side door. Flint was at least good at finding supplies.

Groaning, Lisa grabbed the ladder next to the door. Another addition she had installed which made for easy access to the cargo roof. The space on top of the RV was lined with metal bars. The back half housed the solar panels and batteries. The middle was a large stash of gas cans and a small wooden crate strapped down which held tubes for syphoning gas. The front of the roof was extended into a defensive platform in case they were in a bind. It had a good view of three sides. The back was the least of their worries with the idea being they'd need to plow forward fast to leave anything dangerous behind in the dust. It most often was beneficial when ballsy scrappers came by and tried to loot the RV. They were usually well-armed, but got a quick change of toon anytime Hector had become involved. Something about seeing a zombie Lord was a little terrifying to them.

Lisa climbed up top. The bars of the ladder were warm from the sun. This open space also lent itself to a fresh breeze that smelled of grass and earth. She'd become so accustomed to the smell of death that this refreshing change made her coiled muscles release. She grabbed an empty gas can and syphoning gear, then climbed back down.

Bruno was now by Flint who was handing him piles and piles of stuff. He looked uncertain of what to do as he tried balancing the armfuls. Bruno had a hard past before the zombies, and fought with detoxing after they found him.

Spot was next to them, chewing on a tire. *Stupid dog.* She grinned. The trio drove her crazy, mostly Flint and Spot, but it was a small price to pay to no longer be alone. Her gaze drifted over towards the van. They were making a lot of noise. If something was in there it wouldn't be long before it knew they were there.

She detoured back inside the RV for a moment and grabbed her pistol which she kept tucked under the driver's seat. Strapping it to her belt she made her way over to the cars. The rearended pair both had empty tanks. Her head fell forward a moment. Gas was most often the thing that would drive them into the cities where the bulk of the zombie population rested, and she wanted to avoid that as much as possible.

"Trash, trash, trash!" said Flint, sliding out of the cab of the truck.

"Does it look like scrappers have been through here?" she asked.

Bruno teetered, trying to balance the various sized parts in his arms without dropping them or falling. "I don't think so. There's a lot of good stuff here." He stumbled again. Bruno was a little clumsy and a bit on the unsteady side.

Lisa made her way to the truck in the ditch. It looked more abandoned than crashed like the others. There wasn't much, but she was able to syphon about a gallon from the gas tank. It was old gas, and she had no idea how much moisture was in it. Another problem they often ran into. They'd had more engine trouble from that in the past than she could count.

Stepping back on the road Lisa heard a loud clank. Both Flint and Bruno had stopped dead, giving hint it wasn't either of them. Spot ran to her feet and crouched, bearing his sharp snaggle teeth. Lisa remained calm despite feeling her heart rate begin to climb.

Lisa slowly set the gas down and nodded her head towards the van while making eye contact with Flint.

He nodded and a wide grin spread across his face.

Lisa's back reflexively tightened again, irritating her muscles. Her hand lowered to her pistol. Firing her weapon would be a last-ditch option as the sound would bring out anything nearby, both zombies and scrappers.

In one smooth motion, Flint pulled his machete from the sheath and slinked closer to the van. Another loud bang of metal made all three of them jump.

Bruno, with his arms full, ran to Lisa's side. "Should I get Hector?"

Lisa picked up the gas can and handed it to him, which he took with one free finger. The weight made him sway and the scraps in his arms clattered. "Not yet. Get the stuff back to the RV, close the door, and be prepared to drive."

Bruno nodded and scurried away.

Spot started to creep closer, following Flint. In the pile of trash they had pulled from the car Lisa spotted a tire iron. She snatched it from the ground, keeping one hand on her gun. The tire iron would make less noise, but she still wanted the safety of a bullet if needed.

Flint moved to the back side of the van with Spot now at his feet. He still had a wide grin on his face like he was enjoying the hunt.

You get anyone hurt and I'll strangle you. Lisa clenched her jaw. This was life or death. Every time. No in-betweens. No time for reckless fun.

Flint tapped his machete on the van. A loud thunder of thumps and fast movements came from inside. No doubt there was some sort of zombie in there. It sounded like a rabid animal frantically scraping and attacking the inside. *No wonder cars are abandoned here.*

The scraping sounds moved towards the back, then came a thump hitting the back doors, and then the sounds moved forward again. A disfigured creature burst out of the driver's window. Shattered glass rained like sharp glitter. The zombie had blackened skin and screeched as it hit the sun. Two pairs of hands grabbed the windshield frame and the beast propelled itself up aa good ten feet.

Flint back-peddled fast. Lisa planted her feet and raised the tire iron, still unwilling to use her pistol just yet.

As the thing hit the ground Spot charged, going for what appeared to be a thick neck below a spherical head with pointed leathery ears, but no eyes or nose.

Spot ruthlessly sunk his teeth into blackened flesh and the thing shrieked again. Flint bolted, sweeping in and taking a slash at an arm. The blade hacked into its flesh, but didn't carve completely through.

Flint pulled back, moving with the agility of an MMA fighter.

Lisa bolted in to flank the beast. There seemed to be only one and from the mutations it was at least a fourth turned or later. They were mindless beasts driven by hunger. As Spot hung on, clamping his jaws down on the creature's throat, she swung her tire iron at the thing's stomach. The metal iron connected with its bloody marred body and something inside snapped.

The creature now seemed truly panicked and started slashing at Spot with all four arms. When one clawed hand sunk into Spot's rear haunch he let go with a loud yip. Flint had gotten behind the creature and made two quick swipes with his machete. One at the thing's leg, again sinking his blade down to bone, and the other at its neck. The zombie moved enough that the second swing only grazed its shoulder.

In a frenzied backlash the thing swung, cracking Flint in the chest. He flew back, hitting the van with enough force to dent metal. He slumped to the ground. Lisa backpedaled as fast as she could, grabbing for her pistol. She didn't have any other choice. The later turned were highly infectious. Just one bite could pass on this virus. Spot lunged for the thing's leg, slowing it slightly. Lisa used the time to draw and aim.

Just before she pulled the trigger a loud voice behind her boomed. "Enough!"

Lisa felt the commanding voice ripple through her body and her legs went weak.

The creature froze motionless. Hector came bounding across the concrete with his long animal-like legs taking huge strides. He passed her in a blur and swung a clawed hand at the thing's head, cleaving it from its body.

The zombie's body fell to the ground and twitched a few times before going still. The head bounced off and landed in the grass somewhere out of sight.

With the rush of adrenaline leaving, Lisa fell to her knees, sucking in air. The tire iron clattered to the ground as she fell, making a metallic clunk. Sweat dripped from her face. This was just a simple scrapping. This shouldn't have gone like this.

Hector ran back towards the RV holding his blood covered hand out in front of him. She knew he must be concerned about decontamination. Spreading through blood contact was rare, Hector had once explained, because the virus was transmitted mostly through something that resembled a venom gland in the mouth. But you still couldn't be too careful.

Hector's blood was not infectious, and she'd never seen him bite anyone. The First Turned possessed a non-autonomous poison gland and they actually had to choose to infect someone. Something like a rattlesnake she imagined. But not these abominations. As each wave turned another, the virus repeatedly mutated until some creatures, after being turned, would simply become lumps of hungry flesh that crawled along the ground like slugs.

She knew better. She should have gotten Hector from the start. But he was so tired and had been working without sleep for days. He needed a strong team. He couldn't be expected to protect them every moment.

As these thoughts raced through her head, she saw a flash of movement as Hector burst past her to Flint. She heard him sniff and instantly feared the worst Somehow being a Zombie Lord gave Hector the ability to smell if someone was infected. It wasn't the first time he knew someone had contracted the zombie virus before they even knew.

It was horrible, seeing the life drain from someone's face when they found out they would soon become some kind of zombie monster. She'd seen it before. Seen them change. It was painful as the cells rapidly mutated, often devolving instantly. Bones would snap. Internal organs would burst until they would bleed from every orifice.

Every muscle in Lisa's body tensed. If Flint was infected, they would have to leave him, or worse, kill him. She didn't want that. She didn't want to lose another friend. She didn't want Hector to hold that burden. She pressed her eyes shut and held her breath. She couldn't handle what came next. It was too much. All too much.

It seemed like forever she remained like that without a sound around her except for the grass moving in the breeze. The smell of decay had come back, fouling the air that had, for a moment, given her the sense of peace.

Something touched her arm. She screamed and jerked back, reaching for her pistol. Spots from tears dotted her vision, but she made out Hector's large frame before she drew. She expected he'd be mad, furious. Part of her thought he'd be covered in blood where he had to eliminate an infected Flint.

Instead, he crouched in front of her. His hat shaded his face from the sun. He'd grabbed that, but didn't have his goggles, so she could see his eyes. They were dark, almost like a void. Crouched down, it made the back of his poncho bulge where his wings were well tucked and hidden. He made himself always look as human as possible, stating it was so he didn't scare the others as much. But he didn't and never would scare her.

"I'm... I'm sorry," Lisa muttered.

"Are you alright?" he asked in a smooth gentle tone.

She nodded, ashamed that things went this wrong. "Flint... is he..."

"Unconscious, Mariah suspects a slight concussion. I'll help Mariah tend to him more in a moment... but he is not infected. He should be fine in a day or two."

Lisa let out a breath that turned into several gasps. With his backwards knees Hector was easily able to walk in an unnatural crouched position and moved closer to her. He wrapped his thin arms around her and pulled her close.

She sniffed, catching the scent that could only be described as science equipment, spice, and oldness. Like a nursing home science lab covered up with cheap cologne. She knew he only used the cologne so he didn't smell like other zombies. He was always looking after them, but never himself, and every time she tried to help him it seemed to backfire.

"You need sleep too, you know," he whispered.

She wanted to cry more but fought it. Maybe that was it. Maybe she was just tired and making bad judgments.

He helped her up, lifting her weight with such ease it made her feel like a feather in his arms. He guided her back to the RV where Mariah was crouched by the front seats bandaging Spot's wound.

"He will heal on his own," said Hector.

"Oh, I know, dear, but this makes me feel useful." She stood and gave them both a big smile. "I'm glad you're all okay. Lunch is a little cold, but it's all ready."

Lisa noticed the gas can and Flint's parts stacked between the front seats. Bruno swung around from the driver's seat. He looked nervous, but still mustered a half smile. "I'm glad you're okay too."

"I'm fine," she replied, trying to muster the same attitude the others were putting on. "Flint in the back?"

Mariah nodded. "He'll be fine. The boy has a hard head."

"Well, that's true. Let me get the gas and parts to the roof, then I'll eat."

Hector grabbed her arm. "No, you don't. I'll take them when I go out. That van will need to be moved if we are going to get by."

Even knowing his strength, things like that still shocked her. That one man... creature, could be that strong. It made her feel even less a person than before. More of a burden.

"I'm going to take care of you first." He placed his large hand in the center of her back and escorted her through the RV to the back bunks.

Flint lay in the bed on the bottom right. Other than a little pale, he looked like he was just sleeping. Knowing she could have prevented it if she just had Bruno get Hector made her muscles coil again. The persistent back pain she'd delt with for the last few years reared up until her leg tingled.

Hector reached for the blanket Flint used as a privacy curtain and pulled it down. They each had one which she installed to make their beds a touch more private. He guided her to his bunk, had her sit down, and then handed her a bowl of food she didn't even notice he had picked up. It was some pre-packaged noodles, some spices, and what looked to be chicken. They had found some a while back when raiding an empty farmhouse. Mariah always did push for balanced food to keep them as healthy as possible.

"Thank you," she said, taking the bowl.

"I want you to go to sleep after this. I'll be fine for another day."

"You haven't slept in so long, Hector. You need rest too."

He smiled as he reached for his goggles hanging on the hook at the head of his bunk. "Remember, I'm not human anymore. I can easily go many days without sleep."

"You've already had many days. You can't keep pushing yourself like this."

His shoulders fell. After standing in silence for a minute he crouched down before her. "I don't know why you care so much about a creature like me, but do not worry so much." He got up and left.

Lisa picked at her food. After everything that happened, she didn't have much of an appetite.

HECTOR'S JOURNAL

March 8th, 2037

I have noticed connected mutations. Doctor Liatris's most notable mutation is his extra set of arms. In almost, what I estimate to be, ninety eight percent of those he has turned has developed this mutation. I have yet to find a way to stop it.

Doctor Liatris, along with the others, seems to have no desire in stopping this.

Victoria has mutated to have cranial horns which seems to be a consistent mutation to the men she has turned.

The Janitor, who's name I believe was Mark, unknown last name, has joined forces with Doctor Liatris. They have personally told me their plans to right the political and justice system and have warned me not to interfere. Mark's most distinctive feature seems to be a dislocating mandible. Possible mutation from snake DNA.

Elric, another scientist from the lab, has joined him as well. Noted wolf-like ear mutation.

Difference in virus mutation has been noticed as well. Those infected by those of us first mutated appear to have higher mental processing ability than others. Note: First Turned and Second Turned.

Those infected by the second Turned are more animal like, but still obey a hierarchy. Why?

Note: those turned by others seem to respond to my commands. Hierarchy seems to be based on mutation level.

Chapter 2

Emily wiped her eyes as she awoke to the first rays of sun making their way over the wall. She'd overslept. Jolting up out of bed allowed the cold chill of late spring air to nip at her skin. Her hovel afforded no protection from the elements.

Her space was about seven foot wide by ten foot deep made from scavenged scrap. The walls were partially made from pallets, with one car door as a window, and a tarp over top. The floor was dirt with a few wood planks and cardboard thrown layered on top. Her bed was two pieces of large foam stacked on top of each other and large comforter to keep her warm. Her neighbor, Jim, had helped her procure these things when she first got here.

There was a shelf made from stacked bricks with a board on top which held a few candles. Under it she had a wooden crate and plastic lunch box. The crate held a few of her personal things and the lunch box was where she stored food.

Scrubbing a hand over her face she cursed this existence. "Why? Why did this happen? What did I do to deserve this?" She mumbled to herself, something that had become part of her daily mantra. She was in Chicago when the zombies hit. That's what a lot of people called them, although many people still holding higher authority called them The Turned. Didn't matter. It was the same thing.

They ate their way down the streets to the building where she worked. She ran requisitions for a corporate office back then. She thought she was physically fit and often biked to work. Turns out she was wrong about a lot of things. That was ten years ago. Two of those years she lived in that building, the stairs had been blocked off at the first floor and barricaded. The third floor had a small cafeteria that they scavenged food from.

One by one her coworkers fell. Some to the zombies, some to suicide, and some in fights with the others. Eventually, all that was left was her. Scrappers found her. They were the few people brave enough to venture into the cities for supplies they could sell at a high price.

She had to earn her worth with them, so she became a fighter.

Machete strapped to her hip and pistol in her hand, she became a scrapper. Slowly, she watched them die as well.

Emily strapped on the same machete that Marco, the head of the scrappers back then, had given her. It was a reminder anyone could turn, just like many who followed him did. She also gathered her bag and the small handmade pouch crafted from some old jeans that held her government credits. It was most likely ten in the morning when she ventured out of her hut.

The Outer Rim of Haven was where they put refugees with little value. All together scraping for food and shelter. Almost as good as dead. With the wall so close it took a while for the sun to crest it, like a concrete mountain.

As she shielded her eyes a familiar voice called to her.

"Hey, Emily, you're up late."

She turned to her neighbor Jim, who lived to her left. He was in his mid-forties, had the eyes of a man older, but a gentle and sweet smile. He was medium build and all muscle. Jim was the blacksmith and repair man of the Outer Rim.

His house, an 80's Winnebago, sat behind him. In front he had a few posts and two tarps to make a canopy where he could work. He'd made his own forge, and, according to him, spent a few years working to pay off the anvil some scrappers got him. Jim really was close to being the rich person of the squalor, and he was nice to her.

She smiled and waved back. "Didn't mean to. I'm guessing you were up early as always."

He shrugged and then tried taming a wild lock of hair by sweeping it back with a dirty hand. His hair was dark, and his eyes were a deep brown, but bright. They always seemed to shine with hope and happiness. Something she had lost a long time ago.

"Do you need me to get you anything from the market?" she asked.

"No, no. I'm all stocked up. You go, but be careful."

She rolled her eyes. "You ain't my father." It caught her off guard, as it sometimes did, just to hear the scrapper slang roll off her tongue. So much had changed in ten years.

Emily moved through dirt streets of this residential section of the Outer Rim. People used cardboard and newspaper to help make a path and try to prevent it from becoming nothing more than puddles of mud. Homes were all scrapped together of various sizes and shapes. All were butted up against each other. No one really owned land. Instead, it was an honor system. Or more a, break this frail system and you'll be broken, kind of thing.

It took her months to adjust to the smell. Clean water was a luxury and most often it took a good rain before anyone would bathe anymore. The stench had only worsened over time.

A few homes had planters with small crops as they desperately attempted to grow some food. There was never enough of that. The city existed in sections. The Capitol was most favored with the highest-ranking officials and the last of the government remaining there. Next was the Median where the electrical plants, both the hydroelectric dam and wind turbines and the farmland were. Since food was scare, farmland was well protected. Go all the way down the list and you reach the Outer Rim. Useless people were left here.

Emily passed Yanika's house. It was nice, with some wood walls and carpet inside. Yanika raised chickens and did it so well she had gained recognition in this area. Yanika had hopes that she would be recognized by the Capitol and get to move to the Median. A pipe dream if you asked Emily.

Frowning, she trudged on up the path until the street opened into a huge market. Looming in front of it was the south gate. It was a ginormous metal structure set in the concrete walls. It also was deep, acting like a meurtrière. Anything moving in or out had to pass through two doors. If there are any concerns of infection, those passing through were trapped between the doors and incinerated. The south gate was where the majority of the scrappers came through as the guards here were well paid off.

The market consisted of a mix of low-end scrappers, large shops that got supplies from scrappers, and a few carts of crafts from people trying to make their own way. Among these ramshackle huts and stores, the Haven Outlet stood out. It was a metal building with barred windows and turrets to boot. It was to keep it from getting robbed.

The dollar no longer had value and paper was just paper. Here, trade was king and the government credits it's queen. The government credits were, on the surface, all that the Haven Outlet took for currency, but they made exceptions. Everyone had a price.

Emily headed to the Outlet first. Eric, a lean tall man in the traditional gray government uniform, stood behind the desk. Two others she didn't recognize stood around the room with machine guns slung over their shoulders.

Eric gave her a sly smile and raised his arms as if he was expecting a hug. "Emily, it's good to see you again."

She raised a brow. "What's got you so friendly today?"

"Oh, just the usual." His grin widened.

Emily lifted her head as realization set in. *He got paid something good today.* She nodded and changed the subject. "I need some food."

"Well, you've come to the right place, because boy do I have a snack for you." He leaned over a metal edged glass display and rested his chin on his hand.

"Ugh. I'm using credits. I know there's only trash for that." She crossed her arms. It was frustrating because Eric seemed like the kind of guy who would be pretty chill if he wasn't working for the government. He had short-cut ashy blond hair and bright blue eyes which gave him his boyish charm.

He stepped back and shrugged. "Well," he began as he spread out his hand like a waiter holding a tray, "the spring crops for Haven have been good. We have freeze dried spinach, freeze dried peas, and we still have a few packages of dried cowtail."

She gagged but tried to hide it. *Just like the government to keep all the good stuff for themselves. Bastards.* It was commonplace. The Outer Rim wasn't needed. They thought by selling the food no one else wanted they were being charitable.

"How much for the peas?"

"Ten credits."

"That's robbery!" Emily stomped her foot onto the riveted metal floor.

Eric shrugged. "That's the going price. Winter was hard on us, and food is limited."

Didn't she know it. If it wasn't for Jim she would have starved. The thought of him brought a slight smile to her lips. He was an oaf, but a sweet oaf. She had to eat, and she had the credits, although it wouldn't leave much left. "Fine," she groaned. "I'll take a bag."

Eric pulled a small silver package from the shelf behind him. It was about six inches wide and nine inches long, weighing less than a pound. It would be more filling in a soup, but that meant she'd need extra clean water.

She took ten credits from her little pouch. The things looked like USB chips, but a little flatter. They were made from melted down computer parts from things that no longer worked. Some people had tried to forge their own, but if caught, they were thrown over the fence with nothing to defend themselves. Few had the balls to pull something like that. The ones who did, mostly scrappers, didn't get credits since they weren't part of Haven.

"Thanks," she said with the most sarcastic tone she could muster.

"Come again," said Eric, waving at her as she left.

A little bag of peas wouldn't hold her over, so it was off to trade. She had a few things to trade in her bag that she managed to find, and Jim helped her fix. They weren't worth much out here, but it was enough to get her an outdated package of jerky, a cooked rat, a head of lettuce, and a new jug of fresh water.

Emily returned home. Jim, next door, had his forge going and he was doing some metal work. Feeling a bit bummed, she didn't want small talk, so she tried to slip quietly into her shack. She put the cooked rat and lettuce in the lunch bucket to keep it longer. The freeze-dried peas and old pack of jerky she set on her stand.

As she laid the items down a small trinket caught her eye. It wasn't there before. It was tucked beside a plate she was using to hold candles. Pulling it out she instantly recognized the gear pattern on the copper amulet. *Marco... He's back in town. Is this him trying to contact me? How did...* She shook her head. Of course he found her. Large place, but with everyone packed together, everyone knew everyone.

She snatched the small object up and glanced around for any other traces of someone in her house. She didn't find anything.

HECTOR'S JOURNAL

March 20th, 2037

Mutation level study.

Those caught in the initial explosion, the First Turned, seem to have more stable DNA mutation patterns. Material sample small. Unsure of accuracy.

Confirmed that all First Turned developed a venom gland that allows virus mutation to pass on to others.

Second Turned obey any of the First Turned. No noticeable distinction has been found. Confirmed pattern between how humans mutate and who turned them.

Confirmed that the Second Turned have venom glands as well. Those infected by Second Turned may not. Suspect it has devolved into a salivary gland or less developed venom gland. Upon examination, degenerative changes to frontal lobes have been noted. These people, Third Turned, seem to have an insatiable hunger and 'hunt' humans. Have noted little interest in animals. Why?

Initial attempts by Russian government to quarantine the infected have failed. Number of infected exponentially growing by the day.

Chapter 3

Emily wrung her hands as she rode in the passenger seat of the lead Jeep of Marco's Head Hunters crew of criminals and misfits. She'd felt uneasy since she left which had only gotten worse. Marco was next to her driving with a huge grin on his face. He was cruel, ruthless, and didn't give a fuck about his men. But he did get the biggest paydays and those who lived were rich from it. It was because he did extremely high-risk high reward jobs. Somehow, she had survived the time she spent as part of his crew. That being said, as somewhat of an adopted addition, she was not given the same cut as the others.

Even though he ran through crews like someone would go through a bag of potato chips, people kept coming. Always driven, like her, for a chance at enough riches to claim a better life in this new world. She did question if she made the right choice. If she could just survive one more mission, she could make a new life.

Marco was a muscled man. He had a jagged scar down the left side of his face. Rumor was he got it dealing with one of his own, got into a fight, and killed the man. He had an overly square jaw and short dirty blonde hair. His shoulders were also overly large. Every bit of him lived up to his nickname The Human Tank. It was but one name. Another name he was called was the Grim Reaper because of all the people he'd led to their deaths.

They'd traveled in silence since leaving Haven the next day. Marco needed a crew, so he sought her out while he was stopped at Haven. He said he needed skill. She suspected he was desperate for bodies.

They'd only been on the road for an hour before they pulled over on the shoulder of the road, between two separate piles of cars that had been moved to the sides of the roads.

"Why are we stopping here?"

Marco pointed forward out the windshield. "Sweetness, we're almost there."

She leaned forward and looked out at the line of trees before them. "I don't see anything."

Marco waved his hand and grunted. "Amateur. The city is right over that tree line." He opened his door and slid out. "Boys, get these rigs ready!"

Emily counted seven other crew members as they exited the Jeeps, making their party number nine. The vehicles were modified with metal cattle pushers most likely for zombies, extremely large flood lights, and what looked like a shooting platform on top of each Jeep.

"Wait, are we going in today?"

"You bet your sweet cheeks," said Marcio, fishing a pack of cigarettes from his pocket.

The others were changing places. Two people with guns climbed on each roof. Another pair of men opened the Jeeps' tailgates and started up the generators. One woman slid confidently into the driver's seat of the Jeep behind Marco's. The last two were getting geared up.

"But, are we going to have enough time before nightfall?" She spun towards the sun, guessing they only had a few hours before nightfall. Although she was ready that morning, it had taken Marco a good portion of the day to get supplies.

"Humph. We got plenty of time," said Marco. "This won't take long."

"What are we going after anyway?"

Marco took a long drag off his cigarette and then blew out a large cloud as he smiled. "So, I got word from a reliable source that the walls of Haven arn't quite where they wanted them."

Emily stepped back. "What do you mean?"

"Well, the original blueprints outline a plan for the walls to encapsulate half of Des Moines."

"Why would they do that? Or not do it if that was the original plans."

A young muscular man wearing a bandana scoffed at her as he walked by. "Time, sweet cheeks. They ran out of time."

Marco clapped his hands. "Good work, Dennis. He's not only strong, but smart too. They ran out of time, so they had to make the build smaller. Why do you think they promised so many people sanctuary and then suddenly turned them away?"

"Because the government is corrupt!"

Marco raised a brow and cocked his head to the side. "Well, that too. But the main reason that they couldn't complete the project in time was how fast the zombie horde was encroaching. Something had to be dropped." He glanced left and right before leaning in towards her. "You know what that was?"

She flopped her arms at her sides and huffed with frustration. "I have no idea. I just know you said this job would make me rich."

"Oh, it will. The place that was to be protected was a state-of-the-art DNA research facility. Just a fraction of the stuff in there will make us all rich!" He shouted the last part, enticing excited screams from the others.

"The city is infested with zombies. There's no way we'll get out of there before nightfall."

Marco took another drag from his cigarette. "Not the plan, sweet cheeks. We're going in and looting that place over night."

"That's suicide!" Emily screamed.

"That's money, babe."

"Don't be a pussy," Dennis screamed. He was in the driver's seat, leaning over, and bellowing out the window.

"It's an easy haul. The place has been sealed shut since Des Moines was overrun. We'll get there, break it open, seal ourselves in overnight, and leave with the payload in the morning."

"Oh, just that easy, huh? Not even waiting till daylight?" She threw her arms into the air. She knew this would be tough, but she never expected something like this. Diving straight into the thickest infected area. Was it really worth the chance of riches? All she had was a knife. She was under prepared. Rusty. This wasn't a mission for newbs. And that's all he had. No one here was really prepared. "How many people here have gone into the city? No, how many have gone in and tried to survive the night?"

"They'll do just fine."

Emily started nodding her head as she clenched her jaw, grinding her teeth together. "None. The answer is none, isn't it? You're bringing an entirely new team into that hell pool knowing we're all going to die."

Marco walked over to her and slapped a hand to her shoulder. He laughed, but the deep booming sound and everything about how he moved felt like a threat. Emily tried to step back, but he caught her forearm with his large hand.

His tight grip made her wonder if he could snap her bones with just one hand. She had witnessed his cruelty firsthand. He was colder than ice. Even ice would melt under enough heat. Not him.

"Better not be thinking of running, sweetness. This is your chance." He waved towards the city. "Don't you want a better life? You could have anything you wanted. It's just one mission." He let go of her, stepped back, and chuckled. "This will be the easiest score of your life. Or your last. But do we really want to live as we were?" He turned eyeing the others. "Do any of us really want to keep living like bugs?"

The group replied in a unanimous no. Even though most of them won't come back alive, they still wanted to go. Everyone had already decided that living their current lives were worth the risk.

Emily chewed her bottom lip. Her stomach twisted. She always knew there were risks, but she didn't realize exactly what she was getting into. This was the big one. The last-ditch effort. Every man and woman for themselves to get a piece of that golden pie.

Am I ready for this? Are things really so bad I'm willing to take this risk? She turned back towards Haven, remembering her junk tent. Always on the brink of having no food. More nights than not going to bed hungry. The bugs, the fact people trapped rats for food. Rats! She hated it, hated every little bit of it.

It didn't take long before she started to become just like the rest of them. Hungry for this chance. Desperate. Willing to risk everything. Something must have changed because Marco's grin got bigger.

"Now you're getting it." Marco slinked in, lowering his head over her shoulder. "This is the payload of a lifetime. We're all here because this will make us all rich." He pulled away and stepped to her other side. "Isn't that what you want? Or do you prefer scrounging for scraps in the Outer Rim and eating rat?"

"No!" The desperation to leave that place behind came out in a shrill outburst.

"Good, good." Marco turned back to the group of desperate newbs. "Are we loaded and ready?"

In various ways and accents, they all said yes and started to pile into the Jeeps. Emily slid in next to Marco, who continued to take point. They were so close to the city, it wouldn't take long. And they'd need to move fast to barricade themselves in before dark.

After a while in silence, they ramped on and off the interstate and drove into the city. Cars were mangled, littering the road, which slowed their drive. The buildings were decimated. A broken signpost stood outside what looked to have once been a gas station which had burned down.

Strip malls were bare, with not a window or door left intact and even a whole piece of the brick wall toppled. The foliage had taken over with vines growing over structures and grass coming up through the large cracks in the concrete. The place was more jungle than city.

Their ride became rougher and even slower. There was one guy in the backseat behind her. He rolled down the window and pointed a long barrel rifle out towards the buildings. The city had long ago fallen, yet there was a slight sign of hope. A few birds were flying overhead, and their presence spooked a pack of feral dogs.

"How much further?" she asked, whispering like just the slightest noise would get them killed.

"Not far. Just a touch more towards downtown."

The thought made her skin cold. Downtown was the area thickest with infected. With all the buildings clustered together it was easy for the zombies to group together in the darkness. There had been rumors that hordes lived here. Swarms of undead crawling through the city would make the roads black. Someone had to have lived through it to tell the tale, she hoped.

"There." Marco pointed over the steering wheel and turned on his blinker.

Emily didn't realize how much time had passed as she gazed at the remains of the massacre. They were headed to an unmarked building made of concrete with barred windows. They approached slow, pulling into the parking lot. A few cars were there. Two looked to have been burned years ago. Others were junked.

"Do you think anything is still intact?" asked Emily.

"I'm sure of it. The intel I got was sound. This place is like a fortress."

"Oh, you think any of those zombies are in there?" asked the man from the back.

"We'll find out."

Marco pulled up in front of the building, their headlights beaming on a set of metal doors. Emily leaned forward. There were only a few hours of daylight left. This would either be their ticket to freedom or their tomb. The group unloaded quickly. They might be newcomers, but they were heavily armed and well organized. They formed together like a mini-army in front of the door.

It had stains on it which she could easily guess were old blood stains. Moss and algae had coated the bottom half green and crawled up into monstrous claw marks.

"How do we get in?" asked Emily.

Marco winked and pulled out a small glass vile from a pouch he had strapped to his belt. "Good intel I told you. We won't be able to breach the doors with force. Others have tried." He strode forward with all the confidence of a conquering king returning from a successful campaign. "But a little bit of synthesized acid to the right spot and this baby will open like butter to a hot knife."

She shuddered at the smoothness of his words turning to a growl. It was like his dark soul was pouring from his mouth. He only wanted the profit and didn't care to save a single one of them.

If I'm making it out of this, I'll have to put me first. She glanced around. *No one here cares about anything but themselves.* They were going as a group of individuals, not a team.

Emily bit her lip. "Hey, someone throw me an extra gun."

"Get your own," Dennis yelled from the back.

Marco growled. "Give the girl a damn gun. I gave you thugs plenty of weapons to go around."

Good old Marco coming through. The asshole. She felt the tension. He'd given them something up front so they'd feel indebted to him. She'd seen the trick before. Oldest trick in the book, except for this new blood. They didn't have a clue.

Dennis grunted and then handed her a pistol. One magazine, but it was something. She still had her knife and years of encounters had taught her how to use it.

"Take this too," he growled, handing her a glow stick.

Marco fussed with the door for a bit. Something simmered and the tinge of burnt metal smell drifted to Emily's nose. She sniffed and cringed.

There was a loud clunk before Marco spun around like a prized performer. "See! What did I tell you?" He backed away and waved towards the doors. "Check it out. Your future awaits."

Sending the lambs in first to flush out the wolves. She hated him more every second. He hadn't changed a bit.

She held back, letting two of the others go first. It was safer in the middle. With no one watching her front or her back she could only hope for meat shields. *Is this really the low I've stooped to?*

The insides were dark. The outer windows only let a little light in this first room. They cracked glowsticks and stuck them between various straps to light the way. One person cracked a few and threw them further into the room

They made the softest of noise as they hit, but Emily still flinched. The group quickly became disorganized with the crew sweeping the room in various directions. Marco pulled the door closed behind them.

Emily heard the loud clunk of metal first and spun.

Marco put a finger to his lips. "Don't want any surprise company," he whispered through a toothy grin, lit by a green glowstick in his vest.

She kept right, sweeping the side and keeping an eye on the others. They made for little moving torches that, if she was careful, she could use to her advantage. It quickly became apparent that this building was much larger than what it looked like from the outside.

She pushed open a door half ajar and slid through, gun held at the ready in front of her. This room was filled with computers and desks, covered in a thick layer of dirt. She paused long enough to swipe her fingers through it.

There was a figure at the end of the room, slumped over the desk. It wasn't moving. It looked thin. She pulled her knife. A stab through the skull would be much quieter. If there were zombies in here, she didn't want them all following the sound of her gunshot.

She slinked closer, taking small and quiet steps. The only light was from the one green glowstick she had stuffed in her belt. It was hard to tell what that thing was. The center of the room had desks with folded up laptops and chairs still sitting perfectly in their places. Nothing seemed to have been disturbed, but she couldn't get caught off guard.

Just behind the figure she struck, slamming her knife into a brittle skull. It cracked and pieces of a skeleton fell to the floor.

It's not a zombie. Her hands started to shake, and she fumbled as she pulled her glowstick out and surveyed the body. There were remnants of clothes in the pile of dried flesh and bones. This wasn't a victim of zombie hunger. She'd seen enough to be sure. This was someone trapped in here who died.

And now I'm trapped until morning.

She scanned the computers but decided to come back. Computer parts were valuable but were not enough of a bounty to ensure a new life. Stepping back out she spotted two of the others moving into another room. She followed.

They swept the first floor and then the second. The body count of people who must have been trapped inside grew. Old, aged corpses, eaten by bugs and mice. They found several computer rooms, but the upper levels open into science labs.

Refrigerators, long without power, still held vials and samples inside of them. She slipped into a room with the same amount of dust. One line of walls that led to the hallway were all glass. Tables in the center were covered in beakers and other science equipment. Large computers and other piece of technology she couldn't recognize covered the wall.

What is this place? The others were moving into different rooms. It was apparent that no one was teamed up. They were all on their own. A couple had already started scrapping computers. It was a testimony of their lack of understanding of what real value was out here.

She slipped to one of the fridges and pulled open the old door. A rancid smell hit her. Years of aging and decaying things in bottles made a fume that gagged her so badly that bile hit her throat. It burned and made her gag again.

Emily covered her mouth with the back of her hand and with her other waved the glowstick over the bottles, reading the labels. 'Test Sample' was written on many. She kept scanning, trying to piece together what really had happened here. It was so silent she could hear every breath she took.

There were documents on the tables and other vials labeled with different virus names. After a while, the pieces fit. Her heart began to beat faster as she backed from the room. She bumped into someone and stifled as scream as she spun. Just as she pointed a gun at the figure, she recognized Marco lit in glowstick light.

"What, can't handle the dark?"

"This is a zombie research center."

"You're smarter than you look."

"What are we supposed to do here? What money could this possibly fetch us?"

He raised a brow. "If you don't know, I'm not telling. Better get yourself some better sources." He bumped her shoulder as he strode past and then stopped a few steps away. "Oh, and be careful girly, it's night."

Her whole body went cold and stiff. They were trapped here, in a zombie research center, at night. He closed the door. How secure was it really? They broke in so what's stopping anyone else from coming?

"Shit," Emily mumbled. "Fucker." She rushed back into the room. Luckily, she had grabbed a small bag from the Jeep before entering. Foolishly, she thought they'd be able to go back to the Jeeps for more supplies. She didn't bring food or water, not that she hadn't gone stretches without before, but with all the dust her tongue felt like sandpaper. Her throat ground together each time she tried to swallow a drop of saliva.

She had no idea of the value of any of this. Worse, Marco was right, she didn't have any sources that would buy this shit. *But if he thinks it's valuable, then it must be.* She started grabbing things, wrapping them in the old clothes from the corpses on the floor, and then stuffed them into the bag.

There wasn't time to dally, as the others were already collecting bagsful of loot. Making her way downstairs she snatched anything that looked like flash drives or external hard drives. Maybe what's in the vials wouldn't be worth shit, but information was power. She could leverage it, somehow.

They were spread throughout the building now. Some moving silently and others she could hear stomping around rooms away. If shit went south, she needed something to come of this risk. Just as she reached the base of the stairs across from the front door, something banged from the outside.

She sucked in and then held her breath. This was exactly what she thought would happen. hordes of zombies. If there were any of the smarter ones amongst the lots, then they'd certainly notice new vehicles in their territory.

Emily made tracks, getting herself into the first room she explored just to the right of the door. She put her back to the wall and left the door open a crack. Everything in her body tensed and she felt sick. Her plan was simple, let the zombies flood in, eat the idiots, and she'd make a break for it.

I'm trash. I can't believe I'm doing this, again. Save yourself. Only the strong survive. She'd heard so many scrappers say that swill. But it kept her alive. The bang came again, this time harder, followed by another softer. *They are gathering.*

It was enough to attract attention as she heard someone curse from the direction of the stairs.

"What do we do?" shouted a desperate voice.

Emily cringed. The sound would attract them even more.

"Shut up, asshole," said Marco.

Guns racked and more footsteps converged with the sound of another set more scrambling, fleeting into the distance. The first runner from the fight. *Good, maybe that one will survive.*

The bangs came louder, echoing around her. The sound almost deafening, except the sound of her pounding heart was louder.

"They're getting in!" someone screamed.

That sound was enough. Something outside screeched and the bangs came thundering in.

"Get some balls," said Marco. "We can take them."

A lie and she knew it. In just another moment a bang came before the clattering of metal. Screeching filled the room as the sound of several creatures moved in. She pressed harder against the wall. Gunfire erupted.

All she needed was a gap to save herself. She kept quiet as the zombies flooded in. It sounded like several. Screams joined the chorus of death. One by one she heard the screams start to silence. Taking one more long breath she bolted.

There were three zombies right outside her door. The glowsticks scattered on the floor gave the forms green and red glows. They were misshapen humanoid.

She popped each one in the head before they could spring on her. Cold sweat broke out across her skin. There were more. So many more. A cluster of them were heading upstairs. Most likely following their prey.

She made her escape to the door. More were outside in a cluster. Only moonlight gave the dark forms shape.

Everything in her tensed as she popped off rounds until the magazine was empty. She downed four maybe five, with a whole horde now converging on her.

There were more coming through the door. She dodged one of the more mangled dog-like ones and ducked right. A slug zombie was on the ground. Highly infectious blobs of flesh. She vaulted it only for another to come.

It was all blurs of motion. Panic. Years of fighting for her life. She grabbed her knife and sliced her blade through one's throat and then embedded it in another.

Gunshots rang behind her, coming closer. She didn't dare take time to look back. Scrambling to the Jeep, one made a grab at her. She yanked the door open, slamming the creature in the face. She got inside. Somehow. Lucky. Maybe with skill?

She spotted something dark in the distance away from the building moving their way and realized this was the first wave. These were just the locals, but their commotion was drawing the rest. Emily locked the doors and, just as she went to hotwire the Jeep, she spotted the keys.

She'd gotten into the one closest which was one the newbies were driving. Idiots didn't know the first rule. Always take your keys. The zombies started slamming against the vehicle, rocking it side to side.

She turned it on and then smashed her fist into the headlight button, turning the headlights and the floodlights on. All the creatures around her screeched and backed away. This was her only chance.

Putting it in reverse she sped away. Backing over bodies. The back window shattered, but she had already started moving fast enough the zombie lost grip and didn't get in.

The whole rig tipped a moment as she stopped just enough to throw it in drive and put the pedal to the floor. The lights kept the zombies at bay, but she still spotted them pouring out of buildings. It looked almost like black water moving. There were so many.

She sped up, trying to remember how clear the road was. Estimating how fast she could drive, get away, and not crash. Taking a corner too fast she felt the side of the blocky Jeep lift again. She bit her lip, hard. The tang of blood coming to her mouth.

But the edge of the city was in sight. She gagged again, the fleeting thought of those she left to die striking her right in the gut. But she was getting away. Loot and all. A shred of hope that some of this shit would be worth something. The chance at a better life. It was all she wanted. Not riches, but she wanted out of the swill. Out of starvation. Out of living each day on a road to just die and no one would even care.

She spotted the landmark of the gas station earlier. The sign just an erect black pole in the night. It made her look away from the road, just a moment, and when she looked back a figure was right in front of her. Just a few feet. A man, but it was too fast.

She collided with him, but he stopped her. Like a cement wall. The Jeep collapsing on itself. Glass shattering. Her head snapped forward against the steering wheel. Her body almost propelled out. Arms scraping against glass. Her legs snagging under the wheel. Her body thrashed around like a rag doll all in the split second before everything went black.

HECTOR'S JOURNAL

April 15th 2037

Local forces couldn't contend with the horde that has been created. The virus is spreading and mutating beyond belief. I have been unable to find a cure or a way to stop it. None of those first infected will hear my pleas to stop the madness. I didn't realize the evil in their hearts until now. I feel they are choosing this instead of being driven by some effect of the virus.

I have found many who have been turned into these undead creatures. The virus seems to increase electrical impulses from the brain allowing even the most ravaged and damaged body to continue to mutate. Suspect this is from the testing done with jellyfish DNA.

The Third Turned seem to be like animals, but those later turned are more and more devolved each time. I have collected and caged specimens back in the Chernobyl lab, but I have little equipment to work with. I have been forced to move into the bigger cities to conduct more thorough research on a cure.

I blame myself and my inferiority in not being able to find a cure yet.

Chapter 4

Just at daybreak Jim headed out to his forge. The sky had a pastel blush of red across it with pink wispy clouds. Here, behind the walls, the long shadow kept his workspace dark. Orange coals cast a small bit of light across his workspace. From his Winnebago he had metal pipe supports that connected to posts made from larger metal pipes set in cement. It took a lot of work to get all those items.

He built it tall and tarped the whole thing. He needed shelter from the weather, but enough space that his forge and metal working didn't catch anything on fire. After stretching he grabbed his thick leather apron and moved over to his tool rack. It was made from a large piece of wood sitting on a stack of concrete blocks with a back made from peg board. Most of the pegs were metal and forged by him. It's where he hung his various hammers and pliers.

Most of his work for today was going to be repairs. Many of the people around, mostly other craftsmen, needed tools repaired. It would be simple work that would take more time than anything. Jim walked to the water basin just outside of his house and splashed his face with the cool liquid. He had a small water catch on top of the Winnebago with pipes routed down to this basin to serve as a sink.

After getting the furnace nice and hot he started working, and kept going a few hours until the sun crested the wall. It brought a bright splash of warm color to the dismal slum around him. Somehow, no matter how dismal things looked, he was happy he could be of help. Just that. Not happy to have survived. Not happy to be alive. Just happy he could help. It was a simple existence.

Around twelve years ago, before the zombie apocalypse, he was a simple blacksmith in northern Missouri. His wife had divorced him, angry that he refused to get what she called a real job. In the divorce she left him the house, which she hated, but took everything else including his daughter.

Shared custody went poorly and then after two years the zombies came. When word first hit the US about zombies no one really took it seriously, until the Russian government fell. Then the whole world went into panic. Stores across the US were getting robbed, people were prepping for the worst, and the government started preparing fallout shelters all over the US.

Haven was nearest him and the biggest project. Their goal was to build an impenetrable wall around central Iowa encapsulating farmlands, the wind farm, and the hydroelectric dam. He was able to reconcile with his wife by agreeing to join the project to assure them a place in Haven.

He worked twelve and sometimes fourteen hours a day as a metal worker on the project. Once word got out about the project, people from all over the US flocked here. The government had to intervene and enlisted civilians into an army to protect the project, falsely promising safety within Haven's borders. It was a lie. When the project was finished, Europe had fallen, Japan as well. There were rumors the invasion had reached Australia, and reports of zombies on the US west coast.

When push came to shove there just wasn't enough room in Haven for the amount of people wanting in. It was genocide. Some waiting in long lines outside the gates for a chance at salvation. Many started to perish from the elements and even starvation. A small group tried to take Haven by force. They were all killed. The rest scattered to what he assumed was their death to the zombie horde. His wife and daughter were two that scattered.

They had a day's head start when he found out. No surprise his wife said nothing to him. He spent the good part of a couple years trying to find them. All he found was endless oceans of death. In his despair he almost ended his life, before a group of scrappers took pity on him and picked him up. They took him back to Haven. His work was well enough known that his name alone allowed him entry. Even then, it was to the squalor of the Outer Rim. It was the most minimal payment he could have had.

He started with nothing but his skills and after years of endless hard work he had made somewhat of a home for himself. Helping the others around him gave him purpose, but the hole in his heart from losing his family never healed.

This moment of flashback left him standing at his anvil, holding his hammer in a shaking hand. He came back to his senses with a jolt and shook his head to try and rid himself of those memories.

"I need a break," he mumbled.

The Outer Rim seemed quiet around him, which gave him the

suspicion that there must be scrappers or a new shipment of food at the market. That tended to be the only thing that cleared people from their homes. Emily was there before, but he didn't see her come back and didn't see her yesterday either. If there was a new shipment of food, it would be good to stop by before he ran low. She might have some idea of what was going on.

He walked over to her hut. He helped her build it and, although it wasn't much, he was able to scrounge some luxuries that others didn't have. He knocked on the wood outside her door.

"Emily, you home?" When he heard nothing, he knocked again, assuming she had overslept. "Emily."

"Hey, what up, Jim?"

Jim turned and spotted Noah standing in the street behind him holding a make-shift wooden cage with a rabbit in it. The boy was almost twenty and had spent the last ten years in Haven. He made it in before zombies reached the walls, thanks to his parents. His father was a scrapper who left for supplies and never came home, assumed dead. His mother became ill three or four years ago and passed away. The boy was thin, yet surprisingly healthy, with badly cut blonde hair and youthful blue eyes. His clothes were rags with several patches where it looked like he had tried to mend them himself.

"Looking for Emily. Have you seen her?" asked Jim.

Noah's face paled and his eyes glanced down to the brown fat rabbit in the cage. "Rumor has it she left with some scrappers last night."

"What?" Jim shouted. "Why?"

Noah shrugged. "I heard she was really unhappy. I don't know. Maybe they had a good lead on something."

Jim ran his hand across the back of his neck. He peered into Emily's hut, hoping to find her there despite Noah's claim. His heart was pounding, and he couldn't tell if he was furious or terrified. *What is that girl thinking?* Scrappers seldom came back alive, which made even better profits when a ten-man team ended up only having to split the bounty three or four ways. *She's going to get herself killed out there.*

He knew Emily used to be a scrapper, but he thought that was behind her. He wasn't close to anyone except her. Helping her out brightened his day, and the sudden thought of losing someone else close to him made him sick. Bile worked up into his throat where it burned.

His first instinct was to go after her. Logic said otherwise. Fighting with himself he remained paralyzed in place. Could he just let her go?

Could he handle it if something happened to her? He wasn't close to anyone else. Didn't consider anyone else to be a real friend.

"You okay there, Jim?"

Noah's voice brought him back. The kid looked utterly confused. He was a teenager when he came here and had really only known Haven for most of his life. His late mother had gained entry early on.

Yanika, a woman who lived up the road and raised chickens, had been helping Noah out a lot with his rabbit farm.

The kid never saw what horrors lurked out there. What a horde of zombies could do to an entire army. Jim did.

"Fuck it!"

His outburst made Noah and the rabbit jump. The large rodent thrashed around in the cage and Noah's attention fell from Jim. "It's okay Henny," Noah muttered as he continued along the path.

Jim hopped across the mud to a broken board in front of Emily's door and then headed into his Winnebago. He still had his gear, from when he went searching for his family, tucked into a storage compartment beneath a torn built-in couch seat. He strapped on a tactical vest and slapped his hunting knife in its sheath to the patch of Velcro over the left breast, hilt down. Grabbing his backpack he stashed the pieces of his rifle, a box of rifle rounds, some food, and a canteen in it.

He couldn't go around toting guns in Haven easily without being stopped. Government was slim out here, but brutal. It wasn't the number of guards that kept people in line, but how they dealt with the unruly. Controlling with fear.

It only took him a few minutes to gather everything before he started up the street. A short stroll confirmed his hunch there was scrappers in town selling things. The market was full of makeshift stands with scruffy scarred men and women selling what little they had scavenged from the outside world.

He spotted Walter near the gate. The man was older with long black hair pulled back. He had a thin frame, which Jim knew didn't at all mean he was weak. The man was agile as hell. Walter was part of the crew of scrappers that had saved Jim. He came here often to buy and barter wares. Jim waved as he ran, catching Walter's eye.

Walter turned, only acknowledging him with a suspicious glance. "Jim, you are looking well."

Jim waved his hand, not wanting to waste time with pleasantries. "Not now, Walter. I'm looking for someone."

"Oh?" A single brown lifted above a thin pair of metal rimmed glasses.

"Emily. She used to be scrapper, but has been-"

Walter cut him off. "Oh yes. We all know about Emily. She left last night with Marco."

"What?" Jim moved in and made a grab for Walter's vest.

A flash of movement and Jim found himself on his knees with his arm twisted behind him. "Please don't try something like that again. I am old. Not feeble."

"Why didn't you stop her?"

"Why would I?" Walter let go of Jim's arm and stepped back.

Jim took a long breath. He didn't expect Walter to be quite that fast. It had been a few years, but he didn't think the man was that quick before. Scrambling back to his feet Jim tried to get control of things. "Sorry, okay. I really need to find her. We both know you go out with Marco, you don't come back alive."

"That we can agree on." Walter pointed towards the gate. "They were headed north towards what used to be Des Moines."

"The city! You're joking."

Walter crossed his arms. "I do not joke. They have half a day's head start on you. There will be no way you can reach them on foot."

Jim groaned and looked away. He hated having debts and had spent the better part of these five years getting to the point that he didn't have any more. Now he had to decide. The thought fleeted through his mind, as he realized he had already committed to his decision. He had to bring Emily back. Especially if she was with Marco.

"You got something that will get me there?"

Walt's eyes narrowed. "Perhaps, for a cost."

"I'll owe you one. How's that? You know I'm good for it."

Walter nodded. "Quite. I have a motorcycle just outside the gate with my men. It has a full tank of gas." He pulled a set of keys from his vest pocket and tossed them to Jim. "Bring it back in good shape and there will be no debt."

Walter does still give a shit. I'm surprised. Jim gave him a quick nod. "Thanks. It means a lot." Pivoting on his heels Jim headed to the gate. Getting out was as simple as a shout to the guards who didn't give a shit who left. That meant less people inside in Haven to worry about. There was also a good chance Jim could easily get back in. Pull a few strings, waltz in with some scrappers, and head to his house. None would be the wiser and no one would care enough to question it.

He stepped through the gate into the meurtrière. It hadn't been cleaned in a while and stunk of rotten flesh. He spotted a body swept to the side of the concrete wall that hadn't been taken care of yet. It wasn't uncommon, as the guards would kill anyone suspected of infection without another thought.

The gate before him clucked and cracked as the heavy metal locking mechanism, which he helped build, unlocked. The giant metal gates swung open to the outside. This passage was near an old highway where a group of scrappers had parked.

He counted about ten men and two women wearing a combination of leather and tactical gear. They had two jeeps, one truck, and the motorcycle that Walter promised.

As he approached the group started to move towards him. He raised his hands, holding the key pinched between his fingers. "Walter and I made a deal for the motorcycle."

The group looked uneasy except for Sam. A blond woman with tanned skin who gave off the feeling that she would snap anyone in half that crossed her. She was close with Walter and Jim knew her from when the scrappers saved him.

She strode over and walked her fingers up his chest. "Been a long time, Jim boy."

"Sam." He addressed her bluntly. She gave him the creeps and uncomfortable chills spread across his chest as her fingers flicked the underside of his bristled chin.

"You joining us or leaving us?"

"Leaving," he said, as he sidestepped her. He nodded to the others, hoping to best indicate he was not a threat.

"Too bad," said Sam. "You'd be a great addition."

"Doubtful." Jim made it to the motorcycle. It seemed to be a conglomeration of different bikes, polished to the point the chrome detailing shined. He realized this most likely was Walter's personal ride. *The man will kill me if I don't bring this back.*

He sped off in a northerly direction, curving around the outer wall of Haven, taken a bit out of his way in order to follow the paved roads. Motorcycles were a sought-after item for their speed and maneuverability which allowed them to make their way quickly and easily through the abandoned cars on the road.

The area around Haven had been heavily scrapped. Even car parts such as doors and windshields had been pulled off abandoned vehicles. But the further anyone went from Haven the more crowded the roads were and the more treacherous the terrain was. Glancing up, he cursed the sun. It was midday which only gave him about seven hours before he absolutely had to take shelter. The problem with shelter is that anything fortified enough to keep a zombie horde out was typically dark and a prime place for zombies to hide in the day. Many scrappers died making that mistake. It was a mistake a person only made once.

Jim knew this from the time he spent out alone looking for his wife and daughter. The greater part of him wished they had found their way to Haven, and he was the one that died. Gritting his teeth, he knew he couldn't lose anyone else. He knew he wouldn't have the will to continue on with this miserable life.

The roar of his engine echoed across the overgrown countryside. Years of little traffic allowed nature to flourish. Prairie grasses had come back. When all the farmers fled to Haven their farms were left alone. Cattle, horses, goats, and more got loose and now freely populated the area. It wasn't anything to find a flock of sheep just wandering around.

A lot of food that came into the Outer Rim of Haven was from local hunters, taking advantage of this. It also seemed the zombies didn't care too much for livestock. Just humans. Although animal zombies were rumored, he'd never seen one.

There was a herd of horses in the field near the road which he spooked on the drive by. It comforted him to see animals. Even though he really didn't believe animals could become zombies, he had noticed they would flee from the zombies as they would from any predator. Seeing livestock just roaming around was a good sign this area was clear.

Once he was a good distance from the scrappers and also in an area he felt safe, he stopped for a moment. Just long enough to assemble his rifle and sling it over his shoulder. Loaded to its max with a few extra rounds in his pocket for easy access. It was how he survived while looking for his family. Fire power, and a willingness to do whatever it takes.

In just a couple of minutes he was moving again. If he was lucky, Marco's squad of scrappers would run into some roadblocks that would slow them down enough for him to catch up. If not, then he was prepared to move into the infested city to bring Emily back.

Hector's Journal

April 22nd, 2037

Everything is coming apart. The military has enlisted civilians to fight. It has become the wolves bringing sheep to slaughter. They don't know what they're dealing with.

Humans fear what I have become. All attempts to contact them or provide information have failed. I fear I will not be able to help them. Considering moving to try and contact government officials. I might die in the process.

I pray if anyone finds this journal, they can take what information I have collected and build on it.

Chapter 5

Eric stormed through the North West Compound about a mile away from the Outlet where he was stationed. The building was stone, constructed on the ruins of an old courthouse. The walls were ramshackle composite held together by concrete and iron bars. The entrance still held the broken marble set in a gray and brown stone pattern. The center had a staircase that led upwards to the stories above.

LED light bars flickered above him, powered by the solar panels on the roof. They were dying, as were many things. Today was his last day at the Outer Rim, as his orders were to travel to the capitol. Other guards were pouring in as well, all in their issued non-matching tactical gear, scrounged from before the world fell.

"Um, hello," said a woman.

He paused a moment to see a dark-skinned woman with her curly raven hair pulled up. She was holding a wooden cage with a chicken in it. She wasn't alone. There was a handful of other civilians there.

Coming up behind them were the Sheriffs. Sheriffs were given more authority than guards in this new hierarchy. One large man approached her and slapped the cage from her hands. The wood broke and a wild and terrified yellow chicken sprang forth.

"Catch that bird!" the man screamed.

The woman shirked and grasped for the bird. "Cuddles, no!"

Another Sheriff pulled her back. "Get back in line."

"Hey!" said Eric. He spun on his heels and started a slow approach.

"Mind your business, guard," the large man spat as he said guard, blatantly showing his disdain.

"What's going on? Why are there civilians here?"

The other Sheriff, a smaller man in a Kevlar helmet, walked over and shoved Eric back. "Mind your business."

"These people are my business," Eric snapped. "And until dawn this is still my jurisdiction."

The large man moved in front of Eric. "Well, pretty boy, your people have been chosen to serve a greater cause. As one of your pathetic lot."

"What!" both Eric and the girl shouted at the same time.

"What are you getting at, Sheriff?" Eric closed the gap between them. He was used to dealing with large meatheads at the Gate.

"Stupid. You got your summons, didn't you? Or were you sleeping?"

"Well," Eric cocked his head to the side and back, "unlike you guys at the capitol there isn't much time to sleep."

"What are you saying, pretty boy?"

Just as it looked like they were going to have a brawl right there another figure approached. The well adorned bulky woman wore an army general uniform.

"Break it up. We want this to go smoothly."

The large man looked furious but shoved past Eric anyway and headed up to the next floor. His lackies followed.

The girl sprang loose the moment they were gone. She squatted down and tapped her hand as she called her chicken. "Cuddles, come on."

He watched as the fat bird waddled to her and let her scoop it up in her arms.

"You okay?"

She looked up at him with large eyes. "I... I don't know what's going on. I thought... I thought..." She shook and pulled the bird closer to her chest. The little beasty clucked once and then quieted.

Eric offered her his hand. "I'm not sure what's going on, but I'm not going to let those blockheads hurt you."

She looked at his gesture, chewed her lip a moment, and then took his hand. He helped her up just as a few more guards entered, and another Sheriff started ushering them forwards towards the back of the outpost.

"What is going on?" asked the girl.

"I'm not sure, but I'm going to find out. Stick close to me, okay?"

She gave him a quick nod accompanied by an all over body shake.

"I'm Eric. What's your name?"

"Yanika," she said with a scared squeak.

HECTOR'S JOURNAL

May 15th, 2037

All attempts to contact government officials have failed. I am injured, but there is noted accelerated healing. Running research on this at present. Not all turned seem to have this mutation. People are starting to call this the zombie apocalypse. I fear they are right.

The turned continue to move. Research material is limited. Plan to continue to follow the others.

I can track the movements of Doctor Liatris by the mutated he leaves in his wake. Victoria seems to have moved towards England, as I have not found evidence of her in a while.

Also attempting to track the other First Turned. Many that were caught in the initial explosion, I suspect, had already moved when I gained consciousness. Currently tracking four other mutation patterns that could be from other First Turned. High possibility there are more.

Chapter 6

Lisa awoke to a loud moan. She blinked, clearing the crust from her eyes. Mariah was squatted down trying to tend to Flint who was pushing her away.

"I'm fine, woman," said Flint, waving his hand in her face.

"You have a concussion. Let me help you."

"You and I both know there's nothing you can do for a concussion, so please leave me alone!" Flint pulled himself into a semi-reclined position and then turned to Lisa. "What you want, hoe?"

"Glad to have you back, asshole," said Lisa as she rolled her eyes. She didn't know how long she'd been asleep, but she was over it. Lisa stood up and stumbled past Mariah.

"Oh, wait. Hector wants you to rest."

"I'll rest later when that dickhead gets better."

"I heard that," Flint yelled back.

Lisa stepped out into the RV and froze. It was dark and the sudden realization that she'd slept all day sent her head spinning. Her legs felt rubbery, and she grabbed onto a counter. Hector wasn't anywhere to be seen, leaving her to guess he was on the roof. A corner of Bruno's poncho hung over the edge of the driver's seat.

Soft footsteps came from behind her. When she spun, Lisa spotted Mariah. "Did I really sleep all day?" she asked, her voice shaking.

Mariah nodded. "Hector insisted on letting you and Flint rest."

Lisa grabbed at her hip, trying to find her gun. It was gone. She looked at Mariah with new levels of desperation. Getting taken off guard like this was not okay.

Mariah pointed at Hector's desk. "It's over there."

Lisa nodded. She snatched it up and strapped it to her hip. She popped the door open, grabbed the ladder, and swung around. Mariah hurried behind her to close and bolt the door. As she did, Lisa caught a glimpse of Flint. Hopefully he would take over driving. He might have a concussion, and shouldn't be behind the wheel, but even Spot would be safer than Bruno.

She climbed up. The RV's headlights were beamed on the road and the flood lights affixed on the sides and back. On top of the roof was Hector, crouched in the shadows. He turned towards her as she pulled herself the rest of the way up.

"You should have woken me."

"You needed the rest."

"So do you," she snapped back, stomping her foot as she stepped forward. The impact made a moderate clang in the night.

Hector looked at her, his face seeming turned towards her feet, and then looked back ahead of the RV.

Lisa grabbed the cold metal railing and scanned around them. The lights were enough to illuminate the road just to the grass past the ditches. They were headed down the center of a two-lane highway. The vehicles here were all pushed to the sides and seemed heavily scrapped.

"Where are we?"

"Getting too close to Haven."

Lisa pulled back and then squinted, trying to see past the darkness. She had heard tales of Haven before but had never seen it. For the longest time she thought it was a myth. It was hard to believe there was anywhere safe out there. The only safety she'd known was within the veil of Hector's power to control the undead.

"Why are we headed this way? I thought we were headed to the city." She never liked the idea, but weeks ago it was decided the risk was worth it to get fully stocked. Hector needed new things for his lab, they were short on food and supplies, and the RV needed repairs. With Hector's powers they had a decent chance if they were careful.

"We are, just not directly. We spotted groups of vehicles moving. We've been trying to avoid them." He leaned forward, his thin body craning over. He rested his arms on the railing. From that position the bulge of his wings was more prominent under his poncho.

"Scrappers?"

"Most likely. This area is heavily picked over. They would have started moving further and further away from Haven."

"Is Haven all that I heard?"

"Depends on what you heard." He shrugged.

She grinned. His humor was simple, dry, and fleeting, but it reassured her. Not of his humanity, but of the fact he hadn't given up hope. It kept her hope going. It was why she finally agreed to this trip. Hector was tirelessly working on a cure, and she desperately hoped he would find one.

"Haven could have been great, but I fear it has fallen to politics." He stood and stretched. "Besides, it won't be long before those walls cannot feed the mouths inside. It's a death sentence. It's just a matter of time."

"How close are we to the city?"

"At this pace, maybe an hour or so. I fear the others we spotted were headed to the same place."

Lisa's hand fell to the gun on her hip. Scrappers were their greatest threat. Hector had no power over them aside from brute force Most tended to be heavily armed. "Are you sure this is a good idea?"

"We will not enter the city until I am sure it's safe."

Lisa let out a long breath and gripped the railing. The hum of the RV made a soft vibration below her. With Bruno driving it was surprising they weren't in the ditch yet. "Flint is awake, by the way."

Hector nodded. "Good."

"He's still an asshole."

One puff of a laugh came from Hector. It was hard to catch, but it seemed she had tickled him a bit.

She leaned oved and nudged him with her elbow. "Sure we can't leave him?"

Hector cocked his head to the side. "I had thought about it."

"Look at you. Joking around. You do have a sense of humor."

"Maybe fatigue is setting in."

She laughed. It came from the depths of her stomach and the deepest part of her soul that still had a spark of light, genuine, without thoughts of the reality around them.

The moment was fleeting, and she recognized how she felt. Why she felt that way for a moment. It weighed on her, worse now as it wasn't often she had time to deeply think about these things. Very depressing. But no more depressing than waking up every day in the land of the dead.

The slow drive and deep thoughts were shattered. A little glimpse of light far up the road came into view accompanied by the distant sounds of gunfire. Thankfully, Iowa's mostly flat terrain made it easier to spot things far ahead. Hector straightened fast.

Lisa pulled her pistol and trained it forward. "What is it? Zombies? Scrappers?"

Hector leaned forward, his body hunched like a predator ready to pounce. "Possibly both."

Lisa activated the walkie-talkie strapped to the railing. "Bruno, scrappers and zombies, twelve o' clock."

Bruno's static broken voice came back to her. "What? What should I do?"

She turned to Hector. "They won't survive out there alone."

He crept further forward. His poncho jerked as a thin transparent wing, that looked like a grasshopper's, flicked out and then back in. He pushed the button again to call down into the RV. "Take us on a slow approach."

"Are... are you sure?"

Before anyone could say anything there was rustling, static, and then a new voice. "Hey, boss, I got yah," said Flint.

Lisa grabbed the walkie and yelled at him. "You're a mess. You're supposed to be resting."

"He won't listen," came Maria's voice.

Lisa ground the toe of her shoe into the roof of the RV. That guy was an idiot. *He could crash us. If he blacks out. If his reaction time isn't great. What is he thinking?*

The RV slowed but kept on the approach. More gunshots rang out, getting louder. Loud enough to easily attract any nearby zombies that would have crawled from hiding at nightfall. Even though they seemed far off, they approached fast. Lisa noticed their speed gradually increased, even though Hector ordered a slow approach.

She glanced to Hector, but he seemed completely focused on the vehicle ahead. He stepped forward, placing a large, clawed foot, that looked almost dinosauric, on the railing.

"What are you doing?"

"I'm going to fly ahead while there are still dark areas and try and get the zombies away from that vehicle." He looked down at her. "Will you be all right?"

A quick nod was all it took to reassure him. Hector leapt from the RV. The entire vehicle creaked from the power of his jump. His wings spread out and he flew forward, moving like an insect levitating in the air. His flying was more that of a June bug or grasshopper, and the levitating effect made it even more haunting.

His dark figure quickly disappeared from sight. Lisa chewed her lip. Side stepping, she took the spot where he had been and braced herself against the railing. She felt her back muscles tighten spasmodically. Hector would have the power to protect them from a distance, if he didn't get too far.

A hum arose in the night as they approached faster and faster.

For a moment, she assumed it was the engine again, but a light in the distance said otherwise. One light, converging fast on the vehicle ahead. The hum became a sputtering roar which reminded her of a motorcycle.

Her first instinct was to alert Hector, but that not only might give away his position, but might also attract more attention to them. But why was this lone vehicle heading into certain death? Was this another party?

It must be. She couldn't fathom someone so stupid to drive right into... *Zombies!* Hector must have succeeded because dark figures were now running her way. The lights on the RV parted this mini horde like Moses parting the red sea.

It looked like a combination of walkers and crawlers mostly. It had been a while since she'd seen zombies like this. Early turned, as Hector once referred to them as. Ones that hadn't undergone a lot of mutations. It showed. The group were now aggroed onto the RV but repelled by the light. Unlink the mindless later turned zombies, these seemed smart enough to surround the RV and look for an opening.

The back side! Lisa spun and leapt, trying to get over the solar panels to scout the back of the RV. There was little light back there. To her horror they were converging just a few feet away and coming in fast. She readied her pistol.

They were hesitant to get into the tiny ring of light coming in from the rest of the lamps set around the RV. It bought the fraction of time needed for Hector to return. He landed with a hard thud behind her. The zombies froze and then began backing away.

"What did you find out?" she asked, glancing over her shoulder.

"There's a Jeep out there with two men, alive. Another is coming in a motorcycle."

"Scrappers?"

"It appears so."

"Why is that guy driving right towards them?"

"Why are we driving right towards them?" said Hector, with a drip of humor.

Flint slowed the RV fast, causing a sudden forwards and back motion. She lost her footing, falling into Hector's arms.

The two men now were very aware of their presence, and one started screaming.

"Who the fuck are you?"

Hector helped her get steady. His long fingers could wrap around her arm twice.

"Hey! Hey!" the man below kept shouting.

Lisa reached over and touched Hector's hand. "You stay here out of sight. I'll go down and check this out." She knew he would argue so she added, "You got my back?"

"Always," he said softly but without hesitation.

Lisa made a mad dash for the ladder on the side and slid down to the ground. "We're friendly! We're here to help!" She kept her gun in her hand but raised her arms to make it look like she wasn't a threat.

As she rounded to the front of the RV, the other person on the bike came up on them. It was now the four of them, standing in what looked like a high-noon western shoot out. One of the men was very young, with light blonde hair all coated in blood. His clothes were torn, and his eyes were so wide they looked almost totally white.

The other man was much gruffer with a jagged scar down the side of his face. He had cold eyes, which unnerved her.

The last man stopped his motorcycle and leapt off so fast he didn't even bother to turn it off.

"Marco," he screamed, pointing at the man with the scar.

"Who the fuck are you?" Marco spat blood as he screamed.

All this noise would keep the zombies near. They didn't have a clue the only thing keeping them alive was Hector.

The man from the motorcycle looked furious. He was medium built, but the tight shirt he had on seemed to indicate he was all muscle. He seemed totally focused on the guy he called Marco and screamed again. "Where's Emily?"

"Fuck that bitch. She left us. The damn whore."

"Don't you fucking-" Jim started to rush at Marco, but stopped dead when Marco pulled a gun on him.

"Don't take another step, boy, or I'll blow your head off."

The man from the motorcycle tugged at the strap holding a rifle to his back. "I should kill you right now. I've heard about you. Letting the people you hire die just so you get better pay out. You're the one who should have their head blown off."

"Everyone, calm down," said Lisa.

"Shut up," was the unanimous response from the two men.

Their gaze did travel to her for a second, but they quickly went back to staring each other down like animals.

The boy behind Marco suddenly buckled over and started puking. She hadn't paid him much attention until now.

Marco glanced back over his shoulder at the boy. "What the fuck's wrong with you?"

The boy puked again.

Lisa heard a soft hum. Recognizing it as the sound of Hector's wings she lowered her arms and got a good hold on her pistol. The others weren't paying her much attention. And to think she had the fleeting thought of saving them. She wished, now, that they had just driven away and let them get eaten.

Out of the blackness above just beyond the reach of all the flood lights, Hector descended. He landed hard in front of her.

Marco spun and popped off a round from his pistol. Hector was already moving, as if he knew exactly what would happen. Ducking to the side the bullet just grazed through the flesh of his arm. A bit of blood splattered on the ground behind him.

Lisa ran up beside him. "It's okay. He's with me."

"The fuck. You with that fucking creature!" Marco waved his gun around.

She tensed. He was ready to pop off another round at any moment. She might even have to kill him to protect Hector. It wasn't the first time she'd thought that. Logically, she should prioritize humans. That would be, if it wasn't for the fact that Hector treated her better a hundred times over than most humans.

Hector sniffed and then turned his head towards the boy. "He's infected."

Marco spun, training his gun on his own comrade.

The boy raised his hands. "No. No. I'm okay." His pale face took on a green tinge and he hurled again.

"Fuck. Dennis, I knew it!" Marco popped off a round, blowing the boy's face off.

Lisa jerked, almost pulling her trigger. As the boy's body hit the ground in a wet flop her own stomach heaved.

The man from the motorcycle whipped his rifle around and trained it on Marco. "You sick fuck."

Marco turned, popping another round at the man. As he moved the rifle went off, leaving a boom that echoed through the fields. The rifle bullet, a large caliber, blew a hole through Marco's chest. But Marco did fire his own gun fast enough. Just as Marco hit the ground, the man from the motorcycle also toppled.

Lisa shook. Her stomach heaved. It just happened. There was nothing she could do. It went so fast. The yelling. He just killed the guy he was with. Her head spun. It didn't take long before even her hands shook.

Hector side-stepped to her and rested his hand on hers, pushing her aim down. "Will you be okay?"

She choked on her own words for a moment. "I can't believe..."

Hector sniffed, which made her go silent. He strode over towards the motorcycle man. His gun was out on front of him, and he lay face down on the ground. As Hector rolled the man over, he sniffed again.

"He is still alive, and not infected."

"What?"

"Go get Mariah. He's badly hurt."

Lisa shoved her pistol into her holster and scrambled back to the RV. Her legs felt weak, and she stumbled twice over broken concrete. They were smack in the center of the road, something she barely noticed in the heat of the moment.

The RV door flew open just as she reached it. Bruno stood in front holding a frying pan. Mariah and Spot were next to him.

Flint twisted around in the driver's seat. "What is it?"

"A man," she stuttered. "He's hurt and needs help." Her thoughts were racing, and each word came out broken.

Mariah gave a quick nod. Her motherly face hardened as she pushed past Lisa. Mariah was a doctor before the fall of the world. Although plump, sweet, and caring, when it came to anything medical, she was as focused as a neurosurgeon.

It took Lisa a moment before she shook herself and followed. Flappy footsteps made by sandals told her Bruno was following. There was a lot of light from the three vehicles, but she could still make out the shadows of zombies, staying an abnormal distance. They weren't acting like the light was repelling them, which led her to believe they were acting on direct orders from Hector.

Mariah made it to the man and gave him a quick look over. "I should be able to save him. We need to get him in the RV."

Hector nodded, stepped in, and scooped up the man like he weighed nothing.

Lisa stood for a moment, still shaken. It was a rushed decision to try and help. She knew better. Scrappers were notoriously ruthless and untrustworthy. Even if she tried to argue that it was the right thing to do, endangering her friends was definitely not the right thing to do.

Two mistakes. Why do I keep doing this?

It didn't take long for her to get to her senses. She sucked in a long deep breath to steady her thoughts. There was a motorcycle here and an entire jeep to search for supplies. Turning, she spotted Bruno behind her, wringing his hands. He looked nervous.

"Get Flint. We need to look at that jeep. It'll have gas and other things we need."

Bruno shook his head which looked more like a shiver. As he hurried back to the RV his sandals made loud flap flap sounds against the concrete. She made her way to the Jeep. It looked like it had plowed several zombies. The bumper was bent, and the cattle guard was half broke off and twisted from where it had dragged under the vehicle. The windshield was cracked, and two side windows were broken.

She started on the driver's side. There were bullets in the center console, a knife, and a bag in the passenger seat. It might have been a terror of a night, but there were things here they needed.

Flint was quick to show up. "Hell yeah," he said, as he yanked open the back door. "There's tons of good stuff in here."

She pulled the bag off the passenger seat and started going through it. As she did, Bruno returned with the gas syphoning kit. As they seemed to have things handled, she took some time to rummage through the bag's contents. It was a very worn leather backpack with blood on it.

She reached in, hearing things clink that sounded like glass and other things that sounded plastic. She pulled out a couple of flash drives first. Next, she pulled out a vial. It was thick glass with a black goo inside of it. The label looked to have been damaged by something wet. She grabbed at the bag and felt a wet spot on the bottom. *Something in there must have broken.*

It made her uneasy, and a cold chill crept up her back. It made her already sore muscles tighten more and pain wrapped around her waist.

Hector strode forward, sniffing the air. He had been shot, but for a creature that could heal himself it had never really been a problem. It still made her insides twist. If the world only knew how much he had been through trying to save them.

"You doing okay?" she asked, once he got close.

He reached out towards the bag. "Give me that."

"Gladly."

He sniffed again and his muscles tensed, shoulders rolling forward and his jaw growing taunt. "Where did you find this?"

She nodded towards the Jeep. "In there."

Hector reached in the bag and pulled out another vial. He scanned it intensely and then looked to the one she was holding.

"You know what these are?" she asked.

"Zombie research. I can smell it."

"Like what you do?"

He went silent for a moment as he fished more vials and some flash drives from the bag. "Possibly." He took a quick breath before his gaze seemed to go towards her hands. "This bag is contaminated. You need to clean up." He got behind her, ushering her towards the RV, while not waiting for a response. "Be careful of anything you touch."

Lisa spun and pointed towards the Jeep. "The boys are ransacking it right now. There might be more in there."

Hector gave her a quick nod. "I will take care of it."

Lisa ran back to the RV. It was a struggle to maneuver the outside door and the door to the narrow bathroom. They had a small water tank they used for the sink and a backup for the toilet. Used for emergencies only as they didn't have a good way of cleaning it out.

Spot came up behind her, nudged his chunky chest against her legs, and then ran out behind her. Lisa could hear Mariah mumbling in the bunk room to her left, which made her stomach squirm. They saved him, but who was he? He could be some kind of ruthless scrapper, although that didn't seem to fit. The idea of a lone man riding into danger in the middle of the night didn't track. He did say something about an Emily. *Maybe this is a relationship thing?*

After a while of fussing to get her hands clean, footsteps came from behind her.

Flint wedged his way in. "Don't hog it."

Lisa groaned. He crushed her face first against the wall and forced her to sidestep out and smash her breasts across the doorway. "Well, I could help if you weren't being such a jerk."

"Ugh, why does Hector have to kill the fun?"

Lisa shoved him towards the sink. "He's trying to keep us alive, you jerk."

"Yeah, to do nothing every day." He only ran the water a few seconds before turning as he rolled his eyes. "I'm taking point up top." He shoved past her, forcing her to take a step towards the bunks.

Flint continued his grumpy rampage and shoved Bruno out of the way as he went for the door. Bruno stumbled, catching himself on the driver's seat.

Lisa's shoulders fell. This wasn't the time to fight, even if she was angry. She knew it was fueled by fear. She tilted her head towards the sink where they had an old, modified sanitizer station filled with Hector's alcohol chemical mix for decontaminating. "Bruno, let me help you get cleaned up."

Bruno jumped and slapped a dirty hand on the seat. He jerked his hand back, raising it up like a surgeon ready to operate. His eyes, large and seeming scared, shifted from her to the seat where he left an obvious and potentially contaminated handprint.

"I'll clean it."

"Oh, thanks Lisa. I can always count on you."

She let him by and then cleaned the seat. Hector returned shortly after.

"There you are," said Lisa, as Hector shut the RV door behind him. The squeak of a dry hinge obscured half her words. "What did you find out?"

He clutched the bag in his hands. He looked tense and moved stiffly. "We better rest up here and stay out of the city until dawn." He moved to his desk and set the bag down. He held his shaking hand above it for a moment before clenching his fist and walking back to the RV door. "I'm going up top for some air. Everyone should get some rest."

Although she wanted to protest, seeing how tense he was, she let him go. He wasn't the only one. Her back was now burning, and her legs and feet had started to tingle. There was no point trying to stop him if she couldn't take care of herself right now. It would just make him worry more.

Lisa and Bruno ended up moving to the front seats to get a little sleep. Mariah didn't come out of the bunk room. Flint wasn't around either, so Lisa guessed Mariah had hauled him back to the bunks as well. Since it was becoming a bit of a hospital back there, it made up front not so bad.

HECTOR'S JOURNAL

June 13th, 2037

    I found some survivors. I attempted to help them, but they tried to kill me. I have found I have the power to command any level of turned. I attempted to give them a chance at escaping by commanding the turned to disengage. I found that my powers have a range. The survivors were killed. I'm not sure I will be able to save anyone without a cure.

    I have fallen considerably behind the others. They are getting harder to track. Attempts to reestablish a new lab have proven very difficult. I have been reduced to scrounging the materials I need from fallen cities.

Chapter 7

Dawn came too soon, and the sun was piercing. Lisa groaned, shading her eyes. She tried to sit up when her back cramped. She groaned. An electrical shock went down her leg to her tingling toes. Like her foot had fallen asleep, but worse. Grabbing the passenger seat, she pulled herself up and stumbled forward.

Hector was intently studying something at his desk until she sucked in a quick breath. His head jolted up. She couldn't see his eyes through the goggles, but she felt him scanning her up and down.

He stood slowly, his large lanky body cramped in the small space. "Your back again?"

Lisa glanced at Bruno in the other seat. He was still out cold, head back, and drool running down his chin. It seemed everyone wasn't up yet. She tried to stretch, but the shock happened again. Her knee went out, taking her halfway down to the floor.

Hector moved forward with two long fast steps. He caught her arms. "We need to take care of this. It's only getting worse," he whispered.

She took his arms to help steady herself. "I'm fine. Really."

He leaned closer to her. His breath, hot, brushed her ear. "Please, don't lie to me. I couldn't live with myself if anything happens to you."

"You worry too much." She tried to smile, but another wave wiped it from her face.

Hector wrapped his arms around her, and lifted her like a strong man would lift an atlas. He turned, carrying her through the RV.

He had her arms pinned to her sides and she hurt too much to protest. She rested her head on his shoulder until he set her on his desk chair.

"I'll get Mariah, maybe she can help."

As he turned Lisa grabbed his arm. "Don't bother her. I just need to wake up."

His head lowered. "How about I make you coffee then. I think we still have some muscle relaxers left in the med kit."

"That would be great, honey." She didn't expect that to roll off her tongue and she jolted. The contracture in her back grew so intense that it started bending her backwards. She grabbed his desk, trying not to fall out of his chair.

"I'm getting Mariah."

His voice was distant, drowned out by the blood pounding in her ears.

It didn't take long before Mariah scurried out of the bunk room. She pressed past Hector and moved to Lisa's side. "Back spasms again, huh?"

What do you think? Gritting her teeth, Lisa's response came out a groan instead of words.

"I have some Succinylcholine left over. Give me a moment."

Sucky Chlorine was all that Lisa heard. *Medicines have stupid names.*

Hector moved around to her side closest to the front seats as Mariah raided her medical stash in the back. He crouched by her side and placed his long hand on her knee. "Just hang in there."

"Don't have much of a choice." This was painful but colored with embarrassment. She had called Hector Honey. *What was I thinking? I didn't mean to say that out loud.* Plus, she was trying to protect him. How could she do that if she was bent in half backwards?

Mariah returned with the white metal box they looted at the last city. She had several medications in there. The metal clunked on the desk as she set it down and the glass contents clinked together from the impact. The whole thing smelled like rubbing alcohol.

"Under normal circumstances I would never consider using something we just found." Mariah muttered as she worked. "I don't know how old this is. How long it has gone without refrigeration. I never read anything about shelf life."

"Oh, just do it," said Lisa. "Either it'll kill me, or it won't. Both would be better-" Another wave cut her off. She grabbed Hector's hand and gave it a tight squeeze.

Mariah drew up a syringe of the medication. She wasn't a fighter, but she could reach into a body to pull a bullet out without even flinching.

"What's going on?" asked a male voice.

Hector stood fast.

"What the fuck are you?"

Lisa turned enough to see the motorcycle man. He looked pale and his head was bandaged with a dark spot over the bullet wound where blood had seeped through.

"Sir," said Mariah. "Please be quiet a few more moments. I'm working here. Hector, sit down."

Hector knelt back down, while Mariah administered the medication. A quick IM injection was nothing compared to the spasming.

With a long breath Mariah started to put things back together. "Now, this is fast acting, but not instant. Just sit still."

When she turned towards the man, he backed away from her. She raised her hands, the metal medicine box hooked on her thumb. "I am- was a doctor. And you shouldn't be up yet. I'm still worried you could have cerebral hemorrhaging."

"What's going on here? Who are you people?"

"Shut up and listen," Mariah snapped.

She was loud enough Bruno flapped about in the front seat, startled from sleep.

Mariah grabbed the folding chair she sometimes used when cooking and set it up in front of the man. "Your condition is critical. If you do not listen, you could die. Or worse, become so brain damaged that you might as well have been bitten by a zombie."

The man didn't look entirely scared, but he certainly was shocked. When Mariah fixed him with her mom look and pointed at the chair, he obeyed and sat down.

Mariah leaned against the sink. "Now, quick recap. You were shot, but the bullet glanced off your skull. You have a concussion. A bad one. I suspect cerebral hemorrhaging as well, but the fact you can stand tells me it's not as bad as I suspected. That being said, your blood pressure goes up, and your brain is going to pop like a water balloon in the hands of a toddler. You got it?"

He nodded.

"Now, I'm Mariah. I used to be a doctor. That girl bent in half is Lisa, she used to do home construction."

Great introduction. The girl bent in half. She kept a tight grip on Hector's hand. He comforted her, and she had to be strong for him. She knew how much he worried about them, but she also didn't fail to notice how he worried over her especially.

Mariah waved a hand towards Hector. "This lanky man with horrible fashion taste is Hector. He's a First Turned zombie and our resident scientist and zombie deterrent."

The flop flop sound of sandals drew Lisa's attention to Bruno. He was up now, with crusted drool on his cheek. His hair was wild and the circles under his eyes were dark. He looked like a tired kid.

Mariah smiled and nodded his way. "This kid is Bruno. Flint is on the roof and our zombie dog Spot is outside."

The pain started to ease and Lisa, finally, was able to sink down into the chair.

Hector placed his other hand on top of hers. "Is it getting better?"

"A bit," she groaned. "At least I can feel my toes again."

"Next time don't wait so long," said Mariah.

"I didn't wait at all. I woke up this way."

"Well, then we need to start a regimen to help prevent this. I will look through what medication we have and come up with a treatment plan. Now," she turned back to the man, "who are you?"

"I'm... Jim." He swallowed hard. His eyes looked like those of man twice his age. His short black hair was a mess across his face. Every inch of him was coated with dirt and dried blood.

Bruno waved. "Hi, Jim. Welcome to the family." He smiled awkwardly. As everyone turned to him, Bruno ducked his head down and backed towards the cab.

Jim raised a hand. "Let me get this straight. You're traveling with a first turned zombie and... what? A zombie dog?"

"He's actually kinda cute," said Mariah.

"But... how? How are you all still... human?"

Hector didn't make a sound, but Lisa felt something in him shift. Like that was a direct attack at him. She gave his hand a little shake and smiled. Lisa swiveled the chair around to face him. "Let's get something straight. We're a family here. Hector and Spot included. And, frankly, it was Hector who saved you. If he hadn't intervened the zombies would have swarmed you. Especially with all the commotion you made."

"He—" Jim cut himself off, taking his gaze from her to Hector. "You can control the zombies."

Hector gracefully nodded. "It has its limitations, but yes, I can."

Jim straightened up and leaned forward in the chair. His face flushed red. "So—"

Mariah raised a hand. "No. No. Blood pressure, remember. This is a casual conversation only. When everyone is healed up then you boys can go to fists. But as long as you're my patient you'll behave." She directed the last part pointedly at Jim.

Taking a breath Jim slumped forward and put his face in his hands.

"I'll go and give you all some space," said Hector.

Lisa tried to pull him back to her side, but his strength was nothing she could contend with, and he pulled free of her grip easily.

"I think I'm going to follow him," said Bruno. He scurried out of the RV after Hector.

"How you doing, kiddo?" asked Mariah.

"Bending the correct direction again," said Lisa. "Thanks, by the way. I didn't mean to wake you."

She shook her head. "Oh, you didn't sweetie. I've been monitoring his ass all night." She flashed a quick grin at Jim. "How are your symptoms? Headache? Double vision? Nausea?"

"Yes," said Jim.

"To which?"

"All of them." He touched the bandages and flinched.

"Lucky for you, you literally have a thick skull. I wasn't joking when I said how critical you are. I'm surprise you're conscious."

"Guess I'm hardheaded." A half grin pulled at his lips. "I am thankful you saved me, but you have to understand," his fists clenched, "I have seen so many people die to those things. And you have one here as a pet."

Lisa shot up, her face instantly blazing. "He's not a pet!"

Jim pulled back.

Mariah shook her head. "You must be feeling better."

"Not at all. It hurts like hell." Lisa pointed a finger at Jim. "Let's get this straight. Hector is a good man."

"He's a zombie," said Jim, waving his hand towards the door.

"No! He's a First Turned. You know what that means?"

Jim shrugged. "First infected?"

"Exactly. He was one of the scientists present when this outbreak happened."

"So, he helped make this infection?"

Mariah made a lower-your-tone gesture with her hands. "Blood pressure."

"No," said Lisa "He was researching animal DNA sequences. There was an explosion which mixed the chemicals making this virus."

"Is that what he told you?"

Her heart pounded. "Yes, and we trust him. He's kept us safe in this shit hole existence. It's more than you have."

He chewed his bottom lip and then raised his hands. "I'm not here to start fights. I'm just trying to find Emily"

"Who's that?" asked Mariah.

"She's my neighbor from Haven."

Lisa pulled back. "You're from Haven?"

"Yes. I've lived there for several years."

"How did your neighbor end up out here?" asked Mariah. "Is she part of the scrappers?"

"She used to be, but I thought she gave up that life." Jim pointed a shaking hand towards the cab. "That fuck, Marco, pulled her back into this. I swear, if anything happened to her, I'll kill him."

Raising a brow, Lisa gingerly sat back down. "You're too late for that. You shot him last night."

"Fuck. He was my only lead."

"Maybe not, dear. Hector found some evidence that they were at a lab. He thinks he knows where it's at."

Lisa nodded. "We're heading there today. Or, at least, that was the plan. He wanted to wait until daylight, so it was safer."

Jim's dark chocolate eyes darted up to her. "Where's that? I need to know."

"You'll know when we get there," said Mariah. "And before you argue, you are in no shape to go vigilante out there. Besides, we already packed your bike up. So, I say we travel together. When you're better, you're free to leave as you please."

"So, I'm your hostage."

"You're my patient. I'm not losing anyone else." She took in a quick breath. Her gaze drifted to the window and looked distant. Pained. "I'm going to get some air and then I'll cook breakfast."

Lisa waited for Mariah to leave before turning her attention back to Jim. "Well, you got a knack for clearing a room."

"Then why are you still here?"

"Well, I'm not really a fan of pain."

His chiseled face softened. "What's wrong with you?"

He worded it a bit harshly, but his tone said he was just asking. She guessed he didn't mean anything by it. "My back. I get spasms. Have for years." The RV fell to an uncomfortable silence for a moment. She couldn't handle it. "So, this Emily, she's your girlfriend?"

"No. Just my neighbor."

"What?" Lisa leaned forward and put her hands on her knees to help take the pressure off her back. "You came all the way out here for someone who's just your neighbor?"

"She had a chance at a life in Haven. She doesn't realize how good she has it. It's safe there."

"It's not safe anywhere. Safety is just a way of saying you went soft."

"I guess you'd need that attitude if you've survived out here this long."

Survived... no. Hector protected her. She had survived quite a while, but she wouldn't have made it without Hector and the others. There were so many times she was almost killed. It was just luck.

Spot barked outside and then ran into the RV. Jim jumped, pulling his leg back as if a snake just crawled over his foot.

"Is that Spot?"

"Yup. Goofy, but a good boy. He's gone toe to toe with a lot of Zombies."

"But, he's a zombie too. He looks... a lot more dog-like than I expected."

"He's Hector's experiment. He's working on a cure."

Jim's eyes flashed, like someone lit a light inside of him. "Cure... There's a cure..."

"Not yet. Hector's working day and night on it. Spot was a test. Hector cured him of his photo... whatever. He doesn't burn in sunlight anymore and acts like any other dog. But that's where it ended."

"But... But there could be?"

She nodded. "That's why he wants to find this lab. It might have answers. Hector was the first infected. He knew what they were working on in the lab he was in, and he's been studying this longer than anyone. If any being is going to find a cure, it's going to be him." Hector entered the RV as she was midsentence, so she finished while flashing a smile his way.

"The sun is in our favor," said Hector. "We're going to head on towards the city."

Lisa nodded. "I'll take watch up top."

"No." Hector shook his head. "Lay down for an hour or two and let your back heal. Flint slept through his watch so he's going to drive."

"You don't have to rat a guy out like that," said Flint, coming in behind Hector. He paused and eyed Jim. "Dude with the muscles survived?"

"My name is Jim."

"Well, Jim, glad you didn't get eaten. Hey, wanna take shotgun with me?"

Jim looked around at the others, as if he was afraid to answer.

Hector gave him a calm slow nod. "Check with Mariah. I will not be in the RV if that will make you more comfortable."

"But you need some rest too," said Lisa. "You promised you'd get some sleep today."

"I will go up top with Bruno and nap up there. Can we agree to that?"

Her shoulders fell and her chest tightened. She hated seeing him push so hard, and yet he still was as strong as ever. But for how long? *How long can he push? How long before it's too much?* "I... I guess that will work."

Hector turned back around and headed out, pausing long enough to let Mariah back in. She patted Hector on the shoulder on the way by.

"Well, kids, I'll get cooking." She turned to Lisa. "I told Hector to tell you to lay down."

"Yeah, he told me. I will, but only for an hour. Get me up when we get to our destination."

"I suppose I can agree to it." Mariah turned to Jim with one hand on her hip. "I heard you talking. You going up front with Flint?"

"I guess, since I can't leave."

"Just be careful."

Lisa didn't say anything and awkwardly slipped by Jim to get to the back bunks. She didn't like how things were turning out but stretching out in her bunk alone felt good. A curtain wasn't much, and it let every sound travel in, but it made her muscles uncoil.

HECTOR'S JOURNAL

July 20th, 2037

Little progress made. I'm so lonely. I wish my existence would end, but I must go on if there is any chance I can make a cure for this. I must fix all the pain I caused.

Chapter 8

Yanika and Eric were escorted out the back of the outpost with a large group made up of guards and civilians, and then herded into several vans. It was several hours before they left, as more and more civilians were still coming to the outpost.

She shivered, gripping her chicken cage tightly. Cuddles was her prized pet. She gave everything she had to have scrappers bring her chickens from outside. For the past few years, she selectively bred them. They were the best combination of egg layers and meat that Haven had. She thought she was getting an invitation to bring her chicken to the Capitol. Maybe join the farms in the Median. The middle farmland where, rumor was, there were nice houses and plenty of food. Now she was questioning everything.

She was in just an average minivan with large windows on either side. Dawn had come, bringing with it a red sun that washed over the countryside. The Outer Rim was surrounded by the outside walls on one side and barbed fence on the other. The guards were in charge of keeping those from the Outer Rim from crossing the border into the Median.

She'd never seen anyone get arrested, but people did tend to vanish. There were stories that there was a huge prison where people who try to escape to the Median are kept. Other stories say if you're caught you were executed. She was too afraid to take the risk, so she worked as hard as she could. But this didn't feel like the escape she wanted. Everyone seemed so tense. There were so many civilians mixed with guards, neither seeming to know what was going on.

Outside the windows stretched vast farmlands. Corn, beans, cows, and sheep. Large farmhouses that seemed to be cobbled together with old existing buildings and new construction. They weren't the cute country houses she envisioned. These reminded her of the huts in the Outer Rim, made from whatever was available.

Eric sat next to her and another guard next to him. This van had three rows of seating. Two front seats and two benches in the back. The trunk had someone from the Outer Rim sitting back there with luggage piled on his lap.

Eric seemed nice. Nicer than the rumors she had heard. She knew he was one of guards that distributed food. Rumor had it he was gruff, and some called him a jerk. He was tall and thin with short cut blonde hair and bright blue eyes.

He leaned over and was whispering to the other guard. "You know what's going on?"

"Not sure," said the other man. "I heard this is the first stage of a draft."

"A draft? None of these people would qualify for guards."

"I know, right? Something is up." The other man's voice dropped lower, until she could only hear every other word, but she could still partially read his lips. "I overheard one of the generals. It sounded like they were talking about running out of supplies."

"Like what?"

"Not sure."

Yanika shivered. *Draft?* She gripped the cage. Cuddles eyed her and made a soft cluck. *I'm not a fighter. I just wanted to be a chicken farmer. Have a bed under a roof that didn't leak. And what about Cuddles?* Tears burned at her eyes. *Cuddles is family. I don't want anything happening to her.* She felt like she was being watched, and noticed, out of the corner of her eye, Eric was looking at her.

"You okay? Yanika, right?"

"Yeah. Yeah, I'm fine."

Eric poked at the cage. "She's kinda cute."

A smile tried to tug at her lips but faded fast. Her gut was churning. "I've been breeding chickens since I got here. It took everything I had, but I knew if I wanted a better life, I needed to be good at something. I... I thought I was getting this... summons or whatever to join the other farmers in the Median."

"That makes the most sense. Maybe you will be. Maybe it was easier to send a bunch of vans and take everyone, instead of taking groups."

It sounded promising, but she caught the guard next to Eric shaking his head.

"I'm going to die, aren't I?"

"Not a chance," said Eric quickly. "I'll keep you and... Cuddles you called her?"

"Yeah."

"I'll keep you and Cuddles safe. As soon as we stop, I'll start asking questions."

The other guard chimed in. "You sure that's a good idea?"

"Well, if they are gathering more men, then I doubt they'll kill me. It's worth it to find out more. I have a really bad feeling about this."

"Same, man."

The three of them went quiet again. Yanika looked out the window, wishing she could just jump out and run. This place was far enough away she couldn't see the wall anymore. There was just bright farmland. It looked so warm and welcoming. Fences were mostly barbed wire and butted right up against the two-lane road they were on. It was curvy and they weren't going very fast. It gave her time to really take it all in.

There were black and white cows, eating grass by the fence. It had been years since she saw a cow. A hog farm was on the other side. The rich stench from them drifted though the van vents and filled the space. Someone in the back gagged.

The Capitol was said to have once been a quaint town, but she heard they had turned it into the central hub near the center of Haven. She'd heard tales of mansions still standing like they did before the world ended. A place that a person could forget about the outside madness. A place that was always safe. She knew she most likely would never see it and she was okay with that. She was okay with the idea of just being a good chicken farmer. Not a soldier.

I don't want to die. I'm no fighter. The zombies will just eat me the moment I step outside the wall. I have to find some way out of this.

HECTOR'S JOURNAL

September 8th 2037

I have taken over a fallen government facility. It pains me to see the turned soldiers here. I have ordered them away because I cannot focus with them so close.

I intercepted a satellite transmission from China. It seems the horde has reached the area. The transmission warns people not to enter. I have not heard anything of surrounding countries, but I suspect many have fallen.

I have been synthesizing possible cures, but I have no test subjects. The turned here are too far gone, many having little blood volume and intact organs. I have looked into animal subjects. I have discovered only one animal turned in this area. After observation I have noticed that the turned are not attacking animals.

I do not have a reasonable hypothesis as of yet. Will investigate further.

Chapter 9

The RV rumbled as this rag-tag group headed towards the city. Jim sat in the passenger seat with his arms crossed. His heart still pounded, and he gritted his teeth. This was easily the most troubled he ever felt. Part of him was grateful for being rescued and part of him was angry and revolted by the fact they kept company with zombies.

Flint sat next to him driving the RV. He looked like a used-to-be biker or street racer. He had a naturally cocky face and short-cut hair, longer down the middle like he was starting to grow a mohawk and never finished. He wore a dirty T-shirt with a jean vest over it. His pants were dark jeans and he had scuffed high top biker boots on.

Jim had never seen a creature like the zombie they called Hector. Lisa explained he was a First Turned, and he seemed to be intelligent. Neither he nor the dog attacked him. They weren't grotesquely mutated. It felt like everything he thought he knew about zombies was different.

They are monsters. I never, never saw anyone survive the mutation. But that thing talked to me. He remembered how he acted towards Lisa. How he crouched next to her. No sign of hostility. No sign of being a monster. Trying to figure these things out made his head throb worse. He rubbed just under the bandages. The other woman, Mariah, although he hated to admit it, seemed to be right. Every time he felt a little worked up, his head throbbed to the point his vision blurred.

A sizzling sound came from behind him. Mariah had started cooking something, and the scent of onion, garlic, and some other spice filled the space. Jim's mouth watered. Something metal clanked as well. He relaxed into the white noise of someone cooking. It was a comforting sound. It was hard to get fresh food. Most people didn't even have a pot to cook with. He knew because he was the one who hand made many pots and pans for his neighbors. It was a sound that reminded him of his childhood home.

"So, you're from Haven?" said Flint.

"Yes," said Jim. He noted there was something in Flint's tone. He couldn't quite figure out what it was, but he had a haunting feeling a conversation he didn't want right now was about to commence.

Flint shrugged. "I was on the roof. Heard a little bit. You know I traveled all the way from California to get to Haven." His jaw went taut as he nodded his head. "They wouldn't let me in. Too full, they said."

Jim internally groaned. It wasn't a new story. At first, he hated it. Hated hearing stories of loved ones trapped outside to die. Eventually he accepted that was just the way of things now.

"So how did you manage to get in?" asked Flint.

"I was part of the crew that built Haven."

"Oh, insider. I see. Must be nice getting that little piece of Haven." Flint's tone was level but mocking.

"They let me in, but wouldn't let my wife and daughter in."

"Oh." His tone changed. "Sounds like shit they'd pull. What happened?"

"They died," said Jim. Saying it out loud made a stabbing pain go straight through his chest. He wanted to end this conversation.

"I'm sorry, dude. I guess I'm not surprised. I think everyone has lost someone."

"Who did you lose?" Jim didn't want the answer, but he felt like, to be polite, he needed to ask.

"Sheela. She was a beaut. Curvy and flawless. Old, but not like too old. But I loved her."

"Was she your girlfriend?"

Flint's brow dropped and his lip pulled back into a childish smile. "What? No. She was my car."

Jim groaned, out loud this time. "You got to be kidding me." He got up, planning on getting away from this loon. Once upright the room moved in front of him like he was on a ship in an ocean storm, everything was swaying back and forth. He grabbed the back of the passenger seat and tried to take steps forward. He found himself leaning more and more to the left. The room spun. Little dots speckled his vision like fleas.

"Whoa, big guy." Mariah spotted him, tossed her spatula on the counter, and moved over to his side. As she caught his arm, she hooked Hector's stool with her foot and pulled it over. "Sit down. Sit."

The room still spun. Feeling like he was slowing falling he sat down hard on the stool.

"Stood up too fast, didn't you?"

He groaned as he put his face in his hand. "Yeah. Thank you."

"It's fine dear. It'll take a while for you to heal all up. How about some lunch?"

His mouth was already watering from the smells alone. He felt both hungry and sick to his stomach from his swirling surroundings. "I... Something light maybe."

Mariah went to the skillet and dished up some food into a plastic bowl. "It's not light, but try and eat something." She handed him the bowl. "Here you go honey. Seasoned canned chicken and beans."

Stream rose up from the dish and the hot plastic warmed his hands. The beans were kidney beans, and he could see specks of garlic and onion. "It smells delicious."

"Just wait until you taste it," said Mariah.

"She's even a better cook than a doctor," shouted Flint.

Mariah huffed. "Keep your voice down. Lisa is trying to rest."

The curtain to the bunk room pulled back. Lisa came out, a half grin on her face. "Was asleep."

Jim had found himself in there before. When he first woke up to spots dotting his vision and distant voices that sounded like they were at the end of a long tunnel. He thought he was dead. It was even more shocking to see Hector, a First Turned zombie, and this girl bent unnaturally backwards. Lisa was a blonde medium height petite woman. She wore a brown shirt that had a rip in the side, tight jeans, and boots that were unlaced and looked to have been stretched to be slip-ons. Her eyes were a light green, a color that surprised him. He'd never seen eyes so light and bright before.

Lisa popped up a folding chair and then took a bowl of food that Mariah offered her. The bustle brought him back to the meal in his hands. He stirred it a few times and then took a tiny bite. The flavors melted him like butter in a hot skillet. Unlike the scraps he lived with in Haven, this had flavor. The smells all mixed together with the flavor of actual spices. It made him realize how many times he'd eaten rat to survive.

Smiling, Mariah took bowls of food to Flint and then up to Hector. The RV was moving slowly, and it seemed Flint knee what was going on because he slowed even further when Mariah opened the RV side door. Like usual, she had a small picnic basket balanced in the crook of her arm, making it easier to reach around to the ladder to get to the roof.

Lisa took a couple of bites before turning to Jim. She nodded at him with her cheek stuffed with food. "How you feeling?"

"Like trash. You?"

She shrugged. "Little less trash than before." She slurped up another bite while keeping her eyes on him. "So, you're looking for Emily. Do you think she's in the city?"

"I hope not." He hung his head, pausing with his spoon midway to his mouth. The city— all cities for that matter were death sentences.

"If she used to be a scrapper, she's probably resourceful. She could be held up somewhere."

"There's no way one person can keep those things out," Jim growled. "It's different when you're a group. Especially one already running with the zombies."

"We're not the same as those things out there. Get it through your head."

Her tone was sharp. Not unpleasant but pointed. Jim went back to his food. So many years on scraps made each bite surprise him, like he thought any moment it would start tasting like cooked rat.

The engine of the RV hummed, making a light background noise. Each time the vehicle turned he felt the wheeled stool try to slide. Peeking out the window, he spotted the buildings of the city. It made his muscles tense. Although this wasn't his first time in the city, far from it, it still put him on edge. Even in the day a place filled with dark hiding holes.

He heard a weird animal sound from the bunk room. Pausing, he watched Spot, the zombie dog, wander out through the curtain that divided the bunk room from the rest of the RV. Spot yawned, revealing unnaturally long teeth, and then shook himself. His fur was short, white and brown, with assorted scruffy bald patches.

He had expected him to look like some of the other mutated zombies. They usually looked half mauled, sometimes having revealed bones. Some only had some flesh hanging off their skulls. This guy looked almost cute.

Lisa looked back at Spot and smiled. "Here boy."

Like a normal dog he started to pant and his stubby tail shook. He hopped over to her, whimpering and begging. She fished a pinch of chicken from her bowel and fed it to him. Like an average good boy, he nibbled her fingers for the snack.

Jim lowered his spoon to the bowl in disbelief. "How?"

"How what?" asked Lisa. She raised a brow and gave him a look like he was crazy.

"How is he so... normal?" His voice raised. Usually, he had a little more composure and control than this, but this was crazy.

"He's not really a zombie," said Lisa. "Already told you. Hector was able to mostly cure him."

"That's... That's... incredible." Jim felt both shock and a deep pain in his chest. If this was around years ago maybe he could have saved his family. It was still a deep dark hole in his heart. He worked to forget his loss. Bury himself in his work and just accept the world as it was. Shitty.

The RV slowed, grabbing both of their attention.

Static came from up front followed by Flint's voice. "Yo, we got another of those Jeeps." Flint spoke into a walkie to someone. Jim wasn't sure whom.

Jim sprang up, instantly regretting the decision as the floor spun. Lisa pitched her bowl on the counter and grabbed for his arm. Jim pushed her away, opting to stumble and catch himself on the passenger seat.

"Whoa," said Flint. "What's wrong with you?"

Jim looked out the window at the vehicle in the middle of the road directly in front of them. He dug his finger into the leather seat. "Is there anyone in there?"

"Fuck if I know," said Flint.

Jim turned towards the door and then yanked at the heavy metal latch.

"Hey, where are you going?" asked Lisa.

"To look for Emily. That's one of Marco's Jeeps."

"You're not well enough to go out there."

Jim spun and slammed his fist on the door behind him. "Stop telling me what I'm well enough to do. You don't know me."

Lisa squared up to him, muscles tightening and shoulders rising. He didn't expect her to be so imposing. She stepped forward, looking up directly in his eyes. She was shorter and much thinner than him, yet he felt like he was up against someone his size or bigger.

"Maybe rushing into the zombie thicket worked for you in the past, but here we actually try not to get killed."

He pushed his fist harder against the door. It was daylight. Most likely there wouldn't be any problem going to the Jeep. But he couldn't dismiss there was a zombie Lord on the roof. No one seemed hostile, but it still put him on edge. He didn't know how far he could push his luck.

"You going to stop me?" he asked.

"It's not me you have to worry about. It's Hector."

Jim clenched his jaw. "What? What will your zombie pet do to me?"

"You're being a jerk."

She reached like she planned to shove him in the shoulder, but he grabbed her hand first. "I'm a jerk? I'm the one trapped here."

"You're not trapped, idiot. Hector found some contaminated vials in the last Jeep. He's afraid we'd get infected. But if you want to go join the zombies, go right ahead." She stepped back and crossed her arms.

Flint turned the RV off and then pushed through them, making Jim step away from the door. "If you lovers are done with your quarrel, Hector gave us the all-clear to loot around the vehicle. He's gonna check out the Jeep first."

Lisa looked at Jim as she raised a brow. It was the perfect vision of I told you so. Grunting, she pushed him aside as well and headed out. Spot whimpered and then followed her outside.

Jim paused before following. Despite desperately wanting to look for Emily, he also had another unknown emotion brewing. His stomach felt weird and his head, still cloudy from his injury, struggled with complex thought. He touched his bandages again, debating what was coming from his injury and what was real. Did he actually feel bad... guilty... for how he treated them?

"Staying here isn't going to save Emily," he mumbled to himself. Following the others, he stepped out onto the road, surrounded by the ruins of a world he had almost forgotten.

It was haunting, seeing a once sprawling city in ruins. Malls broken down, burnt, roofs collapsed. Greenery taking back the concrete forest. The few years in Haven he had almost forgot about this place. *No...* He knew it was a lie. *I was hiding from these memories.* He wasn't satisfied with life, he just went with it in order to forget the past. Now it was here, all around him.

The Jeep in front of the RV looked smashed, but not like it had plowed through hordes of zombies. The bumper was caved in like the Jeep had hit a telephone pole, but it was in the center of the road. Hector was standing next to the Jeep with a leather backpack in his hands.

Bruno climbed down the side of the RV with a syphoning kit. The plastic pipes caught the metal rails making a hallow plastic thump, thump, thump. Mariah came up to the RV door. Jim, out of the corner of his eye, caught her standing there watching them.

Flint was ransacking the back of the Jeep, pulling out handfuls of bits and pieces. Lisa was standing at the front of the Jeep rubbing her chin.

Jim glanced around. There were plenty of places for zombies to hide, but no signs of them on the streets or in the parking lots. He approached the Jeep, but felt nervous deep down in his stomach, like something was gripping inside of him and kept tightening and tightening.

Lisa looked over at Hector. "What do you make of this?"

Hector groaned and then moved closer. He was much larger than Jim first thought. He seemed gangly, like a highschooler with a bad growth spurt in tenth grade. He wore a poncho that was humped over his back. His legs were animal like with knees that bent backwards and feet that reminded him of some sort of reptile claw.

Hector examined the Jeep. He had goggles on, which made trying to pick up on facial expressions hard. It was obvious there was no one in the Jeep. At least no one alive. Jim inched forward, still leery of Hector, but mostly praying Emily was not inside. On the other hand he also wished she was, because the alternative was that she was turned and now lurked within the zombie-infested buildings.

This brought him too close to his past and his chest ached. Every muscle in his body went stiff and his fists clenched tight. It was times like this he wanted to lash out. To rid himself of these feelings with his fists. But that was old him. New him didn't care enough to lash out. New him stopped caring.

Hector's voice broke his train of thought.

Hector ran his hand along the crumpled Jeep hood. "Odds are likely this hit a zombie."

Lisa waved at the Jeep. "A zombie couldn't do this."

"Not the kinds that you know. But one early turned could."

Lisa tensed and her shoulders raised towards her ears. "Like the servants you told me about?"

"Servants?" asked Jim. "What are servants."

"They are those turned directly by the First Turned, the Zombie Lords. They are not a force to be taken lightly."

Jim inched up beside Hector. "I have never heard of Servants before."

"Most likely you have never seen one. A First Turned, what people call Lords must be the ones to turn a human. These Servants are almost as strong as I but are subject to the orders of the First Turned. In addition, sunlight effects them minimally and they often maintain their human form." Hector reached into the backpack and pulled out labeled medicine bottle. "Something doesn't feel right."

"Is..." Jim licked his lips. "Is there anyone in the Jeep?"

Hector's head lowered. "No, but there is blood on the dash and windshield. It's a few hours old."

Jim raised his shaking fists and took a long breath to try and steady his emotions.

"Tell me again the name of the woman you seek."

"Her name is Emily," Jim replied through clenched teeth.

"What does she look like?"

"Why? What does it matter?"

Hector straightened and his gaze moved to the buildings around him. "I will go around and search for her. If she has turned, I will know."

Jim jerked, his gaze shooting up to lock on Hector. "You... would do that for me? Why?" Jim took a step back. "You have nothing to gain."

"It is not about gain. It is and always has been about lives."

His voice dripped with years of sadness. The sincerity. The sound. It destroyed any doubt Jim had because he could see himself in Hector's place. It was the voice of someone on the edge of the void of having nothing left to live for. Jim nodded. "She's tall and thin with very pale skin and black hair."

Hector nodded before turning towards each of them one at a time. "Be careful, everyone. I'll make sure the zombies stay away. Try to get what supplies you can." He looked down at the backpack and then handed it to Lisa. "Can you put this on my desk?"

"Of course."

He pulled it back as she reached for it. "Be very careful not to get the contents on you."

Shaking her head, she reached up and took the bag. "Don't worry so much. We'll be fine."

Spot barked and bounded happily over towards Hector. Wagging his stubby tail, he seemed like he wanted to play.

Hector reached down and patted Spot on the head. "Keep everyone safe, buddy."

Hector smiled, which was the first time Jim had ever seen the Zombie have much of a facial expression.

Spot barked back.

Hector turned his attention to the dilapidated buildings, tensed, and then a pair of wings shot out from under his poncho. The top wings were dark, and the bottom ones were translucent, almost like a beetle or grasshopper. He swiftly took to the air.

Lisa took the bag back to the RV, only giving him a quick glance as she walked by. With a few quick steps Mariah came up beside Jim. The squat portly woman in a white coat eyed him for quite some time. Even though he had his head turned, he could feel her looking at him. Jim took a long breath inward. "What do you want?"

"Just checking on things," said Mariah. "I'm still amazed you are alive. How does your head feel?"

He really didn't want to talk about it, but she was his imposed Doctor, whether he liked it or not. "It's hurting."

"When we head back in, I have something that should help a little. I want to keep you off any NSAIDS to prevent any more bleeding."

"How did you get to be part of this group?"

She signed. "It wasn't pretty. I was at a refugee camp in Nebraska. There was a prison there that they used as a stronghold against the zombies. I worked at the local hospital and was the only doctor in the building."

"What happened?"

Mariah shrugged. "Supplies cannot last forever. A mistake was made when a group was trying to do a supply run and the zombies got in. A few of us stayed quiet and boarded ourselves into rooms and cells. Hector and Lisa came through looking for supplies. By then... I was the only one left alive. The others all were turned to zombies."

"You have to be very brave to survive something like that."

"No." She was sharp and abrupt. "It takes cowardice and luck. I hid for two weeks before they rescued me. The infirmary had a little food, but a lot of saline. I stayed silent and alive, all the while I knew the others were dying. It's the others who are truly brave. Even with Hector's help, we've still had many close encounters. They risk their lives every time we do a supply run."

"It looks like you're still a very important part of this crew."

She raised her hands while lowering her head. "Don't take this story as a plea for pity. What I'm saying is it takes an incredible amount of bravery to face the world as it is now."

"I'm not a brave man."

"Well, you are something. Patients with significantly less injuries are in bed for weeks. I'm surprised you are still standing with your faculties about you."

Jim grinned. "I might just be hardheaded."

"We can agree on that."

Jim turned, catching a glimpse of Hector flying from building to building.

"He'll do all he can to find her, hun."

"I don't know why he would help me." He wasn't sure exactly what to say. Their stories were riddled with pain, which he expected, but Hector being the connecting factor was still a hard pill to swallow. They seemed to regard the creature as their savior. *Stockholm syndrome maybe?*

Mariah chuckled. "That's Hector for you. He may be a zombie Lord, but don't judge a book by its cover. He cares deeply." She gave Jim's arm a casual friendly tap. "You seem to have a good head on your shoulders. You should think about staying with us a while. We could use someone like you."

"Sorry, but I can't. I'm only here to bring Emily back to Haven."

Mariah shrugged. "It's our loss. I'm going to start prepping something for supper. Come find me if any of your symptoms get worse."

"You got it, Doctor." He smiled, causing her to smile back as she walked away. She seemed sweet and had a motherly feel to her.

Lisa was returning from the RV and waved at Mariah as they passed. There was a gentle breeze that rustled her blonde hair. Her endless green eyes locked on him. She acknowledged him with a quick tip of her head upwards.

"Hector find anything?" she asked.

"He hasn't come back yet."

Spot whimpered and pawed at Jim's leg.

"I don't have treats. Sorry."

"Don't worry," said Lisa. "He doesn't need it. First zombie I ever knew to get fat."

Spot tilted his head to the side.

"Yes, you. You're getting fat." Lisa laughed for a moment, but then quieted as she started to scan their surroundings.

Jim felt like the old structures had eyes, like something was lurking in every dark corner. How many zombies could be out there. *Most likely hundreds in a city this big. Can Hector really keep them at bay?* It was a gamble. He didn't know any of them, and if he didn't leave here before dark, he'd have to rely on them to survive. There's no way he could get out if the horde moved on him.

He looked at the sun arching over the clear sky, its beams dancing about the overgrown city. It looked hauntingly beautiful. The hair on the back of his neck started to rise. Trees were growing in vast parking lots and up through structures long collapsed. Lush patches of wildflowers edged the broken road. Even the empty husks of cars crashed all around them looked almost swallowed by nature. Vines, mosses, and flowers were overtaking everything human made.

"It's scary, isn't it?" Jim mumbled.

Lisa looked at him and then seemed to follow the direction of his gaze. "To be honest. It's fucking terrifying."

He turned to her, a little surprised by her response. "Thought you were the tough girl?"

"Humph." She rolled her eyes. "Not even. We all do good every day just to survive and try our best to forget places like this." She nodded her head acknowledging Bruno and Flint as they went by.

Bruno was returning to the RV with a gas can heavy enough that he had to lean back while walking to balance the weight. Flint was making several trips, bringing wires and radio parts back to the RV.

He heard Mariah shout at Flint.

"You are not bringing that junk in here."

"Come on. This is good stuff." Flint moaned like a pampered child.

"Not a chance."

Jim was getting a real feel for this group. Family. Unconventional, but a family never-the-less.

Lisa put her hands together in a prayer position and then brought them up to her lips. She looked tense. Her gaze was to the horizon where Hector was passing by.

"Anything I can do to help?" asked Jim.

"Nah, I'm just a bit on edge." She tried to grin, but it looked forced and fake.

They went quiet. Jim wasn't sure what to say. His stomach churned and the muscles in his neck ached. The constant on edge feeling was a well-known pressure he never wanted to experience again.

Flint seemed satisfied with the junk he scrounged and what Mariah would let him take on the RV. Watching over his shoulder, Jim caught sight of Flint, through the windshield of the RV, sliding into the driver's side.

Bruno came by, calling Spot to follow him into the RV. That just left him and Lisa, both intently waiting for Hector.

It didn't take long for Hector to land. His wings fluttered a moment before he pulled them under his poncho. He was large and lanky, but once landed, he hunched over making him appear more a normal human size.

"Anything?" asked Jim, stepping forward.

Hector made his way over to them while shaking his head. "I cannot see, hear, or even sense anything of the woman you are looking for."

An already upset stomach only felt worse with such a huge combination of letdown and complete fear. Saliva filled his mouth and the pressure in his stomach threatened to make him throw up. He'd come all this way to save her only to fail now. *Maybe it's not too late. Maybe she wasn't here.* "Any... Any chance she could be somewhere else?"

"It could be possible," said Hector. "From the samples I found, these scrappers found a research facility."

"She could be there," said Jim, a little hope renewed.

"It is possible." Hector spoke, but he seemed distracted by the Jeep.

"What are you thinking?" asked Lisa.

"Something isn't right here. I don't like how this Jeep crashed, or finding those samples as I did. I'm not sure how to articulate all this."

Jim looked between both of them. "Well, I think we need to head to this lab."

"I'm not sure about that," Hector mumbled, turning towards the city.

"What do you mean?" asked Lisa. "This is exactly what you've been looking for. We can't pass this up."

Hector turned and placed a hand on her shoulder. "It's too dangerous. I cannot risk this group."

Jim felt something release and drop. An uncoiling of emotion. The way Hector spoke set deep into Jim's chest. He felt lighter. He was willing to trust this creature. Maybe not totally. But how he voiced his deep concern for everyone resonated inside Jim.

Emily might be back at that lab. It seems Marco was after the items from the lab. Emily is smart. If she boarded herself up in there, she most likely will still be alive. "We have to go," Jim spit out.

Hector shook his head. "It's too dangerous."

"Why? It seems you can keep the zombies away. What do we have to worry about?"

Lisa tilted her head towards Jim. "He's right. You can keep the zombies away and we can look for Emily and get what we need from the lab."

"Not with the possibility of a servant around here. They are much harder to detect and control. I also don't know if that lab is contaminated. I would need to go in first, leaving you all behind. I'm not comfortable with any of that."

Lisa took his hand. "This is what you've been waiting for. That lab might have what we all need. Information for you." She waved her free hand at Jim. "Maybe we'll find Emily. We'll be able to look for more supplies."

Hector went quiet, his face turned to her. Jim shifted his weight towards his toes, trying to hold his tongue. He absolutely needed to go look for Emily, but he needed Hector's help to do so.

To see such a menacing creature, look genuinely scared, unnerved Jim. He felt chills on his back again with the returning sensation that there were eyes in every corner. The sun was setting, and he was torn. If Emily was still alive, she might not be by the next day. But if he took the risk, knowing she might even be alive, he might die as well. In addition, the others might not survive. He tried to keep his expression neutral and hide his own uncertainties. Still, he shifted his weight back and forth.

"We'll be fine," said Lisa. "We can't miss this opportunity. And we can't risk this lab or research center— whatever it is, getting looted again or trashed by zombies."

Hector sighed. "I can't justify it if it puts you all in so much danger."

Lisa huffed and then crossed her arms. "We came to the city for supplies. We still need more food. Mariah needs more medical supplies." She waved at the concrete wasteland before them. "I hate it, but we needed to head into the city anyway."

"I can help," said Jim quickly. "It might take time to find Emily if she is still alive. I'll work for my keep."

Hector lowered his head, his face now shadowed by the wide brim of his hat. "I can't seem to talk you two out of it."

Lisa shook her head. "I'd rather get this all done. You need rest, and I know you won't until we find this lab."

"You worry so much," Hector mumbled. "Fine. But we do this carefully and safe. No unnecessary risks." He turned to Jim. "That goes for you too. I can command the zombies, but only from a certain range. I'll need you to stay close, with the others."

Jim nodded. He almost saw Hector taking on something akin to a fatherly role, except there was something different in how he treated Lisa. Clearly there was a special bond between them.

The group all headed back into the RV. Flint took the driver's seat with Bruno in the passenger seat, Spot and Mariah in the back. Hector,

Lisa, and Jim all took point on top. Once all in position they headed deeper into the city.

It was such a slim chance that Emily was alive, but Jim held onto the thread of hope. She was strong. If anyone could survive, it would be her.

HECTOR'S JOURNAL

October 31ˢᵗ, 2037

   Halloween feels like it's no longer just one day a year as I am surrounded by the undead. I am moving towards China with the hopes of finding a facility to conduct more research. I have not found anyone alive in weeks.

Chapter 10

Mid-day came and after hours of silence Eric was on edge. Yanika looked terrified and was sweating. The mood was shared among the guards and civilians in the van. They pulled into the Capitol. Eric had been around the Outer Rim so long he had almost forgotten what Capitol looked like. The mud and filth of the Outer Rim clung to a man. It was hard to forget.

The Dutch city here sprawled around them. There were well kept historical buildings and industrial buildings around, all well powered. The nearby hydroelectric dam powered this whole city. There was a lush town square filled with grass, trees, and flowers. All of which were nonexistent in the Outer Rim.

Stores still existed here and before they reached the capitol building, he spotted a bakery, meat shop, and clothing shop. With the world dead, money no longer held value. The government created credits from melting down old coins and useless computer parts. People could sell their wares to the government for credits.

Despite credits being a large part of commerce, the biggest part was trade. Trade ruled, even with the government. Eric himself was in charge of that in the Outer Rim. He was given a list of what different items were worth in credits, but he also did some on the side trading. With so many scrappers coming through the main gate, it was easy to get some good trades.

Eric had built a good bit of wealth on the side, which made coming to the capitol very risky. He couldn't shake the rumors. This was a draft. *A draft for what?*

Once all the busses and Jeeps were parked the generals exited and then the rest of them were ushered from the vehicles. The capitol building was once a factory. He remembered seeing it the first day he became a guard. The first portion was used to house all the government officials. The front had a lush garden and fountain.

There was another portion where the machines had been removed and was used as a stationing area and barracks for the guards with general quarters off of that. The rest was the research and industrial centers were the best scientists and machinists worked.

As few cars were used anymore the parking lots were turned into parks and gardens. The whole thing had a stone wall around it with metal bars on the top. It looked like fortifications, but felt like a prison.

They headed through the main entrance where six guards were posted. They all wore matching black bullet proof vests and carried different variations of AKs in their hands at the ready. The front doors were actually four sets of double doors with white columns between them.

He turned back to Yanika. "Stay close."

She took a couple frantic steps forward, getting herself right to his back. The guards nodded at him as he tried to enter but stopped Yanika.

"No animals allowed!"

"I'm not leaving Cuddles!" she cried. Her wide eyes locked on Eric.

It was just a stupid chicken, but it meant a lot to her. He understood it, living in the Outer Rim for so long. People didn't have much, and desperately clung to what little they had.

Eric raised his hand. "It's okay, she's with me."

The same guard turned to him and repeated, "No animals allowed."

Eric nodded as a show of respect. "This is a gift for General Vandyke." Luckily, the scrappers were wells of information. He had heard in a recent trip outside the walls that General Vandyke was injured and a few of his men were turned. He also heard they were looking for a research facility, but that seemed to be hush-hush information. Eric finished his attempt at convincing this guy by saying, "This is the best beast I could find, and the nutrition will help with his recovery."

Yanika squeaked and he could tell she was heading towards a total outburst. He glanced her way quickly and winked, hoping she would understand the gesture. She pressed her lips together, chewed her bottom lip a moment, and then nodded. "Yes... A gift."

People were backed up behind them and the guard finally groaned and waved them through. "Yeah, whatever."

Eric grabbed Yanika's shoulder and pulled her quicky into the building. The entry was large, at least three stories tall and open all the way to a glass ceiling that was letting in the last rays of the day. The floors seemed to be polished concrete and there were small garden beds and potted plants all along the area. Metal signs were posted around this area, pointing to various locations.

Eric pulled Yanika to the side. There were just too many people flooding in and no real place to hide.

"What... What should I do now?" She trembled.

This girl was small in build, curvy, with skin that looked like smooth chocolate. Her hair was wild, held at bay with a red ribbon. She wore a yellow top with frilly sleeves and a burnt orange skirt he could tell had been patched several times.

She looked to be in her mid-twenties and him being late thirties made him a little uncomfortable. He wasn't sure what she would think of that age gap. The more he looked at her the more he wanted to pull her into his arms. Protect her. Tell her she was beautiful.

This was not the time for that. He knew it. "Does Cuddles really mean that much to you?"

"Of course," she said, quickly. "This is my life's work. I've been breeding chickens since I got here to make the—"

He held up his hand as he spotted a General passing nearby. "Shhhh. We can't get caught. I might have someone who can help."

She gripped the cage so tightly that her knuckles turned white. He caught her arms, just behind her elbow, and pulled her to the left along the wall. They were heading towards the barracks. From here it was obvious that it once was an industrial area. The floors still showed the outlines of the machines that were once here.

Now there were walls built in all directions, making bunk rooms, and some making large rooms which he knew were the lavish General quarters. To his left was a large bathroom with a door by it marked Janitor.

He didn't even bother to knock, opting to slip inside and pull Yanika quickly in behind him. There were shelves of cleaning products and directly in front of him was a man standing over a table. Their sudden presence made him jump and spin towards them. There were bits and pieces of technical equipment behind him which he seemed to be trying to hide.

The caustic stench of cleaning supplies and bleach in a small unventilated area made his lungs suddenly seize and he struggled to take his next breath.

"Eric, what are you doing here?"

Mark was an average man with short brunette hair and brown eyes. He wore a dirty white T-shirt and jeans. Overall average. Eric had made friends with him the short time he was training here before he was deployed to the Outer Rim. Since then, Mark was a partner with him, helping him move goods and funds.

"I need your help," said Eric.

"Who's she?" Mark eyed Yanika. He went from looking startled to a man with a dark shadow over the face. In general, he looked very pissed off.

"She's a friend. With me. I just need you to watch this chicken."

"What the fuck? You're kidding."

Eric shook his head. "It's really important to her and I want Cuddles here to stay safe until I find out more of what is going on."

Mark raised a brow. "Cuddles?"

"Is that all you're caught up on?" asked Eric, groaning.

Mark threw his hands into the air. "Fine. Fine. But I need something from you."

This was their relationship. There was no doing stuff out of kindness. It was all favors and equal shares. "What you want?"

"Information is king now-a-days. I need to know what they're doing and where they're deploying."

"Done." Eric never questioned what Mark wanted before and he wasn't going to do it now. He turned to Yanika who was clutching the cage. "You gotta trust me. Mark will take care of her until we can figure out what's going on."

"But... She's all I have."

"I know." He reached for the cage, gripping it in such a way that his fingers brushed hers. "She'll be safest here."

She let go, her hands shaking. As Eric turned, he fixed Mark with a stern look. "Anything happens to Cuddles and all our deals are off, got it?"

Mark groaned. "Fine. Fine. Nothing will happen to the drumstick."

Yanika squeaked.

Eric put his hand on her arm. She was soft and warm. He was used to the scrappers, who were callused, blunt, and downright mean at times. Or others in the Outer Rim who didn't have a care left. Many seemed one step away from death, just from hating the life they had. Yanika was different. Still scared yes, but seemingly full of life.

"Come on," he said softly. "We need to join the others before anyone finds us."

"I don't want to," said Yanika.

"I know. I don't either. But things will be a lot worse for both of us if we don't." Watching her large eyes widen even more he quickly added, "I'll keep you safe. I promise."

Despite her clenched jaw, she gave him a stiff nod.

He led her back out, keeping close to the wall where the tall potted plants gave them a little cover. There were still civilians and guards heading in, so they easily joined the flow of traffic. They were all heading towards the auditorium. It was part of the old building that had been remodeled.

Eric felt uneasy which left his skin tingling. This area was often used as a briefing space when they deployed large groups. It wasn't overtly out there that they had sent troops outside the walls for supplies. He, luckily, was kept in the Outer Rim and was never called to deploy. Until now.

Entering the space, he found himself in a chaotic mix of civilians, both from the Outer Rim and the Median, and a bunch of guards. Many of which he didn't recognize. The room was the size of a basketball court plus numerous rows of seating around it that stretched up where bleachers might have once been. There was a raised stage built in the middle and chairs that circled out from that.

Close to the stage, all the chairs matched. Further out the folding chairs varied, but not by much. Not like the outer edges where it was obvious that they ran out of seating and just grabbed whatever was available. The farthest rows were wooden dining room chairs of all shapes, sizes, and colors.

He spotted Jance, a dark haired square jawed young man that had worked with Eric at the outpost one summer. Although he wasn't there long, Eric and he hit it off.

Eric waved, getting Jance's attention. He waved back and then jogged towards them. Yanika pulled behind Eric, peering out from around him.

"Bruh, Eric, my man. Where you been?"

Eric shook his head. "Still the same dumb kid I see."

They exchanged punches to the shoulders just like they used to greet each other before.

"What's going on here?" asked Eric.

"My man, this hella sus. I heard we getting deployed to the city."

Eric felt Yanika's fingers dig into his arm.

"Why?" asked Eric.

Jance looked around and then moved so close their chests were touching. "I eavesdropped on a General. Guess Haven is running out of supplies everywhere."

"How is that possible?" Eric whispered back.

"Food isn't the issue. It supposedly is about the power or something to do with computer parts. They need to do repairs."

"Supposedly?"

"Rumor has it that the government is looking for something specific."

"What?"

"Not sure. It's being kept like top secret, you know."

Eric nodded. "Okay. Why are there so many civilians here? They can't be planning on drafting them all."

"Yo man. Told yah this hella sus. I'm takin a shot that they be thinkin' they need meat shields. Yah hear?"

"They wouldn't do that."

Jance nudged him with an elbow. "Then why there so many civilians here, dawg? You know the capitol can't feed them all."

Swallowing hard, Eric took in the crowd of over two hundred people. This mixed group held anything from the most famished from the Outer Rim to the modest farmers of the Median. No one looked like they were from the capitol or surrounding areas. It sure made it look like Jance was right.

Yanika pulled at Eric's sleeve. "What do we do?"

"For right now just be quiet and wait. We need to find out what's going on and try to stay together."

Before she could say anything, a microphone shrieked from excess feedback on the stage. The high pitch faded as someone scrambled at a digital board on the left. Center of the wooden stage stood Admiral Isaac Hammer. Many just called him The Hammer. He was the most ruthless person in all of Haven. His zombie kill count was renowned. He was the first leader of Haven, holding his title of Admiral because he was the only one of that rank alive when Haven reached completion.

He wore his uniform, a bastardized mix of the old army and navy uniform. Medals on his coat glistened from the spotlights above. Medals Eric knew full well were half made up. There was no merits or awards established when Haven was created so it was said that Hammer made up honors for his own accomplishments.

He was seldom seen outside of the capitol, being the unseen face of the Guards. Civilians spread rumors that he would kill anyone for so much as looking the wrong way at him. That might be true. The guards and even the Generals feared him. Deeply. Hammer could end a career without lifting a finger and just as easily could have someone executed.

When his deep voice bellowed over the speakers in the auditorium,

Eric went stiff.

"Everyone, sit!"

Eric grabbed Yanika's hand and pulled her down with him onto a pair of high-backed wooden chairs.

"Who's he?" asked Yanika with a shaky whisper.

"Shhh. I'll tell you later."

"Greetings everyone from the Median to the Outer Rim."

Despite pleasant words his voice rang with the dripping of malevolent intentions.

"You have all been chosen to receive a great honor." Hammer raised his hands towards the metal beamed ceiling. "We have seen the great things you've accomplished here and seen how hard some of you have struggled. I bring you here as we are expanding the Capitol." He paused and looked around, enticing the slow increase of awkward applause from the crowds. "Yes, I knew you would be as excited as I. In order to incorporate you all to our fair city we've set up a training program. All of you will have the pleasure of training with the guards and living in the barracks. Those of you showing good merit will be accumulated into our city."

A few people, obviously not understanding the circumstance, clapped louder. Looking around he could see the desperation in people. People who looked like they would do anything for a new life. Eric bit his lip. *I wonder if that was their selection criteria. Picking people who are so desperate, so they won't question. But then why are there so many guards here?*

It didn't make sense. For the first time in years, he felt scared. Sweat ran down his back against cold skin. He wiggled his toes, trying to quell the sensation without revealing his unease. He knew he was dealing with money under the table. He also knew Jance knew that and was working on his own side enterprises. *Could the guards here be chosen as a way to... cull the heard?*

He heard old farmers talk about that, reminiscing of their days before the zombies when they would tend hundreds of acres of farms. Eric couldn't even imagine that anymore. A landscape safe and beautiful as far as the eye could see. Oh, how just a few years could change the world so much. It took a few years before they reached US soil. How so much loss and suffering could make everyone forget the way the world was. Could make an entire race lose hope.

Hammer continued with a booming voice and wicked grin "We have made an entire hall into a large barracks with luxuries many of you haven't seen in years, and you deserve. You'll be safe, warm, and fed through your training."

Applause intensified. The room was believing what snake oil he was selling. Except, it seemed, Yanika, who was clinging to his arm. Her hands were cold, and she shivered in the seat beside him. Her thin top was nothing to contend with any temperature variation. She was very thin after all and finding clothes that small must have been difficult. Overall, she looked nice, compared to others in the Outer Rim. It attested to the work she had put in while there.

All that hard work just to end up here. Eric took a steadying breath and turned back to Hammer.

"You all will be escorted to the new barracks. Guards who are here today are here to help with training. You will be given new lodgings with our recruits for the duration of their training. Those who do well through this endeavor will be put up for promotion."

Some of the guards started clapping. Jance, sitting next to him, shook his head. He must have been thinking along the same lines as Eric. Promotions weren't just given out. There can only be so many high-ups. Something wasn't right.

The speech finished with another General speaking about the vision of Haven and what it meant to the human race. Pre-generated bullshit is what it was. When it was over, the Generals and their personal guards started herding the group. They weren't even subtle about it. Most everyone was just going along with it.

Others, he noted, who were protesting were getting forcefully herded. He took Yanika's hand and pulled her close to his side. "Just go along with it for now," he whispered.

She nodded.

They were moved through a wide hall that felt cramped from the numerous people who were there. Further down the hall they turned into the area Eric, if remembering correctly, was an old factory. High ceilings, industrial lights, the same worn floor with ruminants where machines, metal walls, and steel beams.

A human factory now.

Eric didn't know what he was expecting, but the end result still made him stop in his tracks. A huge factory area had been converted into cubicles. Tiny areas he estimated were six by six. Signs were up directing people to group bathrooms, showers, and an eating area.

"Let's hurry and grab an area near the bathrooms." He pulled her along, not waiting for a response. From his days in training, he knew how precious bathroom adjacent areas were.

The other guards seemed to have the same thought because the group split. The civilians moved towards the side that was nearest the eating area while the guards booked towards the bathroom area. Showers were the neutral middle ground.

After being cut off twice he spotted two empty cubicles. Spinning Yanika like a dancer he forced her into one area while he took the other adjacent. He didn't notice, but Jance must have been right behind because he shoved someone aside to grab the spot on the other side sharing a wall with Eric. Eric and Yanika were in a line facing the metal wall the bathrooms were on.

Cubicles were two wide going back-to-back and stretching all the way to the back of the room. A narrow two foot walkway divided each two-wide grouping. It looked like they had planned for a few hundred people. He wasn't sure, but it seemed like there was more people than cubicles.

His eight-by-six foot space had a military cot-style bed, makeshift with what looked like ratchet straps for support and a poorly stuffed mattress. Two blankets lay on top with a pillow. He had a nightstand with one drawer, no lamp or any other light beyond what came from the factory lights above.

Underneath the bed was an empty plastic tote he guessed was for personal belongings. None of which he had. Everything was in his room back at the outlet in the Outer Rim. Luckily, locked up tight and hidden.

He sighed and then walked around to Yanika's space. Same size only her bed was an actual military cot with no mattress, two blankets, and a pillow. Where his nightstand was in his cubicle, she had a plastic three drawer organizer. Under her cot was another plastic tote.

"This... This is where we're going to stay?" Her tone indicated she was disappointed.

"Well, it's gotta be a little better than the Outer Rim."

She shook her head, her eyes now glistening with tears. "I worked hard and made myself a home there. I had a lot more than this. I had clothes, my own little kitchen. Decorations that I made myself. It's... It's all gone."

He stepped forward and placed his hand on her shoulder. "It'll still be there."

She shook her head hard enough that dark curls fell from her hairband. "You don't understand. There's so little room out there.

If someone is gone, even for a few days, it makes your home open property."

"Won't anyone watch your place?"

"Maybe. Jim and Emily live by me. They're both very nice. And Noah... silly kid, he lives close. One of them might vouch for me. But they can't just hold my place forever."

Tears now poured from her large eyes. He sobs were quiet, but he could feel each one.

After looking behind him he got close and pulled her into his embrace. She grabbed at his shirt, smothering her face against his chest. She was shorter than him but had appeared taller because of her hair which now tickled his chin.

"I thought I was getting a new life... not... not this."

Her sobs broke her words and cut into his heart. He'd seen so many people suffer, but had only focused on himself until now. Part of him wanting to help others and another part trying to make a better life for himself as well. *I guess we all are just trying to get out of our own hells.*

Jance peered over the cubicle wall and raised his brows as his eyes looked between the two. Eric shook his head. Getting the hint Jance winked and then ducked back down into his own space.

There were few facts to go off of, but Eric couldn't help but feel Jance was right. This felt like a draft. Everything that was said sounded coated with lies. And to be put here in what felt like a concentration camp made it more apparent. Something was wrong. And they were in danger.

HECTOR'S JOURNAL

November 22nd 2037

As I move closer to China I find only carnage. It seems someone, whether military or mercenaries I am not sure, have found ways to kill the zombies. If my research is correct, it is heightened electrical impulses from the brain keeping these rotting corpses walking. Severing the spinal cord completely or destroying the brain seems to be an effective method.

Found many large craters where it appears bombs were set off.

From what I have gathered, I assume China has fallen as well. I plan to move into the city for research, but I also feel I must see how far spread this is and if there is anyone left alive.

I need live subjects for research, but I cannot bring myself to use humans as lab rats. Will have to trial tests in other manners. Animals may be a viable option. I have found few animals that have been turned which will limit my research.

Somehow, I have been able to track Liatris' trail of undead and have found him. Conversations were tense. It seems I can somewhat control the people he has turned, but there is a conflict between my abilities and his as they seem to try and follow both of our orders.

Liatris has revealed his driving force behind this invasion stating that his wife was suspected of being a spy, was arrested, and later was murdered in jail. He blames the government and especially General Komarov who was overseeing the lab. Liatris seems to think his actions are justified. I only ever met his wife once. Liatris is claiming to be the Lord of the zombies. It seems the later turned are also using the term Lord to describe the First Turned.

I sympathize with Liatris' loss but am almost certain this mutation is effecting his judgment. I attempted several times to convince him to stop. Noted heightened anger response from him. With tensions growing I suspect he would have had me killed if I pushed the issue anymore. I was forced to retreat.

I am not sure how to stop Liatris. I am hesitant to risk my life as researching a cure is my ultimate goal.

Chapter 11

Emily felt pain stinging across her face and arms. Groggy, in a dark haze, she tried to move. There was something plush and squishy beneath her. Trying to rise, her body felt too heavy. Spots dotted her vision like static from a TV with poor reception. There were male voices around her, but as she stirred, they went silent. Through her poor vision she caught a large figure moving towards her. She tried to move away and succeeded in scooting back, pushing into something else plush.

"Be still," said a deep male voice.

She froze. *What is going on? That voice... I don't recognize it.* She looked around, making out some shapes and textures. She seemed to be on a large soft surface. It seemed like a mattress with soft blankets on it and another blanket over her legs. Surrounding her was pillows and animal plushies. This was like a lush nest that every child could have only dreamed of.

The figure crouched down in front of her. "Do not fear. You are safe here."

"Who... are..." Her voice was gravely, and it hurt to speak.

"Hush. You were badly hurt, but I will take care of you."

The more she was awake the better her vision got. This man was close to her. His eyes were pale gray blue with creases at the sides set into abnormally pale skin. His skin almost looked translucent as she could see dark lines in his neck that resembled veins. His face had sharp angles which made his gaze intense.

He looked tall and the muscled body on his thin frame was craned over her. He had on a polo, the color seeming to be a dark green or maybe a dark gray. Her vision still wasn't clear. Sucking breath her heart pounded.

Have I been... kidnapped? What's... What's happening?

He reached a hand towards her, but didn't touch her. "Breathe, slow. In and out."

His deep voice was soothing, but as her vision cleared she noticed... *One... Two... Three... Four arms!* She shrieked. This man— creature had four arms. Unnatural skin. Ears that came up a jagged point.

"What are you?" She grabbed the first thing she could find, pulling a large plush cow to her chest. In a panic she didn't realize it at first and when she did she tossed it aside, instead looking for something that could be used as a weapon.

"I am here to help you," he said in his smooth tone laced with some sort of accent. "My name is Lord Edwin Liatris."

"But... you're..."

"I am a Zombie Lord."

She shook in his presence, unsure how she was still alive. Every violent contraction of her muscles made the pain through her head and arms intensify. Now her visions was clear, whether it be due to time or fear she was unsure. Looking down she could see the bandages up and down her arms. "What have you done?"

"I had your wounds bandaged," he said softly. "You were in a car accident and went partially through the windshield. You have been hurt badly so I made this sanctuary for you to recover in. I have my servants working on a hot meal as we speak."

"Meal of what? Rotting flesh?" she spat.

"Hardly. To keep it light for your stomach I have ordered a vegetable beef stew to be made."

"A... what?" Her mouth watered uncontrollably. Just the thought of something that wasn't rat or rotten made her stomach growl.

He glanced down towards the sound and then back up to lock gazes with her again. "How long has it been since you've had a good meal?"

"Since the zombies came."

"A shame. I am furious they would cause you this distress, but I assure you with my presence these mindless slaves will be at your beck and call."

Another man cleared his throat in the distance.

Lord Liatris' eyes narrowed as he glanced over his shoulder. Turning back to her he smiled. "You rest now my dear. I have visitors to deal with."

She could now make out the room she was in the center of. It was some kind of building. There was sunlight coming through windows on one side and another side of windows had piles of furniture in front of them. The glass was all broken out, leaving her to assume they were in a ruined city building. The other two walls were windowless but illuminated by several candles.

She was in a nest of blankets and pillows in the center of the room. Before her triangulated between the two windowless walls and a few feet from her nest was an elaborate wooden chair with a stand on either side. There was also a large table, a couch, and a few other stands with knickknacks on them.

One man had long black hair pulled back, thin frame, and wore a double-breasted vest. The other man next to him seemed more timid with short brunette hair, stained shirt, and was wringing his hands nervously.

"I see you are pleased," said the man in the nice vest.

"Yes, Walter, you have done well. Now why are you still here?"

The man called Walter bowed. "My Lord, I not only bring gifts, but information."

Walter started to turn towards the other man, but paused, looking at Emily. His gazed locked on her for a brief moment, but long enough she felt it. It was a strange look, and she couldn't tell why, but her chest tightened.

Stepping, Walter fully turned towards the other man. "Mark here has word of what's going on in Haven's capitol."

Liatris walked over to his chair, sat, and placed his fingers together on both sets of arms. "Interesting. Go on."

"They are gathering guards and civilians for an expedition into this city," said Mark.

"So, they have taken the bait."

Walter interjected into the conversation. "I am not sure your plan has fully been realized. Mark, will you continue."

"Uhh... Yeah... I heard that Haven's resources are dwindling. So... From what I heard, they are going on a large expedition for supplies, bringing a lot of civilians with them."

Liatris crossed his legs, leaning casually to the side in his large chair. "Why would they do that?"

"I was listening to the generals talk. They're hoping— well planning, on few people coming back. So... get more supplies while decreasing the number of mouths to feed."

"How despicable." Liatris' voice dripping with loathing. "How typical of humans."

Despite all the blankets around Emily, she shivered.

"Have they found the lab?"

"Not as of yet," said Walter. "But phase one and two have been accomplished. As you know Governor Ernando Migel, at my request, did dispatch General Vandyke to this area. His forces unfortunately met their end before reaching the lab."

"Which should never have happened," Liatris growled.

Walter, briefly, cocked his head to the side. "Controlling this city is beyond my capabilities, as you know. And it seems some of the opposition was from their own forces."

Liatris's growl continued, low and primal. "No surprise they would betray their own to keep the lab secret."

"Phase two was partially successful as the scrappers did manage to penetrate the lab. None made it out alive, but I did find her." Walter waved a hand towards Emily.

"What?" she choked out. It still stung to speak. "Me? What... what are you talking about."

Walter smiled, straightening up and then adjusting the collar of his shirt. "Well, my dear I was the one who tipped Marco off to the lab's location and told him you would be a great asset." He looked so proud of himself.

It made her sick. "You... you did this?"

Walter cocked his head to the side. "You wanted a better life. And my Lord here has all the means to provide it."

She turned towards Lord Liatris. Zombie Lord. It finally sunk in with deep sickening fear. But this was not the painful death mauled by monsters she was expecting.

Liatris looked down to her from his throne. "You will never want for anything, my dear, as long as you're in my charge."

"W- why? I don't..." Her heart pounded so fast she had to stop and suck in a few deep breaths.

Liatris stood. "Emily, you need to rest." The way he said her name sounded so formal. He turned to the other two men. "We will continue this conversation downstairs."

Walter nodded and then herded Mark towards a staircase in the far corner of the room where the dark wall met the broken windowed wall blocked up with overturned furniture.

She watched as Liatris followed the two, leaving her alone in a large dark room. Gasping for breath. Panicking. Raking with pain from her legs all the way to the top of her head. The plush nest around her only added to the conflicting emotions. She'd wanted for so long to have a nice soft and warm place to sleep. Here it was. A zombie Lord was promising her that all her needs were going to be taken care of. Food was being made for her.

Emily teetered on the edge. So close to the chance of having everything she wanted and so fearful of where it might lead.

HECTOR'S JOURNAL

March 3rd, 2038

It is the anniversary of the explosion at the DNA research center outside of Chernobyl that started the end of the world. Japan had closed its border early, but a targeted attack has since caused them to fall as well. Unsure who invaded, but suspect Liatris was responsible. The later turned zombies do not seem to have the aptitude for complex thinking.

Europe has fallen, although I have found a few survivors. Each group I have found I secretly brought resources to. I hope they survive. I still need to find a cure.

Chapter 12

Lisa gripped the cool metal railing of the platform on top of the RV. Everything inside of her told her this was wrong. They shouldn't be this deep into the city. They shouldn't let themselves get so surrounded. But she kept it to herself, knowing that the possible reward was worth the risk. Hector needed more supplies. He seemed more eager now-a-days like he was nearing a breakthrough. If Emily was alive, she wouldn't be much longer. They were on a time crunch. She had to rely on their skills and Hector.

There was one problem. Mariah said Flint was not at one hundred percent yet, Jim had a bad concussion, and her back was still not at its best. Mariah and Bruno were not fighters if they got in a pinch. That left Hector and Spot as their main forces. It was a huge risk. Knowing this only made her back ache more.

Jim and Hector both were quiet but standing next to each other. Jim seemed tense, but more accepting of Hector's presence. They would have to be a team in order to make this successful.

It didn't take long before they were able to track down the lab. Trails of half burnt dead zombie bodies led them right to the front door. Using the walkie Hector ordered Flint to park, but for everyone to stay inside the RV.

"What is it?" asked Lisa.

"There are zombies inside. I'll need to clear the building first before anyone leaves this vehicle."

She nodded. The building was tall, concrete, with barred windows and wide-open metal front doors. Hector took off from the platform, flew around the building a few times before heading inside.

"This must have been where Marco was," Jim mumbled.

Lisa looked down at half a zombie sizzling on the concrete. "Good assumption."

The smell reached her. A foul combination of hot rotten flesh. She heaved and then moved over closer to Jim. The smell stayed. It was disgusting. Lingering like skunk smell.

After a minute, like rats from a fire, zombies started pouring through the front door into the sun. Jim jumped, reaching for something that wasn't there. She guessed he was trying to find his rifle or a weapon.

Lisa grabbed his arm. "Wait. We should be fine."

As the mutated creatures fled into the sun their mediocre moans turned to shrill cries and screams. Like dying animals. Their skin smoked as the rays of sun beat down on them. There were various levels of mutated here. Some still held human form with ashen human faces. Most were four armed abominations with faces that looked like a bat and roadkill had a baby. Even a few of the mushy ones slide out, moving like snails. Their bodies were mounds of flesh and goo and they left a wet bloody trail across the pavement. The sun caused instant blisters on most of them.

Jim leaned over the edge, eyeing the creatures with large eyes. They didn't attack. Instead, they moved around them, giving them a wide birth.

"They're... not attacking."

"Benefits of running with a Zombie Lord," said Lisa. "He's been protecting us like this since I met him."

"If he has that power, why has he not helped the survivor camps or Haven."

Lisa chuckled, knowing Jim didn't have a clue about how things really were. "Hector has tried. You know how you reacted. Well, every time he's shown himself to a camp it has been worse. I've seen him try. He gets angry mobbed right out of town. Sometimes shot and other times chased with farm equipment. Either way, no one wants to trust him."

Jim lowered his head, seeming to take in her words. "I see how that could happen. It's hard to fathom a zombie on our side."

"Don't get used to it. Hector is the only one I've ever found."

"How did you two get together?"

His phrasing made warmth move through her body. The memory terrifying, yet the best thing that ever happened to her. It took a while for her to decide what she wanted to say.

When the zombies made land in California all radio updates said pretty much that they were under prepared and overwhelmed. At that time there was no Haven. There was no survivor camp. So, she did the only thing she could think of. She moved up to her father's old cabin in the Colorado mountains. Her father had passed a few years previously and willed it to her. Her mother was never part of their family.

Years in kitchen construction gave her handyman skills and she was able to get the cabin running. Her father was a little bit of a prepper, more in case there was another civil war. It was a saving grace as the cabin was filled with guns and ammunition.

And that's how she became the mountain woman. No people within a hundred miles. Totally off grid. Solar panels charged a couple batteries to keep the radio going. There were a few candles and oil lanterns in there. It didn't take long for the zombies to move across the county until the radio stopped receiving signals. And then she was alone.

The feeling was deeply painful. Years of not seeing another soul. Speaking only to herself. Not even a pet to keep her company. Those memories tore through her. Tears burned at the back of her eyes, and it took all the willpower she had to fight them back.

She chopped wood for the wood fireplace. Hunted the wildlife to survive. Harvested berries and attempted to plant a small garden for the summer. That's how she survived... alone.

Then the zombies came. Gunshots would alert them so hunting became near impossible. She grew skinny and hungry. Many nights spent sitting by the fire debating about whether it would be better to just end it all.

So much shame rested deep inside of her like a heavy boulder set right on top of her stomach. She remembered one night, holding her father's revolver. She debated all night about ending her life. Trying to figure out if she could even survive. What would be better? Starving out here and maybe getting turned by a zombie, or just ending it.

Unable to handle any more memories she shook her head. Jim was still waiting for a response, and she felt like Hector would be back any minute. "It was... by chance I guess you could say."

"Were you in a survivor camp or just on your own—"

"It's complicated," she said, cutting him off. "Hector has been gone too long, I'm going to pop down and get geared up just in case." Hurrying she climbed down and kicked the door a couple times so someone would open up.

As Mariah opened the door Lisa slid inside the RV. Mariah gave Lisa a concerned look and Lisa just smiled.

"Just grabbing some things so I'm ready."

"Fucking things are ugly," said Flint from the driver's seat.

Bruno stood up from the other seat, stepped over Spot, and then paused. "You need help?"

"No. I'm fine. Just getting ready."

Lisa gathered both her pistol from her bunk and Jim's rifle that was leaning against the wall next to Hector's desk. Pausing, she looked back at the bunk room. When she helped design it, she made sure there was a little storage nook in both top bunks and then made two shallow crates with wheels that could roll under the bottom bunks. Hector's bunk crate, which he didn't use, had extra ammunition, a couple guns, and a few knives in it.

What are we getting into? She turned, looking out the narrow view of the windshield at the daunting building in front of them. *Hector was afraid of contamination. What kind of contamination will be in here? What are we really getting into?*

A few more zombies fled from inside. Bruno flinched as a loud moan came from beside the RV. He was shaking, like a small, frightened child. It wasn't common to be so surrounded by zombies. Even with Hector around, it was unnerving.

Lisa took the weaponry and clambered back up to the top of the RV, quickly shutting the door behind her. She pressed her lips together once she reached the top and silently handed Jim his rifle.

"Thank you." His rifle was bolt action and he checked to make sure it was loaded before he slung it over his back. "I'm sorry if I was prying earlier."

"It's... It's fine. Just... bad memories."

He reached over and put a hand on her shoulder. "I understand bad memories. You never need to tell me if you don't want to."

He had strong hands that engulfed her whole shoulder. He was warm and his touch comforting. It made her cheeks flush as if his warmth just rushed into her.

She felt obligated to tell him or at least take up the silence. "What about you? You always been in Haven?"

He took a long breath in and an overly loud exhale. "I spent a few years looking for my wife and daughter."

"Did... you—"

"No. I never found them."

"I'm really sorry." It was a story she had heard many times, but it still made her hurt. She'd lost some friends, but her family was already gone. Even losing family to normal circumstances hurt. Losing them to an apocalypse where their undead forms may wander the world was much worse.

"I was separated from them before the zombies got here. My wife left me and took my daughter with her." He looked down at his hands as he ran his thumbs across his fingertips. "I wanted to be a blacksmith and she wanted me to have a real job. Looking back, I'm not sure what was the right path. My blacksmith skills got myself and my family a place in Haven. But I couldn't find them. I was close to having them safe, but... I just couldn't find them."

His voice cracked. He sounded so hurt. And what he said meant he left the safety of Haven to find them. It gave her a new appreciation for him. That took courage. More courage than she had.

"I... I was hiding in the Colorado mountains." With a deep breath she told him what happened, pushing into her dark memories. She didn't want to relive it, but part of her desperately wanted to tell another soul. She never told the others. It just wasn't something they did. It was like a silent acceptance that their past was gone.

She pushed into the dark memories. It was past the point she thought of ending her life. She still had a thread of will to live, more than she thought. She was out hunting after a deep snowfall when the horde made their way to the mountains. She was bundled in her thick coat, but it was old and tattered. The frosty wind pierced at her cheeks. She still could feel the sting.

Shivers broke out across her body. It was a failed hunting trip, and the deep snow was exhausting. Then she spotted the zombies. They moved slow through the snow. It was a very cloudy day, adding to her bad luck as the sun did not seem to deter them. She came up on them too close. They caught her scent and the cat and mouse game started.

Lisa ran, drudging through knee high snow. The cold was biting at her skin now. If she went home the horde would find her, so her only hope was leading them away. Time was ticking against her as the sun plunged down below the mountains. In the dark with no way to even make a fire and a horde of zombies behind her she had to keep going. Running. Their moans stayed behind her. Either they were catching up or she was slowing down.

It was there she suddenly didn't want to die and was looking at the reality that she might. Turned around, nothing but snow lay before her. With a cloudy sky she couldn't see in the night. That's when she found the cliff. She slipped right off, tumbling down the hill, saved only by the deep snow. Her broken body falling down to where the road used to be.

"I thought I was going to die." Lisa kept her eyes down on the railing, spacing out as she spoke.

"How did you survive?" asked Jim. His voice was hushed and kind.

His inflection hinting that he understood how she felt.

"Hector." Her chest pained. "Hector was following the horde and found me. He can fly and, I guess, he was able to get me to my house. At least that's where I was when I woke up." She licked her dry lips. That part of her memories were good ones. It warmed her like the fire did when she woke from the edge of death. "That's how I hurt my back."

Jim nodded slowly. He glanced down for a moment as the stream of zombies trickled away. The last lingering ones passed by the back of the RV. "That explains a lot. There was nothing anyone could do?"

"Any who? There was no one left alive. Hector was a scientist. He took care of me the best he could."

"You were lucky."

She cocked her head to the side. "Maybe." The time she spent alone with Hector was the best she'd felt in so long. He'd go out hunting for her and chopping wood while she recovered. Her legs were weak, and the pain was intense for several weeks. And he never left her. He prepared meals, washed her clothes. He held her when she thought she couldn't stand the pain. In the end, he needed to move on, and she knew she could no longer survive on her own.

"I've been broken ever since," she mumbled. "My back... Mariah thinks I broke it. There's no way to know for sure, but... I wouldn't have survived without him."

Jim slid his hand over on top of hers. "I think you're a lot stronger than you give yourself credit for."

She glanced up at him and into his dark eyes. "Do you ever miss how things used to be?"

"I don't anymore. It does no good to reach for something so far gone. I just focus on the task at hand."

"Like Emily?"

He lowered his head and his shoulder fell. "She is a friend. I might have been rash in going after her. She chose to go out with the scrappers. She could never be happy where she was at."

The conversation trailed off as Hector headed out of the building. Lisa was left with conflicting emotions. Pain over the past and comfort of where she was in the present. Feeling safe. Feeling like she had a family.

Hector made a plan with them as he felt the whole building was clear of zombies. Mariah and Bruno stayed in the RV while the others split into two parties. Flint and Spot were in one team if you wanted to call it that. Flint had a machete in his hands, pistol on one hip, and Spot staying close to his side.

Lisa and Jim were in the other team. They both had their guns and knives. Decked out ready for a fight they hoped didn't happen. Neither of them had body armor. It was hard to find, harder to keep in decent enough shape, and most of known body armor was being worn by the undead. What luck.

They stood like front wave soldiers about to lay siege on this old building. Hector stood in the middle. He straightened to his full height. A daunting and imposing sight. He looked ready for something to go wrong. It made her uneasy.

"This lab appears to be dedicated to zombie research. Be careful what you touch." Hector turned to Flint.

He raised a hand. "Whoa. Why you looking at me?"

"Because you are the one that tears more things apart than the dog."

Spot whimpered and cocked his head to the side.

"What kind of danger are we looking at?" asked Jim.

"I'm not sure what or how they were working on things." Hector nodded his head towards the lab. "I'm unsure if anything would be harmful to you."

"What about to you?" asked Lisa. She put a hand on her hip. It wasn't like they'd be researching how to make zombies, which means it could be a chemical to kill them. "There could be something toxic to you in there."

"I'm willing to take that risk."

"Well, I'm not," Lisa snapped. "So, you better be careful too." She pointed at him. There was no way she was going to suggest they not go in. Not now after finally getting so close to some answers. This might be the next step Hector needed to make a cure.

Hector nodded. "I have found three stories above ground and there seems to be an underground level. I have cleared the zombies from the upper floors. I will go check underground. Flint, go up to the third floor. Lisa and Jim, you take the second floor. If, by chance, there are any more zombies left below I will try and rush them through the front door."

Jim's brow dropped. "What about everyone on the RV?"

"I will make certain they are safe."

Lisa had no doubt about that. He was obsessively protective of everyone here. That didn't quell her deep-set unease. The group moved into the building, back-to-back in a well-knit unit. Jim seemed very comfortable with this procedure, staying close to her side and sweeping the room.

It was dark, forcing Lisa to break one of her three glow sticks and Flint to flip on his flashlight. They didn't have the batteries to run two flashlights so this would have to do.

The front door led into a decent sized room with a staircase straight in front. There were no windows and instead doors on both side, making it appear that there were rooms all along the outside with this being the central area. There were definitely windows somewhere because she saw the barred windows from the outside.

There was blood splatter along the floor and drag marks. Other places had fresh bloody footprints. The amount of blood and prints made Lisa tense. *How many zombies would have been in here if Hector hadn't gone through first?* Her back tensed and a burning sting traveled down to her left leg.

She wanted to sweep this level but went ahead with Hector's plan. Flint and Spot went in front of them, going upstairs and then turned to go up another set of stairs to the third story. Side by side Lisa and Jim moved into the second story. He had his rifle in his hands, so she took out her knife. Even though Hector said it was safe, this seemed to be preferable for both of them.

The first room to the left seemed to be a computer room. There were desks all along the walls with cobweb covered computers. Chairs were parked up to them and it had the appearance of being frozen in time. Unlike everywhere else, there wasn't the splatters of blood painting the floor.

Each step inside kicked up a small plume of dust. It tickled her nose and left the gritty taste of dirt on her tongue. Holding the glowstick in one hand and knife in the other she swept the room. After rounding a desk, she spotted a figure.

Lisa jolted back, leaping into Jim's arms. He caught her by the shoulders. It was too late to spare her back, which coiled again as if someone was wringing her muscles to death. She gritted her teeth, trying to stay quiet. The pain was enough to make her leg twitch. She stayed in his arms a little longer than she cared too, but needed the support.

Once she was able to recover into standing, she stepped away. He looked her way, his features shadowed from the darkness and the creases around his eyes were highlighted by the green glowstick. He was stoic and hard to read, but she had the sinking feeling that he knew what was going on.

He put one hand on her shoulder and put a finger to his lips and then waved to the body. "It's just a mummy," he said in a hushed voice.

"What?"

"That's what we called people who died, but not by zombies. I've seen many of them." He started walking towards the body. "The people who hid in bunkers and were safe from the zombies, but eventually starved or ran out of water."

"They slowly died."

He nodded. "I'm guessing when the horde came through, they bunkered themselves inside."

She rubbed the edge of her glowstick across her chin. "All the zombie traces we've seen were recent. I'm guessing this place was recently opened up."

"I'd agree." Jim ran a finger across the dust on a desk. "There's no way there were zombies inside for years." He went quiet, looking around with an expression that made him look like he was doing advanced math. "This must have been Marco's haul." He took a deep breath and looked around the room.

"You think Emily might be here?"

His mouth opened. For a brief moment she saw the desperation in his face. He took a deep breath, hiking his shoulders to his ears. It was like a build up to an outburst. And then, with one long breath, it all left. His shoulders sank and his expression returned to neutral. Jim shook his head. "I don't think so. Not alive anyway."

Lisa walked over and ran her fingertips over his forearm. She wanted to take his arm and comfort him but hesitated and made things more awkward. It felt different with Bruno and Flint who were like her brothers. This wasn't the same.

His gaze went from her hand up until they locked eyes briefly. The bridge of her nose heated, and she quickly looked away.

"We should keep moving," said Jim.

She nodded, still not looking at him, and then headed out of the room. Carnage had hit out here and there were a few doors open with bloody footprints leading inwards. The other rooms were closed off. She debated which one to move to first.

There might be a survivor in the blocked off rooms. She turned towards the other side of the room. *But there might be a zombie in the open rooms.* Hector had already swept the space, and he had never missed a zombie. She knew that, but in the darkness the fear still loomed in the background.

She hadn't recovered from the coiling of her muscle in her back. Part of her foot was numb and if anything happened, she'd be hard pressed to move enough to get away. "I think we should sweep the open rooms." Her voice wavered and she hoped he didn't notice.

He walked up behind her, looming. That close to her she felt his size, radiating heat that sent chills across her body. She was strangely uncomfortable around him now. "Good idea," he said in a hushed voice that was deeper and more gravely than before.

She swallowed hard. *It probably was the dust. Don't think anything about it.* They moved into another room. This one had been trampled by zombies. Not a lot. The footprints were almost countable, and it looked like they had wandered in and then out.

This room was a small lab. Equipment was minimal, with tables covered mostly in beakers and small hot plates. It was like a science mini classroom. Jim moved behind her and made a quick sweep. This room had windows that had metal bars on them. The slight wash of light was enough she didn't need her glowstick to see.

He picked up a beaker, peered inside, and then set it back down. "Doesn't look like much. Hector will probably be able to figure this out. I have no idea either."

Jim nodded his head towards the door. "There's a boarded-up room across from us. Let's take a quick look."

"Sooner we can clear this place the better." She followed him out, trying to hide a slight limp.

This room was another closed off one. No bodies. Just a place frozen in dust from the hands of time. A few steps in she had to brace herself on a desk. The pain was growing and spreading. Sweat broke out across her forehead.

Jim turned towards her, and she couldn't hide it any longer. "Your back?"

She gritted her teeth and gripped the edge of the desk. "It's getting bad."

He paused a moment, seeming to be thinking of something with a furrowed brow, and then approached her. "I can't do much, but maybe I can loosen the muscles."

"I... I don't know if that will help."

He shrugged. "Might as well try. At least make it a touch better so we can get back to Mariah."

"I guess. It's worth a try."

Jim stepped around until he was positioned behind her. A gentle hand touched her back, but it was enough to make her flinch. Another ripple of pain shot down her legs.

"Try to relax. I'll be gentle."

She thought he sounded different. *Did his tone change?*

He started with light strokes from the base of her pelvis up her back. She knew he found each tightly coiled rope as he gave these areas careful attention. It might have been his pressure or just the warmth of his hands because it immediately did start to feel better.

She started to melt into the desk. The pain melting away to warmth. Comfort. Even to the point his touch felt good. He didn't stop, paying special attention to her. Lisa sunk down, laying her torso over the desk, using the minimal amount of muscles needed to stay standing.

Jim moved closer as he reached up towards her shoulders. His pelvis right up against her. She froze, feeling him pressed against her, but also the nirvana of getting every tight muscle worked out with meticulous detail. He didn't skimp and he kept going. She expected him to just stop any moment, but he didn't, finding his way up towards her neck and then back down along her spine.

He was pressed against her, and it was making her body hot. The cold of the desk she laid on nipped at her breasts. What started as just keeping her on her feet turned into a soft building lust. Her core was tight and hot. Already a dampness pooled between her legs.

He ran his hands back up and down her back. She accidentally let out a whimper. Jim didn't stop, but she felt his package press against her, getting harder. The next few breaths she took were short. She was pulsating now as her body was acting on its own and begging for him. She didn't realize how much she longed for a physical connection. Until now she just assumed that it would never be possible again.

We... we shouldn't do... She couldn't even finish her thought because at that moment his package throbbed. Her entire body went fiery hot, and her tender buds hardened.

He didn't stop. Didn't move to do anything different. He just continued his massage. As she shifted to get his hands in a different spot along her back she rocked against his package.

Jim took a quick breath in. In response, he pushed against her. He was hard and large.

"Are you okay?" he asked in a soft, but very deep tone.

She hadn't heard his voice like that. It was both surprising and hot.

Enough that her face now felt like fire. "Yes." She accidentally cooed as she spoke.

He jerked, shoving his hard package against her. "I... I can't be this close if... if you're going to make sounds like that."

"Yes, you can."

"I... I..." He steadied himself with a breath. His hand reached around and down the front of her pants. His fingers diving right down between her panties and her hot wet folds. "You do want me," he growled.

It was low, primal, and she spasmed against his fingers. "Yes. I want you."

He leaned over her, taking his free hand and planting it next to her head. His face just inches from her ear and his breath hot against her skin. "Are you sure about this?"

The hot place between her thighs was throbbing. She hadn't felt like this in years. Hadn't been this close to another male that made her this hot. It took her breath away. She didn't want to lose this moment. "Please. Just once. I want to feel you."

"Pull your pants down," he growled.

She did, noting he stayed very close. Pants down along her ankles she laid back over the desk. She heard the sound of his zipper.

He came up behind, rubbing his shaft against her wet valley. She moaned and pushed towards him like a cat stretching its back. She wanted it. Wanted it now. This was a desperation that felt like it was going to kill her.

He held his length, rubbing it up and down. Toying with her.

"Please," she said again.

"Beg more."

It took her by surprise, pleasantly. This was a side of him she didn't expect. "Please. Please."

"Please what?"

"Please fuck me."

"You want it that badly?"

"Yes!"

He reached around and placed his hand over her mouth. As he did, he started to press his length into her. A hand over her mouth was a good thing because she didn't expect his girth. It had been so long, and she was already pulsating with need.

He pushed into her. Spreading her. The waves of pleasure made her quiver and her legs shake. Her core was tightening. She felt like she could cum right now. Her insides grew tighter.

He pressed in deeper as he got his face close to her ear. "Don't you dare cum yet."

She tried to protest, but instead her words were muffled by his hand.

"The only right response is yes sir." He lifted his hand from her mouth.

"Yes... sir," she said, between quick breaths.

He pushed in deeper. His hands took her hips, pushing her towards him like he planned to impale her. "Don't you cum," he growled again.

She couldn't remember ever being with a man like this. There was never a man who told her not to cum yet. It was always the other way around. It was years ago, but she couldn't remember anything as hot as this.

He started to thrust in and out of her. Slow at first. As she whimpered, he put his hand on her mouth again. He muffled her as he moved faster and faster. His head was fat, hitting her G spot each time. She tensed and had to bite her lip to stifle a scream. With a hot rush she squirted on him, the rush of moisture spurting around and out, like a pressure building around a plug then exploding. The liquid dripped all over the floor.

He thrust harder. "Don't... cum... yet." Each word was a sharp command.

"I can't hold it."

"Then you're going to get it all." He reached down, finding her tender jewel with his fingers.

She tried to shriek, but he kept his hand over her mouth. This pleasure was too much. She was going to cum. He rubbed her stiff female spot hard, going in fast circles. He thrust fast. In and out. In and out. He throbbed. Getting bigger. Harder.

"Cum. Cum now," he growled.

Finally. Her insides gushed. Liquid squirting out again. Waves of tension pulsating inside. Then he exploded inside of her. The amount of his hot seed was so much she felt herself stretch more. The euphoria of pleasure raking her in waves made spots dance in front of her eyes.

He kept his hand on her mouth to quiet her. Lisa couldn't stand and collapsed onto the desk. The only thing holding her up was the desk and Jim still pressed against her, his shaft buried inside. He released her mouth and gripped her waist, steadying her.

The pain in her back fled and she felt light and fluffy. Her heart pounded and each breath blew another wave of dust from the old surface.

Without a sound, without warning, Hector strode through the door. "There you..." His voice cut off.

Lisa turned, just able to see him. Hector's face turned between them. He was only there a moment before he left in silence, closing the door behind him.

HECTOR'S JOURNAL

march 3rd 2039

The two-year anniversary. I am so
deeply hurt by what has happened there
are not words. I curved around the coast,
traveled south, went through Spain, and
then moved into Africa. All has fallen.
I have found some survivor camps, but
the reality is simple, there used to be
billions of people and now there are only
thousands.

I finally ran across Victoria seven
months ago. I was surprised that her
following was nearly all second Turned.
They were intelligent with minimal
mutations. It seemed this was her harem.
Through her I learned that the zombies
have moved to the Americas. She was
heading that way as well.

Reluctantly, I went with her by ship.
I would not be able to manage a ship
myself. This was a sacrifice I had to make.
After so long with no one to talk to, I
felt strange being surrounded by other
individuals that could communicate and
carry on a conversation. I felt tempted
to do this myself. Get myself servants to
help with my research.

I felt Victoria's corrupting influence
start to set in as I began to crave human
flesh and desired to make my own army.
Because of this I left. I flew from the

ship. Beforehand I was gifted a pair of goggles from one of her servants. Walter was the most sophisticated of the second Turned and I enjoyed his company. He told me he knew I would need to leave, and the goggles were a parting gift. I miss that man.

Chapter 13

Eric, Yanika, and Jance all piled into Eric's cubical. Yanika sat on his cot, Eric leaned against the wall made from actual industrial cubical divider, and Jance sat on the floor. An announcement came over the speakers in the ceiling that they had an hour until lights out.

"Yo, what us squad gonna do now?" asked Jance.

Yanika glanced at Eric with a brow raised.

"You'll learn to translate," Eric said, laughing. "And I don't know. I'm not comfortable with this."

They kept their voices down as others were piled up close around them within their own cubicles. There haven't been any other announcements, but Eric was more and more feeling like this was a trap.

"This hella sus," said Jance. "I'm going burn rubber out this place if I can."

Yanika pulled her legs up and hugged her knees to her chest. "I don't want to be here."

"Neither do I," said Eric. "I agree, this isn't right. They're planning something."

The overhead speaker announced it was forty-five minutes before lights out.

Jance lifted an eyebrow. "Feels like we're in prison."

"Agreed. Let's make a plan for each other." Eric dropped his voice. "Jance, you have more a in with the other Guards. You should probe them a little for information."

Jance winked. "You got it."

"Yanika?"

She lifted her head. Her eyes were bloodshot with dark bags beneath them.

Eric almost stopped, not wanting to bring her into this, before realizing they were all a part of this whether they wanted it or not. "The other civilians trust you. Can you go around and talk to the people you know? See if they might know anything?"

"I... I think I can do that," said Yanika, with a shaking voice.

Eric nodded. "Okay then. I got a few friends around here I plan to shake down for information. Meet back here tomorrow same time?"

"You got it boss man." Jance did a finger pistol gesture and then vaulted over the wall of the cubicle to land in his own on the other side.

Yanika stood but swayed as she did. Eric caught her arms and then escorted her over to her bed.

"Get as much rest as you can. I can tell this day has been very trying on you."

"I'm sorry. I don't mean to be a burden."

His heart melted. He leaned in, giving her a soft kiss on her forehead. "You're not a burden. I'll keep you safe." He pulled back, so to not be too imposing. He didn't want to scare her. She was already scared enough.

He tried to give her a warming smile as he stepped over into his cubicle. The walls were higher than what you'd expect in something like a call center. These dividers were around six foot tall, so they even gave him some sense of privacy.

He noticed there was a curtain hanging by the opening to his small living space. Upon closer inspection he realized it could be hooked across making something like a privacy curtain. This one was hideous with the look, smell, and texture of something his great great grandmother would have had.

He pulled it across the opening for privacy before pulling the blankets off the cot and laying down. The speakers rang out they were at last call. Without any lights in his space, and the lights above went out, everything went dark.

This was feeling more and more like a prison every moment. He laid there on his back, staring up into the darkness with his hands behind his head. This felt dangerous. How much so, he wasn't sure yet. But they would need to find out more information if they were going make a plan to get out of here.

If he could get back to his stash, he would have the money to high tail it out of Haven. He could pay his way to another settlement or sanctuary, although he knew he would be trading a decent life for one in squalor. He also had Yanika and Jance to think about.

He bit his bottom lip and rolled over in hit cot. He couldn't get them both out. That plan was a one-way one-person ticket. *A last resort, I guess. If everything goes south, I can at least get out of here.*

HECTOR'S JOURNAL

April 18th, 2039

    I flew far enough to reach South America. I have the goggles gifted to me from the second Turned named Walter, my research notes, and this journal. That is all. I had to leave the rest behind. If I hadn't, I fear I would fall prey to desires put upon me by another.

    I have never felt this weak. My body has been feeling cold and fragile. At times I struggle to walk. I wish to continue my research, but I fear I must take refuge and recover for now. Why do I feel this way around Victoria?

Chapter 14

Emily had fallen asleep again, floating in the pile of plush blankets and stuffed animals. Lord Liatris came through with his promise and brought her food. It was well cooked. Delicious. Things she hadn't even tasted in years.

She didn't know how long she was asleep, but from looking at the few windows in the area, it appeared to be night. The room was very dark, only lit by the occasional candle. Liatris sat up on his throne. Clusters of candles around him.

He had one knee crossed, his chin resting on his top right hand. His bottom right hand held a goblet. In his left he held a book, and his other left hand was resting on his leg.

The sight of a four-armed creature still terrified her. As the haze of sleep left and the realization this wasn't a dream set in, she shivered. The motion caught his attention.

He lowered the book and looked at her with a regal stare. "Ah, you've finally awakened. How are you feeling?"

"Um. I..." She paused. *He said I would want for nothing. Do I... Do I dare test it?* He hadn't hurt her, and he definitely had the power to. The other two men were gone. According to the one, everything was part of his design. She rung her hands together under the blanket. *That fucker set me up from the beginning.* She never took her gaze off of Liatris and noticed his eyes narrow for a moment.

"You are angry. Understandably so. This must be a lot for you to take in."

She had a bunch of insults saved up, but all of them were caught in her throat. She just wasn't that brave yet. "I want... a real warm bath."

He tilted his head upwards. "That is to be expected. I have already had my servants working on something that would befit you." He grabbed the arms of his chair with his bottom two arms and pushed himself up. "I will accelerate their progress. When would you like your bath?"

"Uh... soon." She heard her voice shake. It reflected how she felt inside more than she wanted. It felt like there were knots in her chest and stomach, twisting and tightening.

Lord Liatris nodded. "I will make sure they progress quickly. Now, my dear, are there any luxuries you would like? Bath salts perhaps?"

My dear? Luxuries? She partially relaxed into the blankets. It didn't seem she was in immediate danger. "Yes... Bath salts would be... wonderful."

He nodded again. "Then I will give my servants your orders."

"You're a real zombie Lord... aren't you?" The words came out of her mouth completely by accident. As she heard herself speak, she gasped, shaking her head. Her body tensed back up. The knots inside of her coiling and making her heave.

Liatris straightened. He wasn't outrageously tall, but something about his four-armed frame was both imposing and regal. He looked like some kind of warlord people would bow to. Despite obvious mutation, he was not an unattractive man. His light blue eyes were sharp and bright. His gaze, not unkind, still demanded respect.

"I am. My armies conquered entire continents. We freed the people of oppressed nations."

"F—freed. They're... dead." She silently cursed herself. She wanted to at least live through today. She'd pushed her luck so far. In the dark, she couldn't even see a way out. She didn't know how high up she was, so getting out a window most likely wouldn't work. She had seen a staircase before, but now it was completely hidden in the dark.

Liatris strode towards her. She dug her heals into the plush surface below her and pushed herself away from him. Her hands felt for anything that she could use to protect herself. No surprise, everything here was plush.

"They are undead." He spoke with a deep voice, but it sounded smooth without a trace of the anger or rage she was expecting. "They are immortal now with power unlike anything they could have dreamed."

A quiver started in her chin and then worked its way down making her whole body shake.

He crouched down just outside the circles of blankets and pillows. "You fear me now, but I will sway you. You will change your mind when you see what I've created." He stood, towering over her again, and then turned.

Liatris gathered a candle, and she watched as the dim light faded over towards one wall and then down, vanishing in the dark.

She scrunched into a ball, pulling the blankets tight to herself.

Although she didn't see other zombies, she knew they couldn't be far. The lab showed her that. This place was filled beyond the likes of the hordes she has seen before. With white knuckles she gripped a unicorn plushie beside her, pulling until she heard the soft pop of seams ripping. So many zombies rushed the lab all at once. She never fathomed there could be that many nearby.

Trapped in luxury. That's what he was talking about. Maybe food for later. Fatten her up or whatever those zombies like. Yet she pushed him, and he had every chance to retaliate. *Is he just playing with me?*

Liatris returned, holding a candle in an old-fashioned metal holder. "Your bath has been prepared."

"Already?" Emily envisioned an old, rusted bathtub filled with cold water. There was little power around outside of some scrapper camps and Haven. It was just too hard to get. Either you needed to keep looting for old gasoline and oil, or you needed something like a solar panel or windmill. Hot baths were not heard of. You were lucky if you could heat some water for a sponge bath.

"My followers are efficient. I believe this will be up to the standards you deserve."

His wording was strange, but it had been all along. He really expected she'd just stay here in the lion's den and let him, as he said, *treat her the way she deserved.* He was delusional, but she couldn't question it. This whole time she'd pressed her luck. He hadn't retaliated yet, but if he decided to, she couldn't do anything.

Liatris waved, beckoning her to follow him.

Emily stood, feeling the nip of the cool night air against her skin. She looked down at the white pajamas she was wearing. She vaguely noticed before but forgot quickly due to a combination of pain and just the stress of her circumstance.

She patted herself down, feeling that both her bra and underwear were missing. Her chest tightened and a panicked sensation worked its way up from her knees to her neck. "You... undressed me."

Liatris' eyes narrowed. "Not I. That was Walter's doing, as you were this way when he brought you to me. I am not pleased, and I will deal with him later."

Feeling uncomfortable to a level of violated she touched her arms, trying to stave off a shiver. Her arms were sore, gingerly wrapped with bandages like her head.

"You were badly hurt. We did our best, but you will still need time and rest to fully heal."

She glanced back to him, noting his expression had softened as he looked at her. He beckoned again for her to follow and this time she did. The tiled floor felt cold on her bare feet. His candle wasn't much, but it was enough to illuminate the staircase she first spotted during the day.

He offered her one of his hands. "Do you need assistance down?"

"I... I'm fine." She couldn't ignore the irony of having someone meeting her ideals of a dream man, but he was a Zombie Lord. She still half expected a rusted tub, but now pictured the horror movies she had seen as a teenager. Tub full of blood or the serial killer waiting for the girl to become comfortable before murdering her.

They traversed down two flights of stairs which was enough to wind her. She hadn't felt this fatigued in a long time and the exertion made her head pound. Once they left the stairwell she moved to a wall and leaned on it. With one arm up to brace herself she rested her head. Liatris was right behind her, and she heard him take a long breath.

"I was worried this would be too much for you." He moved up behind her, placing two hands on her shoulder.

Emily flinched.

"I know you may never like me, but please, do not fear me."

She couldn't relax with him touching her, although it was a gentle touch. She half expected something rough. Like maybe the next moment he would wrap his fingers around her throat. Instead, he just steadied her and, when she lifted her head from her arm, he let her go.

"A warm bath will do you well. Come, before it gets cold."

Cold? Which means it was hot once? Her skin tingled at the thought of a real hot bath but chastised herself afterwards because in this new world that was absurd. She was still barefoot, and the cold floor felt grainy, like years of decay and dust had accumulated here. On occasion she paused to wipe her feet on the pantleg of her pajamas.

They crossed this story, taking a winding path through hallways that led to what seemed to be different large offices. The roar of a small engine grew louder as they moved, and, after another turn, she could see the dim glow of light at the end of a hallway. The scent of the old moldy building now turned to one of lavender.

Her nerves were now on edge. He was teasing her with the thread of hope that a real bath was waiting for her. It felt cruel as she knew this was too good to be true. Most likely a trap. She slowed her pace, taking more note of her surroundings in case she had to make her escape.

He seemed to notice, slowing his pace as well to stay at her side. The light came from a room two doors down and seemed to shimmer in a mist flowing from the door. The lavender smell was stronger here. Liatris stopped, and, once she spotted a shadow moving, she did as well.

A man left the room. He was dressed nicely with a white button up shirt with the sleeves rolled up. He had short brown hair, cut well. In the dim light she spotted his pointed ears and cast a glance up at Liatris who also had pointed ears.

Liatris looked down at her and gestured with an open hand towards the man. "This is one of my servants, Gerald. He was in charge of preparing your bath."

Gerald nodded. "I believe this will more than suffice." He smiled and seemed totally at ease.

The pair looked like good friends instead of what she only knew as mindless beasts.

Liatris nodded towards the man, seeming to be the dismissal Gerald was waiting for because he left down the hall. Walking like a human. Talking like a human. Looking like a human, for the most part.

There was a loud sound like an engine coming from the room. Liatris beckoned her to go first. She took one more glance around, feeling trapped in the small space. The thought of escape only lasted a moment before she got a real good look of the room. It was a large multi stalled bathroom. In the center was an inflatable hot tub heated by a small gas-powered generator.

There were oil lamps sitting all around the space giving it a warm orange glow. The whole place was warm and filled with sweet smelling steam. The floor was white tile and the sink looked marble. Piles of clothes were laid out on the three-sink long counter. Liatris seemed to be a very observant person as he instantly moved towards the clothes the moment she looked that way.

"I was unsure of what you would like so I sent some of my servants into the city for different outfits. I believe there will be something you like. If not, I will send them again."

It was a daunting thought, that a Zombie Lord who was incredibly intelligent had and could control what seemed to be an entire army of undead. An undead king.

Liatris turned off the generator, causing a silence to wash over the room. He then moved back to the door. "I will have a woman posted outside of this door. Take your time. When you are ready, she will escort you back upstairs." He stepped closer to Emily and ran a gentle fingertip over the bandages on her left arm. "Try not to get these too wet. Your lacerations are deep. I will rebandage you on your return. Do you need anything?"

"Uhh... I don't think so."

He nodded but craned more downward this time in a half bow. "I look forward to seeing you later, Emily."

He left her alone in the large warm space. He came through with everything he promised and more. She moved to the hot tub, noting there was a froth of bubbles along the top. The water was warm and steaming. Everything smelled beautiful.

Tears burned at her eyes as waves of emotions overwhelmed her. She grabbed the inflated edges of the hot tub. She hadn't had a warm bath for over ten years. Her clothes were things the scrappers brought from the city, all bought with blood and sweat. She couldn't sew or repair items. She wasn't good at growing crops or tending animals. That left her one of the poorest in Haven. She had to skimp and save every moment. Many nights going hungry.

Even her nose started to run. The tears broke free and ran down her cheeks. Hot and salty as they rolled across her lips. With all the luxuries surrounding her, it made it worth the chance he would turn on her. She might have to play along. Pretend to be his pet, possibly. But she could have all this. Luxuries. Warm baths. Servants. Clothes. Hot meals.

Emily undressed and slipped into her bath. She'd carefully taken off the bandages along her arms and head, seeing for the first time the deep lacerations from the car crash. No wonder her arms burned. Now knowing the extent of her injuries, she slid into the bath, keeping her arms up above the water.

The warm water brought with it more memories of much better times. She sat there, relishing in the heat and crying. The hurt of the life she lost clawing at her soul. With that she also had to make the final decision. The final step. Try and run or stay in a life of luxury with the very creature that took everything from her.

She soaked until the water started to cool. She washed her body and hair to an extent she felt cleaner than she ever did. Smelling fresh. Hair cleaned and silky. At that point the lacerations in her arms started to burn. That in combination with the cooling water drove her out.

There were two plush towels on the end of the length of sink which she used to dry off. She'd already seen the clothes, but now she spotted all the toiletries gathered for her. Toothbrush and toothpaste, perfume, makeup, a fancy hairbrush with a gold inlay handle.

There plethora of clothes were better than expected. Anything from Abercrombie and Finch to Gucci. The styles were also varied from a silky top fancy pants and some bejeweled tennis shoes to fancy shirts and dresses with various boots and shoes.

She finally chose a sleek black dress with high slits up the side, low neckline, and dainty flats with gold stitched detailing. She also layered necklaces, hoop earrings, and other jewelry. With a hair clip she managed a damp half updo. She relished in what felt like her childhood self playing dress up, hoping someday to meet a billionaire who lived in a mansion.

In the large mirrors of the bathroom, she turned side to side, admiring herself. It felt good. The room was still warm, and she felt so comfortable. The softness of the dress against her skin was soothing.

She took her time just to feel safe and relax. It gave her more confidence. Even before the zombies she would never think of wearing something like this. With this being the end of the world, and the fact she no longer cared what anyone thought, she reveled in it.

Trying to feel beautiful in her new look was difficult with the streaks of tears down her cheeks. The deep unsettling vibration that at any moment she could be killed and there was nothing she could do about it. She hung her head and leaned against the sink.

Is this what prisoners feel like during their last meals? Or like cows right before getting taken to a slaughterhouse? She shook and soon started feeling cold. Goosebumps broke out across her arms despite the warm steam in the room. The deepening unease crawled through her veins, crossing her entire body until it made her squirm.

Giving in that nothing she could do would make her feel better she left the bathroom. Outside the door she was greeted by a young woman. She had silvery eyes and a long cat like tail. She was in a skirt with a bandana on her head. Emily froze, realizing she was a different mutation of zombie.

"You ready to go?" she asked in a broken Russian accent with the wrong parts of words enunciated.

"Go where?"

"Back to my Lord."

This woman was a touch shorter than Emily and attractive, yet seemingly timid. This was another zombie Emily met that had the capacity of thought and even personality.

"You're a zombie."

"Yes." Her tone was flat.

"Why are you here? Why don't you try to escape?"

She pulled her head back. "Why would I?"

That was a good question which made her choke on her own words. If this bath was any indication of what Liatris was capable of why would anyone leave? "But, they killed you..." she stammered.

The woman turned her head to the side. "Lord Liatris saved me." She sounded confused and still kept a furrowed brow expression affixed on Emily.

"Saved you? How is..." She stopped because she didn't really have a good example. This woman wasn't the rotting ball of mindless flesh that Emily associated with zombies.

The woman giggled. "My Lord has saved many of us."

"But how?" Emily waved her hands in front of her.

"My Lord has cured us from the grotesque mutations and our hunger."

"What? That's impossible."

"Difficult yes," said Liatris.

Emily spun, catching sight of Liatris striding up through the dark shadows of the hallway.

The woman leaned, giving Liatris a casual bow.

He nodded. "You are dismissed, Tatyana."

"Thank you, my Lord."

Emily's jaw dropped.

Liatris turned towards Emily, his eyes scanning her up and down. "You look beautiful, but..."

"But what?"

His gaze traveled towards her arms. "Your wounds are not looking well." He cupped her elbow and gave the slightest pull for her to follow him. "I need to rebandage your wounds to prevent infection."

Her shoulder dropped. The tension and fear starting to flee. She was falling in line with his promises of luxury and care. Stupid maybe. She strode alongside him through the halls, heading towards the stairs leading back up the large room she awoke in.

"What did Tatyana mean?"

"About a cure?"

"Yes."

"It's a long story. Let's get upstairs. I have a lot to tell you." He escorted her with care, keeping a hand close to help her up the steps if she needed.

He guided her back to her plush nest. She sat down, legs pulled to the side and together to accommodate how revealing the dress was she chose.

There was a metal cart with wheels here now. It had bandages on it and some other items. Liatris did not waste time in turning all his attention to her wounds. They were red and sore, making her cringe each time he touched her.

"So... the story?" She probed, wanting to know, but was partially distracted by the stinging in her arms.

"Do you know how this all started?"

She shook her head. "Not really. It started by Russia. Everyone thought virus mutation."

His eyes narrowed a moment. "I was a scientist in a secret DNA research lab outside Chernobyl. Most of us were told it was research on medical advancements. It wasn't." He held bandages in one of his hands which he started to squeeze until his knuckles went from his pale ashen color to pure white. "They were trying to make mutations. They specifically wanted something like this."

"That... That can't be true."

His head moved up, locking eyes with her. A bright and fierce look that ripped any doubts from her. His shoulders shook that cause a rippling effect until his hands too did shake.

"It's worse." He took a breath. "I'll come back to that in a minute." He grabbed some antibiotic salve and started the bandaging process on both her arms.

Emily held still, despite how much it stung at times. He seemed to be attentive to that because he lessened his pressure each time she tried to hide a wince.

"I was a scientist there. There was an explosion and the chemicals along with many other things were mixed all at once resulting in this virus. As you may know the greatest bane to zombies are their insatiable hunger."

She nodded. That was one thing that shocked her, seeing zombies that did not attack at the sight of flesh.

"After I attempted to... tie up some loose ends, I started researching a cure." He finished one arm and moved to the other. Seeming distracted he mumbled to himself. "Hector was wrong."

"Who's Hector?" She heard Liatris grind his teeth.

"He's another scientist. We were turned at the same time. The fool has been trying to make a cure ever since. He thinks that turning is the virus." Liatris looked up, locking eyes with Emily again. "He's wrong. The virus is the horrific mutations and the uncontrollable hunger. The rest is a blessing."

The room was dark, and the candlelight danced across his face. Emily winced as he made his way up her arm with gentle and detailed care. "How can you think that?"

"Would you not want to become immortal? Powerful? Wouldn't it be wonderful to never age? Never die? People would never experience a cold again. Never have the flu. Doesn't that sound like a beautiful world?"

She sat there with her mouth open. *It... it would be.* Even as she tried to envision it she couldn't get the images out of her mind of the mutated hordes. Of the people who were torn to shreds alive and dying in the most gruesome way. Those memories were enough to make tears build. She stiffened, trying to compose herself.

Liatris finished and then headed over to the cart where he placed the leftover bandages. "It's hard to believe, I know. You've only seen the dark side. The uncontrolled and uncured mutated beasts with no regard to life. But there is another side. There is another way."

Liatris extended his hand to her. Seeing him function with four arms was not getting any less strange, but her fear was getting better. He painted a wonderful picture of the world. A world free of disease and death. She couldn't even fully believe it was too good to be true anymore because she'd seen with her own eyes the zombies that were only a fraction away from being just normal real people.

"Please, come with me. I have one more thing to show you this night."

Emily stood and, as she pushed to get herself up, a shot of fiery pain went up her arms. The deep cuts were now fighting back, making her regret not taking his advice and soaking her whole body in the tub.

Liatris took two long strides over the blankets and was at her side in the blink of an eye. He wrapped both his right arms around her and lifted her with the ease of a man lifting a feather. "You're still healing. Take it easy for now and let me help you." With ease, he lifted her into his arms and carried her across the room.

She sunk into his grasp. His words were so soft and caring. She had to admit, this night was amazing in some ways. Maybe he was right. Maybe he was wrong. But how could she ignore how good this felt. No one ever literally picked her up just because she needed help. Very few people even acknowledged she was alive.

Her neighbors Yanika and Jim were among the few. And even then, it was the basics she needed for survival. Mostly food. And this zombie Lord had given her food, shelter, a bath, all the clothes and items she could want, and even physical help. He tended her wounds better than anyone around her ever had. Even those people who used to be doctors and nurses had grown cold and uncaring. Even violent though the years. They didn't care if people were in pain. Everyone was in pain now.

He stayed with her as she leaned against him, just for comfort. She could stand. She could make a run for it if she wanted to, even knowing she couldn't outrun him. But she didn't want to.

"Come, let me show you some things."

He kept his arms around her and helped her over the pile of blankets towards the back of the room where the candles were arranged in a way that made them look like they were lighting an altar. Nestled around them, illuminated by a soft orange flickering light, was a worn wooden chest.

"These are my few possessions I have kept since getting infected." He released her and crouched next to the box. He reached for it and paused, almost hesitant to open it.

It was a thread of vulnerability she hadn't seen before. It made him almost human in a way. She got closer and lowered herself down to her knees. That seemed to be enough for him to finally pull the lid back. There were a few items, most notably photographs and newspaper articles on top.

He pulled out the top photograph of a dark-haired woman. Emily leaned in noting that woman looked shockingly like herself.

"Please don't think less of me, but this was my wife."

She didn't say anything but did start to piece things together.

"She was the most precious thing in my life. I had her bring me lunch at the lab a couple times. And while I was at work one day, I got word she was arrested under the suspicion of being a spy." He held the picture in one hand and reached for the newspaper piece with the other. Having four arms he could multitask with ease. The article was about a decorated admiral working for the Japanese government. "This man oversaw our lab. He was also the one who wrongfully turned in my wife. He's also the man that set the charges that blew the lab. He caused all of this."

The man in the news article looked familiar, but she couldn't place him. He had medals all over his Japanese general uniform.

"When I turned, I chased this man down. I thought he was a double agent, but worse, he was a triple agent. He was working in Russia for the Japanese, but he was also undercover in Japan, really working for the United States. The man is true evil."

"I... I think I've seen him before."

"You have. He goes by the name of Isaac Hammer and is the Admiral of Haven."

"But, if you're right he caused the explosion. He caused the zombie apocalypse."

Liatris nodded. "Exactly. Everything you have seen and experienced all leads down to one man. This man." He tapped a finger against the newspaper article.

After a steadying breath he put it down, but still kept the photograph of his wife in one hand. "Walter brought you to me as you are the spitting image of her. I will not deny that it brings me some comfort. Like a piece of her is still with me. But I know you are not her." He set the picture down and turned to Emily. "But it would mean everything to me if you would allow me to cherish you like my precious companion. I know you must hate me, and I can accept that. Just allow me to take care of your every need."

"Am..." She licked her lips. "Am I a prisoner here?"

His eyes moved to the darkness over her head, and he went silent. Her shoulders tightened, apprehensive of the answer and scared how he would react.

"I... don't know how I can protect you outside of these walls." He paced over towards a wall and then back, rubbing his chin. "My ability to command the undead, both those that follow me and those mindless shells out in the streets is limited. If you..." His hand dropped to his side. "If you were to go beyond that point, I won't be able to stop them. I... I can't allow that to happen."

He seemed to still be thinking it over and everything he said seemed to be meant more for him than her. She waited for a direct response. She half expected his response would automatically be for her to be trapped here. His precious thing, given everything except freedom, and she didn't know how to take that. As a person who'd been on her own for so long it was hard to swallow the thought of having her freedom taken away.

"You couldn't go out there alone. Yes. That's it." He raised a finger on each of his right hands in unison. "Accompanied. You can go anywhere you desire as long as myself or one of my servants are with you. They will be able to protect you."

That revelation made him look so happy. His eyes sparked in the candlelight. The persona of a cold Lord had washed away. He was nervous. Begging. Accepting her even if she hated him. Emily got off her knees and walked over to him.

"Promise me... Promise me no one will hurt me."

"Emily... No one will ever lay a hand on you as long as I exist."

She melted as warmth rushed through her body and she felt relaxed. Safe. It was a euphoria she thought she'd never experience.

He extended one hand to her. "It's late. You must still be exhausted. How about we continue this conversation in the morning?"

She closed the space between them and slipped her hand in his. He guided her gently towards the bed, like a man would guide a dancing partner across the dance floor.

"What would you desire for breakfast?"

"I... I don't eat breakfast."

"Why?"

"There's not usually..." She choked on her words. "I never have enough food for that."

He stopped just before the pile of blankets and pillows and leaned closer. "You will never have to experience that again. I promise you a full stomach, warmth, comfort. You name your desire, and I will do everything in my power to make it come true."

"W— waffles. I'd like to taste a waffle again."

He nodded, pulling back a little. A smile on his face. Once fierce and predatory eyes, now as soft and gentle as a small child's.

Emily nestled herself into the plush nest for the night. This time she felt comfortable here. It was soft, warm, comforting. And now she was going to sleep on her old life, ready to move on to an entirely new life.

HECTOR'S JOURNAL

June 4th, 2039

Moving through South America I have found some tribes saved from the zombies. The activity and carnage here is much less than in Europe. I have lost track of the other First Turned and what I've seen here are far gone mindless zombies. Some have devolved to lumps of flesh moving like leaches or even amoebas. I fear North America was a greater target and I'm unsure what I will find as I travel north.

Science equipment is sparce here, although I have started collecting more items I will need for further research. In addition, I have found a dog minimally mutated by the virus. I believe it has been infected by a First or Second turned. This is a new discovery I will investigate further.

I have trapped the dog, and named it Spot.

Chapter 15

Day came after a long night at the lab. Hector found an underground parking garage. With a couple modifications they were able to get the RV inside. One problem was without the solar panels outside they had limited electricity. They chose that compromise for a safer space. The plan was to loot the city in the day and sleep here at night while Hector did his research.

After some exploration they had a good idea of the layout of the building. There was a very scary staircase down to the parking garage. The room closest to the stairs had three windows and let in a good amount of light. It also was a computer room with no bodies. The group made the decision to set up a main base there.

Hector would want to use this lab a while and there was no better place to search for supplies than a huge city few people have survived long enough to loot.

Everything was coming together for everyone, except Lisa.

She stood inside their new home within the lab, staring out the barred window at the dilapidated building across the street. *How could I let that happen?* In the heat of everything, and with such a deep desire just to feel another human being like that, had made her react emotionally, and now all she felt was regret.

Hector caught her. He hadn't really talked to her all day. When he did it was very flat. *I can't believe I did that to him. To both of them.* Jim was kind to her, maybe more so now, but she didn't know him. Since they were caught, he seemed to integrate himself into their group and helped with all the setup of the room and even made himself his own space.

Lisa wanted to ask what he wanted to do about Emily but didn't dare. The man was looking for another woman and she just went right to seducing him. A stranger. But it had been so long since she felt anything like that. The way he touched her. Feeling a touch like that after so long. Years. It had been years. *But Hector. How could I do that?* Clenching and unclenching her hand she mulled it all over.

There was the screeching of furniture being moved across the floor and the clattering of other items behind her. Everyone was still settling in. Being all in one room would be safest, but it seemed like Flint was already breaking that plan.

A few minutes ago, he had asked Jim to help him move a mummified body out of a room so he could claim it as his own. There were six rooms on this first floor along with a storage closet and an old and musty bathroom complete with the bodies of dead rodents.

She could be getting her own space set up, but she couldn't even move. Hector... Hector meant so much to her. But... like how? *What is he to me? Being with Hector feels different than being with Jim. Why?*

The flop flop sound of Bruno's sandals grew louder behind her.

"It looks like we're going to make this a main room, and everyone else is claiming their own... bedrooms. Do... you want a certain space?"

Lisa took a steadying breath before turning to face him. He had dirt smudged across his cheek and across his poncho. She forced herself to smile, despite feeling like she was resting at the end of a bottomless abyss. "I'll take anything. Thank you."

His large dark eyes moved between her and the floor. He was a nervous man, but this time it seemed like he knew something was up. Lisa bit her bottom lip. Hector most likely wouldn't say anything, but could Bruno have found out what happened between her and Jim yesterday?

She now felt uneasy as if they were both avoiding an elephant in the room. Bruno backed away from her a few steps before turning and moving out the door with a quick pace. If she stayed here much longer it'd really tip the group off that she was struggling with something. If she wanted this to stay under wraps, she needed to play it normal.

It took a lot of self-reassurance and deep breaths before she had enough courage to face them. There was a bustle in the central hub around all the rooms.

Flint was out there, looking around for something when he spotted Lisa. "Yo, you got a broom?"

"Haven't seen one," she said, shaking her head.

"Damn. I need to get the dead body dust out of my room," he mumbled. "Now if I was a broom where would I be?" He kept muttering as he headed away into another room.

Bruno was nowhere to be seen and neither was Hector. Mariah and Spot were in the brightest room. With a quick glance she assumed they were prepping it as a main meeting area. She was cleaning it up and fussing with a hot plate. Spot was hopping around her feet like he expected treats.

"Mariah, do you want some help?"

She looked up at Lisa, jumping as if she was startled a little. "Oh sweetie, that would be great. Could you help me clean up this space? I'm trying to make a little kitchen and dining room for us."

The space was huge compared to the RV. It felt more like a home. "Flint was looking for a broom. I'll go look too and see if I can find any other cleaning supplies."

When Lisa left, she spotted Jim and Bruno together at the main door. Jim had some tools and seemed to be repairing it. It was the only thing damaged here, but not bad. It wouldn't lock, which would explain how the zombies got in in the first place. He turned, almost enough to see her, but she scurried away fast. He probably saw her leave, but at least she didn't have to look at him.

Why would something so magical make her feel so horrible in the end. *How could I do that to Hector? I'm a terrible person.*

There was a bathroom nearby and what she thought she remembered was the storage closet. The old door was stiff, and the hinges groaned as she opened it. There were cleaning supplies on several shelves and a plastic cart on wheels that had wet floor signs and a bucket on it.

It smelled old, musty, and chemically which burned her nose. Undertones of old bleach lingered here. The longer she stayed the more she felt her throat burn and grow scratchy. The bottles here expired a minimum of eight years ago. No surprise. Ten years ago, the infection spread to the states. Fifteen years ago, roughly, it started in Europe. The pattern was referred to as targeted as the horde moved in certain distinct directions.

It made sense everything here, even the cleaning products, were expired by now. Who knew what noxious mixture they turned to or how bad the air was she was breathing. Lisa piled the cleaning cart full of supplies including a couple of brooms, a mop, and a few cleaners she thought might not be deadly. As she moved the bottles the stench grew, and the burning deepened in her throat.

Lisa coughed, feeling the soft tissue grind like she had swallowed glass. Everything from her nose up to her eyes felt like someone had sprayed her with pepper spray.

Lisa pushed the cart out of the way and left. The burning from her throat moved into her lungs. She leaned her arms against the wall outside the door. Despite closing the door behind her she could still smell it. The cough grew more intense until it raked through her whole body. Her lungs rattled with fluid. The harsh movements with each cough wrapped its claws around towards her back. The muscles tensed and an electrical shock went down her leg.

Sucking in a breath she tried to stop the cough. The wall she leaned on felt cool, so she leaned her head against it. It only got progressively worse, but if she didn't stop it, she'd be on the ground, immobilized by her coiling back muscles. Her eyes watered and burned.

Something moved behind her, but her burning watering eyes clouded her vision. It was large whatever it was, blocking the little light coming in through the windows of the other rooms.

A hand with long fingers clasped her shoulder. It was Hector. She tensed more which set off a wave of pain. Her knees buckled and part of her leg went numb. She slapped her hands on the wall, feeling the sting of the impact and the rough surface. It wasn't enough to catch her.

Hector's arms wrapped around her. "The fumes are toxic. I need to get you into fresh air."

She couldn't fight him, but also couldn't bring herself to even look at him. Shame had its hold on her. Fear of what he thought of her now. If she hurt him. But no matter how much she wanted to walk away, she couldn't move. Her throat felt tight and swollen. Lungs burning and rattling.

He scooped her up in his thin but strong arms. She held her breath to fight another cough.

"Is she okay?" asked Jim.

Her head was turned towards Hector, but there was no denying it was his voice.

"She's having a reaction to the chemicals in that back room. Bruno, get Mariah. Tell her we need an antihistamine."

"Y— yes." Bruno stuttered.

There was a loud creak followed by an overly bright rush of light. She squinted and that was enough to set off another episode of violent coughing. This time she wheezed. Her lungs burned. It felt like she couldn't breathe. Like she was slowly drowning.

Though she was squinting she caught sight of Jim coming up beside Hector. "What can I do?"

"Go help Mariah and Bruno. They might need supplies from the RV."

She gasped for air. Their voices were sounding distant. The sun above was a squinted beam across the outline of the cityscape.

"Calm," said Hector. "Breathe slowly. You will be okay."

She turned her head, looking up at him. He had his goggles on and large brimmed hat, but his face was still deeply concerned to the point his normally smooth face had deep creases.

It looked like they were alone now. Things were growing dark. It made her heart pound. She gasped for breath, but only a trickle of air came through. *This might be it.* She made it alone for years. Made it through zombie hordes. Survived where few people survived. Only to die from old chemicals.

She opened her mouth trying to speak but choked.

"Be quiet. Everything will be okay."

She rested in his arms. He stroked her hair with on hand. His voice so gentle, but with a slight waver.

Before she couldn't breathe, before it was too late, she needed to make things right. "I'm... sorry..."

"Hush. You have nothing to be sorry for."

She couldn't breathe. There wasn't any more time. She grabbed his hand, pressing him to her cheek. "I... love... you..."

That was it. Everything went dark. She wasn't sure he even could hear her. But if that's how she went, then so be it. She had a good life with him.

HECTOR'S JOURNAL

May 6th, 2040

    I have set up base in mexico south of the united states border. Some signs of zombies, but not what I expected. Radio communication has come through. The united states has not fallen, and they are setting up shelters. Their project, Haven, is a totally enclosed group of cities for the people of the states to fall back on. While great in theory, I know it will not be large enough. The zombies are making their way inwards from the coast. I don't know how long they will survive.

    I have made a breakthrough in my research and am able to reverse some mutations. Notably mild physical mutation and decreased hunger drive. I have tested this on Spot with great results. He almost reminds me of the dog I had growing up.

Chapter 16

Jim sprinted faster than he had running from any zombie in his life. Mariah was on the way to Lisa, and he was charged with grabbing the extra medical supply kit. After Mariah grabbed her small metal med box and ran to Lisa he bolted for the basement. The steps were long, but he managed to leap two at a time to get down there and then back up.

His lungs were burning by then and his heart pounded. Light washed into the room from wide open front door, and he could spot Bruno standing just outside. With the cold metal box clutched tightly in his hand he burst out the front doors.

"Keep compressions steady!" Mariah yelled.

Jim ran into a horror scene that stabbed him clean through the chest. Mariah and Flint were performing CPR on Lisa, with Mariah doing breathing and Flint doing compression.

Jim stopped by Bruno, who was one step from hyperventilating. Each breath he gasped and was wringing his poncho. Jim placed his hand on Bruno's shoulder for some silent comfort. That was all he could do because he couldn't even speak.

Hector stood close by Lisa's body. Jim had almost gotten used to the ashen skinned mutated man. Hector, with his goggles and hat, never seemed to have much expression, until now. The worry was evident in the creases lining his face that usually went unseen. He was crouched nearby with one hand on the concrete for support and the other resting on his leg, notably shaking.

"Pause!" said Mariah. She bent down, giving two more breaths and then rechecking vitals.

There was a complete pause in the air around them. Everyone quiet. Spot hunched down not making a sound. Even the city around them was silent. No breeze and it was a sunny day, but now there was a chill to the air.

Mariah's head popped up. "I got a pulse and she'd breathing, but just barely."

There was a group gasp from held breaths between each of them.

"I need to monitor her closely. That first room, it's still empty?"

Flint nodded quickly. "Yeah."

"I need ventilation. Get the desks together like a bed. I need a hard flat surface in case we need to do CPR again. Bring all my medical supplies to that room. Don't stir up the dust." Mariah spoke fast while huffing. Sweat coated her face.

The group started to scatter but stopped at Hector's voice. "Don't just run around. Jim, push the desks together. Bruno, get the windows open. Flint, run downstairs and start getting supplies. I will go with you."

They nodded and, with Hector's guidance, they were able to organize the job. Jim ran inside and turned to the front office room to the left of the front door. Bruno ran in after him and started to fight with the windows.

It was a hectic panic as everyone did their jobs. Jim pushed four desks together to make a bed like surface. Bruno struggled with the windows, so he hopped in to help while he waited for Hector and Flint.

The pair came back quickly and had more medical supplies, blankets, and pillows. Flint threw a blanket over the four desks. Hector laid out medical supplies on a table. Jim was prying open the last of the five old painted-over windows.

Hector had left and when the last window finally gave and opened with a crackling sound Hector returned. Lisa lay limp in his arms. She looked pale, even compared to him. Mariah was close behind with her arms full of the metal med supply boxes.

Flint and Bruno ran over to help her carry them in. Even Spot came in holding some bandages in his mouth that must have fallen out.

Hector laid Lisa gently on the desk. Jim could finally hear the soft whistle of her trying to breathe. Bruno crept over, looking terrified, and with shaking hands he put a soft blanket over her legs. There was incredible tension in the air.

Mariah went back to Lisa's side. The woman's blonde hair was wet with sweat and sticking to her round face.

"Here," said Hector. He handed Mariah something that looked like a syringe.

Jim got closer and his confusion must have been evident because Mariah chimed in, "This is an old expired EpiPen. It's the last one we have."

"Will it be enough?" asked Jim.

"It will have to be." Mariah pulled a few other items near her. "I'll need to watch her carefully for a while until the swelling is sufficiently down."

"What can we do to help?" asked Jim. He was expecting they needed supplies from the city, and he was ready to take them all. Whether he was projecting on her what he wanted from his wife or was actually developing feelings for her he wasn't sure, and he didn't care. The only complicating issue was Hector knew what had happened and Jim heard, without a doubt, Lisa tell Hector she loved him.

There was a complication between them that wasn't being addressed due to Lisa's condition, but it will need to be. It was a deep conflict that set into Jim's chest like something gripping inside of him ready to pull his insides out. But she had to live first, and that thought made him hurt more.

Hector took a very long breath before turning to the everyone in the room. "Mariah will take care of her so let's not sit idle. I understand everyone has been moving into the rooms here."

Flint shrugged, but his careless attitude was colored with the weight of this incident. "It was kind of fun having my own room." As he spoke, he sounded like a schoolboy telling what he did wrong to a teacher.

"I think you all deserve it. A little more fortification and this could be a very safe place for everyone."

"Safe would be good," said Bruno with a slight waver in his voice. There was also the soft wet glisten on his face where a tear might have been.

"Bruno, Flint, you two clean up the rooms, but do not go into that storage closet. I will take care of that."

Mariah turned to him. "Be careful, sweetie. I don't want you to have a reaction as well."

Hector placed his hand on her shoulder. "Do not worry. I will be fine." He turned his head towards Jim.

It made him instantly straighten.

"Will you be able to reinforce the front door?"

"Should be. Nothing is really broken, but I'm working on a better more stable locking mechanism."

"Very good. Let me know if you need anything. Mariah, you do the same."

"I will sweetie. Just be careful." She glanced around the room. "All of you."

They dispersed. Hector, who started cleaning out the toxic closet, seeming unaffected by the fumes. Jim worked on the door, but kept his eye on Hector, hoping to get him alone. He knew it needed to be addressed, but he was not worried. His biggest concern was others finding out because he felt that would be an intrusion of Lisa's privacy.

He planned on apologizing, explain himself, and promise it wouldn't happen again. *Never again?* He paused, screwdriver still jammed in the door lock and thought it over. Originally, he planned this all out and was fine with it. But really thinking about it. Really thinking about the way she moaned. How hot and wonderful she felt. The primal desire she brought out within him.

Now his entire plan was turned upside down and in addition, he felt bad for even thinking this way. She almost died— no, she was dead. He heard her ribs break as Flint tried chest compressions. Saw sweat drip from Mariah's forehead as she desperately performed rescue breathing.

He dropped his tools and sat back, rubbing his hand across his face. *Shit, I can't believe I'm thinking like this. I'm literally doing the same thing my wife left me for.* He wasn't focused on the most important thing. He was putting one priority first, but not thinking of everything around him. He was good at following that one thing, that one plan, all the way to the end. But he would ignore everything else. His family. His health. Even before the zombie apocalypse he could go days eating almost nothing as he would be wrapped up in another blacksmith project.

The world had changed. He hadn't. He needed to. Lisa might not make it and he couldn't keep overlooking it like it was nothing. He couldn't keep ignoring everything around him like he didn't care. It made his chest tighten and hurt. He didn't like it. He didn't like looking at the whole picture and being exposed to the emotions that came with it.

Jim stood, pushed the door open, and walked out into the open evening. The RV was parked below in the parking garage Hector found so the parking lot was mostly open. Blood stains dotted the concrete and the vehicles around here had been heavily scrapped. Just rusted metal shells. He walked over to a faded orange concrete barrier and sat there.

The sun was falling fast behind the buildings and long shadows were encroaching. He counted the numerous buildings around him, knowing each one was most likely filled to the brim with zombies. He'd been working on the door and hadn't checked on Lisa in a while.

He assumed if anything happened, he would have heard. But what kind of way was that to act?

Nonchalant in the face of her death. *Cold? Have I become numb over the years?* He should be upset. Scared. If he thought about it, he felt the emotions sneaking inwards, but preservation was still too strong. He feared his own feeling. Feared accepting that she could die at any moment.

After so much chaos his head pounded. He touched the bandages around his head. From the way he felt, he assumed the bullet wound was a mild graze. Enough for maybe a concussion, but that's all. He felt better than he assumed a man shot in the head would feel. Nevertheless, his head still hurt.

His muscles were sore. Not from overuse, but more from being tense with stress for so long. Sitting there it became darker and darker. With the city dead, there were no streetlights. No glow on the horizon from distant buildings lit up from top to bottom. Just darkness.

In the distance he could hear the zombies. There was a hum in the air as if hundreds of them out in the city were all moaning at once. Haunting. Impending doom just beyond his sight. And here he was, looking it in the eye, protected by Hector's proximity. Protected by a zombie.

Wringing his hands he felt an uncomfortable sensation slither over him, making him want to squirm where he sat. There had been so many things he decided to let slide due to his hyper focus on finding Emily. Reality was, there was no trace of her. She most likely was dead.

Worse, he started to realize he wasn't saving her for the right reasons. *She doesn't deserve to die out here. I just wanted to protect her... didn't I?* But it didn't feel right. He was too numb to the idea. Like he didn't care about her the same he cared for this newfound group.

Running it through his head he thought of Emily's death and felt it was unfortunate, but thinking of losing a member of this crew, especially Lisa, made a weight drop on his chest followed by a burning sensation and cold shivers that ran out from his stomach all the way to his fingertips.

But... I was just trying to help her. His stomach turned. *She's my friend.* His stomach turned again. He lowered his face to his hands. *I was just trying to make it right.* The pain raked him. Old tears started to build. Emotions long buried now were boiling to the surface. Violent. Bursting out like a geyser.

"I couldn't save my family, so I was going to save her. Who am I kidding?" He mumbled to himself, hearing his own voice crack. "I did all this for myself. I'm trash."

He never saw his daughter much. When his wife left, he tried to get back together, but for his sake, not theirs. *I wanted them back and didn't want to change myself. When I tried, it was too late. But...* A tear broke free and fell from his cheek.

"All I did was slip back into being the person I was before. I don't deserve to be loved." Jim stood, looking at the darkness sweeping the landscape. Taking deep breaths and taking in the smells of the overgrowth and earth around him.

No birds came out for the night. No animals chattering in the distance. Just the faint sounds and traces of the undead hiding in every corner like cockroaches. *I could have saved them if I had really stepped up to be a better father,* he thought while shaking his head. He soaked in the miserable reality he'd been hiding from.

From deep within his core, Lisa pulled out feelings he had long buried. It made him think. It made him face his reality, because the reality was, he cared about her, he lusted for her, and while she is laying on her death bed, he was only thinking of how he'd cut-and-dry clear things with Hector.

At least the sky was clear, and the stars were startingly bright. It was hard to see the stars in Haven. Everything seemed to be in the shadow of the walls. Jim smiled, tasting the salt from his skin as tears rolled over his lips.

He stepped forward towards the darkness. One foot. Then the next. Attracted to the void. A fitting end. He'd never been able to change. Not after everything that happened. He won't be able to change. He took another step, moving across the parking lot and further and further from the lab.

She loved Hector, not him. He didn't blame her. Hector was the better man. He cared for her and fiercely protected her. He obviously cared very deeply for her. *And I just fucked her and then dismissed her. I'm the real monster.*

The tears fell, rolling down his chin and dripping to the ground. The tiniest trail leading away. Like the smallest footprints in the sand of time, as he was leaving the last few traces of his existence. If he got far enough away, then it would just be him and the other monsters.

At the edge of the parking lot, he was far enough to see forms move in the distance. They moved closer, obviously seeing him. He stepped forward, ready to join the creatures he'd become.

Something from behind him grabbed his shoulder. Jim stopped. Not even turning. Frozen and accepting what he deserved. Ready to just have it all end.

"I know what you're trying to do."

Jim jolted at the sound of Hector's voice.

"I heard what you said, but I think you are wrong. Whatever you decide to do, I want you to know, there is always hope to change the future, but first you need to accept that your past is your past." Hector let go of Jim's shoulder.

Jim turned, but even though he moved as fast as he thought he could, Hector was gone. Jim knew the voice. He also noted the zombies in the distance seemed to be moving further away. The night air started to chill him. His legs were shaking. Hands too.

He'd never felt this conflicted. He'd always stayed focused. One thing. One plan. Nothing else. But he couldn't ignore everything else. His insides were like ice and painful like frostbite had set into his soul. Standing there felt like standing on the edge of a cliff. He could go on to his death or head back.

His hands were shaking as his arms twitched. Tingling sensations trailed his arm to his fingertips. Tears kept coming and coming and coming. Darkness came to its entirety, and he stood beneath a bright open sky sparkling like someone had tossed a million pieces of glitter above him.

The horde had moved back and had quieted, allowing the sound of night to set in. Where there had only been undead around him there now was the soft sounds of crickets coming out of the grass and singing their nightly song.

It had been years since he heard crickets. Jim fell to his knees, hitting the rough concrete and not even feeling the impact as the pain in his chest, the pain in his heart, was far greater. Lights flickers around him, and he realized there were fireflies here. Coming from their hiding places they started to decorate the air with their light-yellow glow.

Weight was lifted from him, leaving him lighter as each firefly swirled around him and upwards into the night. Hector's words repeating in his head. *There is always hope to change the future.* If Hector could feel that way, the man turned into a monster trying to find a cure, how could Jim even justify the hopelessness he felt. *If Hector's right... I could try... I could try again to... to be better.*

Jim pushed up from the ground and wiped his tears with the back of his hand. There would be another day to walk into the abyss, but that is a one-way trip. He could take one more try. One more shot.

The front door was open, welcoming him. Just to the left stood Bruno. His head dropped in his usual nervous fashion, but he looked up enough to briefly lock eyes with Jim.

"Hector said you'd be back once you got some air." Bruno nodded towards the door. "I kept it open for you."

Jim's shoulders fell. *Hector already knew what I'd pick. But... He knows what happened with Lisa and I... and he still did that?* "Thanks Bruno, I appreciate it."

Bruno smiled. "Mariah is cooking supper. Join us?"

A slight smile pulled at Jim's lips. "That... that would be good. I want to go check on Lisa real quick."

"Okay. I'll be in the kitchen— living— room thingy." He pointed at the room they cleared up to be a central area.

Jim nodded and then turned towards Lisa's room. Everything was dimly lit with darkness fully set in and the hall was illuminated only by a few candles and the soft glow from the main room. Lisa's room was almost total darkness except for one faint orange glowstick that cast small dancing shadows on the back wall.

Jim headed in. Hector sat on a metal stool next to the desks they had turned into a bed. His large frame was craned over her, and he had his chin resting on his intertwined fingers. He looked to Jim and gave him a slight nod.

Jim moved over to another chair next to Hector. "Will... she make it?"

"Mariah is confident she will recover. Yes."

Jim let out a bated breath. "That's a relief. Uh... Thank you... for earlier."

Hector's head rose, but he kept his gaze on Lisa. "We all fall prey to the darkness now and then. But it's the small light in our lives that keep us going. Lisa is my light."

Jim's chest tightened. This was what he was planning, but now he wanted it differently. He needed this conversation to mean something. "It's a poor excuse, but I had no idea she was in love with you."

Hector took a quick breath inward. "Nor did I. I am glad she found comfort in someone. This life is too short. Every moment should be lived to the fullest."

Jim clenched his jaw. He half expected Hector to be mad or upset, but to be so accepting was surprising, but, Jim realized, reflected who this man really was. Mutated, yes, but still a man. Still, someone with a mind and feelings.

"I..." Jim knew he needed to be honest. He needed things to change in his life. No more running towards something just so he could drown out something else. "I wish to have that comfort again, but I do not want to come between you two. If you wish, I will leave." He turned, finally directly facing Hector. Facing a real man and reminding himself of the monster he almost became.

Hector shook his head. "No. I'm glad you have come into our lives. I..." Hector's head fell. "I may love her, but I can never give her the intimacy you can." He raised his hands and flexed like a child just discovering they have fingers. "I cannot love her like this."

"Why not?" Jim leaned forward. "She loves you already, mutations and all."

"It is too dangerous. One wrong move and I could infect her."

Sighing, Jim lowered his head, taking his gaze to the floor. "You said life's too short. What if she's just waiting for you and you haven't ever taken that step forward? It's just a thought. But I think you two should talk about it when she wakes up."

"Perhaps. I would be a hypocrite if I told you that change is possible, and then plant my feet so deeply due to an event that happened so many years ago."

Jim raised a brow. "Yeah. Yeah, you would be. How about we agree to this? Life is too short, what happens happens, as long as she's okay."

"I think I can agree to this. And I assume that means you have committed to staying?"

"I think I have."

"What about Emily?"

Jim sunk downwards in the chair. "She's my neighbor and a friend, but I don't think she made it. And I... I don't love her."

"Do you love Lisa?"

"I haven't loved in so long... I think so."

"Before you take any next steps be undoubtedly certain: I am not afraid to wipe from existence anyone that hurts her."

"I can respect that."

HECTOR'S JOURNAL

August 3rd 2040

I have set up a lab in Durango in an abandoned building with Spot. The dog is at least company. The horde is thin, and the Mexican government has done well at delaying the invasion. I know it is only a matter of time. Supplies have been plentiful, but I must acquire them under the cover of darkness. Despite my intentions, I am only seen as a monster.

Chapter 17

A few days of grueling training went by, and Yanika was sore, bruised, and scraped. Tactical running drills done, she sat on the edge of her bed. Eric was crouched in front of her, dabbing the deep scrape on her forearm with a cotton ball. He had some bandages next to him he had traded for.

The other civilians were starting to change their tone, most realizing this was more of a draft. The guards brought here had figured things out early and already had started trading for luxuries. Eric was one of them.

From day one he'd been bartering with guards and civilians. He'd take chores given to other guards for money or supplies. He'd do the same to the other civilians, but for food. If food was passed out that was shelf stable, he bartered for as much as he could.

Jance was also helping them, doing more up-trading than trading manual labor. He had taken both Eric's and Yanika's stipend tickets and went to pick up their food. They were first told that food, warmth, and luxuries were being offered to them. In reality, they had to work for them. The better they did or harder they worked the more food stipends or luxuries they got. Just like the medical supplies Eric scored.

Eric glanced up at her. "You doing all right?"

"I guess. Is there any way to just take tomorrow off?"

"Not yet." He dabbed at her wound some more.

She had to speed crawl on the ground under a series of ropes and the surface was solid gravel. Afraid they would kill her if she did not complete the task like they wanted she pushed through, getting scrapes all across her body. Her elbows were the worst, but her knees were also raw and burning.

"You've been incredibly strong," said Eric. "Just hang in there."

"S'up y'all!" said Jance. He had his arms full, and he slid into her cubicle. "Got us some grub." He dumped all the food he was balancing on the bed next to Yanika.

"You have any trouble picking up our food too?" asked Eric.

Jance waved his hand. "Wasn't an issue. The guys know me. Gave

153

me an extra package of wasabi peas."

As Jance reached for the peas Eric slapped his hand. "Don't get greedy. We should save it."

"You're hording food like a chipmunk. What you planning, man?"

Eric put his finger to his mouth. That was cue enough for them to group together.

"Nothing much has changed," said Eric. "It still sounds like the plan is to push into the city."

"I heard rumors that Admiral Hammer is searching for something specific in the city," said Jance.

That seemed to be the trend. There was a lot going on they weren't telling people. Eric and Jance, already being guards, were able to get better information. Yanika was just trying to survive as they pushed her through grueling activities.

She rubbed her arm. "Is this what you guys had to go through to become guards?"

Jance shrugged. "Nah. I was a scrapper. Seems they got some respect for my mad skills."

Eric rolled his eyes and then nodded his head towards Jance. "This kid survived being rushed by twenty zombies. They drafted him after that. I did have to go through training."

"Was it this bad?"

After a slight shrug, Eric started nodding. "Yes. It's not fun." A grin shifted into a soft, yet sad chuckle. "You know I had a business degree and was going for an accounting degree before the zombies came through. Getting drafted as a guard here was the only way to get in. Guess they thought I had some potential."

"I don't want to be here," Yanika muttered. She hurt and was scared. The fear over days has settled itself in her stomach and she'd felt nauseous since she got here. She was used to going without food, but this was different. Eric and Jance made sure she had food, but she could barely stomach it.

Eric reached up and put his hand on her shoulder. She felt a bit stronger with him around. He was soft-spoken with her. He had a whole persona at the outpost that, the few times she had ran into him, she didn't like. She didn't even know his name then and he didn't know her at all. He wasn't the person she thought he would be. His blue eyes were soft and youthful. A business degree didn't fit him. Maybe a tough football player, drafted right out of high school.

"Psst."

The sound of someone just outside of her cubicle made Eric and Jance stand. The cubicles weren't that tall, and Eric was able to peer above the walls. From Eric's calm expression she assumed it was someone he knew. Yanika rolled her shoulders trying to relax.

Eric pulled the curtain away, letting Mark step in. The pale man had dark circles around his eyes and looked like he hadn't slept in days.

"You three doing okay?" asked Mark.

"Yah, bruh. We rollin. You chill?"

Mark raised his brow, shook his head, and then turned back to Eric. "I think I found out something."

Eric and Jance moved closer to him. Not wanting to miss out, Yanika pushed off the bed and stepped closer. Mark smelled like armpit sweat and bleach. Her nose twitched.

Mark looked unnerved and glanced around several times before looking back at the rest of them huddled in this tiny space. "It's a research lab where they were looking up the zombies."

"What?" asked Eric.

"That's the main target."

"No cap? They lookin for a cure?" asked Jance.

Mark's shoulder sunk down. "Haven't heard anything about that. I think it's something else. Data maybe?"

Eric stepped away, hooked his arm in Yanika's and escorted her back to the edge of the bed. "Try to keep resting. You need your strength."

"I'm okay," she protested.

Eric looked her up and down, stopping as their gazes locked. "Your legs are shaking."

"They are?" She looked down, seeing the subtle twitch in her muscles. She didn't even feel it. Deep fatigue had made its way to every inch of her body. Her eyes were dry, sore, and tired. Any closer to her pillow and she might just go to sleep for a week.

Eric sat next to her and placed his hand over hers. She tried to smile, but it was so much effort.

Eric nodded towards Mark. "Thanks. Keep your ears open."

"I will," said Mark.

"Is Cuddles okay?" Yanika mumbled.

"Uhhh." Mark's head lowered. "I couldn't keep it here. I had to give it to a local farmer."

"What?" She jolted to the edge of the bed slapped her hands on her thighs. "Cuddles is gone?" She felt the pain in her knees, but the idea of losing the closest thing to a best friend she had hurt deeper.

Eric turned, putting his hand on her shoulder. "It'll be okay. We'll find Cuddles later. You need to make it out of here first."

Yanika pressed her lips tightly together, trying not to cry. She felt the tears burning and her breath shake.

"You're thinking of leaving?" asked Mark.

Eric fell silent a moment. His gaze was on the floor. "I think so." He looked up to Yanika and then Jance. "I think we need to get out of here."

"No cap? They be hella angry if we get caught. KO mad. We get caught, it's unalive time."

"I know," said Eric. "But I'm not interested in being part of business here. Yanika isn't doing well either."

"Where will you go?" asked Mark.

"I've heard of a few small survivor camps outside of Haven."

"Bruh, most are scrapper camps. Hella sus."

Yanika rubbed her hands together. Her head felt heavy and eyelids heavier. Despite that, she continued to shake. She'd been tricked into a draft. Her life's work, Cuddles, was gone. These head guards, Generals or whatever they were called, were pushing her to death. It made taking their chances with the zombies almost sound appealing. But she did have a bed, food, and shelter.

She shook her head. *That's how they tricked everyone in the first place. I already had all of this and was much happier.* Who knew the Outer Rim would be better than the Capitol? The promise of a better life was as much of a lie now as it was when everyone had tried to get into Haven.

It was not said out loud a lot, but many wished they had taken their chances outside the wall. Risked the danger like many others had just to have a life they controlled. A life where they had a say in the decisions around them.

This cubicle was very close to feeling like a prison. The only privacy she had was the curtain hanging across the opening to the small box and the hopes no one around here was very tall, otherwise they could just turn and look right in on her.

Food was rationed, not given. She had to work harder for food here than she ever did in the Outer Rim. Deep inside, causing her to shake even more, she wondered if she would have even survived without Eric here. He was trapped in this place too but knew the ins and outs of the politics here. He had connections she didn't.

Yanika tried to reach out to the other civilians, even the ones that had lived near her in the Outer Rim. No one wanted to help her, or anyone else for that matter. It was all for themselves and screw the next person. Everyone climbing on top of each other in a pyramid of bodies, trying to be the man on top in the end. But it was the little ones like her that ended up like grains of sand beneath their feet. Walked on. Used. Abused. Unable to stand up for themselves. There were quite a few people like that, but she was too scared to do anything about it.

Yanika opened her lips to speak, feeling them tremble as she did so. "I think we should leave."

Eric turned to her. His eyes were sad, yet gentle. Tired as well. He hadn't had a shower today, or even yesterday, so his hair was greasy and there was a thick deodorant smell trying to cover up the musk of two days of sweat.

She wasn't any better. Showers were limited. They all got shower rations just like they did for food. She hadn't earned one yet. Eric had been trading his shower ration for supplies. They had a good amount, and now she realized why. They'd need all they could get if they were getting out of here.

"We need to be strategic," said Eric. "I have a hunch the punishment for trying to desert would be severe. We don't need to be thrown out into the hoard with no supplies or worse, executed."

Yanika flinched.

"I'm sorry," said Eric. "I won't let that happen to any of us."

"Bruh, you getting sap. Hella sus. Yah boi got this."

Yanika rubbed her forehead. "Do you really know what he's saying?"

"You get used to it," said Eric. "Mark, I'll get you paid back when the coast is clear."

Mark nodded. "Sure. Good luck." He was blunt.

Mark's face held little emotion which unnerved Yanika. He closed the curtain behind him.

She rubbed her eyes, working out a little crusty piece. Blinking, it felt like an eyelash was stuck so she rubbed it more.

"Go to sleep," said Eric. "Meal is just MREs anyway. It'll be here for you when you get up." He lifted her blanket.

Yanika slid under it and laid on her side. He tucked her in and then set her food on the stand next to her bed. Grabbing the rest, he tossed a silver packet to Jance.

Jance ripped it open with his teeth sniffed, and then grimaced. "Sus."

"Military food. What do you expect? See you in the morning, Yanika."

She listened as they left but didn't go far. She could hear every move they made in the adjoining cubicles. All the lights would go off soon and she'd be left, again, in total darkness surrounded by the faint sounds of life around her. Snoring, crying, hushed conversations. At first it was too much to sleep, but the drills seemed to have almost everyone so exhausted that the sounds quieted much faster now after lights out.

With no one around her she let herself cry. Tears rolled from her eyes, soaking into her pillow. She gripped her blanket and pulled it to her mouth to silence any whimpers that may sneak out.

Even this exhausted, she still had the energy to cry. It seemed the only thing she consistently could do. Cry. Plead for something to change. Cry more. This was hell.

Hector's Journal

February 14th, 2041

Valentine's Day again. I was surprised when I remembered, but something this year has me longing for the old days. Back when I was trying to date around my work schedule. I never thought I would miss it.

I've been studying DNA sequence reconstruction. My research has progress, but I feel I must move soon. The hordes have pushed through and are now on the US border. I've been able to listen to radio communication. I'm surprised how long they have held out, but I suspect this is because they had more time to prepare.

It pains me to know they will soon fall as well, just as all the other countries have. The zombies can increase their numbers with every life they take. It won't be long before heavy artillery won't be enough anymore.

I heard on the radio that Haven is nearing completion. There was a message that went out over all radio frequencies informing survivors that they should start retreating towards the midwest to the sanctuary of Haven. I wonder if this place will be enough to protect people or if I'm watching the last of the human race die.

Chapter 18

All she had to do was ask. So, she did. Emily wanted a shopping spree. Something she couldn't afford even before zombies. And it turned into the best day of her life. Liatris gathered some of his female servants who were interested in what he called 'the mission'. These girls, including Tatyana whom she met before, despite being undead, were wonderful. Funny. Lively. Gerald also came with, acting as more of a bodyguard for the group. They went out into the city, safe from any of the other zombies, and they looted everything.

Back in the throne room of the multi-story downtown office building, Emily spun, the lacy black dress spinning around her. Night had fallen, and she moved in and out of candlelight, pausing now and then to admire herself in one of the seven full length mirrors Liatris had brought here for her.

"Do you like it, my dear?" he asked.

"It's beautiful. I love it."

"Are you going to try on the others?" He waved his hand towards the pile of clothes in the far corner. Mirrors, closets, chairs, and anything her whim fancied had been brought here. He had his throne, and she had a pool of riches. She had her nest of blankets and pillows pushed back and claimed a whole corner of this office building as her own.

The wooden closets with gold accents were lined against the wall interspersed with black stained wooden desks. There were three large jewelry boxes and a five-foot-tall organizer that she had started to put her multitudes of makeup into.

The wall of broken windows that originally had piles of furniture packed against it was starting to get bricked up with heavy curtains installed to hide the hideous hodge-podge of stone. His servants were hard and fast workers. Because of their undead status they all were stronger than they looked, but very pleasant.

Emily had talked to several of them, learning that this was the top floor, and the floors below was used as housing for all the servants. This was a newly established home, and they were working on installing more luxuries over the next few weeks.

The women she went out with all lived around this building. One was married to another servant, two others were dating, and the last was single. They had various mutations, but other than physical deformity, Emily felt like she was back in college with her girlfriends.

Something that Emily needed that the others didn't was food. Luckily one of Liatris's servants was a five-star chef and was overjoyed to be able to cook for someone again who still could taste. Fun fact, zombies can only taste a select few things.

She danced over to Liatris. "I'm going to save the rest as a surprise."

He smiled, with a devious spark in his eyes. "You're teasing me again."

She moved forward and straddled his lap. It might have only been a few days since she awoke here, but she was entirely committed to this life. In love with it. In love with him. Showered with everything she ever wanted and more. She had a community here.

He took a finger and ran from her cheek down to chin. "You are stunning."

"And what about you?" She grabbed the collar of his polo and pulled. "You ever going to change up this drab look?"

"Would it please you if I did?"

She turned, raising a brow before shrugging. "I think it would be very attractive."

"I will have my men find something suitable then."

She popped open the top button of his shirt. "It won't be on for long."

He grabbed her hand, wrapping his long fingers around hers.

Her cheeks felt hot, and her breath caught for a moment. Liatris was as charming as he was kind to her. He never raised his voice. Never told her no. And was strict with his servants about protecting her.

She leaned forward, her face a few inches from him. Their gazes locked. She took slow breaths while he didn't seem to take any. His lips parted and he wrapped his hand around her head, lacing his fingers through her hair. He held her there, looking deep into her eyes. This was a commanding powerful man that yielded himself to her. He controlled armies, but not her.

"You are gorgeous," he growled.

Chills trailed down from the base of her skull down her spine like a drop of cold water running across her skin. She shifted uncontrollably, rolling her hips just enough to grind against him.

He gripped her hair and pulled her back as his other hand caught her hip. "I can't take your teasing any longer."

She grinned. "What are you going to do about it?" There was a little panic in the background. One shopping trip and she felt almost invincible. Almost. She'd pushed buttons. Pushed boundaries. Worked her way to each line to see if he was really telling her the truth.

It might have started as a test, then maybe a game, but now she was burning up from the inside. Her breath caught in her lungs and remained stagnant for several seconds.

He held her, eyeing her like someone would examine an expensive gem. On occasion he seemed to take a breath. Or maybe she was taking his breath away. The thought tugged at her lips, pulling a quick smile.

"I want to kiss you," he whispered.

"Then why don't you?"

He tilted his head, his gaze dropping down and to the side for a moment. "I never want to do something to you that you do not desire."

"What if I desire it?"

His eyes snapped up to hers. There was a moment of intense examination before his features softened again. "You are not afraid of me anymore?"

"No. You've given... you've given me everything I dreamed of."

She heard him breath this time, a long drawn-out exhale. "You do not owe me anything for that. Not even your kindness."

"I'm not doing things because I feel like I owe you."

He loosened his hold on her hair. He wasn't pulling tight. It was a pleasurable balance.

Emily ran her knuckles down his cheek, admiring his features. His skin felt soft and looked so pale, like it had never been touched by the sun. His ears came up to a slight point which was oddly attractive.

The way he looked at her felt like a gentle loving caress of the eyes that shifted every time his lips twitched to a look of hunger. Not in a frightening way, but in a way that made her body hot.

Liatris's eyes suddenly shifted past her. Emily turned, seeing movement from the stairs that led downstairs. Emily swung herself around and slipped off Liatris's lap. She spotted the man named Walter moving from the stairwell into the room. He wore a dark pinstriped shirt and contrasting vest today.

Liatris clapped his hands on his knees. "Walter, what brings you here?"

"I have a handful of business to conduct with you."

Liatris's cold exterior set back in and his intense stare lingered on Walter for a time. Emily could have left the room, but she felt required to be at his side. She'd already put a pillow next to his chair. She stepped over and knelt on the pillow with her back erect, trying to seem equally intimidating.

It didn't go unnoticed. Walter locked eyes on her the moment she moved, his expression blank, but tracking her every movement. She fixed him with an equally intense stare, trying to assert that she was the queen here now.

Liatris glanced beside himself, seeming to take note of her presence and position. He gave her a nod before he turned his attention back to Walter. "Speak." His deep tone reverberated around the room.

"The first order of business is an update from my informant. They are training troops to move into this city."

"Are they targeting the lab?"

"Indeed. I have left enough breadcrumbs to bring them right there. But they are taking more time than expected."

"Can you accelerate their progress?"

"It may pose difficult from many fronts. The lab has been taken over by Hector and his crew."

"What!" Liatris sprung from his chair, craning over with his hands still clutched to the armrests. His fingers dug into the wood, making it splinter.

"They arrived a few days ago but have yet to move on."

Liatris groaned. He ground his teeth, his eyes scanning the floor around the room, but unfocused as if he was searching for an idea. "They have to go. They will compromise the whole mission."

"What is the mission?" asked Emily, daring to break into the conversation.

"I'm sorry dear. I forgot to inform you. Admiral Hammer was based at that lab, and I found some incriminating evidence in the documents there. I suspect the old computer files also have incriminating evidence."

"You've been luring him there?"

"More a strategic push to get government officials into the area and making certain the information ends up in the right hands."

Walter clapped his hands together. "That is where I have more information. I have found a small group of trainees that I think would be excellent carrier pigeons to bring that information back to Haven's capitol."

"Excellent. But Hector's presence will make for a much more complicated endeavor."

"Possibly not," said Walter. "My lady Victoria is also here to see you."

Liatris groaned. "And how does that help?"

"She and Hector have been close in the past. We could use that relationship to lure him out. It might be the leverage needed on all sides."

Liatris raised a brow. Emily tried to keep her expression cold like him, but when his expression broke, she pulled back. Glancing between the two she felt present to an inside joke, and she was not on the inside.

"Send Victoria in."

Walter gave a low bow as he grinned. The expression was eerie and devilish.

Emily leaned towards Liatris. "Are we going to be okay?"

"Victoria is harmless. It would be good for you to meet another First Turned."

"She's a Lord— Lady like you?"

He gave her a slight nod.

Nervously, she grabbed at her dress and wrung the material. Her heart fluttered. Liatris was enough of a shocker. His followers were nice, but the thought of another First Turned, someone as strong as him, made her uneasy to the point of squirming on the cushion she knelt on.

He glanced her way and then extended a hand to her. "Be at ease, my queen. No one will ever lay a finger on you."

Her shoulders sunk and the trembling starting to work its way through her body receded like the tide in the ocean. She took his hand and adjusted herself to be more regal and upright, taking notes from his body language.

Queen of the zombies. I like that. It was powerful and that power was addicting. To stand before the monsters she once feared and be unafraid. To mingle among them, safe from any threat. Be around other people and build friendships where before she went long stretches without another soul speaking to her.

This was the life of luxury she had hoped for. She could almost thank Marco, that asshole. He about got her killed, but it seems he was getting played. Walter had set everything up. Marco finding out about the lab and even Marco asking her to join. When she crashed,

164

Walter was the one that saved her and brought her here. She should be furious but couldn't be with how well things turned out in the end. She smiled and, with a deep breath, relaxed. At least until Victoria arrived.

The woman strode up the steps with an entourage of chiseled shirtless men. She was an intimidatingly tall curvy devilish woman. She had a narrow waist, wide hips, and huge breasts that were barely contained by a lacy white top. Her long wavy dark hair had a low side part, and the rest was combed over her head making cascading waterfalls of curls fall down one side. She wore a dark skirt which accentuated her long legs and heels that clicked against the hard floor as she moved.

It was obviously in many ways she was a First Turned Lady of the Dead. She was also mutated with horns that poked through the waves of her hair, wings shaped like a bat's, and a long thin tail. Her followers moved like dedicated guards making three single file lines behind, flanking left and right.

Her eyes were a fierce silver which matched that of all her followers. Walter came up behind them, out of sync with the others and very out of place with his appearance. He pulled to the side, standing off by his own. Despite only seeing him work for Liatris she noticed that he had silver eyes that matched Victoria.

Her face felt tight as she tried to hide all expression. *He's a double agent!* She gave Liatris a quick glance and he seemed unphased by all of this. *He must know.* This was becoming a complicated mess of politics.

Once Victoria was before Liatris, Emily could really see the extent of this woman's size. She was, Emily estimated, a few inches taller than Liatris and she was tall enough to tower over the men behind her.

Victoria grinned with a devious expression. "Liatris, it's been a while." Her head rolled and her deep voice was the most seductive thing Emily had ever heard.

"Victoria." Liatris nodded in acknowledgement to her presence. "What brings you here?"

"We have a deal, and you are late on your end."

His eyes narrowed. "I have been indisposed."

"I don't care. I have men starving."

Men or zombies? Can zombies starve?

"Maybe you should have fewer followers."

She moved forward and leaned over him, overly close, with her face just inches from his, her breasts almost spilling out. "Are you going back on our agreement?"

He didn't flinch. "You wrongfully assume that our agreement was infinite."

She pulled back and crossed her arms. Her tail flicked behind her. "What do you want?"

It was Liatris's turn to lean forward. The power in the room shifted. "The lab in the city on Court Street has been taken over by Hector and his followers."

Victoria's expression broke from the stark emotionless mask to one of wide-eyed surprise with her mouth hanging agape. "Hector is here?"

"He is. And he's in an area I need empty." Liatris stood, pressing his own dominating presence in on her, forcing her back. "So, I'll make a bargain with you. I'll prepare more of the serum if you can get him to vacate that building."

She stood her ground but looked more tense. It felt like an equal fight now. A rock and a hard place finally meeting, but neither budging.

It took her a minute to reply, but when she did it was with all the power of a raging dragon. "We had a deal, Liatris. I have supported your research. I gave you the sample I acquired."

"Mysteriously," he growled. "You never did tell me where you got it."

She dismissed the comment with a wave of her hand. "I supported you with my men. You cannot add onto terms now as I have paid for your wares with the blood of my men."

"Then consider this a renegotiation in our contract." That was his power play, laid out. All in.

It was enough to make Victoria bite her bottom lip and then back down. Her fierce gaze turned soft and sultry. "We could have been great together."

"I have no interest in being another man-slave in your harem. Do we have an accord?"

"Fine. I'll deal with Hector, but I expect you'll get a good deal done for me before the end of the week."

"You think you're in a position to impose deadlines?"

"If you want Hector out of your hair, then you are in no position to refuse."

Liatris's expression remained stern, yet emotionless, while Victoria was now cooing as she spoke, seeming to relish in this debate.

"Good day, Victoria."

"Good day... Liatris." Her smooth coo melted over his name as she spoke it, like a siren trying to lure in her prey. She looked to her crew of muscular shirtless men. "Come, we are leaving."

The power she held and used made chills spread across Emily's body. She was equally afraid and envious. The room was still dimly lit, even with the lamp and candle additions over on her side. Despite this, Victoria vanished into the darkness like a ghost. Emily didn't dare breathe until she was absolutely sure Victoria was gone. Walter had also left, following her men.

Emily didn't move for the first few breaths they were alone, still taking it all in. Mostly the force that was Victoria. In comparison, Emily was nothing. The rush of power she felt earlier had deflated flat. It reminded her that here she was just a human. Weak. Powerless.

Liatris had made becoming a zombie sound like a blessing. She shrugged it off originally, but now was getting a new understanding. Having to follow one leader was no different than a political system, but in this case, everyone had a piece of power and immortality.

"Could... Could you make me like that?"

Liatris's head snapped around as his eyes locked on her like a trained sniper scoping in on his target. The size of his eyes changed, growing larger and then narrowing several times. "That's... complicated..." He stood from his throne and paced. He rubbed his chin with a finger on both right hands.

She'd never seen him so blatantly ruffled. Worried. It was so extreme she felt her own body tense.

"You don't understand what that would entail."

Emily placed her hands on her knees and pushed herself up. Her legs felt like noodles from being in that position, but she tried to hide it. She tried to hold onto all that boss girl energy and strode over to Liatris, high heels and all. "Tell me." She caught the elbow of his lower left arm, stopping his frantic pace.

"My dear, so much can happen, you must jest. Do you mean to be in power, or to be turned?"

"Both." She watched him shiver as she spoke.

He grabbed her hand, pulling it from his elbow only to hold it in front of him like a man ready to propose. "Being turned is not pleasant. While mutations to the Second Turned can be mild, it is not guaranteed."

"I've seen plenty of the others that look human."

"They were lucky. This infection- this virus we carry, it is fully realized only in we First Turned." He pulled away to pace again in front of her. "The Virus has more human DNA to bind with the Second Turned and that's why there are fewer mutations, but after that it becomes unstable. Mutations are random, and messy. And sometimes that instability effects a Second Turned. It's just too much of a risk." He stopped, turning back towards her. His brow was furrowed over a shaded expression of desperation. "You would also not have autonomy around me. All zombies outside the First Turned I can control."

Striding back to her, he caught her chin with a knuckled and guided her eyes to his. "There are just too many risks. I'd take away your own control. The mutations. The hunger and pain of being turned. I cannot risk it."

"Shouldn't it be my choice?" He had good points. It didn't sound pleasant, but from being around the others, she was confident that she could come out stronger than she was now. She was human. Squishy. Mortal. But, on top of having her every wish granted, she could also have power and immortality as well.

He took both her shoulders, looking down on her like a parent would a child. "I promised that nothing would hurt you. That included myself. I cannot do something that I know would harm you."

She moved in. He had plenty of strength to push her away, but his grip crumbled. She placed herself up against him. As she looked up, she trailed a finger down the side of his face. He shivered and she felt it, causing chills to wash from her shoulders down her back like a cape followed by a rush of heat from her toes upwards.

They'd been close the last few days, but not intimate. She was just a treasure to him, but that wasn't good enough. Not after seeing how much power Victoria had over him. Watching her coo at him like she owned him. She had him cornered.

Witnessing that was terrifying and addicting. She chewed her bottom lip. It was a decision, but not that hard. She'd be a slave to his commands. *But aren't I already? I'm at his mercy for food, shelter, protection from the zombies. How much freedom is that? If I was like him, I could go anywhere.*

That thought brought a wide smile to her face. She sidestepped and pushed him back towards his throne. Again, he wouldn't have any trouble stopping her, but he went along. He let her push him back and down into the chair. She hiked her dress and straddled his lap.

Liatris was a chiseled handsome man with sharp eyes and, despite having four arms and pointed ears, he was handsome. Once she saw past her assumptions, she found he was kind. So protective. Doting. This man lived up to every promise. A few days and he was the best man she'd ever met.

He wrapped his two bottom arms around her, gripping her behind. "This isn't like you."

"People change."

"Are you still afraid of me?" He had a slight smile on his face as he asked.

"Not one bit." As she spoke, she walked her fingers up his chest and on the last word booped him on the nose. She giggled at her own action.

His smile grew large and eyes bright. This wasn't just a pretend happy, this looked like genuine happiness. He grabbed her hand and brought it to his lips, gently kissing each finger. His lips felt cool, and his touch was like erotic cold play sending shivers through her body.

He had short hair that felt soft to the touch as she ran her fingers through it. She ground against him feeling a hard bulge grow beneath her. She aroused herself. Each rocking motion rubbing her in a way that made her hot and damp.

His eyes rolled back for a moment as he let out a soft growl. The sound made her suck in a quick breath as another jolt of electricity pulsed through her.

"I...." Another groan from him trailed off.

Emily undid the buttons of his polo to expose his smooth pale chest. She placed her hand flat against him and ran it back and forth over his collar bone. He pushed his hips against her.

Her insides tensed. The dampness grew between her legs. Her breasts tingled and her tender buds hardened, begging to be pleasured.

Liatris's eyes scanned over her, his mouth open. He looked hungry. Ravished. His grip tightened on her, pressing her against his hard length.

"I... want you," said Liatris. His voice was broken.

"I want you too."

"It's... dangerous."

She cupped his face with her hand. "No, it's not."

"I could hurt you."

"You won't." She leaned in close to him and paused.

He remained motionless for a while. He held her close. His hesitance evident in his eyes. He searched her expression, his gaze caressing. Kind. Sensual. It didn't take him long to move in the last inch, pressing his lips to hers.

He was cold, but his lips soft. His kiss gentle for a man that looked as fierce as he did. The chills came again, spreading across her chest and down her arms like icy strings being pulled across her skin.

A soft gentle kiss became a desperate entanglement of lips. They pulled on each other. Rubbing together. Clutching the other as if this was their last moment together.

She felt him get larger and larger beneath her. Unnaturally so. It startled her and she pulled back.

Liatris let out a sigh and his eyes fell. "I'm sorry."

"What? Why?"

"I can't continue this."

"But why?"

"I'm... parts of me are not... human." His words were strained. He squirmed, but this time seeming uncomfortable.

"How... how so?" She stuttered, unsure if she wanted the answer.

Liatris gripped her hip and lifted her off of him. He did so with such ease it startled her.

"I won't hurt you," said Liatris. "And that is why we must stop."

She didn't move once he set her down. *He won't hurt me, but that's why he must stop? I don't understand. What could be so wrong?* The thought brought more with it. She felt his size and slowly began to understand. "If it's... because of your size I'm okay with that."

A soft grin came over his face as his gentle eyes found her again. "It's much more than that." He stepped back, one foot on the edge of the step up to his throne and turned at an angle. He grabbed at his zipper where an extreme bulge was.

Emily's eyes widened, seeing the outline of his length going down his pantleg.

Liatris pulled his pants down revealing his member like that of a stallion. Emily gasped. Once free it began to become fully erect. Protruding like a thick tree branch.

That's... huge... Her legs trembled. There was terror and lust fighting each other. Deep wet need and racing thoughts of how she could handle... that.

"Now you see why we cannot continue," said Liatris.

"No... no..." Emily took an unsure step forward.

"Emily, I appreciate this, but you do not have to do anything to please me."

"What about if it pleases me?"

He pulled back. Her question caught him off guard. "I... I don't know what to say."

Emily pressed her lips together and stepped closer. He was so large she had to move around his length. She didn't want things to end abruptly here. Her body was still burning for him. He was not only long and girthy, but his tip was flared making her more and more think of a stallion.

She hesitated before laying her hand on it. His member felt soft but also was rock hard.

His head tilted as his eyes rolled back.

She pressed herself up against his side as best as she could while working around his arms. Wanting to be close. Wanted to continue this fiery intimacy. She stroked him. Liatris moaned.

Just touch was enough to make her hotter. Moisture growing down below. Her tender buds hard. She stroked him more. Up and down. Slow to start. He didn't resist. Each little moan edging her to continue.

His hand dropped. He caressed a finger down her spine, tracing her body. Around to her hips, her butt, back up and repeating.

She bent slowly, hesitant. Unsure of what he would and wouldn't like. Unexpectedly he smelt good. Like a fresh linen smell. She licked the tip of his length.

His whole body jerked, and his member throbbed. She held her mouth there, waiting for any other reaction while continuing her slow strokes. He put another hand on her and the pair continued the exploration of her body.

She licked him again, this time getting what seemed like a shiver and a soft moan. It encouraged her to keep going. Emily focused on the tip to start. There was so much of it, she wasn't sure she could get it into her mouth.

Her tongue traced the edges. She took his length in both hands. Stroking. His touch felt cold. Arousing. Chills danced across her skin.

"Let's... Let's go somewhere more... comfortable." His voice was strained. He put a hand on her shoulder and started to guide her.

She realized he was heading to the area made up as her bed. The low light made for somewhat of a romantic atmosphere. When she made it to the center of the blankets and pillows, he turned her to face him.

Liatris leaned down and placed a soft kiss on her shoulder. He was delicate. Tender. He slipped his fingers under the straps of her dress and slowly pulled them off. He continued to sample her skin with tender kissed. Up and down her neck.

The dress fell to her ankles. She was completely naked. Earlier she purposely chose not to wear anything under it. She wanted to turn him on. The plan succeeded.

She reached down, taking him in her hands again. He touched her. Embraced her. So gentle. Careful. Slow and teasing. One hand came up, catching a breast.

She took in a quick breath.

"Did I hurt you?"

"No." The moment he froze she bent and put his tip to her lips again. Tracing circles around it. Hands moving. Tongue flicking.

He used his lower set of arms to still reach her despite being bent. Taking soft strokes from the bottom up across her breasts, catching her nipple with a light touch each time.

Emily licked her lips, finally deciding to try his girth. She started lapping the lip with her mouth open. Testing the size. Taking more and more in her mouth like she was sucking a large lollipop. Some. Most. All. The whole head of his length popped in her mouth.

He moaned loudly. His body jerked. She kept her mouth there, stroking him. Pressing her tongue against him. There wasn't any room. He was so large.

"Wait..."

She pulled back and released him.

Liatris lowered himself to the floor on his back. He pointed down his body. "Face that way and sit on my face."

"What?"

"Trust me."

She hesitated. She'd never done something like that before.

"Trust me," he repeated.

Emily turned to face his length, stepped over him, and slowly tried lowering herself.

He reached up taking her waist and hips. Hoisting her weight for a moment before lowering her down on him. She came down on his tongue, instantly pushing inside of her.

She gasped.

He could easily hold her weight and control how high or low she was.

Emily took his shaft again, leaning over to lap and suck. Grip and stroke. She felt him shiver and arch below her. Each action telling her the exact spots to focus on.

He devoured her. Licking her tender jewel as if he was speaking Latin into her and then lowering her down so he could thrust his tongue inside. The mixed stimulation was driving her crazy.

Sweat broke out across her body. Barely able to focus on his length, she gasped. Trying to keep her rhythm. He throbbed to her touch.

He timed with her gasps as well. Finding the best spots. She burned inside and out.

Suddenly he hoisted her up off his face. For a moment she was up in the air, being held like a doll. He was easily able to adjust her and lay her down on her back. He leaned down over top her. His length pressed against her.

He gave her a small peck on the lips and then waited. His face so close to hers. "I won't hurt you," he whispered. Leaning in again he put his lips to hers. Holding longer.

Emily wrapped her hands around him. Their lips tangling. There was a slight odor, but his fresh scent well overwhelmed it. His kissed were deep. Desperate. Fueled with passion.

His length presses against her folds, but instead of trying to enter her he just rubbed it against her. Hitting her tender spots over and over. He was so long that he had to arch his back. Still his length came up all the way to his chest.

He stroked her with his member. Getting faster and faster. Her insides getting tight. Liquid gushing from her. He continued to kiss her. Deeply. As if this might be the last kiss he ever had.

Her body bucked. Getting tighter. Pressure building inside of her. "I... I..."

"Cum for me darling." He broke contact and pulled back. He took a breast in each hand. Kneading her. Flicking her nipples. Still stroking his length against her. Faster and faster.

His head fell back, and he groaned. "I cannot hold on much longer."

"I'm... I'm..."

He thrust fast, driving the orgasm. She bucked under him. Thrashed.

"Infect me."

"I can't," he moaned.

"Do it. Make me like you. Make me live forever."

"There's— There's too much risk."

"I'll take the risk. I'm... I'm going to cum."

He thrust hard. She exploded. Orgasmed. Her body thrashed.

He dropped down, mouth to her shoulder. There was a sting. His length was all the way to her chin. He exploded, shooting his seed over her. She exploded again. Gushing. Hot tingles drenched her. A wave of pleasure swept her to sea. And she drowned in it.

HECTOR'S JOURNAL

March 21st, 2042

Human resilience has astounded me. I also recognize I see them as human and not myself. Many things have changed over the years. Mexico has been bombed by the US to keep the zombies out. Effective against the zombies, but with multitudes of innocent life lost. The zombies have pushed on and I'm starting to see the fall of the US begin. I plan to move into the states because any hope I have at getting supplies here have been, literally, bombed away.

Chapter 19

Lisa clutched at her chest. She had taken a deep breath and the resulting searing pain almost brought her to her knees. Mariah thought Lisa had five, maybe six broken ribs from CPR. It had been a few days she was told, but she was unconscious for most of them.

They had settled well into the Lab, making a large central homeroom and bedrooms of sorts with Hector taking over the top floors for lab equipment. As Hector was doing unstable experiments, he wanted everyone far away to keep them safe.

Lisa sat on the edge of her bed which was four desks pushed together with a foam pad on it, blankets, and pillows. It was tall enough her legs dangled over the edge and made her feel like she was a little kid again. It was amusing for a moment, before another breath sent a stabbing pain through her side.

She had the room just inside the front main doors to the left. She was told that it was because it was a frantic decision to save her life. The corner towards the windows was set up with Jim's bed. He'd grabbed a tarp and made up a hammock over there with a couple blankets thrown into it which were hanging half out.

The darker corner is where Hector set up a bed. His was the simplest, being only a foam pad over some pushed together desks. She'd only caught him sleeping in it once and she didn't think he was there for very long.

Mariah and Bruno had already added their touch of decorations. Lisa was told they made a few supply runs into the city. One desk in front of a barred window had a chipped white ceramic pot with fake flowers in it. There was also a brown teddy bear in relatively good condition along with a few other simple things.

Someone, she guessed Mariah, had also worked on getting her more clothes which were folded and stacked on a desk next to her bed. It was day, so there was light washing through the four barred windows spaced out between two walls. To combat the night there was a collection of candles on one desk positioned the furthest away from anything flammable and a crank charged emergency lamp. It still worked, making it a lucky find. It would fetch a high price about anywhere.

After composing herself, Lisa slid from her bed and slipped on the house slippers someone got her that were warm and fuzzy, but one size too big.

Toddling out into the dark main open space she scanned for the others. Heavy footsteps from the stairs directly before the doors at the opposite end of the building caught her ear.

Turning, Lisa spotted Jim heading down the stairs. He also benefited from the supply run because he was wearing a nice black button up shirt with the sleeves rolled three quarters up his arm. He also had on dark jeans that looked like they were a snug fit for him.

His gaze jolted to hers and he took a quick breath followed by rippling relaxation of every visible muscle in his body. "You're up. How are you feeling?" He descended the last few steps quickly.

"I'm... I'm standing." She smiled. It was genuine, but shadowed with pain.

"You need to take it easy. Mariah said it'll take a long time for you to heal."

Lisa noted that the bandages on his head were gone and there was a bright pink scar. She reached up, running her finger next to it. "Looks like you're healing up well."

He grinned and nodded. "She is still insisting that I not lift anything heavy." He placed his hands on her arms, smiling with what seemed to be building excitement that made his dark eyes twinkle. "I'll get Hector. He's been very worried about you."

"O—oh." She stuttered, feeling a lump form in her stomach and throat. She'd seen Hector on and off through moments of consciousness. He was standing over her, often with her hand in his. She couldn't forget what she said when she thought she was going to die. It wasn't a lie, but Hector also knew what happened between she and Jim.

Jim's brows dropped for a moment, as he gave her intense examination. "I know what you said to Hector, by the way. We talked about it."

"About... It?"

"Hector and I both have feelings for you." Jim glanced around and then lowered his head towards her to whisper in a low deep tone. "If you'll have us, we'll both love you."

Lisa took a quick breath. It made her ribs move and the resulting pain made her shriek. She grabbed at herself, pressing her eyes closed.

The breath snatched from her lungs. Fiery knives stabbing at her sides.

"Lisa?"

She heard Hector's distant voice. Her knees started to fold. It felt like she couldn't hold herself anymore. Fighting it only made the pain worse. It felt slow. A length of time where she desperately wanted to breathe but didn't dare, falling in slow motion.

One set of arms wrapped around her shoulders while another caught her waist. Both lowered her to her knees.

"You need to breathe," said Hector. He was close to her ear with his arms around her waist.

"It... It hurts."

"Easy," said Jim. "We got you."

She drew in a slow breath. It burned. She hadn't left her bed much and this was overdoing it. Cracking her eyes open she spotted Jim on her right, holding her shoulders, and Hector on her left with an arm around her waist.

She pressed her eyes shut, fighting tears. She felt so weak. So useless. *I'm just a burden. I can't even walk without needing help.* Knowing that each breath hurt she tried to hold her breath again. This was more than embarrassing. Ending up like this.

"I'll take her to bed," said Hector.

"I'll see if Mariah has anything for the pain and I'll be right there," said Jim.

They were working together like nothing ever happened. Jim's words haunted her. *We both love you? If you'll have us?* She shuttered causing another wave of pain to rake though her body.

Hector's thin but strong arms wrapped around her, and she felt him lift her with such ease she felt like she was levitating.

"I'm sorry," she whimpered, hoping no one else but him could hear her.

"Hush. You have nothing at all to be sorry for." He strode back towards her room.

Having more windows, her room was brighter than most of the others. She expected him to just put her down, but instead he lifted her into bed and sat down, laying her so her head was cradled in his arm next to his chest. Her face cuddled up against the softness of his poncho.

Tears started building, her eyes growing moist as the waves of emotion and pain boiled together. He held her so effortlessly in a protective way. With his free hand he moved a lock of hair from her face.

"I'm sorry," she whimpered again.

"Why?" He stroked her hair.

His fingers were thin and slid through each lock with ease. Everything about him was calming. The pain slowly subsided like the ocean tide, leaving wakes of fatigue behind.

She drew in a few short breaths. "Everything... I've made a mess of everything."

"No, you haven't." Hector let out a breath. He didn't need to breathe, so she learned those were, strangely, a way of expressing himself. "I thought I had lost you." He lowered his head towards her, positioned as close to having his forehead on hers as his hat and goggles would allow. "I can't lose you. You are everything to me."

Her body warmed. She thought he would reject her. Maybe hate her for what she did. It wasn't like they were in any kind of relationship where she could have cheated on him, but she felt like she did. She felt like she hurt him. The thought of him pulling away, hating her, it was unbearable.

The sound of steps in the distance closed in. "What's happening?" asked Mariah.

Lisa recognized her voice. Cracking her eyes open Lisa turned towards the sound, spotting Mariah holding her medicine tin with Jim beside her. Lisa's brows twitched. She was fighting a breakdown she knew would be painful emotionally and physically. To her relief, Hector took over.

"I think we just need to rest a moment. I think we pushed it too far too fast."

Lisa nodded.

Mariah signed. "Okay then. Call me back over the moment there is any trouble. I'm going to get back to making lunch. Is that okay with you, Lisa?"

Lisa nodded again.

With Mariah gone, it was just Lisa, Hector, and Jim.

Jim grabbed a blanket, hopped up on the bed with them, and threw it over her legs. "You need to take it easy. It'll be a while before you're back on your feet." Jim had one knee pulled up with the other leg hanging off the edge of the collection of desks. One hand he rested on the other side of her legs and his other he placed on top of hers.

Intwined, she lay at the center of them, protected on all sides. Nothing but concern and caring for her. Nothing but understanding.

"I feel so useless."

"You are not," said Hector. He took the blanket Jim brought over and pulled it up to her chin, covering Jim's hand perched atop hers.

"Hector is right. You just need some time to recover. There's no shame in that. We're just grateful that you're alive."

She didn't think she would. Choked and suffocated by her own body. It was terrifying. It wasn't like a zombie attack where she could fight back. It was her own body. There wasn't anything she could do to stop it. She'd be dead without them.

It only made her sadness grow. Scared of what happened, afraid of the pain wrapping her chest, afraid of the consequences of loving two men. She turned her head, hiding her face in Hector's poncho.

Jim gripped her hand. "You're safe. We won't leave you unless you want us to."

Hector stiffened at those words. She could only assume that, maybe, he really didn't want to leave her. And Jim didn't either.

"I'm sorry I... made things so complicated." Afraid of their response she kept her face hidden.

"Nothing is complicated," said Hector. "We have come to balanced accord."

"Accord?" Lisa parroted.

Jim, giving her hand another soft squeeze, elaborated. "Hector and I made a deal to protect you no matter what and... Well, we're here for you in any capacity you want. Friends, lovers, both, neither. You're in control. Just know we both love you. Especially this quiet lanky dude here." He lifted her hand and moved it towards Hector.

Friends? Lovers? Both of them? As the world used to be she wouldn't have ever thought of having two men as lovers. But the world has changed. She had changed. She lusted for Jim before. Loved Hector. And now, in a pile between them, found herself liking the sensation.

Still scared, she continued to think it over. How complicated and messy it could get compared to how complicated and messy she thought she made it before. If this is what resulted in Hector catching them and then an untimely omission of her love for him, then what else really could go wrong?

"Can I... can I fall asleep here..." The words came out slow, cracked, filled with her own fears at what their reaction might be.

"Rest all you need. I will stay with you," said Hector.

The flutter of her heart and waves of warmth that rushed through her body were insurmountable. Hector was a man that focused on work. He never stopped. He never rested. And he was offering to stay there, doing nothing but bringing her comfort.

"I'll be here too," said Jim. "I'm not going anywhere." He nestled down, lying next to her.

Hector also adjusted his legs, getting comfortable next to her. That's where they stayed the next few hours. She drifted off a few times until the room was dark, and she knew night had fallen. It was the most comfortable she'd been in months... years... maybe ever. Relaxed in their embraces.

After a few hours her stomach grumbled. Next to her, in the dark, she heard Jim chuckle.

"I think we missed lunch."

She chuckled, causing Jim to chuckle again.

"We better get you two some food," said Hector.

Jim shifted like he was stretching and moaned. "Yeah, guess you're right. I'll get the lights." He rolled off the bed, his boots hitting the concrete floor with a dull thump.

Lisa shifted, trying to sit up. Just the few muscles it took for a simple action made her hurt.

Hector, arm still around her after all these hours, helped her forward. "Until you heal up, let us help you."

She sighed. "I feel so helpless."

"You're not," said Hector. "You are an amazing and strong woman. I'm sorry I was never brave enough to tell you before this."

A smile pulled at her lips. "I... should have told you how I felt sooner... I... I was just afraid of—"

"You don't have to explain yourself. I'm just humbled that you could love a creature like me."

Lisa tried to turn, her chest now pained from the sadness that dripped from his words. "You're not a creature." She wanted to say more, but the sudden flood of light in the room made her flinch.

"My bad," said Jim, as he fussed with the crank lantern. "Maybe was a little much."

"It's fine," said Hector. "Thank you." He turned his attention back to Lisa. "Let's get you up."

Holding her back he helped her to the edge of the bed. Jim moved in front of her to help her down. Lisa glanced down, feeling one warm foot and one cold, only to realize she was wearing only one slipper.

"I'll get it," said Hector. He stood up on the other side of the bed, his tall frame enough to cast a large shadow across the room. After stretching he took her slipper from the end of the bed and handed it to Jim who crouched and slid it on her foot like a Cinderella fairytale.

Lisa smiled. She didn't want to like it, but this made her so warm and happy. Relaxed. Even with each breath causing pain.

The three of them left, moving into the dark main entry room, and then turning left to the living space they made. The lights from inside cast a warm yellow glow out across the cold concrete. There was a chill in air brining attention to the crisp smell of cooked herbs and spices.

Heading inside Lisa spotted Flint and Bruno at a table playing a dice game. Bruno was leaning over the table with Flint on the other side standing with a fist raised in the air. She'd seen it before as Flint won most games they played together.

Spot was on a rug in the corner, but jumped up as soon as they entered. Trotting over he brought the attention of the room over to them.

Bruno smiled, his large eyes bright and looking like he could cry. "You're up. You're okay."

"Hell yeah. Told you, she'd pull though. Good to see you up," said Flint.

They had made the room homely. Rugs on the floor, decorations on the wall, and candles everywhere for light. Mariah was over to the right at a large area they made into a cooking area. She had a small propane grill and an electric griddle hooked up to a battery.

The tables were pushed together like counters that had spices all across them interspersed with canned goods. She hadn't seen that much food in months. Mariah had a new shirt on and a new apron. She was chopping up something, but stopped as they entered and turned towards her with a smile and nodded.

Lisa smiled back, unsure if Mariah was just happy she was alive or if she knew what was going on between her, Hector, and Jim. Granted, with this small of a group, how could she hide it. It left uncomfortable squirms in her stomach that mixed with the hollow hunger that was now mounting at the delectable combination of smells.

Hector bent so he was closer to Lisa's ear. "Will you be okay here for a while?"

"I'll be fine. Why?"

"I'm going to work in the lab for a little bit, but I'll be back soon to check on you." Hector looked up at Jim who nodded back as if they just had some unspoken conversation.

Jim moved in, taking her arm and then nodded towards a table.

"Mama, shall we dine?"

Flint made a gagging sound. "Yuck. Get a room." His attention on them didn't last long, as he quickly grabbed the dice from the table. "Best eighteen out of twenty."

Bruno groaned. "Sure. Why not. Because the last hundred times you beat me wasn't enough."

"Come on. You were starting to almost get hot."

"Is that supposed to make me feel better?"

Lisa and Jim sat at the table in front of Flint and Bruno, placing themselves between them and Mariah.

"I'm working on supper, but I can make something quick if you two can't wait," said Mariah. "I know you missed lunch."

Jim looked to Lisa to answer, gesturing by widening his eyes and leaning his head towards her.

"I can wait. But thank—" Pain from her broken ribs gave her a quick stab. "You..." she finished as she groaned.

Mariah turned, her brows furrowed. "I can give you something for the pain."

Lisa shook her head. "No. Save it for when we really need it. Sounds like this will be a long process."

"Fucking will!" said Flint, chiming in with a loud boom behind them. "Mine still hurts like a bitch."

She'd forgotten that he'd been tossed like a rag doll and most likely broke a rib as well. With that and Jim having the remnants of a bullet wound to the head, half of the party was in recovery mode.

Jim rolled his eyes and lifted a finger. "One. One rib, Flint. You have several broken."

"He's right," said Mariah. "It'll take a whole month or two for those to heal."

Lisa groaned. "I have to get better sooner than that."

"Why?" asked Jim.

Lisa looked down at the table. "We've got supplies to get. I don't know how long we'll stay here, but if we have to move then there will be things to pack."

Jim raised his hand. "Nothing you have to worry about. Myself, Flint, Bruno, and Hector have done just fine with supply runs. More people would honestly make it more difficult. It's hard enough keeping Flint out of trouble."

"I heard that!"

"You were meant to," said Jim.

Lisa smiled, this time full cheek to cheek. Jim was settling in well with all of them, like he was part of the crew now. But, she remembered, he has his own goals. The smile faded. "What about you? You were trying to find Emily."

Jim's expression wavered a little, but he still held an overall happy look. Like her words hit him for the briefest of moments and then bounced off. "If we haven't found her by now I don't think there's anything to be done."

"I'm sorry."

Jim reached across the table and took her hand. "Don't be. She was a friend, but she made her decision. And that didn't include me. I should have respected that, but I'm glad I didn't because I wouldn't be here now."

This caring Jim seemed different from the man she met before. The angry hardened man, solely focused on one goal. "What about your home in Haven?"

"Pssst. It's a dump. What we've made here in the past few days far surpasses what I was able to do in years back in Haven."

"What do you mean?"

"With Hector's help, supplies are not hard to get. In Haven, the littlest things are outrageously priced." He pointed at the counter. "See that food?"

"Yes."

"That would take months of what I could skimp together. Even with trades, and working for people, and trading the few things I got from the government packages, it would still take me literal months to afford that."

Mariah turned quickly, her expression horrified, and the large butcher knife in her hand added to that look. "What do you all eat there then?"

Jim shrugged. "No one really eats much. Most common item is rats."

"You're joking!" Mariah shouted.

Flint gagged again. "That has to be a lie. Haven is supposed to be like the best place on earth now."

Jim shook his head. "It's far from that. Unless you're part of Capitol or the farmers in the Median, then you're in the slums of the Outer Rim. Most people live there. Food has been scarce for years."

Outer Rim? Median? "I don't understand. I thought it was like a big city."

"Nope. People with no use get put in the Outer Rim, never to be heard from again. People with connections and skills get the Median. Might have a decent life there. The uppity assholes, government, last few rich people all get the Inner Circle. The Capitol city I mean. It's a real city, still standing and functioning, but the government makes sure only the people they like get in. I was a black smith. I helped build the damn place. Only got me to the Outer Rim."

Bruno turned in his seat, having a similar horrified expression on his face. "That's... horrible. How can they do that to people?"

"It's a bad system. Always was." Jim made an exaggerated stretch, groaning loudly before pounding his fists on the table and locking Lisa's gaze with a wide smile. "Doesn't matter now. I found a good place to be." He nodded his head towards the table behind them. "And these assholes seem to like me. So, I got that going."

"Seem," repeated Flint. "Might just hate your guts too."

"As long as you don't eat them, then I'm fine with that."

Nervous laughter started, but it was contagious and one by one they all chimed in with a genuine laugh. The tension in the air broke and Lisa could feel the calm wash back over the room. Flint, easily distracted, got back to the game. She had her back to him, but could hear him rolling dice and still managing to make that an overly loud sound.

Mariah, with a smile, turned back to her cooking. The only one still a little blue was Bruno, but as long as he kept losing game after game, that wouldn't change much.

Jim started chatting, casually like they were on a first date, asking her about her past, moving on to likes and dislikes, then setting into rhythm with general happy conversation. The boys played games while Mariah finished cooking.

Not to long after she had a meal prepped with canned beans and season canned chicken with individual packaged cakes for dessert. Desert! For the first time in months. Her mouth watered from the sweet chocolaty pastry. Before they were done Hector came back down, just like he promised.

Sliding in next to her he too took a pastry and chatted a little. It didn't take long for her small store of energy to expire, and she sat there feeling like a wilting plant

Hector reached over and placed his hand on her back. "You're getting tired. How about we get you back to bed?"

"But I just got up," she protested. Feeling this weak, no matter how much help she had, was still frustrating.

"He's right," said Mariah, as she started gathering dirty dishes and cake wrappers.

"I suppose."

Jim smiled and then looked to Hector, giving him a nod again.

That has to be something to do with their accord. Something about me. I don't know if I should ask... She yawned, which cut off her thought.

"Yup," said Jim. "Time for bed."

Hector stood and offered her a hand to help her up. The pair escorted her back to her room. The crank lamp was running out of charge and was now a dim white light in the corner.

Jim paused, looking around the room. "Might be a little overstepping, but what do you think of making a huge bed in the center of the room?"

"For... all of us?" asked Lisa.

Jim shrugged. "If you like. It's up to you."

The nap she had earlier in their arms was wonderful, she couldn't deny that. And she'd already been stripped naked by Jim before, minus the socks. It was silly to try to be modest now after that. The memory of that ecstasy, now stripped of the guilt that was clouding it, made her whole body warm. *If you'll have us. Have both of them?*

She was tired, but a new wave of erotic energy was growing. She felt herself dampen at the thought. Heat flushed into her cheeks. Her core tensed along with the muscles in her chest which sent a wave of pain through her.

Hector turned, wrapping his arms around her and lowering his head towards her shoulder. He whispered softly in her ear. "Don't be embarrassed, but I can smell you. I can guess what you want, but now isn't the time. You need to heal first."

Her face was now fire. Don't be embarrassed was the key phrase to make the embarrassment worse. *He could smell me? He knows...* Her heard spun with the thought he could smell her arousal. Another burst of quaking pain pushed the thought aside. Lisa grabbed his arms for support. He didn't budge, holding her there.

"We should think of moving furniture another night," said Jim.

"No," Lisa squeaked, face against Hector's chest. "I like the idea."

There was silence. Not even looking she could almost bet the two were doing their head nod thing again.

"You take care of her, and I can move things," said Jim.

"No. I can move things easier, if you can help her."

Jim slipped in as Hector slid away. They were cautious to stay away from her ribs. Jim outstretched a hand for her to take and with his other he took her shoulder to help steady her.

Hector moved with a flourish around the room. Like the Tetris game Flint and Bruno played, he moved the desks, making a bed six desks wide and a desk and a half long. The size was bigger than a California king. He then gathered all the blankets and pillows around making a large sleeping area. "Will this suffice for now?"

Lisa looked around Jim who was standing between her and the bed. She guessed the surfaces would be hard since they didn't have mattresses, but overall it looked comfortable. "It looks fine."

"On our next run I'll get more pads and blankets for it," said Hector, looking over his work.

"But that's another day," Jim added. "Let's get you in bed. Want some pajamas or something?"

"I don't have any."

"You do now," said Jim, smiling. "I found some I thought you'd like while we were out. Hector found the slippers and some blankets he thought you'd like."

"I... guess. I mean, I haven't had anything like that in so long."

"Well, let's indulge then." Jim pulled her over to the desk where they had all her new clothes folded up. "I can help you change."

Hector started to turn towards the door when Jim held out the pajama pants. "Can you hold this?"

"Oh, yes." Hector seemed apprehensive.

Lisa felt the same. Hector most likely had seen her naked before because he was the one who tended her wounds when he found her. It had been so long though that she never thought about it until now. But if she really wanted a night with the three of them, she'd have to accept it.

Hector took the piece of clothing from Jim.

"Perfect." Jim turned back to her. "I know it's going to hurt, but I'll help you get your shirt off."

She couldn't argue with that as moving her arms was enough to snatch her breath away. She lifted her arms, flinching with every little movement. Her inside squirmed as Jim took the bottom of her shirt and started pulling upwards.

She caught Hector looking at the ground just before the material was pulled over her head. The chill in the air nipped at her breasts. Jim was pleasant, but made no comment, simply sticking to task. With her arms still up, holding her breath to reduce the pain, he pulled the silky blue pajama top over her head. Lowering her arms, she felt every muscle in her chest coil.

"Don't forget to breath," said Jim. He reached his hand to Hector, who gave him back the pajama pants. "You relax, I got this." Jim crouched in front of her, taking the waist band of her pants between two fingers.

She wasn't wearing anything under them. Her face heated and saying breathe was useless help. She couldn't. Her nerves were on end. She knew the help would make this less painful, but to just get naked in front of them now was such a quick step.

Before he pulled them down, he gave her shirt a tug, giving her a little more coverage over her intimate parts. It did help. She tried not to look directly at Hector, but she still tried to watch his reaction out of the corner of her eye. His eyes were adverted, seeming just as nervous as she was.

Jim pulled open the top of the pants and held it by her feet. She slipped her legs in, quickly getting them pulled up and encompassed in the coverage and comfort they provided. They fit well and were a silky light blue material.

Hector seemed more relaxed once she was dressed.

Jim took her hand and guided her over to the bed. "You want big spoon or little spoon?"

"What?"

Jim laughed. "Never mind. You hop in the center, and we'll crawl in next to you."

She was stiff, partially a protective mechanism for the pain and partially because this was really happening. Her. Them. Together. The love lust combo that has given her headaches and panic for days until now.

Getting her first knee up she felt the hardness of the desks under the thin blanket. Moving towards the center she felt the cushion of her foam pad. Jim stripped his shirt and pants off in a flash leaving nothing but a brown pair of boxers. He crawled in after her, tucking her in first before throwing a blanket over himself.

The comforter he covered her with had an old plastic and dust smell. Nothing she wasn't used to. Nothing was really new anymore. Even unopened things from the store had aged poorly in their packaging.

Hector moved around to the other side. He took his hat and goggles off, setting them on a nearby table. Even with the desks they pushed together there were still several tables and desks along the outer wall, their shapes just visible in the dying light. Hector, with the elegance of a cat, slipped into bed on the other side of her. He laid next to her, putting an arm over her hips, and whispered in her ear. "I'll need to work tonight, but I'll stay until you're asleep."

Focused on work Hector was the side of him she knew best, and knowing he was putting that on hold for her was comforting.

Jim rolled so he was facing her and took her hand in his. "And I'll be here all night if you need anything." He paused and then continued. "And I can get Hector for you anytime. You just have to ask."

The crank lamp finally ran out of charge and the room when black. The outside world was silent, but she could just hear Flint and Bruno in the other room. She felt warm, cozy in the space with blankets and pillows around her. Breathing hurt still, but much less than before.

The two men were quiet, letting her slip asleep fast.

HECTOR'S JOURNAL

December 3rd, 2042

Dallas, Texas has been a good place to hold up. My heart is heavy as the US has fallen as well. The zombies have made their way through the borders. I fear I am watching the end days of humanity.

I continue my research for a cure. I fear it may be the only option we have. I am trying to isolate DNA sequences but so far have failed. During the explosion that created the First Turned numerous animal DNA variations were released. I don't know if I can isolate them all.

Chapter 20

It took only moment for the virus to infect Emily. She writhed in Liatris's arms, screaming between tears. A sharp pain ripped through his heart as he regretted giving in to her desire. "I'm sorry," he whispered, pulling her tightly to him. His extra set of arms helped to hold her as she thrashed.

This mutation was hitting her hard. He didn't want to leave her, but he also needed the vaccine immediately to head off mutations. He wasn't prepared for this. He cursed himself for giving in. If she wanted turned, he could have done this safely. Emily felt cold in his arms yet covered with sweat. Her eyes were darkening as the virus spread through her body.

Tears exploded from his eyes in a single instance. He gritted his teeth. *Why did I do this? Emily, my beautiful queen. Why did I do this do you?*

She wanted this, he knew that. She was hungry for that chance at immortality. He wanted that too. To never lose her. To never see her grow old. To have someone at his side until the end of days. But seeing her in this pain was heart wrenching.

Liatris scooped her up in his arms. She pushed against him, thrashing uncontrollably. Bones were cracking in her body, breaking and rebuilding rapidly. He'd see it happen to the multitudes of his followers he turned and knew that the end result was one he was told was worth the pain.

He could heft weights far beyond hers, making her thin body feel like nothing. With four arms he was able to cradle her, overcome her thrashing, and made a mad dash for his lab. Down the stairs he ran as fast as he could, jumping down several at once.

As he twisted and turned through the layout of what once was an office building, he gained concerned attention from his underlings.

"Sir?"

"My Lord, what's wrong?"

He was moving too fast and didn't bother to respond, but his intentions must have been made clear because they started moving things from his path and opening doors for him. He needed to get to the basement and now cursed how far away he put his lab.

Even at the fastest pace he could take through this place, it still took a good ten or more agonizing minutes as she screamed and thrashed. With each sound it gouged another piece from his broken heat. He loathed himself more and more.

Down in the basement there was a loud hum from the generator. The first room which led to the generator room, smelt of burnt oil. He rushed inwards, bursting through doors with his shoulder. There was a large room with desks, lamps, and paperwork all around it.

Past that he rushed into the lab. A dim glow of light strips that surrounded the outside of the room shone through vials and beakers of various size and color. The mix made a kaleidoscope of rainbow colors on the floor and ceiling with blue being the most dominating. His completed serum was a sapphire blue and new batches lined one table.

His three most trusted scientists all spun towards him. Miku, a scientist he found in China and turned, lost her hold on an empty beaker. It crashed to the concrete floor, shattering into pieces that picked up the sparkle of the lights as the shrapnel stilled. She was a minimally mutated Second Turned, only inheriting his pointed ears.

"Lord Liatris!" Another man, Evan, trapped in youth for eternity, a Second Turned, with Liatris's tell tell four arms, stepped forward like he wanted to help, but froze, unsure what to do. His eyes were large and darting up and down from Emily to him.

"Move!" The last of the three, and old man with long white hair pulled back and a long gotee, pushed the others out of the way. He was Elric, a First Turned like Liatris. Elric had black furred wolf ears, golden wolf eyes, and furry brown prehensile tail behind him.

Elric was Liatris's most trusted friend. Even though their paths have separated and intertwined over the years, he eventually came back to help Liatris with his research.

"You turned her?" Elric's tone was sharp and cut deeply.

Liatris turned away from his gaze away. "She wanted me too. I... Please help me." Tears were running down his cheeks. It was like watching his wife die, which he never did, so instead he dreamt over and over the different ways they might have killed her. This was touching to close to bleeding wounds.

Elric knocked papers from a table, scattering them across the floor. "Lay her hear. Evan, help hold her down."

"Yes sir." Evan moved forward, grabbing her arms and legs with his four arms and was easily able to restrain her.

"I'll get the serum," said Miku. She ran to a large glass door refrigerator and pulled out one of the vials.

Emily shrieked. Her arms and legs were growing longer. As they did, the bones cracked. She was completely naked and it was easy to see the mutations ripple through her body.

"She's mutating fast!" Elric screamed. "Hurry up!"

"Yes Sir," said Miku. She ran to Emily's side with the vile and syringe in her hand.

Evan held tight, but Emily's thrashing grew more violent, almost knocking him off a few times. Her strength was exponentially increasing.

"Give me that!" Liatris snatched the vile and syringe from her hands. An extra set of arms was beneficial as he was able to draw the serum, hold down Emily's arm, and administer it.

Her screaming did not subside as now the new substance was fighting the viral mutations. She kicked with a leg, breaking Evan's grasp. Miku dove in to help restrain her.

As the pair of younger looking Second Turned tended to Emily, Elric and Liatris backed off into the shadows of the room. Liatris had to turn away. He smeared the tears away with the back of his shaking hand. His stomach was rolling and, for the first time in years, he felt as if he could throw up.

"I didn't think you would turn her," said Elric. He had his arms crossed. The white haired wolfen man huffed. He was an old scientist back in Chernobyl with long unresolved issues. He used to enter into weightlifting competitions until his health started to fail and he began to grow frail. The zombie mutation was a blessing for him. He was not a person who wanted to ever save humanity, but did join Liatris under similar beliefs.

"She begged me. I made certain multiple times that she truly wanted this."

"Then why didn't you bring her to the lab to turn her? It would have been a controlled setting. There would be a much higher chance of her having few if any mutations."

Liatris clenched all his four fists. Still shaking he remained quiet with his heard turned.

Elric grunted. "I see. It was a heat of passion decision. Thinking with the wrong head isn't like you."

"I thought I had things under control," Liatris snapped.

"You're going to have a lot to sort out if you don't get your head on straight."

"What do you mean by that?" Liatris was feeling the build of frustration. Elric, being another First Turned, meant neither of them had power over the other. It was something Liatris did not deal with often.

"You're replacing you dead wife with this woman, still trying to avenge her though. Your wife that is. You got us producing mass amounts of this serum, but with no solid plan to dispense it to the other zombies." He raised a bushy white brow, his wolf ears twitching. "You're an unorganized mess."

"What would you have me do then?"

"Razvaluha! You need to sort your priorities out, but more importantly your duty to your people."

Emily's cries settled. Liatris fought the urge to run to her side. He hated to admit it, but Elric was right. He was distracted from his goals. Touching on them here and there was not enough. He tried to envision how Emily fit in the picture. The justice his wife deserves. Hector and the complication with the lab.

It came together more thoroughly that he expected. He would no longer have to fear Emily's demise to his own kind. Not matter what the final end result was, she would now be a Second Turned. She had power and her position had merit. He could more easily focus on his end goals.

Liatris headed to Emily's side, bumping into Elric's shoulder, but not saying a word. Emily was still on the table. Her skin was a shade paler than before. Her ears curved up to a dainty point, legs longer with longer fingers.

He took her hand. Even though he thought he had it together another quake of uncomfortable unease rippled through his body. He physically shook for a moment. This woman started as just eye candy, a distant substitute to his wife he could look at to motivate him in his cause. She quickly became far more.

He expected the fear, that was typical, but he wasn't prepared for how fast that fear faded. The fierce look in her eyes, calculating, as she questioned, and she probed. It took him by surprise, each time, watching her approach him with more and more confidence and, in a short flash of time, she was walking beside him like his queen. Every bit as confident as a First Turned.

He loved his wife, but she was the sweet housewife type. They were childhood lovers. In life and undeath he'd never faced a woman who carried so much force behind her as Emily did. She didn't even seem to know it. Never thinking he would be attracted to that, he found himself quickly smitten.

"Emily, can you hear me?"

She stirred.

"My Lord, she seems stable," said Miku.

"Shut up!" Liatris snapped. It was far too harsh, but it was said.

Miku slinked off into the darkness with her head lowered.

Liatris slide one arm under Emily's shoulder and pulled her torso up against his chest, head cradled in the crook of his elbow.

She let out a soft moan while stirring slightly, like a child awakening from a long nap.

"Wake up. It's time to wake up," he whispered.

Her eyes slowly fluttered open, changed from a deep dark brown to a bright blue. They sparkled in the array of colored light around the room. A spotted pattern of red, orange, and blue light lit her skin.

Liatris felt his shoulders fall and heard a breath leave his lungs. He didn't breathe and the reaction took him by surprise. "Can you hear me? How are you feeling?"

"I—" Just one syllable and she choked on her words.

She had been screaming for some time and it wasn't a surprise. He stoked the side of her face. "Take it easy. It's all over now."

Her mouth opened and shut twice before she laid a hand on her bare chest. Her eyes widened, seeming to realize what had happened. There was a flash of fear as she sucked in air, but in an awkward, uncontrolled way. She recoiled from his grasp, grabbing the edge of the desk steady herself.

Liatris pulled his hands back, giving her space. There was a war going on in her body and mind which was evident in the features of her face, changing from horror and surprise.

Emily started to look at her body, examining her hands, then her arms, and following across the rest of her. It was like she was discovering herself for the first time. She was completely in the nude which seemed to terrify her at first. She covered her breasts and pulled her legs together. This took only a fraction to process before her gaze darted back to the subtle mutations. She ran a finger over her pointed ear.

Then the feral queen set in. Emily fixed stares with Liatris, and her force was that of a raging storm. She grabbed the table for a moment and then stood up before him. She was too tall, almost hitting the ceiling, but without missing a beat her body seemed to roll like that of a cat. She stood before him knelt down, but not like a servant. More like a predator. She reached out and gripped his shoulder.

"How are you feeling?" He kept his voice low, but this primal look was pulling him from the depths of regret and fear.

"Different."

Her voice was a touch deeper and much smoother. Chills ran down his spine. "Is there any pain?"

She glanced down a moment before bringing her eyes back to his. "No."

Elric strode over, arms still crossed. "How about your hunger?" he growled.

Emily did not back off. Despite being naked, she held a feral fierceness and confidence he had not seen in any other creature.

"Oh, I'm hungry." She grinned, looking Liatris up and down.

"What do you mean?" asked Liatris. His mouth felt rough and dry.

She stepped forward and reached right for his package.

He jolted.

Emily bent to his ear. "I want you to fuck me."

"W— what?" Liatris shouted, his whole body stiffening, even his package.

Her eyes drifted over to Elric and then Miku and Evan. "I want them all."

Liatris strutted. Shocked. Maybe panicked mumbled. He didn't know what to think. His length was getting harder, and he couldn't control it.

Elric stepped forward. "It's just part of turning the first time. Maybe you should go—"

She cut him off by grabbing his hand and pulling it to her mouth. She ran it across her bottom lip as she stroked Liatris through his pants. His fly was still unzipped, and she quickly found the space to thrust her hand and grab his length.

He burned for her and was getting harder and harder, until the confines of his pants hurt.

Elric stilled as she sucked a finger. His wolf ears pulled back. "This is... unexpected."

Evan, over by the table, shifted and pulled at his pants.

Liatris swallowed hard before grabbing her shoulders. "Emily, you need to stop."

"No. Everyone should get naked now."

Liatris felt a hard pounding in his chest and an instant deep desire to strip all his clothes off.

Miku and Evan grabbed their shirts and began to undress.

"What are you two doing?" asked Liatris.

"Sorry, sir," Evan mumbled. "I just... I have to... I don't know why."

Elric came forward. She still held his hand close to her lips. "You're controlling them."

"Am I?" Emily made it sound like a question, but a grin pulled at her lips as she raised a brow. She gave Liatris's length a firm grip and stroked up.

He groaned, for a moment his head tilted back. He struggled to stay focused.

Emily grabbed Liatris and pushed him over to the table. "On your back," she commanded.

The four of them were all naked. Hard shafts all around except for Miku. She had her legs together and one hand kneading her breast. She was quivering.

Liatris felt this push. Felt this commend. He couldn't fight it. Maybe he didn't want to. He bit his lip as he slid on the table and laid down. He had nearly two feet of hard length pointed upwards. He dribbled from his flared tip. His package was also that of a horse. Large. Throbbing. The pressure was unbearable.

Emily grabbed Elric's shoulder and pulled him to the end of the table. "Wait here." She glanced over at the other two. She seemed less interested in them. "You two just go ahead and fuck if you want."

Evan spun to Miku. His length had similar shape to Liatris's but a few inches shorter.

Miku looked shocked. Her eyes wide. "I... I can't take that." Even as she spoke she touched herself. The light was low here but the moisture running down her legs still glistened.

"I think you can," said Evan. He held his length. The tip dripped. He shoved some files off the corner of a desk. "Just bend over here."

"I... I don't think we should." Miku quivered. She was a small, petite thing.

"Don't make them do this," said Liatris.

"Let them do it," said Elric. "They've been boning for each other for years." He grinned. "She especially has been as horny as a cat in heat. It'll finally get it out of their system."

Evan grabbed Miku and turned her to the desk. She bent over. Exposed. A fine woman, small and curvy. Between her legs looked soft, wet, and pink. Almost no hair.

They were positioned to the side from where Liatris lay. Evan moved in behind her, two hands on her hips and one on his length. He rubbed the tip on her, getting it moist. Guiding it with another hand he pressed it to her.

Miku gasped. "It's too big. It won't fit."

"It will," said Evan. He pushed inwards.

Miku shrieked as he entered her. There was an audible sloppy pop sound as his flared tip entered.

Liatris felt panicked, hard, painfully lusting for relief. Elric began to stroke himself. Emily grabbed and kneaded one of her breasts.

"It's too big," said Miku.

"The biggest part is already in," said Evan. His head fell back. "You are so tight. Miku you are amazing." He pushed in further.

Miku arched her back. "No. Slower. You're ruining me." Her voice went from high pitched to sultry.

"I know," said Evan. "I guess that makes this my pussy now." He pushed in more. She took another inch, and her shrieks became screams. Evan reached around to her tender jewel and began to rub it.

Miku shook. Her whole body jerking beyond control. "Not there. I might... If you touch me there, I'm going to cum."

Evan pulled his hand away. "I'm not in yet. Can't have that." He pushed another inch inside of her.

Miku threw her head back. "You're in! You're in! You can't go deeper."

It looked like she had already sucked in a good eight or nine inches. Her fists were balled up. Her body shaking. Moisture running down her thighs.

"I can feel your cervix," Eric moaned. He finally pulled back. There was a brief moment where she almost relaxed before he thrust in again.

He began to thrust in and out of her. The combination of a large member in a small space made a wet sucking sound.

She screamed and moaned with each thrust. Her body jerked. He reached around again and started rubbing her tender jewel.

"No," Miku mutter. "I'm going to... I'll cum," she said between gasps of breath. She didn't even need to breath, but still needed air to make sound. And she was making a lot. "If you keeping going, I'm going to cum!" she screamed again.

Evan groaned. "Good. You feel so good. Cum. Cum on me."

"You'll tear me apart!"

"You're already ruined." He thrust harder. Deeper. Pushing in another inch.

Miku clawed at the table. "I'm going to cum! I'm going to cum!"

Evan thrust himself in deep. Miku screeched. Her body shook and convulsed. Evan's head fell back. He jerked, holding himself inside. Suddenly thick white liquid exploded out of her around his shaft. So much. A pint's worth. Maybe more.

"My turn," Emily muttered. She stood up on the table, legs on either side of Liatris. "Let's do this right this time."

"I don't want to hurt you," said Liatris.

"You won't you know."

She lowered herself over his shaft.

It had been years since he had been intimate like this with anyone. He thought just being able to rub and hold her was all he would be able to do. He was too large. Too long. He'd hurt whoever he was with, so he withheld all this time.

Her wet center touched his tip. He chewed his lip, not wanting her to stop. He never fathomed this would happen. Never thought this would be the result of turning her. *Does she really want this? Is she going to regret this?* But he was compelled by her words. He didn't feel like he could move even if he wanted to.

She pressed against him. He was so large compared to her. His tip larger. She was wet and warm. The heat of her body hadn't left yet from turning. There was so much resistance.

She seemed to control her motions with ease. Strong legs holding herself there poised over him. Emily reached down and grasped his length, holding it to her.

She lowered herself more and he felt himself start to slide in. The tightness immense. Crushing him in the best way possible. He slipped inside. She moaned. He made it. Made it inside. It was so impossibly tight. He'd destroy her.

Slowly she lowered onto him. Taking an inch. Two. Three. Every few moments she came up and lowered again. Each time taking more of him.

He felt her insides grip him. So moist. So tight. Every nerve ending in his body was on fire. Tingling. He wanted to thrust inside of her so badly, but held control. Fearing he would hurt her. He had to let her have all control.

Up again. Lowering again. Another inch. And then another. He felt her core. Felt the end of what he thought she could take of him. She moaned and cooed. Her gaze lustful, yet kind. Gentle. Locked with him.

She came up again and back down. Another inch. He bucked, unable to control himself.

She groaned. He didn't hurt her. Then she took another inch. His length was bulging out from her belly, very obviously. It was so much that her insides were stretching.

Another inch. Somehow. He felt her core. There was no way she could get him deeper, but she did. He could see his length deeper and deeper inside her body.

Mutation... It must have... changed her... He couldn't think straight anymore. Couldn't speak. With all four hands he grabbed the table. Bracing himself. "Command me not to thrust!" he blurted out. "Command me not to hurt you!"

She grinned. "Thrust. Thrust inside of me."

Something inside of him broke. Almost like he could cry. He wanted to fill her. Make love to her. And here she was giving him permission. No. Commanding him. He couldn't fight it anymore. He started thrusting in and out of her.

She bounced on top of him. Moaning with pleasure. Not pain. Taking him inside her. Letting him move impossibly deep. He thought he could never be with a woman like this again and the happiness made him want to cry. Made him want to thank her over and over.

He watched himself move up and down inside her belly. Above the belly button. Up higher. Up her whole stomach to her ribs. She gripped him. Tightened over and over. Pulsating with him.

He thrust, timing with her bounces. It felt like he was as deep as possible. Deeper than any human could take. He made her this. Turning her made her into a match for him.

"Don't cum until I tell you," she cooed.

He moaned, feeling the command. "So much pressure."

"You cum when I come. That's an order."

"I... I don't know if I can. You... feel so good. So... tight." His words were broken. Cut short by gasps and groans of pleasure.

"Wait," she commanded again.

He continued to thrust, feeling himself pulsate. The growing pressure inside him, wanting to spill over inside of her. Explode. He was like a lit keg. The fuse burning, faster and faster. He wanted to let loose, but couldn't. Bound by her command.

"Please," he begged. "Please let me finish."

"Almost."

He groaned. The pressure was too much. He was going to explode. Going to die. Every muscle was taut. His back arching to try and push deeper. To pound her. Harder. Harder.

"Please," he begged again.

She tightened on him harder. Her insides pulsated. "Now! Cum now!"

He screamed. Hands digging into the table. He thrust inside of her. All the way to her ribs. Every inch buried. Blowing like dynamite. He dumped himself inside of her. Gushing. So much. He burned. Tingles and shocks of pleasure popping over every nerve.

The bulge he created inside of her grew. Inflated. Until she looked almost pregnant. The fluid still coming until it exploded out where they were connected. His seed coming out of her with such force. Splattering.

Emily screamed with pleasure. "Yes! Yes! Yes!"

He kept coming, unable to control it. Twitching. Thrashing. Gasping. Clutched in the rapture of shock and pleasure. She was a queen. His queen. And amazing woman. So perfect. So hot. So amazing.

He wanted to scream all of this to her, but all that came out was incomprehensible babble. Gasps and groans.

She swayed on top of him. Her eyes rolled back in her head. He jolted, reaching up and catching her. Balancing her on his shaft. Her head rolled around. Her soft moans making him continue to throb.

"Emily?" he breathed. "Emily, are you okay?"

"That..." She licked her lips. "That was amazing."

"You are—" He gulped as she tightened on him again. "Amazing."

Another voice in the room broke his concentration.

"Well, that happened."

Liatris glanced over, seeing Elric holding a sticky hand over his limp member.

"If you don't mind my Lord, I'm going to clean up."

"Uh... yes. Yes, that's fine."

Emily giggled.

"You're trouble," Liatris mumbled.

Elric shouted across the room. "Either fuck again you too or get cleaned up and get back to work."

"You want to go again?" asked Evan.

"Yes," Miku breathed.

Liatris closed his eyes a moment. It would have been nicer if this first moment had been just between the two of them, but, nevertheless, he was glad to have this moment.

"We should get cleaned up," said Liatris.

"I don't want to move," said Emily.

"Me either, but we can't stay here all night."

There were moans across the room as Evan and Miku went at it again.

"I want some time to ourselves," Liatris whispered.

"That would be nice," said Emily. Her eyes looked tired. Her smile weak. She swayed on him as if she was high on some drug.

Liatris helped her off of him, shocked by how deep he was inside of her. After getting to the floor, he scooped up her body and they headed to the bathroom, Liatris commanding a bath be drawn as they went.

HECTOR'S JOURNAL

April 1st, 2043

This is no joke. Humanity is at its end. Spot and I left Texas and started moving north. I am in need of not only supplies, but also uninfected human DNA samples. I don't know how I'm going to accomplish this. My only thought is looking for those that died uninfected.

Chapter 21

Secrecy was a must as Walter moved along the dark paths and hidden passages to reach Haven's capitol. As unrest had increased so did the length and size of a massive underground tunnel system that wove in and out of existing underground structures to reach the capitol. It was a project that started around seven years ago. Because of its massive size there were even small vehicles hidden at entrances. Mostly small motorcycles and mopeds to make travel faster.

The tunnels were heavily protected and, as everyone was more worried about zombies on the outside, no one had discovered it yet. It was the best way to reach contacts at Haven without being detected.

Walter made the long trek from the city here. He left his group of scrappers far beyond the walls where Sam and the rest of them were safe. They were paid well to not ask questions.

He stood in a hidden hall in the old brick building, tucked behind a large painting, waiting in the old building nestled in the middle of Haven. Victoria's words haunted him. Her direct orders were to get Hector and his party to vacate.

The command gripped his chest and fighting it made him ill. It was not under specified time, but just a general command. That was where he could slide by. He was always one to be less affected by the First Turned orders, but it was still there. Especially Victoria, who turned him.

This was complex and elaborate and far deeper than she had any clue about. She was focused on her people and keeping all those turned from being mindless hungry mutated monsters. He ran a long fingernail across his chin and then smoothed his hair to try and gain more composure.

This passage was dark and cold, scented of dust and mildew. It disgusted him. He kept himself in the center, making sure not to touch his clothes to the dirty walls. This waiting did give him time to think more things through. He would still need to follow her command, but the unrest in Haven was a much higher priority to him.

There was a coup d'état at foot. This place was on the verge of collapse from the inside out. Military forces were growing, unsteadily, to the point where lines were getting crossed, and command was a fragile position. One tip and this place would crumble.

Although he didn't care for the politics of humans anymore, there was something here he needed. A place clean from the destruction. One not soiled by the lowest of undead. His scrappers were loyal. He had a small following of skilled men and women. He had the means. It was just a matter of timing for him to take what he wanted.

There was the click of a latch and the soft squeak of a door from the room adjacent to his hiding place. Walter had keen hearing and an over developed sense of smell. Everything was foul. As foot falls echoed through the space, he could smell the spicy musk of an outdated cologne. He recognized it and crinkled his nose.

"Walter? Walter, are you here?" said a hushed male voice with a moderate Hispanic accent.

Walter stretched and then took his cue like an actor striding onto stage. He flicked the lock holding the painting in place, swung it out, and stepped through the threshold.

Ernando Migel, a governor of Haven, looked rattled. The man's tanned skin looked paler than normal. His pitch-black hair was slicked down, wet with grease and sweat. He wore a tan vest with a muted yellow long sleeve polo. It had pit sweat stains.

The smell all made sense to Walter, who took a step back. The cologne was to cover the sweat and that accounted for the under tones of musk.

"I'm glad you could come," said Ernando as he fiddled with the two large gold rings on his left hand.

"You said it has begun?"

"My men have been trying to infiltrate Admiral Hammer's forces, but they are getting disposed of." He leaned forward, whispering. "Along with many of the civilians and guards he drafted. The board has no idea. They're in favor of this push."

"The board is nothing but a group of high class and low intelligent old bats." This room was large, but sparsely decorated with lighter spots on the burgundy carpet where furniture used to be. He was able to spot a bar built into a large bookcase that still held a few books. Striding over he perused the area for a drink.

"There's no one to stop him," said Ernando, waving his hands around. "He's not going to stop until he wipes out or drafts everyone but the upper class."

Walter found a liquor bottle with a glass stopper. He dared take a whiff, finding it poorly aged and foul. He grimaced and set it down on a shelf next to a tattered copy of a dictionary. "He already has the board and any other members of status under his control."

"I am not," Ernando sputtered.

"Aren't you?" Walter raised a brow. "You bring me here. An outsider and undead, to help this problem because he has stripped you of all ability to do anything against him."

"The men loyal to me are dwindling daily. Most are disappearing. I know Hammer is behind this, but I don't have proof."

Walter's eyes narrowed. He had played four sides since arriving. Being Victoria's Second Turned and servant to her, a spy for Liatris, the head of his scrapper crew, and an undead force for Ernando to utilize to prevent the overthrow of power. He had the pawns. The chess pieces were in position. Now he needed to put them in motion.

"I'm working on proof that will reveal Admiral Hammer as being a traitor and war criminal."

"What?" Ernando spun to face Water.

The curtains were pulled in this room, but small beams of light still penetrated the edges. The glow giving more depth to the worried lines on Ernando's face. Dust particles swirled around him. It tickled Walter's nose and added a new level of irritation. *I can't wait to live in a place that is actually clean.* "I'm working on exposing him as we speak, but I need to know I can trust your forces to make the push necessary to overthrow him when this happens."

"Well... my forces, I'll do what I can." He stumbled over his words like a bumbling idiot.

"Exposing him will do no good, if nothing can be done about it," Walter growled.

"I... I will see what I can do."

Walter rolled his eyes. This conversation was useless and dragging on far longer than he desired. Mark was working on finding candidates Walter could use to expose Admiral Hammer. That was his main task while here. Ernando was part of the puzzle, but a pawn next to his knights and bishops.

"You are part of the council, the founding men and women of Haven. You've been in the bastardized politics from the beginning." Walter stepped towards Ernando as his voice progressively grew deeper. "You've had ten years since those monsters reached your shores. Longer than that since word of the infection spread across the world. I don't want excuses. You are either strong enough to lead your men, or just another weakling under Hammer's foot."

Ernando quivered like a cold chihuahua, which did not instill a grain of confidence. Walter chose to work with Ernando because the man had visions for a brighter future. He wanted to change, not just Haven, but spread that change into the world. Reclaim the outside instead of hiding inside.

Ernando also knew Walter was a Second Turned zombie and, although he seemed to fear Walter, he also seemed to understand that not all zombies were mindless, and those of the First and Second Turned could protect humanity from the monsters that roam with simple hungry desires. Walter, though, had not mentioned there may be a cure that would grant further mutated autonomy again. That there is a chance to make a superhuman race of immortals and free an entire world of death and starvation.

Liatris's serum was unique as it rebuilt some of the frontal lobe damage, reversed some of the mutations, and significantly reduced the primal hunger. In doing that he decreased hunger all across the board. Those he cured typically ate as a treat, not as a need. With Hector in play now, even more could change. Walter was not opposed to working multiple sides.

The conversation was cut short. Walter heard fast approaching footsteps outside the large wooden door. Before he could say anything, the door burst open. Ernando screamed. Disgusted, Walter slipped back, hoping to obscure himself in the shadows.

The intruder was a young boy, late teens, with badly cut blonde hair. He was out of breath and grabbed his knees as soon as he got inside the room, sucking air as if he'd ran the longest marathon in the world.

Walter took another step back, sensing that the boy hadn't seen him.

"Councilman Migel," the boy wheezed.

"Noah?"

"I..." He took another breath. "Admiral Hammer is executing the recruits."

"What?" There was a sudden flare of furry from Ernando.

Walter stroked his chin. *Maybe he will be useful.*

"What do you mean? Are you sure?"

Noah wiped sweat from his forehead with the back of his hand. "Well... He's making the training purposefully dangerous. I heard him tell his men he was planning on weeding out the weak ones."

"Are you certain?" Ernando stepped towards Noah, suddenly appearing more imposing that before.

Interesting. So, it's his fear of me that makes him act like a pathetic little bug.

"I'm sure," said Noah. "I... I think I figured out where he's keeping the bodies, but it's too heavily guarded."

Ernando raised his hand. "Don't worry about this. We need to stop Hammer." He turned to Walter. "Can you expose Admiral Hammer?"

"With certainty." A tiny lie, but those were his orders from his Master, and he could not fail that, even if total certainty wasn't guaranteed.

Noah's wide eyes moved to the dark corner where Walter was, but his gaze never fell on him for any length of time. It seemed he followed the sound, but still could not see Walter.

"Do it!" said Ernando.

Walter said nothing, waiting to see how this angry leader Ernando reacted.

Ernando turned back to Noah, moving quickly like he was about to rush the man. "I want everyone keeping a close eye on him. I need every man and woman at the ready."

"Y— yes sir."

Walter slid along the walls in the shadows as the pair interacted. Noah had his attention back on Ernando and did not notice Walter's movements. Not wanting to deal with this conversation anymore he slipped silently back into the secret tunnel behind the painting and made his way out.

Mark was trusted with the task of finding some people who would be willing to help expose Admiral Hammer. Since Walter was here already, it made sense to check in. Mark was a skittish man, but easy to corner. Easier to manipulate.

The only deterrent now was the disgusting dirty tunnels he would have to travel to make it to Mark unseen. The day when he could walk freely anywhere could not come soon enough.

Hector's Journal

May 3rd, 2043

I've been collecting specimens from the recently dead, but I have no way to keep them. I'm forced to research *in situ*. With my limited equipment it's near impossible.

Adding different mediums has yielded different results, with the current combination that works the best creating a liquid with a curious pink coloration.

Chapter 22

Four more days passed in the large lab as they all settled in, gathering more and more items.

Lisa slipped the bunch of fake flowers into a red vase that Hector found her. Jim came up behind her, taking her shoulders and planting a kiss on the back of her neck. His hot breath and slight scruff of his chin gave her chills.

The small wake of pain from the sudden motion reminded her Mariah wasn't wrong when she said it would be a month or two before Lisa's ribs would heal. After a couple days of pain, she finally gave into taking some pain killers. Each breath was sore, but manageable. She was able to do more and spend more time with Hector and Jim as they had time. Another thing she noticed is they both would drop anything for her.

"How are you feeling?" Jim whispered.

"Better." She ran her finger along the convex cool edge of the vase. "I'd really like to go on a supply run with you."

"You're still healing. You need to take your time."

"So are you, and you are going out."

"You're right. But mine is very manageable and has had time to heal. Yours just happened. You need time." He ran his hand from her shoulder down her arm. "We can't lose you."

She shuddered, ached, and then accepted the fact she was not totally well. It was a frustration, not being on the front lines like before. She was more reliable than Flint and better under pressure than Bruno. Hector's right hand woman. In reality, she took that place to be there for him and close to him, and he most likely did the same for similar reasons. Each going years, never revealing their feelings.

"Place is looking pretty nice," said Jim.

Lisa sighed. "I wish it could last."

"Why can't it?"

"Well... we can't stay here forever."

Jim shrugged. "Why not? There's plenty of resources around here. This place is safe and locked up enough that I bet even if Hector had to leave, we'd still be fine."

It was warm and pleasant today. The sun had reached its peak, letting beams of light flow through the windows. Temperature was cool at night, comfortable during the day, but that wouldn't last long as the seasons changed. They had the RV set up for all seasons, but winter was the worst. And this place wasn't set up for winter at all. *Maybe I'm thinking ahead too far. The supplies here are so extensive. We'd have to scramble for food if we left.*

Jim turned her towards him, placing his hands on her shoulders. "Hey, don't worry so much. We're here for you..." He swallowed, harder than normal. "I'm here for you."

There was a touch of strain in his voice she hadn't noticed before. Why, she didn't know, but it made her pause. *Is he not sure he'll be here? Is he lying?*

He touched her forehead, smoothing her furrowed brow. "What's got you so stressed?"

"Just a lot of things. So much is changing."

"We'll just take it one day at a time." He rubbed her shoulders.

It was comforting when so many things were uncomfortable. Her room had come a long way. The boys had been working hard on rechargeable batteries. Jim had been installing a solar panel on the roof to charge them. She knew how to do it, and wanted to help, but the boys were insistent on following Mariah's advice. Lots of rest.

"Hector said he'd be done—"

He was cut off as Hector entered the room. He had to duck to get into the room. Jim ran his hands across her shoulder, and she shivered.

"You're up," said Hector. "I'm glad. You're looking better."

"I feel better," said Lisa.

Jim continued his massage right behind her. Pressed so close.

"I've made some good breakthroughs and I wanted to come check on you," said Hector.

"You're getting a lot further here," said Lisa.

Hector smiled. "I am. But I'm more interested in you now."

She warmed and shivered.

Jim leaned in placing a kiss on her shoulder.

Hector walked over to her and glanced at Jim. "Your back hurt?"

"Not... Not bad," said Lisa. She was getting warmer. Having them so close. Jim pressed against her, reminded her of their first time. It started like this. A back rub leading to... She leaned back and again felt the bulge in his pants.

There was a knowing look in Hector's eyes.

"I can leave you two."

"Stay," said Jim, his voice level. "Would you like that?"

He breathed into her ear as he spoke. Hot breath. A low growl in his tone.

"I'd like that," she said. Her voice a quiver.

Hector stepped closer. He traced his finger from her cheek down her neck. Chills followed his touch. Down her back. Expanding out across her body like tiny explosions. Despite the chills, she felt hot, and it was growing. Across the bridge of her nose. Her breasts. Her core.

"May I kiss you?"

She nodded.

Hector leaned in, the motion stealing her breath with anticipation. First kiss. She closed her eyes and waited. Unlike Jim, Hector didn't breathe. She had no warning before his cool thin lips touched hers. The kiss was so gentle. Timid.

It was brief. She exhaled. It felt like she was holding her breath for ages. There wasn't much time to inhale as he returned for another kiss. Longer. Deeper. This one held more passion. He warped his arms around her and pulled her into his embrace.

Jim held her from behind. His lips exploring the nape of her neck. Hector held her by the waist. Jim held her by her shoulders. It was exciting. Comforting. Protective and in some ways desperate. Hector's lips seem to practice some forgotten speech as he kissed her.

They touched her. Up and down. Hector cool. Jim hot. Their hands exploring all over her body.

Jim broke contact first and then Hector shortly after. She opened her eyes. Hector was right there. He reached up and cupped her cheek. He still had his goggles on which she wanted off. She wanted to see him. All of him.

Lisa reached up between his arms. She took his hat off first and gave it a gentle toss to the nearest table. Next, she went to his goggles and gently started to pull then off. Slowly. Tenderly. Just to see him. The true person he was. Not the mask he wore. Using his hat and goggles was always his way of hiding his true self. But his true self was what she loved.

Jim took her shoulders and turned her to face him. In the time she was involved with Hector, Jim had undressed. His muscled form stood before her. A soft covering of dark hair across his chest. His unshaven face. Gruff in a handsome way.

He moved close enough that his length pressed against her. He cradled her head with one hand and held her hips with the other.

He glanced past her. "Lay a blanket down please?"

She caught Hector's hand out of the corner of her eye snatching a blanket from their bed.

"You trust me?" asked Jim.

"Yes." The question caught her off guard which made his next motion surprise her.

Jim lowered her down to her back. Slowly. Taking her weight with ease and for a moment she felt weightless in his grasp.

He knelt with her, lowering himself on top of her, while holding the bulk of his weight off of her. He started at her collar bone, taking a deep breath until he made it to her lips. Not missing a beat, he kissed her. This time his lips tangled with hers. His hot breath brushed her skin.

He pulled back, sucking her bottom lip, and then returning. They kissed differently. While Hector was gentle and sweet, Jim was more intense and dominating.

Jim rolled, pulling her on top of him. She had his length pinned against her. So hard and throbbing.

"You ride me, and Hector will come behind. Is that okay?"

"B— both of you?"

Jim grinned. "You can take us."

"Don't pressure her," Hector snapped.

"It's fine," she said quickly. "I... I want to try." *Take them both? At the same time? Can I?*

Jim lifted her up on her knees, encouraging her lift to her weight. She moved up and he positioned his tip at her entrance.

"Go slow," he whispered. "This is about you. Your pleasure."

She sucked in a quick breath. Her jewel was hard and tender. She was hungry for them. Even though her mind was unsure, her body was burning. On fire. She wanted to have them. Wanted them inside of her.

Jim raised his hip, pushing his tip into her. He kept his hands on her. Guiding her down on him. He was thick and felt good as she slowly slid on top of him. He filled her. Rubbed her inside.

He kept it slow and instead of thrusting he just let gravity help impale her. Until she was resting on him, his whole length inside of her. Throbbing. Each twitch making her throb as well.

"Lean forward," said Jim.

She laid her chest onto him, his length inside of her, her bottom up.

Jim reached around and gripped her cheek. "You ever take anyone there before."

"No." She shook her head.

"We'll be careful."

There was rustling behind her until she felt another shaft pressed up again her other hole.

She took a quick breath.

"I don't want to hurt you," said Hector.

Lisa glanced back. Hector was knelt behind her, his length pressed up against her. He looked stiff.

"Relax and it won't hurt," said Jim.

Lisa took a few long breaths until she felt Jim nod.

Hector slid back and put the tip of his ribbed length against her.

Relax. I can take them. She felt so tight. So wet. Wanting them to just pound her.

Hector pushed. It felt so tight. There was no way—

Hector laid a hand on her shoulder. "Breathe. Relax. I'll go slow. I can stop at any time."

"No," Lisa whispered. "I want to feel you inside of me."

He pressed his tip into her. It burned. She tensed and it burned more.

Jim ran his hands across her back. "Easy." He was inside of her, but not moving.

Hector pressed into her, slowly. Every time she tensed, he stopped. It was better when she relaxed. It felt hot, but not painful. He went inside her deeper and deeper. Filling that space.

Her insides felt so full. So stretched. Taking Hector from behind made Jim feel thicker.

"You move," said Jim. "You're in control."

She ground against him, making both lengths move out and in. Hector moaned. His hands dropped to her waist. She rocked again, feeling them on both sides. Rubbing inside of her.

The pressure hit her insides just right. Wakes of pleasure with each motion. With each grind.

Jim slowly started to move with her. Hector second. In and out of her. Both of them felt different. Different girths, lengths, and shapes. She lost her own rhythm as they took over. Pounding her as she just held herself there. Pleasuring her. In and out. In and out. Both ways.

Sometimes she could breathe and other times each breath was like an uncoordinated gasp that just barely held back a scream of pleasure. Spots dotted her vision.

The waves of pleasure far overpowered any lingering pain or soreness from her ribs. Her back. Her legs. Everything was pain-free and filled to the brim with pleasure instead. Her skin tingled. Nipples hard, brushing Jim's chest as her body rocked forwards and back.

Jim let out small moans below her. It drove her wild. Crazy. Over the top. Pressure built inside of her. Built. And built. And built. She tightened with each gasp. They were going faster. Harder. Beating her insides.

She lowered her head, unable to breathe. Her body twitching. Spasming. Jim thrust hard and groaned. He throbbed before exploding inside of her. The sudden change in pressure and the feeling of his hot seed sent her over the edge. Her whole body tensed over and over, sending waves of pleasure between each nerve ending.

Hector jerked and suddenly he exploded too. Filling her from behind. It sent another cascade of pleasure through her. It kept coming. Waves hitting her over and over. She tried to breathe, shrieked, and held her breath again to try and remain silent.

Her whole body shook. Limbs going totally limp. Unable to hold her own weight she collapsed on top of Jim. Quaking. Floating. Dancing in a new dimension she'd never been to before and never wanted to leave.

HECTOR'S JOURNAL

July 15th, 2043

   I have been attempting to test my serum on slides holding infected tissues and compared the results to uninfected human cells. I have conducted thirty-four tests in the past few months. There is no easy way to get uninfected human samples. The two I've used have been from freshly decreased that were not turned. I'm noticing some progress as my serum does seem to attach itself to infected DNA. I'm starting to make progress.

Chapter 23

"Move! Move! Move!" a drill sergeant screamed.

There were cries across the dirt compound of the training fields. Yanika was panting, covered in sweat and cuts. Dirt caked to her skin with smaller grittier particles scratching in her eyes. Her lungs were burning.

The course was agility, strength, and pain. Everywhere pain. She stood at the precipice after failing three times. Taking in a painful deep breath she either needed to do it or die. *I might die doing it.*

The thought was quick, as more cries broke out around her. The civilians were breaking one by one. People realized now that the promise of home and comfort was a lie. The guards, serving the generals, were dragging people out left and right. Even some of the other guards dumped into this mess with the civilians were breaking. Breaking hard.

Those who were failing were getting dragged away. Worse, she never saw them again. If she didn't finish this, she would become another of the lost. They were being told people who don't make it are getting returned to the Outer Rim. Eric's sources say there's no traffic from here that way, hinting these people haven't left the area.

"Move it!" a man screamed behind her.

She thought he was screaming at her, but, as she turned, a man shoved Jance forward.

He glanced at her and shrugged. There was blood running down his face and his left arm looked torn up, the sleeve tattered and bloody.

With time running out she had to head forward. The first challenge looked like a giant gazebo easily stretching thirty feet in front of her, with multitudes of electrified wires hanging from it. She'd tried to get through it already and found each one had a different level of shock.

Jance bolted headfirst into it. Feeling the pulsating pressure to move or be dragged from the training field, she ran after him. Her steps were fast and then slow, as she hesitated over and over. The first couple wires tapped her skin carried a little static shock.

The next one slapped her on the cheek. A white light flashed. At the same time, she heard the loud snap as she felt the sting of pain. Her left ear rung. A moment later the realization let waves of pain slam into her.

She screamed, buckling to her knees. Spots danced before her right eye. Left eye black. Other people around here were screaming as well. She didn't remember the electricity being so strong. *Did they turn it up? Are they trying to kill us?*

Hands grabbed her.

"No! Please!" She thrashed, trying to break the person's grasp.

"It's me, bruh. Shut it and scoot."

She knew Jance's voice. He hefted her up and pushed her forward, hooking one of his arms in hers. The wires kept slapping her and she couldn't see where they were going. Small shocks. Painful shocks.

There was a loud pop.

"Fuck!"

Jance stumbled, pulling her forwards. She lost control. Another wire slapped her shoulder. The bolt felt like it traveled all the way through her body, burning a painful trail like someone drawing a sash across her with fire. She collapsed. Just as her knees hit, she felt someone yanking her up again.

"Please. Make it stop. Make it stop."

"Move or we're both K.O. Hamburger. Fuck this!"

Each little wire dealt so much pain she felt like her chest was going to explode. No matter how much she cried, no matter how many tears poured, there was no stopping it if she wanted to survive.

It seemed liked they had run miles, but were only halfway through. Jance cussed with each zap at first, but now he was moaning. The shocks were definitely getting stronger. Her vision grew darker.

They stumbled forward. Shock. Shock. Then nothing. Jance lost his grip, his body tumbling to the side. Yanika fell forward, flat on her face. Dirt and gravel scraping the skin of her arms and chin as they hit. Her body convulsed, popping as if the electricity was still hitting her. Her vision in her left eye hadn't come back. The horror of the mixed screams filled the area with a unanimous terror.

Someone behind her with a deep voice like one of the General's guards started screaming. "What do you mean we blew a fuse."

"I— I'm sorry sir. There was too much electrical pull—"

"Shut up and just get it fixed!"

Someone wrapped their arms around her. Hot breath hit the nape of her neck. "We need to go while he's distracted."

She recognized Eric's voice, although his blurry form could have been anyone. He struggled to heft her weight, staggering as he did so. There was another form on the ground she couldn't make out.

Eric kicked at it. "We have to go," he hissed.

"Fuck, bro."

Their drill sergeant was still occupied with the other man. "Mark. You are a total waste of air! It needs to be working now!"

The other man stuttered.

Their heated conversation melded with the screams and cries around them. Yanika felt her body go numb, running with little control of her limbs. She had to rely on Eric, who guided her. Foot falls and groans beside them told her where Jance most likely was.

More and more Eric had to help her, taking most of her weight. Every inch of scraped raw skin burned. It was one of the few sensations she could still feel. They made their way off the dirt course onto a hard floor. Their footfalls echoing in what sounded like a hallway.

"We have to hurry," said Eric. "Hang in there."

He was reassuring, but she was fading fast. Her knees buckling. They turned, crashing through a doorway into a small room. The walls seemed lined with something that was blurred and too hard to make out. She held her left eye shut and blinked the other, trying to clear her vision. It was like looking out a steamy window.

Eric lowered her down. She felt a chair and touched the edge, not balanced enough to keep from falling. She tipped. The small split second of panic wrenched a shrill chirp that lasted not even a fraction of a second. Eric was already there, arms around her, and pulling all her weight onto the hard chair.

"Shit, what happened to you?"

He touched her face, but she could only feel the pressure of his fingertips against her mostly numb skin.

"Bruh, that shocking shirt bout K.O.'d us."

"You doing okay, Jance?"

He groaned. "Bruh, I think I'm going to be sick."

"Lay down then. We'll be safe here."

"Where are we?" asked Yanika. Her voice was soft and broken. Her throat burned and grated with trying to speak three simple words. She felt pressure on her face again and could see the shadowed outside of his hand.

"Can you see me?"

"Not... really."

He moved side to side in front of her, maybe looking at her eyes. All she could make out was the edges of his face and a little detail around his nose, all out of her right eye. Her chest tightened and that spread through her body. Her fists balled together. Leaning over she opened her mouth, silently screaming. Tensing. Hearing the sound in her head. But kept the whole thing silent. Sight hadn't come back to her left eye. It was gone.

"Easy. You're safe now." Eric wrapped his arms around her. He pulled her forward and her face found the softness of his shirt.

She could only feel the fabric on the right side of her face. She could still smell his sweaty musk. Every time she thought of those electrical cords she twitched. Each muscle in her body felt both sore and like wet noodles. Resting on him was the relief she needed. Just to lay. Be safe.

She still wanted to cry though. Scream. *Will the sight ever come back in my eye? How... How could they do this to me? To us.* Her hands shook. Friends. Neighbors. They were all missing now. *They must be dead. That's the only explanation. How... This was supposed to be better.*

"Easy," Eric whispered, his hot breath brushing her ear. He rubbed her back and swayed side to side, rocking her gently.

"Bruh, you gonna rock me next?"

"Shut up, Jance."

"Rude." Jance grunted.

Yanika could make out a person's shape on the floor. Most likely was him. She couldn't care less anymore. She was almost dead. She knew it. Eric continued to hold her close, and that was nice. If she had to die, that was better than in the Capitol's execution grounds.

"Hey." Eric stopped rocking and gave her a slight shake. "Stay with me."

"Just... let me die."

"I'm not going to do that. We're going to make it out of this."

"Six feet under," Jance chimed in.

"Shut the fuck up, Jance. You're not helping."

"Bruh, I feel like I'm dying."

"Me too," said Yanika. The same if not less food than she had at the Outer Rim and a thousand times more activity had already left her exhausted. Most nights sick to her stomach. Eric was doing everything he could to save up favors and tradable items to get them out of here while also trying to get them enough protein to survive this training.

There was the creek and slam of a metal door opening and closing with footsteps. "Are you three all right?"

The voice was male, shaky, and slightly familiar. She didn't have enough energy to care. Keeping her head against Eric's chest she started to gain more and more feeling throughout her body. All of it pain. Burning. Throbbing in some places. As the pain built, her stomach grew more and more sour.

"They're not doing well. Do you have a med kit, bandages, anything?" asked Eric.

"I have a little stashed away."

Yanika turned, making out a general form and listening to his footfalls as he moved past them. There was rustling behind them like boxes and metal objects being moved on a metal shelf before he returned.

"This is all I have."

Eric sighed. "Thanks, Mark. It'll do." He pushed Yanika off his chest, trying to brace her upright with one hand.

She grabbed his forearm. "I think I'm going to be sick."

"Trash can. Trash can," said Mark.

She heaved.

Something rattled next to her and then something metal hit the back of her chair with a clang.

"Here."

A trash can shaped object appeared in front of her. She didn't bother holding it anymore. She heaved again, this time spilling wet burning bile. Quickly it became a painful dry heave. Eric kept a hand on her shoulder to steady her. Another pair of hands came up behind her, steadying her in the other direction.

If felt as if it would never end. She couldn't even breath after a while. Her hands shook as she clutched the cold trash can. It felt like metal with a dint in one side. Horrific. That wasn't even a strong enough word to describe everything. When it finally subsided, she wished she had just died.

"Shit, bruh, I'll get some water," said Jance.

"Thanks," Eric muttered. "Hey, breath. Everything will be okay," he whispered in her ear.

"Just let me die."

"I can't do that. You're strong. You can make it through this."

She clutched him tighter. "I can't. I can't do it."

"Yes, you can. I know you can. Breath with me. In. Out."

He guided her and she tried breathing with him. The burning of bile in her throat kept her gagging. She had to rely on both of them to keep her on the chair.

"Open your eyes. Look at me."

She tried. Her left eye was still black. Her right eye was blurry, seeing only muddled shapes and shadows. "I— I can't."

"Keep your eyes on me."

She felt pressure again on the left side of her face, like he was touching her again.

"You can't see out of this eye still?"

"No." Her voiced cracked. She thought she was too tired to cry, but tears started to spill over. The warm liquid ran down her cheeks.

"It's okay. You got hit very hard." He touched next to her right eye. "Can you see out of this eye?"

"Not really."

"What do you see. Talk to me."

"It's blurry."

The pair of hands behind her left and the shadow of a figure moved in front of her.

"Let me look," said Mark. Her touched her face as well. "There's a lot of tissue damage from the shocks. You have a burn here too. Let's get you laying down. Shit, I wish I had some ice."

There were footsteps again, moving around the room, a shape shifting with the sound. "Bruh, I got— Barf, what happened?"

"Grab a washcloth off the shelf over there," said Mark. "Eric, help me get her to the floor."

"Okay. I got her," said Eric.

They helped lift her from the chair and then lowered her to the floor. There was rustling and Eric's blurry form moved around her. Something soft was placed under her head. The other form, she guessed was Mark, laid a cool washcloth over her eyes.

It felt soothing as did just lying there. The floor was cool as well. At first it felt good, but soon she started to shiver. The chill working through her small body.

"Give me a coat, blanket, or something," said Eric.

"I have towels here," said Mark. "Some are pretty good sized."

There was more rustling before she felt the men start to bundle her in the rough fabric. It calmed her a bit, but it took time for her to warm. Time for the pain to become tolerable. The aching in her stomach. Throbbing in her head.

Every second stretching to minutes and beyond. She just wanted to cry. Scream. Pray, even though no amount of prayer ever helped her before. Watching everyone and everything she ever knew get swallowed by zombies. Moving to Haven only to find it was a hell. Then coming here with a glint of hope, only to find it was worse than hell.

Eric sat down beside her and placed his hand on her arm. He seemed to stay there the whole time, the best as she could tell, as she waxed and waned from consciousness. She didn't know how long she just laid there.

They talked a little off and on. Nothing she really listened to. She didn't care. Part of her still wanted to die right there. Be done with it all. End the pain. End the suffering. End the trying over and over to have a better life only to have every hope and dream she had dashed over and over.

It wasn't fair. She tried to help people. Tried to be a good person. While others cheated and scammed around her, she tried to be fair. Look where it got her. Naïve. Falling for this trap. People were just evil. No one cared for anyone but themselves. There were exceptions. Eric. Maybe Jance. A few of her neighbors seemed genuinely good. But the rest were trash. Horrible people. If she could just do to them what they did to her. *Shock that fucker right in the balls.*

Groaning, she pulled the washcloth from her face.

"Bruh. No cap. She's alive." said Jance.

She blinked, staring up at the ceiling. She still could not see from her left eye, but the vision in her right was clearer. The ceiling light above her had a slight glow around it, but now she could make out the stained ceiling tiles.

"Hey." Eric leaned over her, his brows deeply creased. "How are you feeling?"

"I hurt," said Yanika, through clenched teeth.

"I know. You were super brave."

She pushed herself up, fighting the pain in every joint. The more she hurt the angrier she got. "I wasn't brave. I was weak." She slammed a fist on the floor. There was enough pain coursing through her that she didn't even feel the impact.

"I think they were seri tryin to kill us. No cap. Like that was, fuck, so cranked up."

It took a moment of processing to decern what he said, and he made a good point. "Yeah... Yeah, no cap."

"I think we got a plan that's bussin," said Jance.

Eric groaned. "Not now." He cast a worried glance at Yanika.

"Yes, now, bruh. We need to bust out of here or we're gonna be fried chicken for sure. Yah hear?"

Yanika felt a deep lump set into her stomach. "Cuddles..." she muttered. "Is he..." She pressed her lips together and then shook her head. "Don't tell me. I... I don't want to know."

Eric raised his hand. "See what you did, idiot."

"What? I'm just sayin' we need to make tracks."

Yanika brought her balled up fists to her chest. "So, are we getting out of here or what?"

Eric groaned again and leaned back against a metal cabinet. "Maybe. What were you saying again, Mark?"

"I was saying I found out why they are making such a hard push to get more military units. The lab in the city has records of research studies, but it also might have evidence that Admiral Hammer is a war criminal."

"No cap!" Jance shot up, looking at Mark with wide eyes.

"I heard them talking about it," said Mark. "Rumor is he was a double agent. Anyway, he's trying to get to this lab as a cover up."

Eric rubbed his chin. "I hate that man a lot, but this seems like a stretch. You said you heard this?"

Mark looked uneasy, but he was that way the first time she met him as well.

"I did," said Mark. "There's more rumors too, but that's the best I can glean."

"Makin sense," said Jance. "Man be actin hella sus."

"Well, there's nothing we can do about it," said Eric.

"I was hoping to find someone willing to go first. If we could get this information, Admiral Hammer could be outed. All this could stop." Mark rubbed his hands together in front of him like a fly trying to clean itself.

Eric shook his head. "We'd never survive out there. We have almost no supplies. Hands down not enough weapons or ammunition—"

There was a sound of tapping on metal from the back of the room which cut Eric off. Mark's eyes widened and his face became paler, intensifying his sunken cheeks.

Jance, who was sprawled out on the floor with his feet propped up on a shelf, jolted, spinning to his hands and knees like an alligator.

Eric grabbed Yanika's arm, sliding closer to her side. "What is that?"

The tapping came again.

"Well... Uh..." Mark looked towards the back of the room. "I have a friend— coworker— colleague..." He kept stuttering.

Eric pulled his legs in until he was crouching like he was preparing to spring at any moment.

Yanika gritted her teeth, following suit. She pushed herself into a crouch. Her body still ached, making every movement feel like swimming through wet concrete.

Mark backed away. "I... I really need to answer this."

"Do you?" asked Eric.

His eyes were narrow, and Yanika could tell he was suspicious of Mark's actions.

"I..." He waved his hands in front of him. "He can help. Trust me."

Eric pressed his lips together and shifted his weight. He didn't answer, instead just nodding to Mark. Jance got the rest of the way up and pulled a toilet plunger off the shelf next to him. He brandished it as his weapon of choice, enticing an exaggerated eye roll from Eric.

Mark moved to the back of the room. Yanika could just see him around the metal shelving. He messed with a lock on a double door metal cabinet on the wall. She thought she heard the lock click, but she wasn't sure.

The doors opened with a loud creak and in strode a tall man with dark hair pulled back, thin chiseled face, and wearing fine clothes put together with a double-breasted vest. He stopped and brushed his sleeves off.

"My Lord— master— I wasn't expecting you so early." Mark clasped his hands together and bowed several times.

Master? Lord? What is he talking about? Is that man some kind of Haven official?

"I heard about the commotion Admiral Hammer has caused. Since I was in the area I came by." He stepped around the shelf, eyeing the three of them gathered together. "You all look horrible," he grunted.

Eric stood. "I didn't expect to ever find you this far in the city walls, Walter." Eric groaned as he spoke, words tainted with frustration and disdain.

"You know him?" asked Yanika. She straightened, unsure now if this was going to lead to friendly conversation or running for their lives again.

"Yeah," said Eric. "Walter is the leader of a group of scrappers. He comes by every few months to sell and barter their junk."

Walter crossed his arms. "I needed a hobby."

"Why are you here?" Eric snapped.

"I'm working on overthrowing Admiral Hammer." He ran a finger across his chin. "I know where there is incriminating evidence that will reveal him as a war criminal."

"Why are you telling us this?" Eric stepped forward. He didn't show any signs of being afraid of the man.

Still, Yanika backed against the shelf, feeling the cold of the metal against her shoulders. Eric's fists were tight balls. Jance kinda had a weapon. This prompted her to glance at the shelf behind her. This place was like a huge janitor closet. The best she could find was a toilet brush that was a little brown around the edges. She gagged and turned back towards Walter.

Walter turned his attention to Mark, who was backing himself into a corner. "Are these the ones you told me of?"

Mark shrugged and then nodded. "Yeah. Plus, one. Uh... Eric, Yanika, and Jance." He waved his shaking hand towards the three of them.

Eric's head snapped towards Mark. "What have you been planning?"

Walter raised his hand. He looked completely unphased and there wasn't a spec of emotion in his cold expression. "I need people from the inside to help pluck this criminal from his ranks. Mark said you all might be willing to help."

"Yo, bruh, we don't even know yah. Like, no cap, you might be tellin' tales on us."

"Perhaps he was wrong." Walter lifted a brow and glared at Mark.

"No. No, I swear. They can help," said Mark.

Jance stepped up, his glare telling the whole story how he planned to take on both these men with just a toilet plunger and win.

Yanika also felt something inside of her shift. She was already wounded. Already almost died. What was there to lose? She scooted forward up to Eric's side. He cast her a quick surprised glance twice, like he was checking to make sure he wasn't hallucinating. His gaze quickly moved back to Walter.

"They need to leave," said Mark. "But I think they will help." He turned to them. "Won't you?"

"Bruh, we not helpin some strangah out here. You be trippin.'"

Walter raised his hands. He turned away from Mark and sighed. Maybe he had had enough. Yanika couldn't tell, but he didn't appear like he wanted to hurt them.

"There is a lab in the city with evidence of Admiral Hammer's involvement in espionage and war crimes. I have the means to easily get there, but I will need connections on the inside to get the information through Haven smoothly."

"Bruh, you trippin'. No cap. We bussin, but not that OP."

Walter snarled. "Please stop speaking. You are giving me a headache."

"Hey," said Eric. "You don't get to talk like that to him."

Jance shrugged. "No stressin'. This guy psycho."

Walter pinched the bridge of his nose. "There is still a radio system here in Haven. We can use that to expose Admiral Hammer."

Eric tilted his chin up. "Then what? Huh?"

"Then those on the inside will make their move." Walter straightened and tucked his hands behind his back. "The Admiral is not loved, he is feared. It will not take long before the people turn on him."

"What you're suggesting is a complete uprising," said Eric.

Walter raised a brow. "And?"

"Bruh. This dawg for real?" Jance pointed his thumb at Walter.

Walter seemed to ripple as muscles tensed from his shoulders down. "Are you telling me you like the filth they've created? The squalor they force the majority to live in?"

Yanika's attention narrowed on Walter, those key words that had been repeating in her head now spoken aloud. *The filth the majority is living in. That's it.* She sucked in a breath and then clenched her jaw. This was never Haven. It was born on power and favors. The ones that made it to the Capitol had enough power, influence, or had enough money out there that they could buy their way in. Median was tolerated because the Capitol needed the food and supplies they produced. It made so much sense now. It wasn't about hard workers or qualified workers. It was about who knew who and how much power you had.

Another corrupt political system. Now. The world has pretty much ended, and the wealthy are still trying to become wealthier. It enraged her. The pain enraged her. The fact she no longer could see out of one eye enraged her.

Walter was still eyeing the group, seeming to take notice of every little motion and action, until his gaze fell on her. His eyes narrowed for a brief moment, and she felt as if he knew instantly how she felt. Empowered, she stretched to her full petite height and put a foot forward, stomping it down hard enough there was echo around the small room.

It startled both Eric and Jance. While Jance just looked dumbfounded, Eric held out his arms like he was either planning on catching her or rushing between her and Walter. His eyes were wide and even his face paled a little.

"I'm in," said Yanika.

Eric gasped. "What? No. We're not doing this."

She turned to him, now tingling with anger. Her skin felt hot like she had a sunburn over her whole body. "This has to stop, Eric. This place is hell. All of Haven is just hell. You were the one trying to get us out of here. You decided that we'd be better off in zombie land than here." She waved a hand towards the storage room door. "So, what, we leave and everyone else just suffers here until they die too?"

"There's three of us, barely surviving," said Eric. "There's no way we can save them."

Yanika turned to Walter. He seemed smug, like a part of him was enjoying this exchange. "You said there's for sure evidence there."

"Without a doubt. Getting the evidence is a simple matter." He pulled a hand from behind his back and examined his fingernails as he spoke. "My only hold up has been implementing those on the inside that can help distribute this evidence."

"Bruh, why should we trust you?" Jance thrust the toilet plunger towards him. "What you got to gain for this?"

Walter paused and then raised a brow. He kept his head low and looked up towards Jance and Eric. "Haven could become what it was envisioned. There are enough people here, enough forces here, to build a better city. Expand the borders. Tell me, with all the supply runs this government has done, why has no one decided to expand the borders?"

"There are hordes of zombies out there!" Eric screamed.

"Are there? The scrappers do pretty good. Why can't a whole government make it?" Walter leaned forward. "Let me ask you this, if people wanted a life, wanted to have a family, how can they accommodate an increasing population when they had to turn away so many on the very first day this place was finished?"

Eric closed his mouth. He looked stiff and continued to hold an intense glare, but quieted.

Jance cast him a sideways glance and then, with his head down, he shrugged. "Gotta give it. Dude makes sense."

Yanika could see Eric grinding his teeth and the veins on his neck bulge. He looked like an angry bull ready to charge. Maybe he should be. Maybe not. He had his reasons to stand his ground. He always had an escape plan. Yanika's escape plan was to get to the Capitol just by working hard and doing the best she could. Look where that got her. Almost dead. No one in this shitty society cared. She was exploited, just like everyone else. Meat. A number. Even if Walter was full of bullshit, what was there to lose?

HECTOR'S JOURNAL

August 21st, 2043

I have been monitoring a few survivor camps. I planned to further my research nearby, but that has proven impossible. These small camps are becoming feral. Each one I've found has started to create a tyrannical hierarchy. It's brutal and cruel. I cannot understand how after everything that has happened to the world, that some still prioritize power over people's lives.

Chapter 24

Horrible. Traumatic. Shitty. Stressful.

There weren't words strong enough to describe the day Eric had. How it spiraled out of control. How he was certain he saw people die today. Dumped into the janitor closet now with two crazy decisions. Go back and continue to try and survive long enough they can make their escape or go now with nothing but blind faith.

The thought made his stomach sink as he glanced at Yanika. Burns covered half of her face. Her left eye was open, but glassed over and pale. Fuck. Shit. Damn. There really weren't any options.

Eric slid over and slipped an arm behind Yanika's back. "You going to make it?"

"Can't get any worse," she mumbled.

The three of them followed Walter over to the metal cabinet. Mark followed behind them, casting nervous glances at the door. The bottom of the cabinet was open to a straight drop down into darkness. Walter strode off the end, falling into that dark without a sound.

Eric grabbed Yanika's shoulders and stepped around her, trying to keep himself between her and this mysterious drop. Once closer he could see a small ladder that led down.

"Here? Really?" asked Eric.

Mark kept himself turned towards the door as he backed towards them. "It leads down into the tunnel system. It's the only safe way out of Haven."

"A tunnel system? Something like that to get out of Haven has to be huge. There's no way the government doesn't know about it."

"It's a heavily guarded secret," said Mark. He squirmed. "I mean, if the wrong people find out... they... they die."

"Bruh, what's that mean for us?" Jance came up beside him, elbowing his way into the space past a large metal shelf.

Walter's voice came from in the tunnel, distant with soft echo. "Quit squabbling and make a decision."

Eric groaned. This wasn't the decision he wanted to make. Yes, he was planning on breaking out of here, but not like this. Sudden.

No supplies. He still didn't trust Walter, but did he have any other choice? Mark hinted if the wrong people found out about this tunnel they would die. *If I refuse are we going to become the wrong people?* Everything added together to him not having a choice.

"I'll go first," he said to Yanika. "Jance will help you down and I'll be at the bottom to help as well."

She nodded. This frail precious woman that he had been protecting was different now. He felt an unmovable need to keep her near and safe. But she changed since he saw her this morning. The look on her face was not fear, more of a vacancy. He made a note to keep a close eye on her, but knew they were out of time.

He climbed down first. His boots made a clunk on steps. As he descended, he wrapped his hands around the ladder rungs feeling that they were made out of metal pipe.

He stepped into total darkness that extended an unknown distance ahead of him. The tunnel was deep. When he looked up the entry was just a small square of light. The only sign of Walter was a shadow that shifted in front of him. Walter's cologne was what gave him away.

"Send her down," said Eric. He looked up, watching as Yanika slowly made her way down.

Before she made it halfway down he was already reaching for her, in case she needed him, or worse, if she slipped. She descended into his outstretched hands where he guided her to the ground.

"It's dark," she muttered.

"How are we supposed to see?" asked Eric, her comment prompting him to find out. The thought of blindly following someone in complete blackness made a lump form in his throat.

There was muttering above before Jance descended, illuminated by a green glow. He hopped off the ladder, landing on the dirt floor. It kicked up a damp earthen smell that tickled Eric's nose.

Jance held up a green glowstick which lit his unsure expression. He cocked his head and gave Eric a questioning glance.

"This is it?" asked Eric. He looked from Jance to Walter. As he did, he pulled Yanika closer to him. He noticed that something was off. Usually he could feel her tremble, but now she felt abnormally still.

The trio all looked to the darkness where Walter stirred. He stepped forward briefly into the glowstick light before retreating back into the darkness. "That's all you need. We must walk some way, but there will be other transport soon."

As Walter finished speaking the light above vanished with a metal clunk. They were sealed in. The bang was enough to make Eric flinch, yet Yanika remained still in his grasp.

He reached for her hand. "Stay between Jance and I."

"I'll be fine," she said, with flat affect.

It was unnerving. Not long ago she wanted to die. *Does she still want that? Has she given up?* They began following Walter into the darkness. No other options. The air felt cold and damp. It smelled like a cave. The walls were carved out earth and stone, but only for a short bit before they ducked into what looked like a large old sewer.

The smell here was acrid. Water stepped to the side where there was a small lip in the rounded tunnel. It barely kept him out of the water. Eric followed suit, not wanting to know what that water really was, even though he had a good guess from the smell.

Jance gagged. "Bruh, really?"

"We don't have any choice," Eric mumbled.

Eric gave Yanika's hand a little squeeze and continued on. The tunnel was mostly straight with only one slight angle before they turned off into a larger tunnel. This one was similar to the first but only four times larger. The walls were supported with wooden beams larger than his thighs. The tunnel was squared off like it could have once been a mineshaft. There was still no light, so Eric had to rely on where Jance waved the glow stick.

"How much further?" asked Eric.

"That is an open question," Walter muttered. He was moving in and out of the shadows before them.

The sewer smell faded back to that of the moist earth. Even Jance held back any comments he had. It was a long silent walk before the tunnel widened again. The green glowstick light just caught the gleam of something ahead. Something reflective.

It made Eric uneasy. His muscles tightened as a cold chill tingled across his skin with icy pieces of string being pulled across him. He glanced back at Jance who was looking ahead as well, just as concerned. The party slowed, letting Walter get further ahead.

Walter stopped which almost made Eric stop as well. He stiffened again, taking a step in what felt like slow motion. He made himself continue to move even through everything inside of him told him to run.

The glint he saw earlier was the light reflecting off the back taillight of a motorcycle. There were three of them. One a large, nice bike and the other two looked like dirt bikes.

"What are these?" asked Eric.

"What do they look like?" Walter retorted.

Eric knew Walter knew what he meant, and this was just the attitude he was getting back. His face warmed despite the cool underground air. "Why are there motorcycles here? What the hell is going on? And what is this damn tunnel?" He finally lost it, unable to just go along with things anymore. He had to catch himself as he balled his fists to make sure he didn't crush Yanika's hand. Walter was still mostly in the dark, but he could see the man roll his eyes.

"This is how we get around. Do you know how miserably long it is to get outside the walls?"

Eric shook his head. "There is no way someone hasn't found this."

"They have," said Walter in a flat tone that was almost haunting. "They all died."

"Bruh, what the fuck. No cap this sus. I call vibe check."

"Please never speak again," said Walter.

Eric released Yanika's hand and stomped forward. "You don't talk to him like that. You talk to me."

"Fine," said Walter, with a snarl on his face.

"Where are we going and what are we doing?"

"Ugh. You've already been told. The plan is to reveal Admiral Hammer is a war criminal."

Eric nodded. "By going to this place in the city to get information. If you have this tunnel, why do you need us? Huh?"

"Great. Underground. I can completely reveal this information to the rats with the same effect." He paused a moment, scowling at the group. "You are a guard. You can move above ground with little concern. I cannot. You can take this information directly into the radio station. You might meet some resistance once in there." Walter shrugged. "But I would be shot down in the streets."

Eric felt the muscles in his shoulders loosen. That actually made sense, which he wasn't expecting. "How are we supposed to get into the city? It's swarming with zombies."

"My crew is waiting for us at the exit point. The city has been no issue."

Something a scrapper would say. They were used to going into the hordes to loot old buildings just to resell things for fortunes in Haven and other survivor camps. That's how they always had well-working vehicles. Plenty of food. Clothing. Luxuries. Thinking about it, they were doing better than the recruits going through what Haven was calling training. *More like the purge.*

Eric didn't look back at Yanika, but what happened to her sat sour in his stomach. He knew scrappers didn't often survive, but in the years he'd spent at the outpost he'd seen a lot of return business. Walter being one of them. In fact, he'd always seen the same crew with him every time. It should have put him a little more at ease, but the situation still made him tense.

"So, we get in and get out?" Eric asked.

"Like always," said Walter. "Now please shut up. We don't have decades to get this done." Walter straddled the motorcycle.

"Bruh, won't someone hear that thing?"

"We're too deep for that," said Walter, as he started the engine.

Eric took Yanika's hand and pulled her towards the larger of the two dirt bikes.

Walter turned back and groaned. "Leave one behind. You..." He trailed off, his voice strained. "You ride with me."

"Bruh, no way."

"That's not a request!" His voice managed to get loud yet deep and the sound vibrated through the space. "We need to conserve gas and leave vehicles behind if we can."

Jance glanced at Eric. Eric shrugged. He wasn't going to be the one rocking the boat. Not now. They were in no position for that. Maybe later. Maybe if things go south. He could feel out how much room to move they had.

Jance wasn't happy, but joined Walter anyway as Eric got on the dirt bike and then Yanika. Everything weighed heavily on him. They started forward, slow, but still much faster than walking. He thought things through. What Walter had said. What Mark had said. Even everything he had seen and heard over the past few days while they were going through their so-called training. It was all coming back to one deep feeling.

Hate. Hate for that man who instigated what happened to Yanika. The longer they spent in the winding tunnels the greater that hate grew. The more unnerved he felt. Hell, he just wanted to run, not be a hero.

It took what felt like forever moving through dark tunnels lit by the headlights. Twists and turns. Dirt to stone. Large to small and back. Who knew how long it really was, but he was relieved when Walter finally pulled over at a dead end.

Jance jumped off so fast you would have thought he was sitting on thorns the whole time. Yanika slipped off from behind him. As she did, he felt the chill of the air wrap around him where her arms were. The seat was small and the whole way she had been pressed up against him. Something he would have liked at a time other than this.

They shut the bikes off, plunging them into darkness again. There was rustling and then Jance pulled out his dulled glowstick. It was minimal light, but enough to reveal Walter was missing.

Eric spun around and then back, eyes scanning the shadows this man loved to hide in. Something metal clanked. Eric turned towards the sound. Jance thrust his glowstick up to illuminate it. Eyes all turned to the sounds as they were suddenly blinded by a wave of bright light.

Yanika hissed and backpedaled. Eric turned, following her as she backed into the dirt wall.

"What the hell man," said Jance.

There was no response.

"Are you okay?" asked Eric.

Yanika covered her face. "The... light hurts..." She mumbled and her voice was soft.

"I know. I'll take a better look at it soon." *I hope.*

The two men shuffled over and looked up at what appeared to be an opening to the surface. Best guess, Walter was the one who opened it and was already up there.

Jance glanced at the pair of them and huffed. "Fine, I'll go first."

"You don't have to," said Eric, quickly.

Jance held up a hand. "Nah, nah, nah. Bruh, you got her. I'm just a solo. I'll give it a once over." He winked.

Eric waited as Jance found another metal ladder and headed up. After a moment and getting the okay they all went to the surface. They were in a thick brush-covered area. Glancing around Eric realized they were outside the walls. Just like that. They were out of Haven. He knew they'd traveled a long way, but he didn't realize just how far.

Walter was standing under a nearby oak tree. His arms were crossed, and he looked frustrated. Another round of griping got them nowhere and they were again left following him. Eric did ponder the thought of taking off and leaving Walter, but without any weapons, supplies, or really anything he knew none of them would survive.

The walk was shorter, and the warm sun was refreshing in comparison to the dank underground. Walter led them away to where a team of scrappers were parked. One jeep, one battered car, and one truck.

It would have put Eric on edge if he hadn't recognized it as Walter's crew. He knew Sam, who was perched on the hood of the jeep eating something. There were three other men around relaxing. They saw them coming, but none of the group bothered to get up.

Walter walked up to Sam and said something that Eric couldn't pick up.

"Bruh." Jance stepped closer to Eric. "This is sus."

"It's his crew. I think we're fine," said Eric.

Sam slipped off of the jeep, touched Walter on the shoulder, and then sauntered forward. Eric had seen her a few times, but wasn't ready for her sultry catwalk up to him or the glance she gave Jance with a little grin.

"You all are a sight for sore eyes. Except you." She kept her gaze on Jance.

"Uh, no cap. I'm not interested."

She rolled her eyes. "And I wasn't on the table."

"Skip it," said Eric as he tried to force his tone to be neutral. "What's next? Are we going to the city or not?"

Sam shook her head. "Not now. We bunker here for the night then we'll head in."

"Here!" Eric lost his composure. "It's wide out in the open. We're sitting ducks out—"

"Please stop yelling," said Walter. "We are fine here. Now shut up and sit down." He turned to Sam and his harsh tone faded. "Get them some supplies. Do we have any med kits left?"

Sam nodded.

"Good. Get them patched up. I'm going to take a nap."

The other three, Mario, Lambert, and Joe introduced themselves rather rudely as Sam got the supplies. Finally, the trio hunkered down on a blanket in front of a fire Mario was trying to start. It was too much to deal with everything, so Eric turned his attention to Yanika and Jance opted for a nap.

Yanika sat next to him on the blanket leaning back with a blank stare. Eric got stuff out of a med kit and scooted towards her. "Let's clean you up a bit. Does it still hurt?"

She shrugged. "I'm not sure anymore."

"What do you mean?"

"I feel numb. I... I wanted to die..." She trailed off a moment, never breaking her distant stare. "I got so mad afterward... but now I don't feel anything."

Eric nodded. "I think that's called shock."

"I don't think so. Well... maybe you're right."

Eric tried cleaning her up, mostly removing the dirt from her face. The burns were looking worse. The area around her left eye was bruised with streaks of bright pink from raw skin. The eye was open and white. It gave him chills, which he tried to hide from her.

Conflicting emotions made him sick. The trapped sensation. The anger that someone hurt her. Realizing just how deeply he cared for her. Worried that something drastic had changed, like she was ready to give up. She wasn't the girl he first met anymore. Deep inside he knew, after all this, she would never be again.

That didn't deter him. Instead, it made him want to be by her side more. Wanted to be there to support her. To help her continue on. For the first time he was presented with a goal beyond himself. Beyond his little scheme to trade under the table until he could make a solo break from this place.

Now he was free, in a way. It wasn't the feeling he expected. Eric started trying to make some kind of bandage for Yanika. His hands shook and it was hard to push past his foggy thoughts and come up with something that would work. Her gaze stayed distant. Like a robot that had gone into sleep mode.

He used a gauze roll combined with an ace wrap to start. The kit also had the items to do sutures, but he used this like a sewing kit. He couldn't sew, so it looked terrible, but somehow he fashioned an eye patch.

He held it up, trying to catch her attention. "This should protect your eye. I know it doesn't look good, but I'll find something better later."

She turned slowly, her one good eye drifting to what he made and then to him. "It looks great," she said in a barely audible tone.

He forced a half smile, but could feel how awkward it was. He struggled to be her support. To reassure her. He already struggled to protect her. Eric went to Mark during that electrical trap and got him to get it to malfunction. During that time Jance dove in to protect her. They were both too late.

Eric bandaged her up. It would cover the wound at least and protect the eye. He knew she'd never see out of it again, and that hurt him. They were silent for a while. The others got a fire started and the crackling warmth was comforting at a small level. No one was talking. There was just this cold divide.

Eric scooted over towards Yanika and wrapped his arm around her. She laid against him, and they sat there as the sun set. The only lights were a couple on top of the vehicles and the campfire. Not enough to keep the zombies away. Before all of this he would never let himself get into such a dangerous situation. Now he just let it happen as he kept aware of how the scrappers acted.

The more they seemed relaxed the more he accepted they were most likely safe. In the dark he glanced over at Jance. He was still laying down, but with eyes wide open. The man was stiff. Overly alert. The only one of the three that seemed truly calm was Yanika. She had her eye closed now and seemed to be asleep. Not wanting to disturb her he stayed there all night. Eyes open and alert. Waiting to see if they survived to the morning.

HECTOR'S JOURNAL

October 4th, 2043

   I am going back to my roots for my research. The Chernobyl Lab had various animal DNA samples in bulk within it. After years of research, I can confirm the explosion created a vaporized and bastardized version of those samples. Some of the samples within the lab were designed to be mixed with the DNA to make it more aggressive. This created, not one, but multiple virus mutations. I hypothesize that the mutation variations correlate with the position of the first Turned within the lab in relation to the different research area. Photosensitivity seems to be part of the virus mutating from being passed from one host to the other, but becoming more and more unstable. These are educated guesses, but should allow me to further my research.

Chapter 25

Lisa was finally able to take a deep breath without feeling like she would die. All together they had healed up pretty well. There was a soft pink line on Jim's head where the bullet grazed him. Flint was the same pain in the ass as normal, and no one would ever know he had a mild concussion.

They had made the lab a home. Jim and Flint had moved some more solar panels to the roof along with finding one more in the city. Food supplies were stocked full. They had wash bins on the roof to collect rainwater to wash clothes and blankets. Luxuries were starting to pile up. They'd gathered new clothes, books, board games, snacks, and more.

Lisa sat in her room in a bucket chair covered in a fuzzy blue blanket. It was morning and the sun was shining in, catching the tiny dust particles floating around within its bright rays. She had a nightstand next to her with a blue coneflower in a vase. The stand was scratched and weathered, and the vase had a chip on the top. Nothing was really new, but it still felt new. Even more importantly she felt like it was hers.

Out in the wild, just trying to survive, getting attached to material things couldn't happen. She had to be ready to move at any minute. To flee an area as fast as she could, never looking back. Now she could enjoy having a few things to herself.

She was reading a thick book about a group of space travelers stranded in an asteroid belt. The book was worn with page ends tattered and the paper weathered to a cream color. It had a smell that could only be described as a very old dusty library. The book wasn't bad so far.

When her door creaked open, she lowered the book to her lap. Hector entered, bending slightly to clear the doorway and fit into the room. The outer entry space had taller ceilings as did many parts of the lab above them. Her room was made from an old office, so it had a drop ceiling. Granted, it was missing many tiles now and long dead wires hung from above.

Hector had a metal tray in his hands with a stainless carafe and coffee cup. As he neared, she noticed the cup had a small tea bag strung over the side.

Hector had on new pants today. They had to be modified to accommodate his backwards raptor like legs. He still had his hat and goggles on. Despite everything, he still seemed more comfortable covering up his zombie features instead of embracing them.

From what she understood, the first turned zombies, or Lords as he called them, were mutated based on what part of vaporized genetic material was released in the air. It made her chest hurt thinking of the kind of person Hector was and the deformities that made him so insecure.

"I brought you some tea," said Hector. "I was able to find some in the city that was still good."

Lisa scooted forward. "That's sweet. You didn't have to."

"But I wanted to."

Although he remained expressionless, his voice vibrated with a soothing deepness that made a cascade of warm tingles cover her body.

"How are you feeling?" he asked.

She shook her head. "Just like yesterday, I'm feeling fine."

He turned towards her, seeming to examine her with some amount of intensity, but mostly it was a guess because his goggles hid his eyes and his hat masked most of his expression.

"I've seen you flinch at deep breaths. I know you're still in pain."

She sighed. "It hurts a little, but nothing like it did."

"How's your back?"

"Mariah thinks I'm improving." Lisa frowned, rolled her eyes, and then rocked her head side to side. "She said I needed time to rest it. I guess she was right all along."

Hector chuckled. She didn't hear it often, but when she did, she couldn't help but feel happy.

"That happens," he said. He set the tray on the stand next to her. He paused, running a long finger across the coneflower petals. "This is lovely. Did Jim find it for you?"

"Yes. I'm surprised he got it back in one piece."

"He picked well. It's very fitting of you."

"You two are spoiling me too much. I can do stuff for myself you know."

Hector moved back far enough so that he had room to squat in front of her. Craning his body over to be eye to eye to her also made an awkward bump on his back underneath his poncho where his insect-like wings lay hidden.

"I know how capable you are. I've seen you survive things that would have taken the lives of many others. I know you are strong, but that doesn't mean you don't deserve better. We do what we do because we care. Not because we don't think you are capable."

His tone dropped, deep yet serious, which resonated with her. Tears burned behind her eyes, and she pressed her lips together, trying to fight them back.

Hector stood, craning over her again. "I want to get back to the lab. I think Jim is around somewhere. Either way, we won't be far."

"Are you making any progress?"

"Actually, yes. I was able to isolate the DNA sequence that causes photosensitivity in more mutated zombies. I've also done a little investigating into the hierarchy."

"What do you mean?"

"A first turned zombie can control lesser zombies by way of pheromone emission." He cocked his head to the side. "To zombies, we are very stinky."

Lisa laughed, enjoying both his humor and the fact that a simple laugh no longer hurt.

"We have pheromone glands and from what research I have done it seems the more mutated, or a better way of putting it is those turned later have much less developed pheromone glands. I think I may be on to a way to reverse that, basically rendering a pheromone gland useless."

"But..." She rubbed a finger on her temple. "Isn't that how you keep the zombies away from us."

"Yes, and I have no intentions on testing it on myself. I'm simply researching the individual mutation components. If I can isolate a good portion of them, I may be able to develop a serum that would treat nearly all the effects of mutation. I'm already working on some samples, but with limited resources it is slow." He hung his head and his shoulder slumped. "If I had done things differently earlier, this might not have been an issue."

Lisa shoved her book down on her chair and stood. As Hector's head snapped up, she took a long stride forward and wrapped her arms around him. She laid her head on his chest and gently ran her hands across his back, being careful of his wings. He stiffened as they made contact, but in just seconds she could feel the tension evaporate, and his whole body relaxed.

He wrapped his arms around her in return. His body was thin, but not emaciated. Instead, it was more a very lean feeling of muscle over a bony structure. His poncho softened the sensation, but really, she couldn't care less about any of that. All that mattered was them and these precious moments together.

"You did the best you could. You always tell us that's all we can do."

He sighed. "That I do." He bent forward.

She felt the brim of his hat bump her head and then his forehead rested on hers. He had her wrapped up tight in his embrace. This was a safe place. A comforting place. She could relax in his arms knowing he would never let anything hurt her. But she also knew he respected her. He thought of her as strong. He saw her as beautiful.

"I need to go get some more work done. You should drink your tea while it's still hot," he whispered in her ear.

"I'll miss you," she whispered back.

He let her go with a soft subtle smile on his face.

He still had his hands on her when a loud pounding came from the front of the lab somewhere outside her door. She looked at him, waiting for an answer. Maybe the boys were working on something. His gaze snapped to her door and his body stiffened, telling her that was unexpected for him. It unnerved her and she felt her muscles start to coil and cold chills trickle down her back.

"What is it?" She clasped his hand tighter, guessing any minute he'd go after the sound.

"A zombie. I can smell him." He pulled, trying to get free from her grasp as she tried to hold him tight. "Stay here. I'll go check it out."

"I'm not letting you go alone."

He took a breath, and she expected a strong protest.

Instead, he sighed. "Watch my back then, but stay behind me. There shouldn't be any zombies near here."

She nodded, letting go of his hand. She didn't have any of her weapons handy. Something she should have thought of before declaring she'd come along. Lisa bit her lip and clenched her fists. If things went south, she'd have to rely on agility. Hector pushed her door open, and she followed close on his heels.

Bruno and Mariah were both in the entry space, standing outside the door of their main room. Their eyes were fixed on the front door. Bruno had his hands clasped together, standing behind Mariah, slightly hunched.

Jim and Flint came from the back of the building where the staircase to the underground parking garage was.

"Was that you two?" asked Jim.

Hector held up his hand, indicating for the pair to stop. He shook his head and then turned his attention back to the front door.

Jim stopped and grabbed Flint's arm to keep him from going forward further. Spot bounded up behind them. He seemed to also know something was happening because he halted at Jim's side and crouched down like he was ready to attack anything that moved.

The bang came again, the sound loud, but a steady pattern. It wasn't like anything she'd expect to hear if it was just a rogue zombie trying to get in. They tended to wail, claw, and knock themselves against doors. She stayed at the doorway. Together they could flank anything that came through the door. But it was daytime. What kind of zombie creature would be here in the daylight?

She heard Hector sniff the air as he approached the front door. Jim had it locked up in several places. Hector peered through the barred window next to the door and then pulled back abruptly.

Lisa jumped.

Jim took one quick step forward and then stopped. "What is it?"

Hector grabbed the locks and started to undo each one, not saying a word.

"You're not going to open that?" Bruno's voice cracked. He took a step back into the shadows. His body blended in with the darkness except of the whites of his eyes.

Spot dashed over to Bruno and then back by Jim. His nails making a clickity-clackety sound on the floor. Other than that, he was surprisingly quiet.

Lisa raised a hand and lowered it, trying to indicate for both of them to be calm. "Everything will be fine," she whispered. It was directed mostly to Bruno, but partially to herself as well.

While Mariah and Bruno looked scared and on edge, Jim was sharp as a hawk ready to attack. Flint was a step in front of him, a smirk on his face looking like he wanted a fight.

She gritted her teeth as she turned her attention back to Hector.

He undid the last lock and then pulled both large metal doors open. A flood of sunlight rushed in, blinding her for a moment. She shielded her eyes and stepped back, pressing her back against the wall next to her door.

"Walter?" said Hector, a waver in his voice.

"Long time, old friend." A man pushed his way past Hector into the open lobby. He had on a button-down shirt with a vest over it and nice dress pants. They were perfectly clean and even looked pressed. His long dark hair was pulled back without a strand out of place.

"Walter!" Jim shouted loud enough his voice echoed around the space. He stormed forward, stopping right before the man, blocking his path so he couldn't enter further into the space.

Spot barked and bounced back and forth.

The man, Walter, raised a brow as he looked at Jim. Jim was taller and much more muscular, but this man had something about him that made her feel like in a fight, Jim would lose.

"You know each other?" asked Hector.

Jim gave a sharp tilt of his head upwards. "Yeah. He runs a scrapper team. How do you know him?"

Hector stepped to the side and glanced back at the door. A group of people were outside.

One, a woman with smooth chocolate skin and curly dark hair rushed in. She wore a patch over one eye and there were lines across her face like she had recently been burned. "Jim?"

Jim jolted, his eyes went wide, and his focus turned completely to her. He sidestepped Walter, bumping him on the shoulder on the way by. "Yanika? What... What are you doing here?"

"You know her?" asked Lisa. She kept her voice steady, but this whole situation unnerved her. *Could she be an old girlfriend?* It was a sudden intrusive and unwarranted thought. Recognizing this, she shook her head, trying to get it out of her mind.

"Yanika was my neighbor in Haven." Jim gave Lisa a quick glance and then turned back to this woman. "What happened to you? Why are you here?"

Hector raised his hands. "Everyone be quiet. There are too many questions for all of us to be talking at once." He turned to Walter.

Walter slightly turned towards him and glanced over his shoulder, looking out the corner of his eye. It was like he was too proud to address Hector directly.

Hector seemed tense. His back twitched causing his wings to push on the poncho which made the material flutter. "It's not safe to just mingle out in the open." He turned, looking at the group in the parking lot.

Walter strode forward next to Hector. He was much smaller than

Hector in size, but he felt like a much larger threat. He waved his hand, beckoning them inwards. "Eric, Jance, and Sam, you three come in. The rest guard the front."

One man groaned. "I always get stuck out here."

The others made no protest as the three approached the front door.

Jim's dark eyes scanned the group with what looked to be either fear or desperation. "Eric, I didn't expect to see you here."

Eric shook his head. "Didn't expect to see you either."

"I see there are many connections here," Hector muttered. "Let's all adjourn to our main room. I have questions."

"As do I," said Walter back to him.

The pair locked into an intense staring contest. Walter not blinking and Hector, with his goggles on, seeming to meet the same energy. After a moment, Hector escorted the group to the main living space. Mariah and Bruno took a step back before ducking inside the room before everyone got there. Walter kept on Hector's heels with Flint and Sam behind thems elbows shoving each other, and Jance behind them.

Eric waited for Yanika who had paused as she watched Jim.

Jim didn't seem to notice. He held out a hand towards Lisa. "You going to be okay?"

"I'm fine." She took his hand, stepped closer, and nestling her head near his shoulder. "What's going on?" she whispered.

He nuzzled against her, brushing the stubble of his chin across her cheek. "I'm not sure. Keep your eyes peeled."

She nodded against him, hoping it looked more like a cuddle to onlooking eyes. He took her hand and led her towards the room. Yanika gave them one more glance before letting Eric escort her into the room as well.

The space that once seemed open, with the large kitchen area and tables for games, was now crowded. Mariah and Bruno had moved towards the counters to the left that Mariah cooked at. Flint had joined them and was sitting on a desk next to a pile of pans.

Sam, Eric, Yanika, and Jance were all around the far table to the right where Flint's checkerboard was. Sam had spun a chair around and was sitting backwards with her chin on the backrest. Jance was sprawled in a chair next to her. They were watching, but seemed somewhat uninterested.

Eric and Yanika were standing, both intently focused on the group.

Lisa and Jim slipped in, both pressing their backs against the wall, staying close to the door, their only exit if things went south. Spot was quick to follow, keeping himself by Lisa's leg where he sat like a good guard dog, growling. It was low and quiet, but an obvious sign of how unnerved this creature was.

Hector and Walter were paired up in the center of the room like two fighters in a ring just waiting for the bell. This room had higher ceilings and Hector stretched up. Walter didn't even flinch, and instead his eyes narrowed, and he fixed Hector with a dark stare.

"Why are you here?" asked Hector.

"Why are we here?" Walter corrected, waving to his small group.

Hector stayed silent and the conversation fell into another staring contest for a moment.

Walter broke first, grunted and then continued on. "To sum it all up quickly, this lab has information that will prove one of Haven's high officials, Admiral Hammer, is a war criminal. Lord Liatris wants you all out of the picture so the data here that's needed to overthrow Admiral Hammer can be retrieved. My Lady Victoria wanted me to perform the task as a favor to Lord Liatris to secure more of his trait-suppressing serum."

"What are you talking about?" Jim interjected with a crisp sharp tone.

Hector held up his hand and Jim quieted. "Why?"

Lisa caught Yanika leaning forward, her mouth open like she planned to say something, but Eric grabbed her arm and pulled her back. She closed her mouth, looked at him, and nodded.

Walter waved his hand in a fanciful motion. "That is part of the long story."

"Long or short, I want the whole story." Hector's tone dropped.

Walter stiffened and his eyes locked to Hector in a different way. She hadn't seen him move like that. Stiff. Like he was being... *Controlled. Is he the zombie? Is Hector controlling him?* Her heart started beating faster and the wall against her back suddenly felt cold. She grasped Jim's hand and gave it a tight squeeze.

Lisa didn't say anything, but having Jim close was calming. She felt more in control. Maybe it was because she felt safer. Maybe it was because she knew she had backup if needed. She wasn't sure and was too distracted to even bother figuring it out now.

"Don't... do... that," said Walter. His words were broken, but each sounded like a command.

Hector pulled back. "You must understand, I have people here to protect."

"So do I!" Walter's composed expression broke, and he snarled.

"You spoke of Lord Liatris and Lady Victoria. Are they both in this area?"

"Yes, here in the city. But with different agendas." By the way Walter stiffened, Lisa guessed he really did not like the question.

Hector stepped back, his foot bumping into a chair making the metal legs squeak on the floor. There was tension that felt like taffy in the air. Uncuttable, but pulling taut over and over.

"What do you know of Admiral Hammer?" asked Walter. His voice had a low hiss now that wasn't there before.

Hector cocked his head to the side. "I am unfamiliar of that name."

"What about General Komarov?"

Lisa watched as every muscle in Hector's body rippled.

Walter grinned. "You do know that name." He straightened, now taking a proud stance with his chin turned up. "Admiral Hammer and General Komarov are the same person. General Komarov was a triple agent, which is a story for another day. He was responsible for the explosion at the lab. He's also the one who mistook Liatris's wife as a potential witness and had her framed and murdered."

Hector tilted his head back and then slowly nodded. "And Liatris is here for revenge."

Walter shrugged. "Of sorts. Hammer worked for the Japanese government, or at least was connected because that's where he retreated to after the lab blew up. When Liatris found he was the one that had his wife killed Liatris pursued him across the world. That is how he learned of Hammer's connection to the US. From what is known, the only evidence of his connection to the explosion and the creation of... our kind, is here."

"Our kind!" shouted Flint. He slipped from the desk. His face was a contorted mix of excitement and surprise. "You're a zombie?"

Walter's lip twitched. "I... am a Second Turned." He spoke as if that was a royal title and even tilted his nose up to Flint as he spoke.

Lisa licked her lips. "Is that how you know him?" she asked Hector.

Hector nodded, and, as he did so, his shoulders sunk, and his body relaxed. "Walter is a Second Turned of Victoria's creation. They both are... friends."

As he spoke, the smug expression on Walter's face faded. He too relaxed. "I see you're still wearing the present I gave you."

Hector nodded, touching his goggles. "I cherish them as I do our time together."

There was a moment of pause where they both seemed to be relaxed. The pair existing more like old friends than potential enemies, but that quickly ended as Hector's voice changed once again. Intense and deep.

"Tell me about this serum."

"An army of mindless hunger-driven bags of flesh is useless," said Water. "After Admiral Hammer was too far from Liatris's grasp, Liatris started researching how to suppress the more negative traits of the Walkers. He was successful."

Walkers... The third turned, Lisa remembered. The ones that looked like mangled humans. Haunting effigies of the people they once were. They were also more mutated. She remembered ones with extra arms, tails, and even wings.

Walter crossed his arms and lifted a brow. "Liatris has created a new generation. Somehow, and I am no scientist, he was able to suppress the primal hunger, reverse a portion of the mutations, and decrease their light sensitivity. Really, he created a better human."

Lisa looked between the two. Walter was more relaxed, but still proud in his stance in a better-than-thou kind of way. Hector was now a still blank slate. She couldn't tell if the information was good or bad for him. Walter fixated on Hector, waiting for a response. Hector was quiet, not giving him any.

Their silent quarrel over dominance was broken by a whispered voice to her left.

"Bruh, this is getting tense dawg," said Jance.

Eric kicked the chair Jance sat in. "Shut up."

Hector clenched and unclenched his fits. "I'm not surprised Liatris continued his research as well, or how he has gone about it. You spoke of evidence. If that is true, and there is evidence here of what Hammer has done, then what does Liatris plan to do with it?"

Both of Walter's brows now rose as a crooked grin pulled at his lips. "Why, he plans to tear down Haven's corrupt government."

"I cannot allow that," said Hector.

Yanika jumped forward, her arms snapping down to her sides. "Well, it's going to happen!"

Hector lowered himself, making himself shorter in the room as he eyed her. Tension was high and Lisa could feel that everyone wanted to shout out their own thoughts and opinions.

"He almost killed me," said Yanika. "He's killing people. Lots of people. My neighbors are either begging to get away or vanishing.

Probably dead, because as far as I know, no one is making it home alive." Her voice started to shake.

Jim tightened his grip on Lisa's hand. "What do you mean? The Outer Rimmers?"

Yanika nodded. "They drafted a bunch of us. Told us we'd go through training and get a place in the Median or Capitol, but it's a lie. Look at my eye!" She pointed at her face, her hand now shaking violently. "This was a result of the training. If it wasn't for Mark doing his shit, and Jance, and Eric, I'd be dead. They weren't planning on stopping. They were going to push us until everyone who couldn't take it just dropped dead."

"Damn straight. Gurl making a point," said Jance. He nodded towards Eric. "This blockhead pulled my ass outta that execution. Big man don't give a shit bout us. No cap."

Confused glances were cast towards him, along with raised eyebrows.

Eric rolled his eyes and the cleared his throat. "What Jance means is they are actively trying to weed out the lower class. I hate to admit it, but I also agree with Walter. I did some spying back in the Capitol and what I heard seems to track. They're massing forces and it seems like this could be their target."

Walter raised a finger. "Oh yes. I forgot that part. Admiral Hammer plans to launch an attack on this place."

Lisa's stomach dropped so low her whole body slumped. The blow instantly made her eyes start to dampen with tears. She knew living here couldn't be permanent, but for a while she thought maybe she was wrong. Maybe they had a chance to stay here and make a home. A safe place. Only to have that hope ripped away from her.

Jim pulled on her, bringing her a step closer to him. She could tell he was trying to comfort her, but this time it wasn't enough. "Marco and his team were also targeting this place. It might have been related."

"Oh, it quite was," said Walter. "I was hoping to exploit their foolish greed with the hopes they would retrieve information and return to Haven to sell it. Easy extract and delivery."

"You!" Jim jerked forward. He kept his grasp on Lisa and stopped when he tugged her arm. "Emily was part of that group. You led them to the slaughter."

"Only because I underestimated their foolish greed," said Walter "I had plans to intercept them if I could have gotten there in time."

"You got Emily killed," Jim growled.

"On the contrary." Walter crossed his arms. "She was part of my plan. I brought her to Lord Liatris."

Jim jerked forward, breaking his grasp from Lisa. Lisa had a sinking feel that, without Hector, if a fight broke out Jim would easily lose to the Second Turned zombie.

Jim shook. The veins on his arms were more defined and he looked like it was taking everything inside of him not to attack Walter. "Why would you do that? Why?"

Hector took a step over and placed his hand Jim's shoulder. "Breath." Turning to Walter, his wings twitched beneath his poncho. "Explain yourself."

Walter stepped back, putting more space between him and the other two. Lisa glanced at Hector, unsure what was about to happen. Unsure of a lot of things if she took the time to think about it. The information bounced around her head, like an advanced mathematic lecture that was far beyond her understanding.

Hector angled himself directly at Walter, but kept his position between Walter, and Lisa and Jim.

Walter straightened. His eyes were fierce and facial expression taut. Lisa's stomach twisted. A quick intake of breath made her still-healing ribs burn. The tension was settling into her back as well, and she could feel the old tightness start to return like a snake coiling around her spine.

"Emily was a gift, as she very much resembled Liatris's late wife," said Walter.

Jim stomped his foot as he stepped forward again, trying to get closer to Walter. "You monster. You just threw her away. Tossed her to the wolves like a sack of meat."

"I doubt it," said Hector in a hushed tone. "Am I right?"

Walter rolled his eyes. "Someone at least has some capability of intelligent thought."

Jim lunged, but in that very instance Hector caught Jim's arm and held him firm. Jim tried to shake him off, but Hector was far stronger.

"Lord Liatris will give her every comfort," said Walter "I can guarantee that."

"She'll be fine," Hector reiterated. "Liatris was devastated when he lost his wife. If he sees even a fraction of her in Emily, she will be the most protected being on earth."

"How am I supposed to know that?" Jim snapped, turning an intense glare on Hector.

"Trust," Hector said simply. He cocked his head to the side and then cast a glance at Walter. "Let me process." He lowered his head and rubbed his hand across his face. "Liatris pursued Admiral Hammer, was unable to reach him, and in the time being, has created a serum that suppresses most zombie traits. He's targeting Haven to stop Hammer? What of the innocent people there?"

"He has no interest in turning them, if that's what you mean," said Walter. He backed away and leaned against a table. "Unless they want to be turned."

"This guy is crazy!" Flint waved his hand in the air.

His sudden outburst and motion were enough to make the tension in the room crackle. The group jumped, some more than others. Bruno especially, who seemed to be drowning in his small corner of the room.

"Be quiet," said Hector. His voice was low, calm, and gentle. "I'll address that comment later. Liatris needs this information, why? If he knows Hammer is at fault, why is he bothering with this?"

"Simply put, how is a zombie supposed to saunter into Haven to kill an official? Or, a better way of saying it, my Lord Liatris does not want to be the enemy in this endeavor. That title should fall on Hammer."

"So am I to assume his strategy is to use this information to make Admiral Hammer's own people turn on him?"

Walter tilted his head towards Yanika and Eric. "He has already started that process. This information is simply to solidify the deal."

"And your master, Victoria? She's involved how?"

"She wants to enlist more men on her side, but refuses to do so without his serum. My Lady has no need for mindless disgusting beasts."

"And ordering you to get rid of us is her payment to Liatris?"

"Of sorts."

Hector straightened again until his hat touched the ceiling. He was imposing and his entire demeanor changed. "Then why should we trust you?"

Walter did not flinch. It was terrifying. Hector was larger and much more imposing, but Walter acted like he was nothing more than a small inconvenience. Like he could overthrow Hector at any moment.

It still made Lisa hold her breath as she waited this exchange out. She felt her ribs sting if she breathed. Her back ached and the longer she stood, the more the muscles burned. *Hector can control Walter if needed. Everything will be okay.*

Despite it being an intense conversation, Lisa was solely focused on her ramshackle family, her new home, and the two men she loved. All that was in jeopardy right now. This wasn't something she could control with brute force. This was a debate with their lives hanging in the balance. She didn't understand half of it. She was never in Haven. She had no idea before now of any of these connections.

Walter pushed off his table, matching Hector's energy. He didn't care what Hector did or said, that was obvious. "Don't trust me. I could care less. They're the ones you should trust." He tilted his head again towards his group. "They're the ones that almost died."

Hector turned his attention to them, his posture slowly changing. She looked between him and the group. Yanika was still shaking. She was a little thing and Lisa could guess those recent injuries were from the event with Hammer they spoke of.

On closer examination she could see Jance constantly shifting his weight off to one side. He looked pale, with dark circles around his eyes. Eric was in similar shape. The trio looked exhausted and thin. Sam was the exception. She had caramel sun-tanned skin, a testimony to the hours she spent in the hot sun. While the others were in scraped-together uniforms and tattered clothes, Sam was more of a typical scrapper. Tank top. Belts around her waist with several pouches. High top leather boots.

Lisa could tell Hector was caving. He had a deep soft spot for people in need, most likely driven by his enormous guilt.

Hector stepped forward, now ignoring Walter's presence. "If there is indeed information here that will incriminate this Admiral, what will you do with it?"

"Dawg, we bringin' the whole capitol monopoly down."

Eric sighed and then pointed at Jance. "What he said. If we can get this information out to the people, if we can get the Outer Rim and others on our side, we can get rid of this entire hierarchy."

"You would be creating a war," said Hector.

"Mr.... Lord Hector... We're already at war. And..." Eric shrugged, his gaze moving over towards Walter. "Walter's right. Haven is too full. We can't take in any survivors. If anyone wants to have a family at all in the future there's no way Haven can support them. I worked at the outlet distributing rations. There's been less and less every month. Many of us guards have been stockpiling. Those of us who know of other survivor camps or maybe some scrappers we can team with... well, we've been moving out." He glanced at Yanika, his brows dropping and his eyes softening, giving him a sad childlike expression. "Everyone in the Outer Rim doesn't have that chance. You know that too, Jim, don't you?"

Jim lowered his head, his eyes traveling to the floor and his gaze distant. There was some kind of struggle there. Lisa glanced back to Eric. *Something he said must really be getting to Jim. Is he worried about the people he lived with?* She could assume a lot of things, but all she really could do now was be a comfort to him.

A long breath turned into a soft groan before Jim spoke. "Eric is right. I hate to say it. I saw it. I saw it the moment I settled there, I just didn't want to accept it."

"We're at critical mass," said Eric. "Something has to be done."

"And killing everyone isn't it," Yanika snapped.

"It will still be a fight," said Hector. "Governments do not fold easily. People will die."

Walter rolled his eyes. "People will die either way. But this gives them the power to decide how they die and how they live. I have a governing source on the inside I have been working with. He is willing to fill Admiral Hammer's shoes and move Haven towards being a stable community."

Eric turned with a questioning stare he fixed on him. "You didn't tell us that. Who is it?"

Jim leaned towards Lisa. "That's typical for Walter," he whispered.

Walter turned, looking over the group. It was more a parade in front of them than anything else. "It was not pertinent at the time."

"It's pertinent now," said Eric. His tone lowered and was harsh and gravely. He leaned onto his front foot as his shoulders tensed.

"Ernando Migel," Walter grunted. "Happy?"

Bruno choked. Hector spun towards him and the whole room turned to his position. He looked so pale at the moment that he appeared more like a zombie than the ones in the room. His back was pressed so hard against the table that part of his hip was sliding on top, like at any moment he'd just vault over it and make a break for the window. Barred or not.

Hector lowered himself, making him much less imposing. He moved his hands, indicating for him to calm. "Breathe first."

Bruno gasped and clutched his chest. Mariah clasped his arm in one hand and placed the other on his back. She guided him a few steps over to a wooden barstool. He still gasped. His eyes were large and bouncing all around the room.

"Tell us what is wrong," said Hector.

"Well... Uh... not wrong... I guess," Bruno stuttered. He grabbed at his poncho and began to twist the material. "It's just that..." He started to rock.

Mariah kept her hands close, guarding him from tipping off the stool.

"It's... Well... Ernando Migel... He's..." Bruno looked up at Hector with large tear fill eyes. Desperation mixed with too many emotions to distinguish marring his expression. "He's my dad."

"Your what?" Walter's tone was harsh. He lowered his head so that he was peering out at Bruno.

Bruno flinched, pulling back from Walter despite the distance between them. Mariah caught his back, keeping him steady in place.

"This complicates things," Hector mumbled.

"Not at all." Walter pulled a small pocket watch out from his vest and glanced at it. It was gold, with elaborate metal work, on a gold chain. "Hmmm, we'll have to finish this debate soon. It is getting too late."

"Be a good time to leave," Flint spat. He clung to the table, and it looked like that grip was the only thing keeping him from springing into the group and starting a fight. The vein on his forehead was bulging, highlighted by the sun now partially set.

Things were getting dim in the room as, indeed, nightfall was coming. Despite how much they cleaned this room, the amount of people moving around caused the remaining dust to stir. Little particles made large loops in the light. She knew how dangerous it was to be out at night even with a zombie Lord at their side. Walter was a second turned.

Hector had explained it all before a few times, although it still confused her. The Second Turned should be able to command everyone turned below them. The further mutations. But nothing above that, if she was getting it right. Now wasn't the time to ask, but she knew there were people outside. They looked human, but so did Walter.

Walter turned to Hector. He straightened, but this time kept a level stare. "My people will need to come in for the night if we plan to uncover this evidence. Time is also of the essence as we have no way of knowing when Admiral Hammer's forces will arrive."

"Not right away," said Eric. "At least I don't think so."

"No cap," said Jance. "Overheard two oldies having a discuss. They seem really hesitant to head into the city."

"The fact the city is thick with other zombies might be our only benefit," said Hector. "Fine. Bring your people in. But know, I will protect my people over any of them. If something happens, I will not hesitate to match force."

"Always the lone protector," said Walter.

That hit right on Lisa's last button. She stepped forward, stopping her foot on the floor. "Hey, we've smacked zombies around for entertainment. The only one who needs protecting is you." She waited for him to make a much better comeback, but, for once in years, Flint chimed in at the right time.

"Boy, this is our turf. So, you just keep your overly fancy pants in line, cause it doesn't look like you have any idea how to get down and dirty."

It was a small victory and Lisa cheered inside.

Walter's silver eyes became large and his brow low for a brief moment until Hector stepped up to his side.

"You better get them inside before dark. My protection extends to this building, only."

There was more tension than ever before, but Walter said nothing. It seemed Hector had finally settled the pecking order and their team was on top.

HECTOR'S JOURNAL

October 21ˢᵗ, 2043

   I have crossed paths with Victoria again
in the former states. She was not hard
to miss. I estimate that she has collected
a force of two to three hundred undead.
While before her forces were mostly second
Turned, but now she is gathering more.
She will not explain why. She asked if I
would join her again. I refused. I made the
encounter brief and later noticed one of
my serums missing. I suspect she stole it,
but when I tried to trace her movements,
she was nowhere to be found.

Chapter 26

It was decided the main area in the lab where they had set up the kitchen dining and recreation area would become the central point for the new people. At Hector's orders, the rest of the doors to the rooms they had turned into bedrooms were closed and the newcomers ordered to not enter.

There was some scrambling to get things done that usually would be done hours ago. Mariah started cooking for the large group. Yanika offered to help.

Lisa paused to watch. The petite woman looked to have several recent injuries across her face and wore a thick bandage over one eye. She looked very thin and frail, yet she was moving fine as if she didn't have any injuries. It was perplexing, but Lisa lost focus quickly as her gaze drifted to Bruno in the corner.

He sat in a chair which he had scooted against the wall furthest from the other scrappers. She didn't remember their names exactly as introductions were brief. Hector had pushed Walter from the room quickly, and Jim and Flint had to go get batteries for both lights around this place, and to power things upstairs. Hector said something about the computers.

Lisa slipped over towards Bruno. He kept his face to the floor. He was wringing the end of his poncho. She remembered Hector's poncho was a gift from Bruno. His mother had made Bruno two of them before she died. He gave Hector one to thank Hector for saving his life. Bruno had never mentioned his father.

"Hey." She kept her tone soft and as gentle as she could.

Bruno glanced up at her for a brief moment, but quickly returned his gaze to the floor.

Lisa put her back against the wall next to him and slid down to the floor. "I think we should talk about this."

"About what?" he whispered.

"Your dad."

He flinched.

"You didn't think he was alive, did you?

"No."

"What happened?" She didn't want to push too hard, but she knew he'd stay like this for days if she didn't. "Did you two get separated?"

Bruno shook his head.

"So? What happened?"

Bruno let out a long breath. "Papa— dad, kicked me out when I was eighteen. Mom still talked to me, but he wanted nothing to do with me?"

Lisa straightened against the wall. "Why?"

"Dad was the governor and I got arrested on drug charges when I was seventeen. He stopped talking to me after that. When the zombies came... well, I never found him. Figured he was dead."

Lisa scooted over and put a hand on his arm. "A lot has changed in the world. I bet he would love to see you again."

Bruno shrugged. "Maybe. But if he's a high up in Haven then... I bet nothing will be different."

"Bet you're wrong."

Bruno turned his gaze to her. His large eyes were damp, his cheeks and nose red.

"We'll find him. You can talk to him. If he's still an asshole, then he'll have to deal with me."

There was a brief grin that crossed Bruno's face before the dark shadow returned. "We'd never get close enough to even talk to him."

"Don't bet on it. Hector can accomplish anything, and I know he'd do anything for us." *For me.* She realized it had been a while since she'd seen Hector. Jim and Flint hadn't come back in either. "Will you be okay for a few?"

Bruno nodded.

Lisa went to find the others, but stopped by Mariah first. "Will you watch Bruno?" she whispered.

Mariah gave Bruno a quick look. "Sure thing sweetie."

Lisa ran into Jim outside partially up the stairs going to the next story. Jim stopped. Flint, who was ahead of him, kept walking and she caught a quick glimpse of what looked like Spot's butt.

"Everything okay?" asked Jim.

"What's going on?"

He descended the stairs back to her. "There are computers upstairs that might have some information on them. We're going to try and get them running."

"I'll come with."

Jim took her hand. His fingers were oddly cool, as if he had been holding cold metal. "Okay, but stay close. I don't trust Walter."

That wasn't a surprise since they all just found out that Walter gave his neighbor to a Zombie Lord like a little meat present. Hector seemed certain that she would be getting fine treatment. In any other situation that would sound mad, but if this Zombie Lord treated Jim's neighbor Emily even half as good as Hector treated her then it didn't sound like a bad change from what she had learned was the squalor of Haven.

She followed Jim upstairs to the third floor into the darkness. Jim pulled out a glowstick and held it up to cast some light in the area. There was an overtone odor that reminded her of burnt metal and an undertone of bleach. Lisa stopped and stiffened as the last time she smelt anything like this it almost killed her.

Hector was to her right in a large room with glass walls. There were spots of white light giving off a soft glow in a few places and casting long dark ominous shadows in others. The entire place was silent except for the soft sound of bubbling liquid in Hector's direction and the sound of her own breath.

Jim was moving past her now, seeming unphased by the smell. His eyes were glancing from one side to the other, examining the glassed-in rooms, his gaze lingering on areas that were semi lit. This floor was large, but seemed more crowded as the rooms here were much larger than below.

She didn't want to interrupt, but wanted to be involved as well. Lisa held her breath, trying to make the decision. She was already here now. Most likely, if this smell would kill her, it would have already started. She assumed, but wasn't sure.

Hector turned her way and immediately abandoned whatever he was doing, striding with long graceful steps to her side. "What is wrong?"

She placed a hand on her chest. "Is it safe?"

Hector moved close and brushed his knuckles across her cheek. "It should be, but if you are feeling unwell, even in the slightest, I want you to go back downstairs and get Mariah."

She lowered her head. "I'm sorry. I think I'm just on edge."

"So should you be. A lot has happened."

"Have you found anything yet?"

"All the computers are old. We're struggling to get any turned on. There are files here as well, but I'm guessing if Walter if correct, the real information will be well hidden."

It made sense. Evidence a person is a war criminal wouldn't be something someone would just leave laying around. "What can I do to help?" asked Lisa.

"We'll need help looking for these files, if they're here. Look for anything like a secret compartment, a safe or vault."

"I'll help too," said Jim. Once Hector had come over Jim took notice and headed back.

Lisa glanced between the two, afraid to leave either of them. Hector seemed to have control with Walter, but it continued to unnerve her. She wanted Hector close to her. Even if she couldn't do anything, she wanted to try and protect him. It was a foolish whim because she knew what was safer, and that was Hector keeping close tabs on Walter.

Jim stood in front of her, but his gaze was sharp like a predator looking for prey, swiveling between the doors and rooms around them. Lisa accepted it with a deep sigh and then side stepped towards Jim. Hector seemed to understand the gesture, nodded, and then headed back into the room with Walter. A new blue light came from a monitor. She guessed they were finally getting the computers running.

Jim reached his hand out towards her. "Let's check the filing cabinets in the offices."

She didn't know how cold she was until he took his hand. Even with his cool touch she was now colder, and his gasp felt warming.

They moved over to a table pushed up against another windowed wall. There were a few flashlights that they had left there. This level, most likely because it was more of a lab set up, had few windows. Corners were black and the floors were difficult to distinguish from the walls.

It was a big contrast to the room Hector cleared out for his research. Lisa was up there a few times and remembered how well-lit it was, the chemical smell, and the rows of beakers with pink liquid in them. Although the chemical smell was different than what caused her to almost die before.

The flashlight was self-rechargeable by shaking it. The action of the battery sliding inside a coil created a charge. Jim took it and started shaking it vigorously up and down.

The motion reminded her of something else which made her grin. The area was lit from the lights back down the hall where Hector was, which put dark shadows around them. Despite this, Jim seemed to take notice of her expression.

He smiled. "Get your mind out of the gutter."

She pulled back. "What?"

"I saw that look."

"It's pitch black over here. That's impossible."

His smile widened. "Talent. Not much light in the Outer Rim. You get used to the dark." He seemed playful and happy, but at the mention of the Outer Rim his smile faded.

She could see the lines and features of his face intensify in the shadows.

He kept shaking, but now with his gaze towards the floor. The flashlight made a clattery sound accompanied by a sliding metallic sound of the battery moving inside. Another minute went by and then he flicked the switch.

A bright light, yellowed by old glass, lit up the hallway. Jim waved it around and they both turned, trying to get their bearings. The hall they were in went down to a T, going left and right. They were both quiet as they walked. The right turn looked more like bathrooms, elevator, and emergency exit. The offices seemed to be towards the left, so they headed down that way.

This area was like others frozen in time and dust. Cobwebs clung to corners, but hung tattered, the builders long gone. There was enough dust that just walking the hall was enough to kick it up. It was an irritant, making her nose burn and her mouth taste like dirt.

They followed the hall around into a small office area. There were solid walls with glass doors, and it looked like the only two offices on this level. She thought, for a moment, they could split up, but quickly dismissed it.

"Are you doing okay?" asked Jim.

"Yeah, fine. Just a little creeped out."

"You and me both." He panned the flashlight around the room.

This office had one large desk with a dual monitor computer and an old desk chair with cracked leather. There was a bookcase on the back wall, covered in dust and webs. There was also a line of filing cabinets on the wall to their left.

Now they split, Lisa taking the desk and Jim the filing cabinets. The more they looked around the more they both started to sneeze. The dust was immense. Unlike some of the lower-level rooms, there were no bodies. It looked like this place was closed years ago and never opened again.

It didn't take long to confirm this lab was deep into the genetic study of zombies. The files they found were signed by several different people. This place must have been huge. Lisa flipped through one folder. The pages were yellowed with a few tattered edges that looked like insects might have gotten to it.

She didn't understand most of the files. They were technical and far over her head. There were a few places she could get a general idea. They were definitely doing in-depth research. Things to do with cellular structure and some outlines of mutations.

They spent the rest of the time in the room finding more of the same until they had massive piles of files on the desk and floor. With no real finds the pair retreated to the hallway, where they gasped for cleaner air. It wasn't clean. Everything smelt of years of dust, but the hallway was still better.

After a few gasps they tried getting into the other room. This one had a locked door. It was strange as most areas here were not locked up. When they found that, it seemed that only the outside doors were locked and there were signs that nothing had gotten in for years until recently.

Even then, the few zombies that had broken in recently hadn't touched many areas of the building. It gave her a little bubble of hope that this room might lead to something. Jim handed her the light. His brows were drawn and his gazed focused, like he was on a mission.

"Can you pick the lock?" asked Lisa.

"Don't think I need to." Jim pulled back and then landed a hard kick right by the doorknob.

The whole door rattled and cracked, the locks splintering from the wall. The thick wooden door flew open and slammed into the inside wall.

Lisa felt her eyes widen and her mouth fall open.

Jim turned to her and winked. "I have a few skills."

"I didn't know drop kicking a door was one of them."

"Had a lot of practice on undead." He waved towards the open door. "After you."

She rolled her eyes. "Such a gentleman, for once."

He placed a hand on his chest. "Ouch. That one hurt."

This room was set up similar to the previous one except it had more filing cabinets. Stacks of files laid in the corner of the room. The desk was cluttered with the drawers half open as if someone had moved things in a hurry.

Lisa went to the desk and fanned out some old folders.

"Everything okay?" Hector wrapped his hand around the door

frame and leaned in. It looked like he used the door frame to swing inside.

Lisa jumped, at first only seeing the dark shadow slip in. Realizing it was Hector, her shoulders fell. A good feeling, but one she needed to control as she couldn't keep him at her side all the time. There were things that needed done. "Jim had to break down the door."

"Sorry about that," said Jim. He was further in the room, sweeping it with his flashlight.

"There aren't many rooms that are locked," Hector mumbled.

"A lot more information stored here it seems," said Jim.

Lisa spread out more files, flipping some open that looked more important. With what little light there was she had to wait for Jim to pan over in her direction to read the file labels better.

Hector went to a cabinet in the corner and flicked through the numerous files. "I have been so focused on using the equipment that I didn't even go into some of these rooms," he mumbled.

It didn't take long for Walter to follow inside. "Anything?"

"These files are more promising," said Hector. "Any luck on the computer?"

Walter shook his head. "It looks like they were wiped. I also noticed some areas that seemed ransacked."

"Marco's crew was here, right?" asked Jim.

"Yes. I sent them here with the hopes of gathering information."

"How'd that work for you?" Jim's tone was pointed, like he was trying to make a verbal stab.

"Quite well, in some respects." He cocked his head upwards.

Jim balled his fist and moved towards him with a loud stomp.

Hector moved in a flash, putting himself between the men. "Let's go back," said Hector. "There are other things in that office we haven't checked out yet."

"Fine." Walter was blunt, like usual, but still not rattled.

His calmness was unnerving.

Hector turned towards Lisa. "Be careful." His voice was low, and he spoke quickly before leaving after Walter.

"I hate that man — zombie fuck," said Jim. He uncurled his fists and then took a long breath.

"Hopefully we won't have to deal with him much longer," said Lisa.

They spent a little more time here before the group started bringing things down to the main room. Lisa balanced a large pile of files in her arms. Which, coincidentally, was only half of what Jim held. She stuck her tongue out at him as he passed her going downstairs. He grinned.

Inside the main room she spotted Hector as he was setting down a computer tower. Flint was attaching a battery to a converter to get them powered with Spot circling his legs.

Mariah and Yanika were over by the cooking area talking. Two scrappers had moved to the corner and were playing checkers. Another, a younger guy that was named Charles— Charlie— Chuck, something like that, was sitting by Bruno and they were having a quiet conversation. Eric and Jance were at another table sorting papers into piles.

She and Jim took another table, laying out the files they collected and going through them. Eric and Jance seemed to have a good idea so the two of them also organized them into piles. The information here was immense. Several files were detailed reports on the zombie virus and mutation. Many listed test subjects, giving hint that they used zombies and maybe live humans for research. Chills crawled across her skin as she read.

A computer lit up and the clacking of a keyboard became background noise as their individual piles grew.

"There it is," said Walter. He shoved Hector aside and slipped in towards the table Flint sat at. "This flash drive should have it." He pushed Flint over and stuck it into the USB port in the back of the tower.

The group quieted, with most everyone slipping close to the computer. It was crowded with Hector, Walter, Jim, and herself all trying to get a good look, the others huddled behind.

She had divided her files into two main stacks. One looked like personnel files that listed many government officials that held office before the zombie apocalypse. The other was a compilation of various studies on the virus. The computer had similar information pulled up.

Lisa slid in front of Hector. She was small compared to him, so she didn't block his view. It was a good idea in theory, to be able to get a better view. In execution her body rubbed up against him. Instead of moving and giving her more room, he pressed against her wrapping one arm across her shoulders and the other around her upper chest.

It was a tight embrace, protective, yet it still made warmth flush over her cheeks and the bridge of her nose. It didn't go unnoticed either. Jim's head tilted up and his gaze casually traveled her way. It was enough to attract Walter's attention. He glanced from Jim to her and rolled his eyes.

Lisa's face grew hotter. Embarrassed. There was no doubt that Walter knew exactly what was going on.

"This what we need?" asked Jim.

"What do we got?" Eric's voice drifted up from behind the huddle. Jance and Yanika followed, and the trio huddled up around Jim.

Walter grabbed a handful of files, flung them in front of him, and popped each one open. "It's all here."

What it all meant, Lisa wasn't sure, but there was a pretty blatant picture. Admiral Hammer's file was there listing him as an undercover Japanese operative. The government official files each listed whether payment was received and if it was their file was marked for acceptance to Haven. The genetic testing and lab files listed a first encounter date which was recorded by Admiral Hammer. It wasn't much of a stretch to correlate that with him being there.

The computer had even more information including a whole tracking program outlining the progress of the zombie horde. There were even evacuation requests for various other people with their files marked paid.

The more Lisa read the more she leaned into Hector for support. He kept a tight hold and on occasion gave her shoulder a gentle squeeze. "They knew what was coming so they sold entrance to Haven."

Eric punched his fist into his palm, making a sharp smack sound. "Those bastards. Haven was never about protecting the people."

A low growl from Jim joined the mix. "It was all just a big plan. Admiral Hammer as their agent, the government, rich bastards. It was all of them." He slapped the back of his hand on the files.

Walter kept moving various pieces from other files all together in a pile in front of him. "This is everything I needed."

"You needed?" asked Hector.

"My Lord Liatris needed."

It was the first time Lisa had heard Walter stumble over his words. Her stomach twisted. There was definitely something he wasn't telling them.

HECTOR'S JOURNAL

November 25th, 2043

   I have finally confirmed the basis
behind an interesting finding, that some
zombies bleed, and some don't. The
earlier turned zombies have significantly
higher electrical impulses going from
their brains to their body which partially
circulates blood, and many have shown
signs of advanced healing. I have traced
the increased electrical impulses back to
jellyfish DNA and the enhanced ability
of starfish to heal. The later turned have
significantly less electrical impulses from
the brain which does not circulate blood
causing blood pooling. This includes the
abdomen and limbs. This leads me to
believe that later turned do not bleed,
more exactly, they leak.

Chapter 27

Sleep for Lisa was stressful. Jim slept with her while Hector remained on guard. Just in case, Jim propped a chair against the doorhandle to keep anyone from sneaking in. If Hector wanted in, he was supposed to knock three time. Lisa lay awake most of the night. Which led to a miserable morning. Aching back. Headache. Sore eyes.

They reconvened in the main room. It looked like all the scrappers had slept here. Mariah, Bruno, and Spot were all around the cooking section. Something was sizzling on a hot plate and smelled sweet. The trio separate from the scrappers, Eric, Jance, and Yanika, were sitting at a table thumbing through some files.

Hector was sitting at a table, a pile of records in front of him as well. He seemed immersed in his reading and didn't seem to notice them until Lisa started to sit across from him. He jolted, and then relaxed, as if relieved by her presence.

"Lisa, it's good to see you. You look tired."

"Didn't sleep well."

"I understand." He had his goggles on, obscuring his eyes, but by the way his head moved it looked like he was giving the room a once over.

There was a quiet pause for a minute of two and then Hector suddenly shot up from his seat. His hand grabbed blindly at Lisa's arm over the table, jerking her upright and off her seat. The chair tipped and clattered to the floor. His quick actions caused the entire room to scramble to their feet.

"What is it?" asked Jim.

There was no need for an answer. Just as he spoke the roar of several engines could be heard.

"Scrappers?" asked Flint.

Walter took long strides over to the window. "Most likely the Admiral's forces." He tried to peek out the window, but the tables and bars got in the way. He cursed and stormed towards the door.

Hector side stepped and grabbed the corner of Walter's shirt. He shook his head. "We have too many people here. We need to get them out."

Walter paused and squinted. There was a small silent fight over authority which quickly led to Walter giving a quick nod. "What are you planning?"

"The underground garage is well hidden. I doubt they will find it right away. We can escape there."

Jim stepped up to the pair, throwing his own authority into the mix. "The RV is in no shape to outrun them. I know that sound. They're running jeeps."

"And Humvees," said Eric. "I know for a fact they've been stocking vehicles, making them ready to move into the cities. Unless that RV is magical there is no way we'll outrun them."

"I still have my motorcycle," said Jim. "If we hurry, I could try luring them away."

"It won't work," said Walter. "They're not here for you."

Hector raised his hands, pushing his palms towards both of them. "We can't outrun them. We need to sneak into the city and get everyone out of here."

"I'm not into sneaking," snapped Sam. She was standing now, gun in her hand. It was the first time she'd spoken all morning.

"Enough," said Walter. "We have nowhere near the firepower to combat a full force." He gritted his teeth. "Hector's right."

Yanika ran up to the group. Her eyes were wide and her motions jerky. "What about the evidence? The papers?"

"Grab them," said Walter. "Quickly."

"What about our stuff?" asked Flint.

His voice was a loud outburst which Lisa felt inside. Their stuff. Their home. This little piece of the world they managed to carve out and feel safe in. The thought had almost made her sick before, but now it was here. The end, all over again.

Lisa clenched her fists. It was one thing leaving the cabin. Getting forced from place to place as things got too dangerous. Just surviving. But lately she had been living. That was thanks to friends. Thanks to the men she loved. All that was in danger now.

"You have twenty seconds," snapped Hector. "Grab what you can."

The room exploded into a flurry including members of Walter's crew. Lisa bolted for her room. A metal clatter of canned goods echoed behind her. Inside her room, Lisa closed the distance to her bedside table in a few large steps. They had gotten comfortable here, but not complacent. Her belt lay there, outfitted with her loaded pistol in its holster, a small pouch containing backup magazines, and a sheath for the knife lying beside it.

She snatched her belt off the table and scrambled to put it on as Jim ran up next to her and grabbed his rifle.

"Are you ready for this?" asked Jim.

"I have to be," she exclaimed, slamming the knife home in its sheath.

They didn't take any more time. She didn't look at anything else. Not her new clothes. Not the blankets and plush luxuries. Not the gifts that Hector and Jim gave her. Nothing. This was a time to focus. She could mourn this loss later.

The cluster of people regrouped in the main lobby. Vehicles were sliding into the parking lot now. Tires screeching from abrupt stops.

"Shit," said Sam. "Our Jeep is out there. They'll know we're here."

"All the more reason to make haste," said Hector.

Mariah had her metal medical tin clutched in her hands. She wore her long doctor's coat which had pockets stuffed full of various items. Flint had a backpack slung over his shoulder with the barrel of a rifle poking out from inside. Bruno held a can of beans in each hand. Out of everyone here he looked the most terrified. Eric, Yanika, and Jance seemed to have collected the bulk of the files and threw them into whatever they could find.

"Jim, lead them to the underground exit. I'll cover us," said Hector.

Jim gave a quick nod and took long strides to the back stairwell. Everyone clustered together, making a forced pecking order. Walter was quick on Jim's heels with Sam behind him. Eric, Yanika, and Jace were next followed by the other three scrappers that were with him. Lisa stayed back, letting Mariah, Bruno, Flint, and Spot go in front. That put her right before Hector. It was an optimal place. She felt both safe, but also confident that if anything happened, she could help. This time, she was going to do something. She was ready to take a stand and not be the damsel in distress.

They narrowed down single file at the stairway and were halfway down before something banged on the front doors. Half of the party in front of her jumped. She kept her hand on her gun. The hallway, windowless and powerless, was pitch black.

Jim popped a glowstick, giving the narrow metal hallway a sickly green hue. They were smashed together. Lisa could smell the spice from Hector's cologne mix with the thick stench of unbathed skin, made more intense by the tight space.

Speed was now a priority and the group clattered down like a herd of cattle. Each clank of metal on metal or hard foot falls made her tense. The pounding kept coming from above as the intruders were still trying to penetrate the door. It was made to keep out a mindless hoard, but not an army that knows what they're doing.

They descended towards the basement. As it was a parking garage the last story was tall and the steps steep. Footfalls became heavier and uncoordinated as the group pushed against each other. The stairs ended in a metal door with a small broken glass window.

Jim shoved it open, revealing a vast ocean of darkness. His glowstick gave off so little light that not everyone could fit inside the perimeter of its greenish glow. Lisa held back with Hector behind her. It gave the others more room. Flint, seeming to understand the gesture, fell back as well. The light just barely lighting Lisa's and Flint's face. Spot bounded a few steps forward, but as soon as he looked back at the trailing group, he turned and bounded back to them. Hector was lost in the darkness with only the sound of his steps and smell of his cologne to remind Lisa he was still nearby.

"Where are we going?" Walter hissed.

"The exit is over here," said Jim.

They moved through the open space in a diamond formation, Jim being the point. The spear cutting the darkness. All the steps together echoed over the concrete perimeter making a pounding parade that continued on over the expanse. Anyone near had to have heard them. Never did she think that she would be running through the dark more afraid of the living than the dead.

Jim reached the end of the parking garage. His glow stick shown on a door with an old, faded exit sign on it. To his left were the solid metal garage doors. The door had a heavy metal lock and two additional ones that Jim had installed since they arrived.

With a clattering of overly loud latches the door finally swung open. The creaking of the old hinges was so loud it made her cringe. Jim pulled up his rifle and stepped out. His movements were slow. Walter went out next, sliding to the right out of her sight.

She breathed, relying on sound. The others funneled out, making their way left. Midday sun struck her eyes like a spotlight. She lifted a hand to shield out the light. The cool brisk air nipped at her skin. Side stepping, she joined the rest of them, back up against the garage doors.

The vehicles above were still running and the engine hum drifted to her. She glanced to the right up the concrete alley. Exhaust made light clouds from the back of a truck. She couldn't see anything else, and it didn't seem like anyone was there.

Walter stepped away from the building, clenched his fist, and pulled it towards him.

"What are you doing?" Hector hissed, his tone just above a whisper.

"I'm buying us time."

Hector stepped forward, stretching to his full height. "You're going to get people killed."

"But we'll be alive."

"I can't let you do that."

Flint leaned towards Lisa. "What the hell are they doing?"

She shook her head. The movement more of a thrash from one side to the other. Every muscle was tight. She pressed her finger against the gun's upper slide to keep it away from the trigger just in case she accidentally jerked. The combination of a rising heartbeat and sudden cardio had her ribs burning.

A voice cut through everything, and she gasped.

"Hey, you!"

Someone in black tactical gear appeared by the tailgate up the alley.

Walter spun towards them. "Run!"

That one command was enough to send humans bounding like frightened deer. Spot barked, riled by the commotion but unknowing what was to come. Hector took large leaps to get to their side, acting like a rancher herding cattle. Jim made it to the end of the building first. As he did, he pulled up his rifle.

A gunshot skipped off the concrete near him. He returned fire.

The other scrappers moved around him and opened fire. Lisa pulled up her pistol and made a move to join them when a bullet bounced off the building up the alley. She turned, catching more people spilling out from behind the truck. Guns readied.

Another barrage of fire broke out. Bullets flew around her. Hitting metal. Skipping across concrete. She went to return fire when Hector leapt in front of her. Crouched. Arms up, like he planned to be her shield.

"Move!" She couldn't get a good line of sight.

Screams came from behind her. She turned again. Blood was splattered everywhere. One of the scrappers fell to the side. Limp. Sam screamed. Bullets flew in. Bang. Bang. Bang. Three more shots skipping across the concrete by her feet.

There was a wet gargled sound. She glanced over her other shoulder in time to see another of the scrappers go down. Walter pushed in, forcing Sam to the wall with himself out like a meat shield.

Mariah screamed. "No. No. No."

Lisa whipped around to look over her other shoulder. Flint staggered around to face her. His hand on his chest. Blood coated him. Chest. Mouth. Dripping to the ground.

"Flint?" Her voice cracked. Suddenly the pounding in her head muffled everything.

Bullets flew over them, each round glinting in the sunlight. They were sandwiched. Fire coming in from both fronts. Sam let out an enraged scream.

Yanika. Jace. Bruno. Mariah scrambled to catch Flint. His body falling towards her. His gaze fixed on Lisa. He grinned as he went down. Bits of cement flew into the air. Tiny pieces of shrapnel.

The figures around her blurred together. How many were still alive? How many dead? This is where everything led to. This was the price of freedom. The price of trying to put down some roots. To live without fear. And it wasn't even zombies. It wasn't other scrappers just trying to survive. No. Military. Like nothing in the world really changed. Just the political dynamics.

Flint was done for. The look in his face. He knew it. She knew it. Chest shot. At their best they didn't have the medical supplies to save him. Mariah screamed. She was clambering to stop his fall and still clutch her medical supplies. She would try to save him. But it wouldn't work.

Lisa turned to the approaching forces. They were a decent distance. Their weapons shit. Just like their aim. And they had the audacity to fire on them. She raised her pistol and let loose her own retort. Each bullet laced with her anger. Dripping with anguish. Her aim fueled with revenge.

She shoved Hector aside, no longer letting him get in her way. Five men versus her. Decent odds. Three rounds and one fell. Two more and another. The fire continued. She felt a bullet whiz by her face. She didn't blink. In what felt like time had frozen she fired her whole magazine, but she wasn't done.

Magazine ejected, she slapped another in and continued. Pushed forward. Popping round after round. Taking down the last of the five. Not stopping. It wasn't enough to wound them. They shot Flint, so she was going to take every one of them down. Even when she ran out, she continued to pull the trigger. The gun clicking. Dry firing.

Hector's hand came down on hers. "Enough."

She shook, unwilling to stop. Still pulling the trigger.

"They're dead. You can stop."

She turned to him, shaking. His poncho was coated with blood. "You're hurt," she squeaked.

"I'm fine." He grabbed her and pulled her to him. Embracing her tightly, then he pulled away just as quickly.

"Hang in there," said Mariah. "Just hang in there." Her voice was high and cracked.

Sam still screamed, raking her clawed hands across her face. Jim lowered his rifle and pushed past the others towards Flint. He looked at the body and then to Lisa. Both of them acknowledging they could not save him.

Jim's brows dropped. He hesitated, leaning towards her and then back several times. Gunfire continued, but she didn't hear the bullets pelting around them anymore. Screams that drowned out their own came from up around the lab building.

Hector made a quick motion towards Walter with his fist raised.

"It had to be done," Walter snapped.

"What's happening? What's going on?" Yanika spun in place, sandwiched between Eric and Jance.

"I've ordered the surrounding horde to engage them. That will buy us time." Walter's fierce gaze traveled from Hector to the ground where his men lay. He snatched Sam's arm and pulled her away. "They're beyond saving. Leave them."

"Fuck!" she screamed.

Mariah had half a roll of gauze pressed against Flint's chest. Blood had already soaked it through and pooled on the ground. "No! No, it can't end like this." Mariah shook her head. Tears rolling down her cheeks. Her whole body quivering.

"We need to take this opportunity to get out of here," said Walter.

"We can't leave him!" Mariah screamed.

"He's dead. Dead is dead. Even a zombie can't save him," Walter growled.

Jim shoved his way through to her side. He gripped her shoulder and gave her a gentle shake. "If we don't go, we'll lose more people. We have to take care of the living now."

"I... I'm a doctor... I'm supposed to save people..."

"Save the ones standing here. We need you."

It took some coercion, but she moved away from Flint's body. "We can't leave him here like this."

Jim put his hand on her back, pushing her away. He slung his rifle over his shoulder and then grabbed Bruno as well. "We have to. I know, it sucks, but we need to move."

Sam followed close behind Walter. Eric and Jance kept Yanika between them and guided her in the same direction. Spot was limping and whimpering, his shaggy coat covered in blood.

Jim paused, glancing from Hector back towards Walter and Sam.

"Where are you going?" asked Hector.

"My Lady Victoria's nest is not far. That will be our safest place."

Hector didn't respond, but he did nod to Jim before wrapping his arm around Lisa. "Are you okay?" he whispered.

"I'm fine. But we need to get you somewhere safe."

A soft sad smile crossed his face. "Don't worry about me."

Screams and gunfire continued from above, now mixed with shrieks and moans. It was the undeniable sound of an enraged horde. No matter how many people were up there, they were no match for that kind of force.

"I tried to turn them away," Hector mumbled. "Why... Walter's orders went over mine—"

He was cut off as Spot bumped into his leg.

The group darted across the road and continued weaving from building to building. The war behind them growing quieter. But they were not alone. Every shadow had movement. Faces in windows. Shifting creatures in every crack and crevice. Walter must have only called on part of the horde because this place was infested. Zombies thick like lice.

Hector kept her close to his side. His wings were flared, protecting her back. She was out of ammo so anything from here would be an outright brawl. She holstered her pistol as they walked and pulled her knife.

Jim kept Mariah and Bruno moving forward, Spot guarding their side. They traveled blocks like that. Silent except for soft sobs from various members of the group. Like a yawn it was contagious. One whimper made the others break.

Lisa felt numb. Her ribs. Her back. Every muscle just tense and like plaster that had hardened inside of her. The pain was somewhere, but all she could feel was the weight. They ended up cutting right through downtown. Large buildings towered in pieces. Windows broken with moss and vines pouring out through them. Foundations cracked.

Piles of rubble that they had to clamber over. The concrete roads were broken with tall grass growing up through them. Street signs were bent and aged from time.

To add to the decimation, they cut through a suburban area. Homes left to rot. Some cars crashed around the expanse and others just abandoned. Swing sets creaking in the breeze, void of all living things. A modern-day ghost town. She could see signs of the people once here who most certainly died. Toys. Playgrounds. Trash cans overturned with plants growing out of them. The horror reclaimed by nature, like a bad attempt from the world to throw a Band-Aid over the scar. They had a thick, overgrown hedge to get through before coming out on a four-lane road.

Walter pointed ahead. "There. That's where we're headed."

"To a mall?" asked Eric. He stepped up a few feet, leaving Yanika's side for the first time.

"Correct," said Walter. "My Lady likes things a little finer and a mall has presented as the perfect lair."

"Are we going to be safe there?" asked Yanika.

"Quite," said Walter. "My Lady has no use for turning anyone into some mindless monster."

Hector remained silent and when Walter moved, he followed. Jim continued to take cues from him, frequently glancing at Lisa.

Lisa didn't care where they ended up. She just needed everything to stop for a moment. A safe place to regroup her thoughts. *But is any place really safe anymore?*

They walked right to the front doors. More figures moved, but they did not look like mutated monsters. Some were disfigured, but not grotesquely. The mall front was broken, glass doors shattered. Broken furniture was in a pile out in a parking spot.

Walter, in the lead, strode right through the front. Sam followed. The ones inside separated, making a wide path for them. Everyone slowed and moved to follow. Jim and Eric were especially on edge. Their heads swiveling around to take in the ones around them. The zombies.

Most of them were men, well chiseled. Each had their own handsome feature from strong jawlines to perfect abs. Almost all looked human and the ones that were different looked almost like someone had put a costume on them.

A few had tails that bobbed behind them and others had wings and animal-like ears. If this was before the end of the world it would have looked like a haunted house party.

Many of the shops had broken windows, but the place was surprisingly clean. The tiled floors were free of debris. Seating areas were arranged with rugs and decorations. A few men were off to the side at a large table playing some kind of board game. They cast curious looks at the group, but none of them showed any signs of aggression.

Is that because of Walter or Hector, or are they just like this? More like Hector is? They traveled down a long-broken escalator and down to what looked like it once was a food court. There was a huge couch at one end where a woman sat, surrounded by other men. Rugs were laid out all across the expanse. Desks, stands, and tables were all placed around with various decorations piled on them. Eloquently placed mannequins modeled fancy prom dresses. Despite no windows, the expanse was well lit. Lamps, lanterns, and candles were scattered everywhere.

Walter raised a hand and everyone behind him stopped while he continued forward. Before the woman he knelt.

When she stood, it didn't take much of a guess to realize she had to be Victoria. She stood well over Walter with a curvaceous figure and large bust accentuated by a tight cream-colored dress. Dark wavy hair cascaded over her shoulders. She had sharp cheeks bones, pale skin, and piercing dark eyes.

"What's the meaning of this?" she asked as she scanned the group.

"We were forced from the lab by Haven forces. We came—"

She pushed past him, shoving an open hand towards Hector which made Walter instantly go silent. Her heels hit on the occasionally exposed tiled floor with a loud clack. "Hector, it's been a long time."

Hector lowered his head as she approached. "Victoria, you are looking well."

She was tall enough to match Hector's height. Intimidating from a distance, yes, but when she moved next to Lisa she felt herself cowering. The woman had a thin tail, horns, and large bat-like wings tucked in behind her. It was like the most sexual and intimidating Halloween costume anyone could have ever dreamt up.

"You look like trash," said Victoria. She took a painted nail and picked at a bloody spot on Hector's poncho.

"We need a safe place to regroup," said Hector.

She flicked the piece of dried blood off her finger and scoffed. "I should have known nothing would go smoothly."

Just as she had approached, she strode back to her couch. Her presence alone forcing everyone to give her a wide birth. Walter stayed in a knelt position, his gaze fixed on the black and gold swirled rug beneath him.

"I suppose all is well. You're not in the lab anymore," Victoria muttered.

"Me?" asked Hector.

"Yes, you," she said, purring as she spoke. She raised a fine brow. "Liatris made me get you out of there. The fool gets himself a woman and can't even follow through with his obligations."

"Emily, I'm assuming," said Hector.

"I think that was her name. Pretty little thing. He should turn her before that face starts to age. He'd be doing her a favor."

Jim leaned towards her. Lisa could see his neck muscles tightened.

"Why did Liatris want me out of there?" asked Hector.

"You were in the way of him getting..." She rolled her eyes. "Some information he wanted. I don't know. I'm not interested in his petty feuds."

"Yet here you are," said Hector.

Her eyes slowly tracked to him. Lisa felt it, cold chills darting down her back.

"Be careful. Don't give me a headache." She looked at his injuries and half her lip curled up. "You all are disgusting. Walter."

"Yes, my lady."

"Get our guests a room and make sure they can wash up. They stink."

"Yes, my lady."

Lisa had never seen Walter so submissive. It came as a shock, which she tried to keep hidden. It felt like every minute motion was being tracked. All the eyes around them taking note of every little detail.

Walter stood and turned, taking a quick glance Sam's way. She followed right in line with him with her head lowered.

"Follow me," said Walter to the rest of them.

There was no protest from anyone. The silent group all seeming in shock and following him like mindless... zombies. It was a term that no longer held the same meaning. Zombies were better than people. People were more dangerous than zombies. It made her head throb, the first sensation she felt through their entire walk here that really registered.

Walter led them through the mall into a small sports store. He moved around, flipping on some battery lights that cast small white glows around the space. This place had also been cleaned. Floors were cleared. Many of the sporting items were stacked up behind the front desk. It also had a back room positioned towards on end behind another desk.

"You all can stay here," said Walter. "I'll get the others to arrange food, places to sleep..." he raised a brow. "A bath."

Hector lowered his head. This time it looked more like a soft bow in Walter's direction. "Thank you."

Walter also seemed to soften. His harsh greater-than-thou exterior shed. He looked tired now, with dark shadows cast across his face from the dim lamp light. It was still day, but little light penetrated the darkened mall.

Walter turned to Sam and put a hand on her shoulder. "You should stay here as well. I'll go get whatever you need."

"A drink," she muttered, her speech broken.

"Done. I'll grab you something sweet as well. And don't forget to eat." He leaned in and gave her a peck on the cheek.

Lisa stood, stunned at what she witnessed. She didn't think the man was capable of emotion. Observing the group was her way of avoiding any of her own feelings. Disassociating. Acting like a fly on the wall that was just a witness, not a victim.

When Walter left, Sam snatched up a sports hoodie, slid onto the checkout counter, and laid back using the hoodie as a pillow.

Eric, Jance, and Yanika huddled down on the floor, leaning against the back wall. To their right were two dark changing rooms.

Jim had gotten Mariah and Bruno to the other side where the wall was made to have shelves at coffee table height for displaying items. It was cleaned off, so he sat Mariah down there. Her face was beat red as were her eyes. Tears had streaked through dirt down her cheeks and her clothes were coated in dried blood. She didn't have her med kit anymore either. They must have left it behind.

Bruno was just a statue, that Jim moved and posed as desired. Bruno's gaze was so distant and devoid that he looked more like a mannequin in the store. Jim was still strong. Focused.

Looking around the room she caught the reflection of herself with Hector behind her. It pulled her back into reality. She was there. This was real. Flint was dead. All at once she felt gut shot. She hugged herself, bending forward. No, falling. Her knees were rubber. Tears were ready to explode.

Long thin arms wrapped around her and lowered her to the floor.

"Take it easy," Hector whispered.

He crouched down behind her. Holding her tightly. Lisa rocked herself back and forth, reliant on his grasp to keep her from falling face first to the floor.

"Breathe," said Hector.

"He's... Flint's gone."

Hector was silent. Like he didn't have anything else comforting to say. The emotions once dead inside her were breaking to the surface with all the violence of a raging storm. With everyone so close, all mourning, she screamed silently. Her mouth open but not making a sound on the outside. On the inside she wailed with all her strength. She could hear the scream in her head. Felt it vibrate through her. But it was silent to the rest of the world.

It wasn't long before there were more footsteps coming towards them. Lisa kept her blurred vision to the floor. Not caring who it was or why.

"You all look like you've been through a lot," said a soft sweet female voice.

There was a rustle on the other side of the room before Eric spoke. "It's been a very... intense day."

"We brought some bandages, water, food. Liam grabbed some blankets and pillows as well. It's not much, but if you give us a list, we'll try and get whatever you need."

"Clean clothes," said Jim. "Maybe another couple of lamps. I don't know how long the batteries last."

"We can do that. The mall has plenty of clothes. Think you and the guys can handle that?"

An accented male voice chimed in. "Shouldn't be a problem."

Irish. It was a strange thing to note, but that's what popped in her head.

She still had her back to them, but heard the clunk-clunk of something that sounded like plastic jugs with liquid getting set down.

"This one is for drinking," said the woman. "The other three with the tape over the tops are so you can wash up. Here are some rags and towels."

Hector shifted behind her. "Thank you. And thank Lady Victoria for her kindness."

"I will do that, Lord Hector."

Lisa's eyes widened. Bloodshot and teary, the motion made them burn. She never heard anyone address him like that. Lord. He was a

First Turned. A Lord. She knew it, but it still stunned her. She knew the group left by the foot falls that drifted off in the distance.

"How about we both get cleaned up," said Hector.

Lisa opened her mouth, but nothing came out.

Hector hooked his arms around her and pulled her to her feet. He pointed at the back room behind the front desk. "Let's go in there."

She didn't argue. He did have to help her walk as she still was fighting part of her body feeling limp and other parts feeling numb.

The back room was larger than expected with racks on all sides that sported various old shoe boxes and some stacks of shirts. It appeared to be the storeroom. Inside also was a small wooden bench. The kind you would find in clothing stores where people could sit to try shoes on.

Hector sat her there and then disappeared back to the main area. The lamp light was very dim here, as it just barely came around the corner from the front desk. She blinked a few times, trying to adjust her already blurry vision. The floor didn't feel like the rest, and she couldn't quite see why, but after rubbing her shoes against it she guessed it was a dark colored rug.

Hector returned with piles of various things in his arms which he sat on the floor next to her. One of them was a glow stick which he cracked and set to the side. It was blue and cast a strange hue around the space. The pile looked to be washcloths, towels, a small red med bag, a jug of water, a metal bowel, and something wrapped in plastic.

"Let's get cleaned up first. Were you injured at all?"

Lisa didn't move at first. It took a while for her to process he was even talking. When it did sink in, all she could do was shake her head. He was hurt though. There was a huge blood stain on his poncho. She remembered now he had been shot.

"Yo— your— you're hurt," she muttered.

"Not bad."

She reached forward and touched lightly near the tear in the material. He grabbed her fingers and leaned in to give them a kiss. His thin lips were cool, but the sensation made her warm.

They went silent, which was a relief because it took everything within her to try and force out sensible words. Hector pulled off his poncho and set it to the side and the removed his tattered gray shirt. They were both bloodstained from what she could now see was a bullet wound in his shoulder.

He took to the medicine bag and turned from her. "I need to get the bullet out," he whispered. "Then will you help me bandage it?"

"Of course," she said with a gasp. She pushed herself up, still feeling the lack of working joints in her body. She took his shoulder and pressed her body close to his, trying to give him support like he did her. She waited, unable to even look at what he was doing. Just the thought of him digging a bullet from his shoulder himself made her want to cry.

She felt him move and then he hissed. She flinched, imagining the pain he must be in.

It took a little bit before he spoke. "I'm okay."

She pulled away and lowered herself down on her knees as he turned to face her. The blue light of the glow stick highlighted his thin lankly body. The bullet wound was round and seeping dark blood. She hadn't seen him bleed much and this reminded her of how different he was from her. His blood was dark and thick. From what he explained before only the first few zombies turned were even capable of bleeding. It was because the high electrical impulses that kept them moving often would keep a mild amount of blood flow going as well. They by no means needed blood to survive.

"What do you need me to do?" she asked. It was the first time she could force out a whole sentence.

Hector grabbed a washcloth off the floor and handed it to her. "Can you help clean me up?"

"Yes. Of course, I can." She grabbed the jug of water and pulled the tape off the top. Wetting the rag, she began to clean him. She felt his boney structure. Although he had a long trunk, it was still proportional to him. Like a tall basketball player.

He knelt in front of her, silent. As she began to move up towards his shoulder, she noted something on his face and wiped that away. The cloth moving against his smooth features. She paused a moment just too take in how he looked.

She took his hat off and set it on the bench behind her. He had no hair, and his head was round. It made the goggles he wore look bulky and out of place. She slid her fingertips along the band to the back of his head. Her body was hot. Her breasts tingling. All the pain, sorrow, and loss pushed far back in her mind that only desire remained. Desire for any positive sensation. Desire to never think of those things again.

Her insides tensed. Between her legs felt damp and hot. She took his goggles and slowly pulled them off. Once she had thought Hector to be featureless, but now she knew him so much better. His black eyes, larger than a normal human's, were sad. Fixated on her. He had no eyebrows, but his browline was still crinkled inwards. Deep concern set on his face.

She leaned in, almost close enough to touch. He still held that spicy smell she loved. A scent she associated with safety. Warmth. Her hands ran from his shoulders inward across his chest. Feeling his defined collar bone. His ribs. Down to his stomach where his pelvic bones made a V down into his pants.

He lowered his head and took her hands, pulling her off of him. "If you continue my reaction will not be appropriate to this endeavor."

She glanced, catching sight of the bulge in his pants. It only made it hotter. The others were just outside the room. They had to whisper just to make sure they weren't heard. Her own heartbeat drowned out any noise out there. The heat building inside her made so she didn't care.

She pushed towards him, getting her lips right next to his head. "I want you."

"Now isn't the time," he whispered back.

"Please. I... I need something good. I need you."

He shifted, lowering his head down to her shoulder. "I never want to tell you no, but I also do not want to do anything to you that you may regret."

"I won't regret this."

He let out a breath. That little sound he made, not because he needed to breathe, but a sound that seemed to be his way of communicating so much without a word. He ran his long fingers down her back.

"Do you truly want this?"

"Yes."

He took off her top slowly, exposing her breasts. She hadn't had time for a bra before they left. Her tender buds were hard. Tingles crossing her chest. Next, he just as slowly and gently removed her pants. Stripping her down completely naked.

His top was already off, but removing his pants over his long legs was awkward. It didn't take him long before he sat back down. Stripped to the flesh as she was. Exposed.

Hector pulled her into his lap, long ribbed shaft pressed against her. His large form compared to her was able to cradle her body. "If you make a sound they will hear."

She pressed her lips together and shook her head.

He looked hesitant, but his member throbbed against her. It was obvious he was fighting his own desires against what he thought was right. And maybe it wasn't, but she wanted him.

"I'll be gentle," he whispered. His words so hushed she wasn't sure if he spoke or if she just read his lips.

He lifted her up, clutching both her cheeks, and poised her over his shaft. All thirteen ribbed inches. She'd felt him inside her from the back, but not like this. The anticipation made her insides throb. She could feel the hot liquid from her core start to run down her inner thigh.

He lowered her slowly. His tip sliding against her lips to her opening. Hector kept his gaze fixated on her as he began to lower.

The tip penetrated and slipped inside. She tilted her head back, wanting to moan, but stifled any sound. She reached for his arms. So very slowly he lowered her. Her body ratcheting down each ridge of his shaft. It was so different than anything she'd felt in her life. And the ridges were just right that every one of them brushed her G-spot.

A couple inches, and then three, four. He kept lowering until she realized just how massively long he was. His tip hit her core and he wasn't even halfway inside. She felt the pressure. It burned a little, but also made her more aroused. Wet. Throbbing.

Hector was tense, his gaze locked on her. Watching every movement. He lifted her up. A slow motion that made every ridge notch rub inside her. Then back down, all the way to her core again. Pressing against it. Her heart was racing. She never thought keeping quiet would be so hard. She wanted to moan. Wanted to scream. Wanted to beg him. More. More. More.

He kept everything slow and controlled, lifting her up again with ease and then back down, pressing at the end again until she took another inch of his length. It felt like he was shifting her insides around. He continued. Up and down. Up and down. Each ridge sending jolts of pleasure though her. Each time at the end he pressed to get deeper inside of her.

The end hurt a little each time, but she felt him stretch her. Felt him getting deeper each time. He was wrestling her cervix for space. No matter how much it burned she wanted more. Wanted to take him. All of him. But he was driving her whole body crazy. Hot. Throbbing.

She moved her hands to his shoulders and squeezed. "More. Please." She whispered, trying with everything she had to keep as quiet as possible.

He lifted her again and then back down. Faster. Harder. His tip slammed into her core this time. She flinched.

"Did I hurt you?" he whispered in her ear.

"More." That's all she could choke out without letting herself freely moan.

He raised her up and down again. And again. And again. Faster. Harder. Hitting her core every time, but somehow slowing just before impact so that it was a pleasurable burn. She took more and more of him inside of her. She felt him stir her insides. His shaft was poking through, making her belly bulge from his length.

Looking down, she could see each thrust as it moved her insides around, his shaft a visible bulge in her midrift. He continued moving her with ease. Using her like a little toy casually bouncing up and down.

His brows were taut. His grip tight on her. She felt his shaft getting thicker. His length was starting to swell. Stretch her. She had almost all of him inside of her. The last few inches she just couldn't take, but he kept trying to push inside. Hitting every sensitive spot over and over. She was so wet that both her thighs were soaked. Dripping.

He was moving faster and faster. She mouthed to him. I'm going to cum. I'm going to cum. His motions went faster. With four hard thrusts until he pushed her down on him. She felt him explode inside of her right on her core and lost it.

She came with such force her body jerked. Waves of heat and pleasure rippling through her. Her inside stretching as he filled her up with his seed. Her head fell forward towards his chest. Her body convulsing.

The pain left her body. Thoughts. Memories. She floated for a moment and in that moment nothing else existed. It was the best she'd felt in a long time. Purposefully, she grounded herself in this moment. She made herself forget and just enjoy this time. This pleasure.

Hector was also shaking. His body. His hands. His eyes were closed, and his head tilted back. His wings twitching, occasionally making a soft buzz that he seemed to still quickly each time.

Jim came around the corner to their small space. Lisa jerked up, eyes wide. Her first instinct was they were caught, but that faded fast.

"I see what's taking so long," said Jim. He grinned. "Hector, you've been shot. Let me help." He spoke loudly before moving in.

Lisa still was in Hector's lap with his length inside of her. Jim came around behind her and moved so that his lips were next to her face. "Having fun without me, I see."

"I—"

He cut her off by reaching his hand around and covering her mouth. "Nod if you would be willing to go another round."

Another round? Now? I just came. She stiffened a moment. Thinking it over, but her body was still hot. Hector was still hard. Pleasure was still raking through her.

She nodded.

"Hector," said Jim. "May I help?"

There was playful inuendo in his tone and she guessed how loud words were chosen for eavesdropping ears.

Hector nodded. "Of course. Just, be gentle."

Be gentle. What are these men up to?

Jim pulled away. She glanced over her shoulder to see him strip. His thick length was already rock hard.

Lisa was still straddling Hector, facing him, with Hector's hands on her cheeks supporting her weight so she didn't just fall on the last few inches she couldn't take.

Jim came up right behind her and pressed his hot length to her back. "I was worried you two might have been badly hurt," he whispered. "But seeing this made me so hard." He wrapped his hand around her mouth again. "You have to be quiet, is that okay?"

She nodded.

"If you need me to stop all you have to do is pull my hand away. Understand?"

She nodded, but this time tremored with small electrical shocks going through her body.

Jim positioned himself behind and she expected they would take a similar position as last time.

She jerked when she felt his tip at her folds like he planned to enter the same place as Hector.

Her eyes widened. There was no way she could fit both men inside of her.

"Relax," Jim whispered. "I'll go slow."

Relaxing was far from possible. She was already so tight from just having an orgasm. Hector was buried inside of her. She was still dripping where he filled every bit of her insides. Jim's tip rubbed around the wetness a few times before coming to the entrance. He pushed, trying to make his way into the same space as Hector.

She felt herself start stretching like she never had felt before. It burned. He was going ever so slowly, pushing just to penetrate. He was trying to completely ruin her.

Lisa lowered her head, but nodded at the same time so he wouldn't stop. It hurt, but she wanted to take him. Wanted to take them both. So focused on all these sensations. All her mind could do was scream they both couldn't fit.

Jim kept pushing until his tip popped inside. She jerked, feeling her entrance stretched to its max. She kept her hands on Hector. Jim's hand on her mouth. She knew why now. He pushed a little further inward. Stretching. Pushing her beyond her max. She thought just taking Hector's length was impossible. Now she was taking both men at the same time, the same hole.

Hector had a tight hold on her, keeping himself buried deep as Jim took her from behind. He was ever so slow. So careful. They both seemed overly aware of her every reaction, adjusting accordingly.

She was so wet, Jim was sliding in with ease. Little by little. Pushing. Stretching. Ruining her. His tip went further inside of her. He didn't try to smother her with his hand, but kept it against her lips. She had control of this. It didn't scare her in a way that made her want to stop. But her heart pounded, unsure if she could take them both.

Jim went deeper. His head forcing Hector's hard length aside. Stretching her all the way around. "Is this okay?" Jim whispered in her ear.

She waited a moment. When she didn't respond right away both men froze. Finally, after a few breaths, she nodded.

Something changed because Hector started lifting her up and down in small motions. Dragging her inside across them both. Jim's thickness made Hector's length push harder against her G-spot. It was immense pleasure. Too much to take. She was gushing fluid. Some of hers. Some was Hector's seed being pushed out to make more room for the pair of men to enter her.

Jim was shorter and he shoved his whole length inside of her. Hector's cock bulging through her stomach like he might just poke through.

She held onto Hector tightly, just trying to stay on for the whole ride as they both destroyed her. She didn't want to just explode right there. She wanted to enjoy it. Wanted to continue a while, but she felt her insides grow tighter. An orgasm right on the brink.

She couldn't take it any longer and tried to warn Hector with her eyes. She was getting tighter. And tighter. And they were getting harder inside of her. She was going to break. Rip. Explode. She couldn't take it any longer and lost it. Cumming so hard on their cocks that her insides just burst.

Jim let out a small groan and shoved his whole shaft inside of her and exploded. In doing so Hector let loose another time. The two men dumped all their seed inside of her and the space already stretched to the max couldn't contain it. She felt the hot rush and all their juice explode out of her. Gushing down her leg.

Jim still had his hand over her mouth which was the only thing that kept her from letting out a gasp. Maybe a scream. She fell forward onto Hector. Her whole body convulsing with pleasure. Everything floating for a moment. Spots danced across her vision. This was much more intense than the last time.

"Breathe," Hector whispered, though his voice was strained.

Jim leaned in and pressed his body against her. The small motion made her tense again. Another convulsion of pleasure taking her body. "I'm going to stay here until you're ready." Jim pulled his hand away.

Her first reaction was to gasp. She held her breath a moment to stop it. The feeling of euphoria lasted. She didn't know how long she stayed there, Hector holding her. He still kept her up and prevented her from falling those last few inches she couldn't take. Or could she? She wasn't sure anymore.

Jim was inside her, but he was softening. The pressure on her insides was decreasing. Both men were getting smaller, and each little twitch made her convulse.

"I'm going to pull out," Jim whispered. He didn't wait for an answer as he slipped out.

There was a wet sound and more liquid fell from her insides. They ruined her. Filled her. She was gushing. Jim clattered around, getting a few things. Lisa kept her head resting on Hector. Just breathing. Just letting her body relax. The pleasure remained. Happiness. Comfort. It was all washing around inside of her hot body.

"Let's get you cleaned up," said Hector.

Jim wrapped his arms around her from behind and Hector shifted to help. Jim lifted her from Hector's length. She was destroyed, still dumping their seed from inside of her. She couldn't stand, but somehow he got her sitting on the bench.

"Well, Hector's finally taken care of," said Jim. Again, he was loud as if he was trying to cover up what they were really doing. "Now, we better get you cleaned up, Lisa."

He wasn't talking about a bath. Her eyes widened as she stared at him. They'd destroyed her. What else could they do? Jim walked over and knelt in front of her. "I'll take care of this," he said, pointing at her pussy. "Hector, you want to take care of that?" He then pointed to her breasts.

"Are you sure?" asked Hector, looking to Lisa.

She wiggled back and forth, fighting desire, shock, and still trying to process how they just kept making her cum. She licked her lips and looked down at Jim between her legs.

He grinned. "You'll feel better afterwards."

"Oh... Okay."

Jim waved Hector forward and then put his finger on her tender breast. "You work there." He scooted back and then bent down, his gaze still up and locked on her. His voice dropped to low growl just loud enough she could hear. "Don't make a sound."

Before she could reply he leaned down and ran his tongue through her folds. Her head jerked back. Everything was so sensitive that it made her whole body jolt.

Hector took his cue. He seemed less hesitant and instead hungry. His shaft hardened. He lowered himself, taking one of her hard tender buds into his mouth. His tongue alternated between lapping it and circling the sensitive area.

Jim kept exploring with his tongue as well, slurping her juices and then pushing his tongue inside of her. Before two orgasms it would be pleasurable, but after she was so sensitive that every movement made her want to gasp.

Hector reached for her other breast and fondled it. The two sensations were meeting in the middle as her inside tightened again.

"But... It's dirty..." she managed to whisper between breaths.

"I don't care," said Jim. "I love you. All of you." He went back down on her.

Hector pulled away for a brief moment. "As do I."

It was so warming as she fell into the sea of pleasure as he returned his mouth to her breasts.

Jim was speaking Latin against her tender bud. Up. Down. Around. Playing her with his tongue like a controller. She was jerking against him. Making him plunge his tongue inside of her.

He came up, stretching back enough she could see his length was hard once more. He grabbed it and pointed the tip towards her. "May I?"

She clenched her jaw and nodded.

Jim moved him, putting his tip against her again. He paused there, taking her hand, and then resting it on Hector's shaft. She felt the hard ribs. The wet skin. Wet from what they just did. "You handle that," Jim whispered. "I'll handle you."

Jim pressed inside of her. From being so stretched he penetrated her with ease and suddenly his entire length was buried inside of her. He grabbed her hip, pulling her forward and tightly against him.

She tried to stroke Hector, but she couldn't think. Couldn't control any movement. Jim paused, deep inside of her. "We've almost pushed you to the brink. Let's change positions."

She couldn't speak. Only watched. Jim gestured to Hector to move away and then he sat beside her. He made a motion with his hands to Hector. They must have understood each other because Hector came over and helped lift her. Jim slid under her, and Hector helped lower her onto his shaft and into his lap.

Hector then moved in and took her breasts, pressing each one to the sides of his length. Jim made small thrusts inside of her, pushing against her core. Hector made long strokes, making the ribs of his shaft move up and down between her breasts. A new sensation. Somehow these two men found another way to pleasure her.

She was seeing spots. Her insides were getting stirred. Destroyed. She was so sensitive. Her insides. Her tender bud. Her breasts. All these sensations were sending her over the edge of the world.

She got tighter and tighter on the inside. Jim grasped her harder. Hector stroked faster. She was going to cum. Again. Suddenly she exploded in another wave of convulsions. Hector made two quick thrusts and exploded, his hot seed covering her face and chest.

Jim was so deep, but he pressed harder and exploded. Again there was so much sticky liquid she couldn't contain it. It ran out of her. Hot again. The spots collected together until everything was a blur. She came three times. They came inside of her three times. She couldn't take anymore. Couldn't breathe.

They didn't wait for answers this time. After a few breaths Hector hefted her again, sliding Jim out of her. He pulled her forward onto him. Part of her expected them to push for a round four, but instead Hector just cradled her.

She closed her eyes. Barely conscious. Her body still tingled. Felt hot inside and out. She was still leaking as well, although she was barely aware of it at this point.

Time was nonexistent. It might have been minutes. Maybe hours.

Jim whispered something to her before a damp cloth ran across her inner thigh. She shivered. He was cleaning her. Thighs. Chest. Even her folds.

After a while the two men shifted her, and she found herself in Jim's lap this time. They were cleaning themselves up, she guessed. She didn't open her eyes. It was euphoria, but to an extreme she never could have dreamed of.

They wrapped her up in a blanket and laid her on the floor. They whispered something along the lines of they would be back, and left.

She wanted to fall asleep, but didn't. Instead, she listened for a short period of time. Most everyone was quiet, but she could hear Jim and Hector both encouraging the others to eat and drink.

Other voices came, but they were distant and muddled. She still had no concept of time, but the two did return. Cracking an eye open she noticed they had clean clothes.

She still couldn't stand, so they treated her like a precious doll and helped her get dressed. They had a pair of soft yoga pants and jeans.

Jim paused and then whispered. "Better put some underwear on you. You're still dripping."

Her cheeks heated.

Hector was at her side, still helping her move. "It is arousing," he muttered.

They got some underwear on her and the leggings. Hector helped pull a thin gray shirt over her head and then wrapped her up with a blanket again.

"Can you stand?" he asked.

"I think so."

The pair helped her to her feet. Once steadied, Jim presented her with a pair of slippers which he helped her get on. He also had tennis shoes which he said she could put on later.

Finally, once she could stand somewhat decently, Hector escorted her out to the others.

Sam was curled up on the front desk with a blanket over her, facing towards the room. Walter was sitting next to her in a wooden chair, one leg crossed in a figure four position and a book in one hand. His other hand he had reached over and was resting by Sam's head.

Eric was sitting on the floor reading over a file. Yanika had her head in his lap and seemed to be asleep. Jance was certainly asleep with his head craned back, snoring, and drool running down the side of his face.

Each time he snorted Walter looked his way and scowled. Bruno was curled up against the wall, his knees pulled to his chest, and his head down, hiding his face. Mariah was cleaned up, wearing a light blue shirt. Her gaze was distant and her face pale.

Lisa's stomach rolled because she knew her friends were hurting, but she chose to take care of her own needs first. The waves of pleasure numbed her a while, and then later allowed her to think through the situation. As much as she hated it, and it hurt, she knew when it happened that Flint wasn't going to make it. Smiling at her. Like that was how he wanted to go out.

Spot was by Bruno curled up next to him.

Hector escorted her to an open spot across the room. She sat on the floor awkwardly, adjusting from the feeling of taking both men. "What do we do now?"

"Nothing," said Bruno. He waved one hand above his head, but kept his face buried. "Home is gone. RV is gone. We've already lost everything."

"That's not true," said Hector. "We lost a dear friend, but we're all still here together."

Eric raised the file he was reading. "What we need to do next is get these to Haven before anyone else dies."

His voice woke Yanika, who jerked.

"Sorry." Eric took his hand and ran it across her hair.

Jance snorted, like he might have been disturbed, but then continued to snore.

Walter groaned. "Can you please shut him up?"

Yanika kicked her foot against Jance's leg.

This time he woke up with a loud snort. "What, yah. Hell... Bruh?" His eyes were half open as he looked around the room. "Fuck, that wasn't a dream."

"No, it wasn't you lout," Walter groaned. He set his book down on the counter and then stroked Sam's hair.

She didn't move, but her eyes were open now.

Hector turned more towards Walter. "Do you have a way to get this information back to Haven?"

"The tunnel system should still be safe. Much less chance of getting caught. We can get to Ernando. From there we'll have to make it above ground to the radio tower. If we can, we can broadcast everything we have found."

"Will the people believe you?" asked Hector.

"I bet they will," Eric answered. "They're exploiting everyone in the Outer Rim. I don't think it will take much to get people on our side. Even most of the Guards are getting weeded out."

"There is the issue with Lord Liatris," said Walter.

Hector quickly lifted his head at the mention of that name. "Why?"

"If Haven is making their move, I suspect he will as well."

HECTOR'S JOURNAL

January 2nd, 2044

The survivor camp nearest me has fallen. Not to zombies, but to civil unrest. It only took one gunshot to turn them all against each other. The few who survived at the moment, fled. By the time I realized what was happening those survivors had already been turned. The casualties of this catastrophe are wearing on me. I wonder if I really do have purpose or if I'm just fooling myself.

Chapter 28

Yanika dozed on and off all night. No one ever slept at the same time so there was always some disruption. Eric was finally asleep. He held her the whole time. She started the night feeling cold. Void. So many people just died. She thought she was numb, but now those images haunted her.

She felt the wounded skin on her face burning. A first since they left Haven. Trying to be quiet was difficult as she moved from his lap, stood, and then stretched. She was sore everywhere.

Jance was still asleep snoring loudly. It was mostly quiet and dark out in the mall except for the lamps and other lights that dotted the area. She guessed it was night. She looked at the others she just recently met.

Sam was on the checkout counter covered in a stiff blanket. Walter was gone. Lisa was stretched out on the floor with her head in Jim's lap and Hector at her feet. She spotted a man in a green poncho. Bruno maybe. He was laying on the floor and Mariah was leaning against the wall. They were both asleep with the zombie dog thing curled up next to them.

Other than Walter, that was all of them. That was all that survived. The crew that got them to Haven was pretty much dead. All their supplies gone. Yanika didn't have anything left. That was a cold thought. She hung her head. At least in the Outer Rim she had some things. Hope was one of them.

Yanika silently walked out of the shop. She knew this was a zombie lair. Didn't care. The mall was large and there were many figures meandering about. She got the feeling that some were looking at her. She still didn't care.

This was strange. She could remember how she felt before. How crippling her fear was. Not wanting hurt. Not wanting to die. All that was different now. It was like she was a totally different person than what she was before.

Yanika wandered the halls, glancing at the old stores. Some of the signs were still there. Lingerie. Dress Shop. Signs of the old world. She started to think of a world without zombies, but that no longer had effect. She met Walter, who was a zombie. Hector. This Lady Victoria. All these zombies around her that looked a lot like everyday people. And it was her own people, humans, who hurt her.

Voices caught her attention. It was faint, but because it was so quiet it was very obvious. She moved towards it, now sliding over to the outer wall along the stores. It was a man and a woman's voice. Both were somewhat familiar.

She slowed more, almost sneaking towards the conversation. Closer, she could recognize Walter's voice and the smooth sound of Lady Victoria that she met briefly.

"So, this was your plan," said Victoria. "Are you going to overthrow Haven or liberate it?"

"A little of both," said Walter.

Yanika stiffened and then started to back away. *What was that about? Overthrow and liberate? Is that good? Bad?* She still felt eyes on her, but also was not afraid of it. Even what she just heard. It was strange, what he said. She wanted to know more, but also both sounded good. Liberate the people who were trapped. Overthrow the Capitol. She wasn't sure if that's what he meant, but that's what she wanted to do.

It was starting to get lighter as she returned to the small sports shop that everyone was gathered in. Eric was awake and jumped towards her the moment he spotted her.

"Yanika, I was worried. Are you okay?"

She reached out and took his arm. "Don't worry so much about me."

He placed his hand on top of hers. "Don't tell me that. If you haven't got it yet, I care. I care a lot about you."

She lowered her head, trying to feel something. But did she dare? After everything? *Everyone keeps dying and nothing is safe. Do I... Do I dare let myself feel something?*

"Yanika..." Eric gripped both her shoulders and gave her a slight shake. "You can talk to me. I'm here for you. And that's not going to change."

Her stomach churned. *For how long?* Everything was a fight inside her now. Fighting the sinking feeling that everything would just go away, and the hollow acceptance that there's nothing she can do. It left her cold. Left her unwilling to feel anything. But what life is that? She was basically living as if she was already dead.

They let the conversation fall to silence between them. The others were starting to wake up, making a soft scuffle in the store. Jance woke with a snort. There was a soft whimper from the dog and another that sounded like a stifled sob.

Eric let out a sigh and then fished for something in his pocket. "I made something for you while you were asleep." He pulled out a rounded piece of leather on a long brown piece of cloth.

"What's that?" she asked, her voice almost a whisper.

"It's an eye patch. I'm not that good at sewing." He lowered his head and shrugged. "But I've been teaching myself over the years so I can fix my own clothes."

She held out her hands, allowing him to pass the item to her. "You made this for me?"

"Well, yeah. I thought it might be more practical that the bandages, but I made it so we can tie it. I was thinking we could put bandages under it while you're healing and then... well..."

"I can use it to cover my eye. That's what you're saying?"

He choked. "I... I was just trying to help. I didn't mean anything bad about it. I just thought—"

She gripped it in her hand and smiled. "Thank you," she said, cutting him off before he could stutter through any more explanation. She stepped towards him, stopping just before touching him.

Yanika didn't need to ask for anything. Eric closed the gap and wrapped his arms around her, gently cradling her in his warm embrace. It was nice. Comforting. She allowed herself to relax there a while, not saying a word.

In that time the others got going. Yanika and Eric pulled away when one of Lady Victoria's zombies brought breakfast. After everyone gathered something to eat, they convened in a circle around the room. Walter strode in, casting a glance at Yanika, and then heading over to Sam.

The look he gave her made chills travel down her back. She turned her gaze to the ground. It seemed like he knew.

There was some light conversation before Hector gathered the attention of the room. "We need a plan."

"I have a plan," Walter grunted.

But what kind of plan is it though? Overthrow and liberate. Those words kept echoing in her head.

"You're planning on getting the information to Haven," said Hector. It sounded more like a recap than him really interacting with Walter.

The pair had a moment of seeming like old friends, and other times they acted like bitter enemies.

"We need to move quickly as well," said Walter. "Do we have everything we need?"

Eric moved away from her slowly, seemingly reluctantly. "We have the files here and the flash drives."

"Divide up the information."

"What are you planning?" asked Eric.

Walter shook his head. "How many times must I lay this out? You three can go through the city easier than either of us." He waved towards Sam. "Three parties are better odds as well. You all take some information. I get you into the city. From there you head to the radio tower and broadcast the information."

"Bruh, what if they give us the slam? Jailbirding."

Walter ran a finger across his eyebrow. "What is that man saying?"

"What if we get caught?" said Eric. "He's saying, what the hell do we do if we get caught? And, I mean, we're breaking into a radio tower. We're most likely going to get caught."

"Then I guess you rely on getting rescued by the others."

Hector took a sharp step forward, slamming his foot against the ground. "That is too steep a risk."

"Then you come up with a better plan! Or do you think you..." He glanced Hector up and down... "can infiltrate the city better? Or any of your motley crew for that matter? Eric and Jance are both guards. Yanika was enlisted. Do you think all of Haven has seen them go missing? Don't you think they have better odds of talking their way out of it or getting away than any of us do?"

Walter's voice progressively got louder. Hector backed away, his head slowly lowering. Yanika chewed her bottom lip. Everything he said made sense. Everything he'd said from the beginning made sense. She'd felt the pain. Saw the damages. She knew he was right about that place.

There was some more talk that she tuned out for a moment. Her fingers ran across the soft material of her eye patch. This was her life now. It wasn't the life she wanted. But her old life was a lie. It was all a lie. This at least was real. This was a purpose.

She strapped the eyepatch over her bandages. "I'm fine with this plan."

Eric glanced at her, but didn't say anything this time.

"Then it's settled," said Walter. "Gather your things. We'll retrieve the vehicles and head to the city."

Jim approached Hector, seeming to ignore Walter's presence. "What should we do?"

Hector was silent a while. He only looked at the floor. He was a strange creature compared to his counterparts. More mutated. More monster-like than human or zombie, but he acted more human than most people she'd met.

"I need to speak to Liatris," he muttered.

Walter huffed. "You're not going to change his mind."

"I need to try something," said Hector. "I cannot allow him to ravage the city. I understand what he wants to do... but I do not trust his execution." He finally looked up, turning to Jim. "What's our supply and weapons situation?"

Jim shook his head. "Pretty much nothing. I've got a few rounds. I checked Lisa's stuff. She's out of ammo."

"Do we have anything else?" asked Hector.

"Not really. We lost all of our medical supplies as well."

"I'll see if I can ask Lady Victoria for some things."

The conversation was no longer about her group so she tuned it out. They did agree weapons might be needed and within the hour they had some supplies for the travel. They were all going. All going to liberate Haven in one way or another.

Chapter 29

With the directions Walter gave them, Hector was easily able to navigate them all towards Liatris's lair. Mariah and Bruno remained silent, almost as if in a state of shock. As they followed, Lisa kept closer to Mariah. Jim kept his eyes on Bruno.

Mariah was still pale, and they got little sleep last night. She did grab her blood-stained doctor's coat and was wearing it again.

"We could try and get the stains out," said Lisa, attempting to distract Mariah a little with conversation.

"No. I want them to stay."

"Why?"

Mariah pulled at the coat. "I need this reminder."

"Of Flint?"

"Of what being a doctor now means. There will be a lot more people dying if this war breaks out."

"You can't save them all," said Lisa.

"But I can save as many as I can." She turned to Lisa with a tense stare and sparks of renewed determination. "I'm a doctor, not a God. But no matter how things turn out, I don't see this ending any way without bloodshed."

"The odds are in that favor," said Hector. "But I hope you are wrong."

Jim moved closer to Bruno and bumped his shoulder. "Are you sure you didn't want to go with them to see your dad?"

Bruno shuttered. "I mean... I want to see my dad, but... I doubt he'd want to see me. Besides, this is my family now."

"Yes, we are," said Jim. "But when this is all done, I'm going to get you to your dad, and if he gives you shit, he's dealing with me."

Bruno smiled and for the first time relaxed. His sandals made a soft slap on the broken concrete. The early morning air felt crisp and was almost silent. A sheen of dew glistened on the surrounding foliage. They were making their way deep downtown and it was a long walk that took the better part of an hour before they were faced with a towering office building.

"Is this it?" asked Lisa.

"Without a doubt. I can smell him," Hector mumbled.

There was commotion inside and many figures were darting back and forth in the shadowy cracks between boarded up windows. As Hector neared, they all stopped. He didn't hesitate, and strode straight through the front door.

Lisa picked up pace to get closer, entering just after him. Jim kept himself on the tail, guarding Mariah and Bruno. Spot was weaving in and out of the group, sniffing like a bird dog on the hunt.

They were surrounded by creatures just like they were with Victoria. Human-like people with horns, extra arms, wings, and claws.

"Fetch Liatris," Hector boomed.

His voice was so commanding it gave her chills. Everyone around scattered.

They were all zombies too. "What are you planning?"

"Liatris cannot invade Haven. It will be nothing but bloodshed."

"They're basically starting another civil war," said Jim. "No matter what, there will be causalities."

"I cannot stop that. But I can prevent innocent humans getting turned into part of the horde."

There were footsteps from afar in the building. Two women came forward, both holding a small battery lantern. They were like escorts to the pair behind them.

She could guess the man was Lord Liatris. He had a second set of arms and jagged ears. His face was human in appearance with piercing eyes that locked instantly on Hector. The woman next to him had similar ears, but seemed elongated. Slim and tall like Victoria. Her skin pale and flawless, and her dark hair hanging in waves over her shoulder.

They were a dynamic, powerful duo. Like king and queen. The presence bringing a chill in the air. All creatures around them parted to make way, like a royal court.

"Liatris," Hector growled.

Jim lunged forward, shoving Hector to the side. "Emily! Emily is that you?"

She raised her head. "Jim, it's been a long time."

"What— what happened to you?"

She ran her hands across her breasts and down her body. "Oh this. Nothing much. I asked Lord Liatris to turn me so I could become his true immortal bride."

Jim staggered back, his face paled, and eyes wide.

"Liatris, how could you?" said Hector.

Liatris shook his head. "Always trying to chase your tail and never seeing what is right in front of you. Emily chose this path of her own accord."

"You've made her your slave."

Emily stepped forward, slamming her heel down on the tiled floor. The impact revibrated about the shell of a building. "I am no slave, nor do I have any intentions of being one."

"But you are still bound by his will," said Hector.

"No, I'm not."

She looked fierce and angry. Liatris was silent behind her.

She approached Hector, fists curled into tight balls. "Now you step back."

Her tone was deep, commanding, and echoed around them. Hector stiffened to her words. He did not take a step, but he pulled his trunk away from her.

"How is this possible?"

Liatris strode forward to Emily's side. "This is the result of real research. Emily has the minimal mutations of a Second Turned and the power to command of a First Turned. She is a marvel of evolution."

"Evolution is not some mutating virus," Hector hissed.

Emily waved her hand in front of her in a sharp cutting motion. "Neither is rotting and dying. Sickness. Hunger. Thirst. A common cold. Humanity is so frail. So why not give them a chance at power? At immortality."

Jim hung his head. "You were never one to be content as just a survivor."

Emily pointed at him. "And you always had your head in the sand, so you didn't have to deal with anything. You had skills enough to keep your belly full. Not all of us had that ability."

Jim pulled back, his stunned face dropped to a saddened distant gaze. "I guess things have changed for both of us."

Liatris gave the two a glance before returning his attention to Hector. "Why are you here?"

"I'm here to stop you from invading Haven."

"You do not have that kind of power."

"If you bring your troops in there the city will be decimated. They have no way of defending themselves against a horde. They are barely surviving as is."

Liatris raised a brow. "A horde? What kind of monster do you take me for?"

He was insulted. No doubt about it. The dark shadow that crossed his face with the deep loathing in his eyes made Lisa's skin cold.

"Do they look like mindless a horde to you?" Liatris roared.

From all corners different people approached. Zombies that were strongly human. In fact, she had seldom seen the monsters she knew lately. The mindless ones were monsters. Flesh hanging from bones. Old wounds gaping and still dripping. Hunger driven, attacking anything that moves without thought. Without care.

These people were not the monsters that hunted her. They were like Hector, Victoria, Walter. Looking around she could see emotion. Thoughts. People.

Lisa stepped forward past Jim and Hector, to the front of the group.

"Lisa, what are you doing?" asked Hector.

Lisa bowed at the waist. "Lord Liatris, what are your plans?"

His brow unfurrowed and he looked at her with curiosity. "My plan is to give Admiral Hammer a taste of his own medicine."

"What about the people there?" Lisa asked.

"I have no interest in them."

His words gave her a sudden panic and she felt her whole body tense before regaining control.

He must have noticed because he continued quickly, "I do not mean them harm. Only Admiral Hammer and those who serve him."

"Those who serve him are innocent humans," Hector snapped.

A shadow crossed Liatris's face again. "Those who serve him are not innocent."

Lisa raised her hands like she was trying to keep the pair of zombie lords apart. "

Maybe, maybe not. There..." She paused to take a breath and steady herself and her thoughts. That man was the cause of everything. Every life lost. The whole world falling. Humanity almost wiped out. She may have different reasons than Liatris to loathe the man, but she understood his stance.

Yanika, Eric and Jance are going to try and expose him. If it works, there will be some sort of fall out. If anyone is still on his side, wouldn't they be just as wrong? It was a moral debate. Who to risk and who to save? But from what I know they're killing innocent people. Destroying anyone that they consider less or not having enough worth. Zombies are mindless but these people are killing by choice.

"No." Lisa shook her head. "I think Walter is right, and Liatris too." She turned to address Liatris directly. Looking into his cold gray eyes. "I'm not... I'm not a fan of running into danger." She clenched her fists. Her jaw tightened. "We lost one of our group already. But... but it wasn't because of zombies. It was because of his men. That Admiral Hammer-head or whatever is responsible for Flint's death. His men fired at us on sight."

Jim groaned. "I hate to admit you're right. And I know Haven has never been a great place, not even a good place, but the people there don't deserve to be treated like cattle. Haven was supposed to be a safe place."

Emily tilted her head up. With her height it made her look down on Jim like some raptor looking at a curiosity, decided if it is friend or food. "Nothing in that hell hole is going to get better unless something is done. We lived like rats because of the government there." She raised her hands. "Before, as a mortal, I'd look the other way. There was nothing I could do. But that has changed. We have plenty of forces to overthrow their government and wipe their slate clean."

"You don't realize how many people could die," Hector snapped.

"Already died!" Emily screamed back at him. "It's too late to play good cop zombie Lord. We already were starved near to death. Dying of disease. Eating cooked rat to survive and many of us getting sick. You're blind if you think the people wouldn't risk their lives for a better life." She pointed at Jim. "Even that head in the sand ostrich didn't stay there."

"I left to find you," Jim grunted.

Emily's hand slowly lowered, and she stared at him a moment almost like he had spoken another language. "Why?"

Jim shrugged. "You are my friend. I know you were unhappy, but when I heard you left with Marco's squad I couldn't just stand around. Joining him was a suicide mission. I had planned on trying to find you and convince you to go back."

"And what? You got a taste of freedom and changed your mind?"

He glanced at Lisa. Initially he had a similar dark shadow across his face, with the creases and wrinkles of his expression making him look aged. Once their gazes locked the wrinkles softened. Even his eyes softened, and a small smile tugged at his lips. "It took a while, but I guess things have finally opened my eyes."

There was an awkward span of silence around them. Tension tight. She could hear the breath of all the beings that still breathed in the room. The others were silent. Her own heartbeat, pounding fast and hard in her chest, roared like an old engine. To the point she was sure a few of them heard it.

There were glares and even what felt like a power struggle. Hector was trying to stand his ground, but something about the slight change in his posture hinted at the ground falling out from under him. She couldn't quite place it. Maybe his shoulders were a little different. How he had his feet. But she felt it.

Lisa didn't want to go against him. Side with the enemy in a way. But she wasn't sure what side she was on. This catastrophe caused by this Admiral, a human. *A normal fucking human did this.* She balled and unclenched her fists several times.

Fighting against zombies for years and watching so many people die, to now be here. Surrounded by zombies. *New zombies? Hybrids?* She wasn't sure how to take this all. Before it was just Hector. An anomaly. She saw him as a person. Saw him for his actions. So, it was easy to put her trust in him. Scrappers had been killing each other since the beginning. It was war. Bloodshed. In her chest she could feel the weight of what Hector was trying to prevent.

After a while, after Liatris glanced around the group several times, he strode forward, stopping next to Lisa and in front of Hector.

She stiffened and held her breath. He wasn't looking at her, maybe not even acknowledging her, as he seemed intensely focused on Hector.

"You're not going to stop me, so move out of my way."

"This is going to be a war," said Hector. His words were strained now.

"It already is," Liatris hissed. "So, make your decision. You can let the last few humans butcher each other, or you can help end this efficiently. If you weren't such a coward, you could go and help. Instead of being so blindly focused on your stupid serum that will never work, you could have been trying to save people."

Hector stiffened. "I have been trying. At least I've been looking for a cure. What have you done? Fed your single-minded need for revenge."

Compared to Hector's lanky height, Liatris was smaller, but the four-armed zombie was far more muscular. Not a body builder by any means, but he definitely looked like if they were in a fight, he might snap Hector in two.

"I have perfected my serum. You keep trying to bring the dead back. Idiot. There is no reviving the dead. A scientist like you should know that."

"It's a virus mutation. If caught early on we could reverse it!"

"With whom?" Liatris screamed back at Hector. "You come at me like there weren't hundreds of employees in that lab. Like I was the only one spreading this virus."

"You led an army through Russia!"

"Yes. I crushed them. I crushed their government. But I also took in all the zombies wandering in the wake of others. I controlled them until I could give them back their will. Now look at them." He outstretched all arms and turned around the room before screaming to the zombies around him. "Does anyone here wish to be human again?"

"That is not a fair question," said Hector.

"Oh, because I'm their Lord? Fine." He spun towards Lisa.

His sudden movement in her direction made her flinch. Out of the corner of her eye she saw Hector and Jim both stepped forward and froze.

"You," said Liatris. "Ask them. Any of them. Go on. Go ahead."

"She doesn't have to do that," said Hector. He stepped forward in one large stride and shoved himself between her and Liatris, stretching to his full height again. This time his wings buzzed behind him.

Liatris lifted a brow and turned his head. He glanced from Lisa to Hector. "I see you found something else to focus on instead of your stupid research."

"Back off," Hector hissed.

He was imposing, more so than ever before. Like two elk ready to tangle together in heated battle. Jim was right behind him, his eyes zeroed in on Liatris. He moved slowly, but she could tell he was also trying to position himself between him and her.

Lisa glanced behind her. Usually, Flint was there. He covered Bruno and Mariah. They were a team, and now the team was broken. Spot stood guard as the only thing between them and the zombie army before them. Mariah and Bruno were terrified. Pale faces. Wide eyes. The look she had seen many times as hordes moved through catching people off guard. Survivors. Scrappers. Military. They didn't care. But now the military had taken that spot. It was terrifying and infuriating. She both quaked in her shoes and tensed. Her stomach turned in the middle.

Taking a steady breath, she reached up and took Hector's arm. *When did I get afraid? When did things get to the point I couldn't step up? This isn't me.*

She took another breath. "Does anyone here want to be human again?" She screamed loudly. Her heart was pounding harder than before.

The group around them looked at each other. Some shrugging. Next was the unanimous no from the group around them. Men and women. Young and old. Not a person in the group said yes. It made chills go down her back.

Hector hung his head which elicited a smug grin from Liatris. The ball changed courts again.

"Make up your mind," said Liatris.

"I'm a scientist," said Hector. "Not a soldier."

"You are a Zombie Lord, even if you act like some pet." Liatris cast a quick glance at Spot as he spoke.

Lisa tightened her grip on Hector's arm. "We can go like... like field medics." She struggled with her words, unsure of where she was going with this line of dialogue. "We can... we can at least try and help."

"It's too dangerous," said Hector as he shook his head.

"Maybe... But... But there's a lot of things outside this family that's also important." Was she really going— Yes. She couldn't question it anymore. They almost had a home. Their family. Safety. That was taken from them by these people in Haven. And those government officials were taking that from many other people as well. "We need to do something."

"Are you sure?" Hector's voice was low and soft. He turned to her, hovering like a sentry. Like her protector, craning over her.

"I'm sure. We should do this."

HECTOR'S JOURNAL

march 1st, 2044

I traced an aggroed horde to find a woman unconscious and injured in the mountain snow. There was only one nearby building, so I brought her there. It was a cozy cabin that looked well prepped and lived in. I suspected this was her home. There was no other explanation for why she would be out in the snow in the middle of nowhere. She's still unconscious, but I am starting to feel something. protective, maybe? I feel like I must save her.

Chapter 30

Emily moved second with the army of zombies around them with Liatris in the lead. Liatris had more vehicles than she ever expected, and they moved their army quicky. Vehicles parked, the group was converging on Haven. Gunshots rang out from inside the walls, along with screams both high pitched and low. It sounded like a war had already broken out before they even got there.

She felt the shift into being undead. There was tension in her chest where she once would have felt her pounding heart. They were all out on the road before a towering gate. They were moving faster than planned, but there was no sign of guards or security in the area. That never happened.

These gates were always heavily guarded. She took long strides to catch up to Liatris. He flung his arms forward and barked an order she couldn't quite make out.

At his command the zombies moved. The gate was metal set in what looked like a concrete dam, except it managed people not water. The chemin de ronde atop the walls were empty. Coils of barbed wire clung to the sides just below the electrical cables. Even without guards, getting in would be a challenge.

"What's the plan?" she asked, reaching Liatris's side.

"Penetrate, diffuse, and move to the capitol."

"How are we going to diffuse?"

"From the screams I anticipate it will be easy. Those weapons are not from the people you used to live with."

She shook her head. "We barely had food."

His zombie army began to pile before the gate. One on top of another like a pyramid, each body helping the next reach higher. It was a ladder of undead flesh and bone. The whole place looked more like a castle from this side. This first gate was just hurdle one. There was the second gate. At any time, if the kill switch was activated anyone that was caught in between the two gates would be evaporated. It was designed specially to kill the undead.

"How are they going to get in?" She felt herself shutter. There was this overwhelming euphoria of power coursing through her, but enough common sense to make her realize that things could still kill her.

"I'm having them scale up and try to go around. If we can disable the switch and open the doors from the inside, our forces should be safe to enter."

Another round of gunfire came with an even more shrill round of screams. Her stomach knotted. "How long will it take?"

He glanced at her a moment. Reaching up, he cupped her cheek in his hand. "We'll both do the best we can. I know you want to save those people."

She nodded. Save. Liberate. Set free. All around the same thing. But definitely not let them all die. She swallowed, feeling her dry throat grate against itself. The Outer Rim stretched the whole wall that encompassed several former towns. Thousands of people lived there. It wasn't like in one day they all could be wiped out, she hoped.

The undead troops reached the top and scrambled to get a foothold on the wall. A few hit the electrical cables and were blown off. Their bodies literally propelled away like missiles trailed by a shower of sparks. Others that were caught in the wire stayed there and worked at holding it back so the others could get past.

Carnage.

It took far longer than she liked. Every passing minute made her squirm. The other zombies around them all were standing guard. Eyes panning between the top of the wall and around them. Normally she'd expect opposition by now. Everything was wet from recent rains and the zombies struggled in the mud to send one after another over the wall. Every step around them made a slick slush of noise.

She must have been visibly uneasy because Liatris put both his left arms around her, one at her shoulder and one at her hip.

"As much as I feel pride in having you at my side, you do not need to be here."

"Yes, I do. These people were my neighbors. I didn't know them well, but they deserve better."

He slowly nodded.

Gunfire erupted close by, she guessed just on the other side of the wall. Liatris's grip tightened on her. At the same time more of their forces moved forward. The telltale clunk of the door mechanism made her jump. Slowly the gates began to open.

Emily tried to make a break for them, but Liatris pulled her back.

"Not yet. Let the troops see if it's safe."

"But—"

He dropped his gaze to her. The full light gave his blues eyes the most intense look she'd ever seen. "I cannot live if I lose you," he growled.

She shivered.

The forces flooded into the city. They had at least two hundred zombies with them. A small force compared to how many guards might be awaiting them.

She waited, shifting her weight on and off her toes. She wore black leather boots and a dark purple jumpsuit. Something easy to move in. The pantlegs were already splattered with mud.

As soon as the first few moved in, she felt Liatris pull her forward.

"Now."

She bolted, Liatris keeping pace with her. They slid around the corner to see both gates wide open. Zombies were already engaged with the guards. It was a blood bath. Bodies piled up just within the gate. It struck her right in the chest. She instantly realized this was a chokepoint of people trying to flee and get out, only to be shot down. The guards were killing the people here.

As she and the forces ran in people were bolting out, uncaring of the zombies flooding inward. Complete primal fear driving them. Emily slid in the mud and caught Liatris's attention. "Will they be safe out there?"

"I'll make sure my men keep the devolved away."

Devolved. Good way to put it. Houses were trashed and small fires had broken out, but were growing. A group of five guards turned and followed the fleeing people. She thought, for a moment, they were running, but they raised their guns to the innocent bystanders.

"Stop them!" Emily screamed.

A large group of zombies instantly bolted at her command. Gun fire erupted as they were piled upon. Zombies of Liatris's creation were stronger than humans. Gunshots hurt, but seldom killed. The guards were quickly torn apart.

"Help get the civilians out to safety!"

Again, they obeyed her command. Zombies with the look anywhere from human to costume character lined up, guiding people out. They were acting as walls. The ground was all slick mud. The outlet here had been heavily damaged. Outerwall pitted with bullets.

An orange glow on the horizon grew nearer. Smoke began to fill the sky.

An old woman with a small child slipped in the mud a few feet away. Emily darted to her side, grabbing her arm. The woman smelt of smoke. Her floral-patterned dress was stained different colors from aged wear and little ability to clean clothes.

She looked up at Emily and jerked back.

Emily raised a hand. "We're here to help. How many more are trapped back there?"

"I— I don't—"

Seeing the fear in her eyes, Emily cut her off. "Don't worry. You two get out of here. There are men and women outside the walls that will protect you."

The woman gave her a quick nod. "Thank— thank you."

"Get the survivors out and push inward!" she screamed.

A man came out of the outlet, rifle trained on her. She caught the glint of the barrel out of the corner of her eye. She flinched.

No gunfire. Cracking open an eye she just caught the man soaring upwards in the air. Rifle flying off to the side. Liatris was below him, arms up.

"Don't you dare point a gun at my wife!"

Wife? The word startled and warmed her. There was little time to dwell on it. Their forces were moving through the narrow streets and acting as cover as people fled to the gate. They were taking fire, but as undead, they were able to keep going.

Emily joined the fray. She bolted for a guard's body, laying on the ground bent backwards. She broke the strap holding his rifle and snatched it off his corpse. She wasn't very familiar with it, but the basics of point and shoot should be enough.

Guards in this area were dwindling. Bodies lay in the mud around the area. Civilians dead in bloody muddy pools, trampled in place. The distant fire was growing and now a cloud of smoke was rolling her way.

Slopping in the mud, she backed towards the outlet. A group of three guards were coming up the street. Two in uniform and one in tactical gear. There was no point in playing nice. She unleashed a volley of rounds at their heads, popping the three men like watermelons.

Blood splattered like cranberry juice. Her stomach churned. The twisting bile making her gag. Fewer people were coming their way and the other zombies were converging.

"What now?" she yelled at Liatris.

Liatris clenched his fists. Blood splatter dotted him head to toe. His gaze shot around from the zombies to the civilians, back to her. Over and over. "I need to move towards the capitol," he said. He looked distracted and sounded as if he was telling himself and not her.

"Hammer is there, right?"

His gaze snapped back to her. He sloshed through the crimson mud to her. "If I go, will you go with me?"

The fire was coming closer. The smell of burnt wood and trash heavy on the air. Mixed with the well-known stench of slum living, it made her gag. There were still people coming. Maybe more along the miles of the Outer Rim.

Liatris groaned. "You're going to try and save them, aren't you?"

Emily bit her lip. "I think I have to. There's no one else who can."

Liatris pulled her into his tight embrace. "I can't lose you."

She wrapped her arms around him. Felt the cold wet of his clothes against her. The strength of tight muscles on a man ready for the fight of his life.

"You won't," she whispered. "I'm not the scared little bird that was dropped into your nest before."

"I know. But I'm so afraid of losing you, nevertheless."

Getting his revenge and killing Admiral Hammer was his ultimate goal. Avenging his wife. It was what he had lived for all this time.

Emily gripped his shirt, pulling him in tighter. "You need to finish this. I will be fine." She felt him tense.

"I... Can you promise you will be careful?"

"I promise, love."

He gripped her tighter, squeezing the air from her. Liatris looked up towards the fire moving their way. "It's too dangerous," he muttered.

Emily ran her hand across his cheek. "I can move around the Rim away from the fire."

"You? No, you're taking the army with you."

She shook her head. "You'll need them to get to Haven."

"Not everyone. I'd rather leave the forces with you."

"Let's split up then. Evenly. I don't want anything to happen to you either."

He took her hand and kissed it. "I can promise you that I will come back unharmed."

"I'll hold you to that."

He looked so hesitant. Concerned. An expression that struck her right in the chest. She desperately wanted to rid him of it. There would be time later. Flames licked at the edge of this area. Smoke grew thicker and fouler. The heat radiating from it now heated her skin.

Emily snatched two of Liatris's arms and yanked him to her. She planted a deep, but quick kiss on his lips. "Go. I'll be fine."

Still hesitant, he gave her a nod. "You!" He pointed at a small group of zombies to his left. "You're with me. The rest of you are under Lady Emily's command."

Even heading off down the path, he cast several glances back her way.

With the fire approaching there was no time left. "How many survivors did we get out?"

"Fifty or more," replied one of the troops.

"Send some people out to protect them. The rest of you follow me."

They gathered a group and their forces split again. Emily led them down the slum streets away from the fire. She spotted more civilians in the distance, all headed her way. Gunfire followed them. She pulled her rifle tight and prepared to take down every last fucker that would dare kill innocent people for no reason.

HECTOR'S JOURNAL

May 5th, 2044

    Her name is Lisa. She is a very
interesting person and does not seem
to be afraid of me. I enjoyed the time I
spent with her while she was recovering.
When I planned to leave, she insisted on
coming with me. Although my first instinct
was to deny this request, I could not
voice those words. It was easier to protect
her if she was near, and, I realized, I
desperately want to keep her safe.

Chapter 31

The morning was a bit long but then everything moved in a flash. Yanika, Eric, and Jance were teamed with Walker and Sam. The group had made their way, uneventful, across the city back to the lab.

There was a hum in the air. A distant chorus of moans. Blood splattered across the concrete. It chilled her. Even now she felt the icy tingle down her back. They had grabbed the jeep they originally traveled to the lab in, gathered weapons that still had some ammunition, and had headed towards Haven.

Once they were within walking distance but far enough not to get spotted, Walter had Sam pull the jeep into a ditch. Once they were out a zombie crawled from the bushes. It was a shredded, burnt, fleshless figure with exposed muscles and tendons. At Walter's command it crawled into the Jeep.

It was his plan that if the Jeep was found with the zombie inside people would just assume that's what happened to the previous drivers. Next was the real task. Getting into Haven.

The landscape was wet from recent rains which now hung as a haze against a gray sky with the walls of Haven standing as a thin line across the horizon. Her first thought was this might be what the great wall of China would look like. But it was a death trap.

The five of them stood on what once was the northbound highway to the city. Cracks were filled with weeds, and moss was slowly swallowing all traces this road ever existed except for worn wheel ruts.

There used to be a lot of farmlands, she remembered. Now it was overgrown waist-high grass, thick trees, and brush all around them. A jungle of sorts. The cold mist in the air had already started to sink in through her clothes.

"We're walking from here?" she asked. Her voice cracked from a sudden shiver.

"It will be our safest course," said Walter. He held out a hand and Sam handed him an umbrella.

Jance stepped forward, his mouth open and eyes bugged. "What? Bruh where you get that?"

"Really?" said Eric. Frustration and disgust evident in his tone.

"I am not planning on getting wet," said Walter.

It seemed away from Victoria he was back to his pompous self. It wasn't ideal, but nothing was. Yanika stood there watching this go down like she once would have sat down and watched a boring movie. It wasn't just the cold outside. It was a cold inside.

Eric turned to her and took her hand. "You going to be okay?"

He looked so concerned. Sweet. Until she lost her eye, she felt reliant on him. It felt like there was no way to stay alive. That was her then. He reached up brushing his fingers across the strap of the eye patch he made her.

She reached up, cupping his face in her hand. He stiffened, surprised, but quickly melted into her touch. She'd never done that before, and only realized it after she saw his expression. She felt different. He felt different.

"I'm fine. How about you?"

His brow furrowed as his gaze went from her eye to her patch and quickly back. "I'm worried."

"I can tell." She leaned to the side, glancing at Walter. "This might be the most dangerous thing I've done in my life."

His fingers ran from her ear down her neck. "You don't have to come."

"But you're going no matter what?"

"I have to."

"Why?"

He lowered his head. His eyes narrowed and his gaze distant, like he was searching the rocks and grass for answers. The mist has collected on his forehead and ran down his face to his chin. "I don't want to... but I feel like I have to." He lifted his head. There was desperation in his eyes. Sadness. "I don't think I can run from this."

"Neither can I. They're killing good people just for their own agenda." She paused and then chuckled. "To think I once was so afraid of the creatures outside the walls." She nodded towards Walter. "Look at that pompous poodle. Can you believe he's a zombie?"

Eric shook his head. "I never thought that was possible. I saw him with the scrappers on and off for years and never thought about it."

"You wonder how many like him have walked right under our noses?"

"Not until recently. Those Lords... They're terrifying yet, I felt safer there than I did in Haven."

"Our own government is the nightmare now."

Eric lowered his hand and balled it into a fist. "I've seen the zombies. Not like him. Like that one he called into the jeep. I never thought I would hate anything more than I hated them." Biting his lip, he nodded. "I guess things are changing."

They were wet, water running down their faces. Walter strode away from them with Sam behind him like a bodyguard. Pistols on her hips. Jance was following, but stopped to look back at the pair. He had an AR strapped to his side, buckled to his waist and thigh.

"We better go," said Yanika. She grabbed his hand and started pulling him with her. Taking the lead. Taking the next steps. Wet and cold. Blind in one eye. Scarred. Angry.

They strode across the lush landscape of lost memories. Through the traces of humans past. Families. Innocent people. The gray sky a background to it all. Thick mist. She passed Jance. Passed Sam. Strode right up to Walter's side and matched pace.

When he looked at her, she nodded. There was a pause before he nodded back. Yanika kept a hold of Eric and pulled him behind her. Jance stayed back with Sam. Walter seemed to be walking casually, but somehow was covering ground fast. Yanika had to take quick long strides to keep up.

The walls before them grew and grew. Haven. A trap. A human cage. Yanika's chest tightened and cold chills ran across her skin like lightening. They still had a lot of ground to cover. It didn't take long before she felt accustomed to the cold. Back in Haven winters were deadly. Many didn't make it. Her roof leaked in the summer. She was no stranger to being cold. Being wet.

It was funny that after all that, it took being tortured and almost dying to get her here. *Is it good or bad that I don't care now? I feel so cold inside, but... No, I'm just not scared.* If she didn't care, she wouldn't be going through with this. She really just wasn't scared.

Jance was the most vocal during the long traversal, moaning and complaining about the rain, the walk, and a blister on his toe. Walter threw a few quipped comments back to him. Beyond that, it was just nature.

It took a while of walking in the misty haze. The walls grew larger as they neared. Daunting. To keep zombies out, the tops were outfitted with spotlights, and electrified cable. There was a walking platform that the guards patrolled. Yanika had watched then from afar once feeling security in their presence. Now, she wished each one would fall off and break. She clenched her fists.

Jance turned and ran after them. He'd been falling behind and catching up the whole time. "Bruh, this isn't where we left."

Walter turned and put a finger to his lips. "Shhh. Be quiet you fool."

"Dawg don't you shush me. Where d fuq we goin?"

"This way will get us to the Capitol faster."

They continued through thick brush. She didn't notice guards on the wall, and they could easily hide themselves in the grass. The thought of the wall being unguarded anywhere seemed odd.

Eric kept looking up the wall. His brow deeply furrowed. He stared, only blinking when a drop of water rolled into his eyes.

"What is it?" she whispered.

"There should always be guards on the wall. No matter what. It's the most standard protocol we follow."

Jance jogged up beside them and waved a hand in front of his face. "Bruh, you smell that?"

Walter froze. He had his umbrella up, but the green blended into the grassy cover. Weeds up to his waist. It was strangely like camouflage, and it took Yanika a moment to notice he stopped.

Sam had stopped behind him with her hand on the pistol strapped to her side. She was looking around and didn't seem to know why they stopped either.

"What is it?" asked Eric, his tone hushed. He crouched as he spoke.

"I know that foul smell," Walter hissed. "Death."

He glanced at the wall, straightened, and then strode forward with his umbrella protecting him from rain dripping within the mist.

"What are you doing?" asked Eric.

The rest of them started to follow him. There was a stench. Rotten. It reminded her of old eggs when Cuddles would lay one and she wouldn't find it for days. But worse. Stronger. Acrid in a way that made her want to run from it. It was getting stronger as they walked, which gave no mystery to the fact they were nearing the source.

The five of them emerged into an open clearing of grass and dirt leading up to a large pit. There was no warning. They all just sauntered into it.

A mass grave filled with layers upon layers of rotting corpses.

Jance spun, bolted away, only to puke after a few steps. Sam collapsed where she stood, covering her mouth and heaving.

Eric grabbed at Yanika, trying to turn her away. She pushed him back. Her body shook. Stomach turning and turning. Her eye drifting from one rotten form to the next. Mutilated bodies, but not in a way that would indicate a zombie had made a meal of them. Those attacks had a distinct pattern. The fresher bodies on top were not bitten or chewed. Some looked like they had been shot.

Amongst them she spotted Noah. The sudden twisting of her muscles made her body jerk, uncontrolled. He was a neighbor. A sweet young boy trying to raise rabbits. She'd given him advice in the past. She traded eggs for rabbit meat with him. He was a good boy. He deserved better. They all deserved better.

A thin mist twirled around the hole, but she could still see the maggots crawling on flesh. On occasion something small and furry would skitter from corpse to corpse. There were guards in uniform in there too. Men, women, kids. Clothing hinted of all ranks being lumped together in one dead pile.

Her gaze fell back on Noah. The kid, like many, still had his clouded white eyes open. Not a shred of respect was given to these lives. His body limp and contorted on the pile. On top. He most likely didn't die too long ago. Maybe a day or two.

She bit her bottom lip. Her head spun. This whole ordeal made her body feel light and uncontrollable. She listed to the side, unable to stop herself. Eric swooped on, wrapping his arms around her. He kept her from falling.

She took a moment to bury her face into his wet shirt. She could hear the duet of Sam and Jance both still heaving. A soft hiss accompanying them she guessed was from Walter.

"They killed them, didn't they?" she muttered.

Eric shifted his weight, but didn't answer.

"Why?" Yanika screamed.

"Shhhh," said Eric. He ran his hand down her back. "I... I don't know." His voice cracked several times.

Wet squishy footsteps grew louder as did the soft tunk-tunk sound of water hitting an umbrella. She pulled away enough to glance at Walter.

"We need to hurry," he said. There was a glint in his eye. A darkness across the bridge of his nose.

"Why?" asked Eric.

"I fear the war has already begun."

Even though Eric tried to pull her closer, Yanika pulled away. She wanted the warmth. Wanted the comfort. But not right now. Those desires were distant, like dreams. Right now, for the first time, she felt the burn of seething anger. Fists balled and muscle tight, she wanted a fight.

"If… If… Bruh…" Jance wiped his mouth with the back of his hand. "If they're… they're already at war…" He bent forward and grabbed his knees, heaving again. "Why are we still going?"

"Nitwit," Walter growled. "The majority of governors and the military are behind Hammer. This information may make some switch sides."

"What do I have to do?" asked Yanika. Although she struggled with how she felt, she heard her own emotion come out in her cracked voice. The sound of her own desperation.

"The passage inside isn't far." Walter turned towards the wall. "We need to infiltrate Haven. This tunnel will take us directly there."

The first passageway was nestled outside the wall. It was a bunker covered with brush to hide it from prying eyes. The passage led to a dirt tunnel with water running down the center. Two dirt bikes were there. Less than ideal, but they didn't have time to find something else. Yanika was forced on the handlebars. Luckily, she was small. Walter on a bike with Sam behind him, and Eric on a bike with Jance desperately holding onto the back. The combination made travel slower than last time.

It was muddy, miserable, unsafe. Many times, she felt as if she might slide right off the bars. They made it with what had to be pure luck. The trip didn't give them a moment to breath afterwards. The pressure of time was now compressing against her.

They snuck into a residential area through an old hatch situated in the middle of a park. Cute houses lined the streets with signs of families there. Playgrounds. Toys in a well-kept front yard. There were signs of life. Happy life.

She felt the threads that held her together snap one by one. The people here had all this. All this space. Safety. Shelter. And everyone else was just left to die. Fed scraps to keep them docile. Threatened with death so no one ever rose up.

"That's going to change," she muttered.

"What?" Eric glanced at her with one eye squinted.

"Nothing."

They moved down another street and stopped when Walter abruptly put his hand up. He was peering around a corner. There was the low sound of several engines running. Distant pops and booms from what sounded like gunfire.

Eric crept close, ducked around Walter, and looked around the two-story brick building. They were somewhat hidden by bushes. Somehow, they hadn't been spotted yet. Or if they had, not one cared.

"Vehicles," Eric whispered.

"The guards here are assembling. This is going to be much harder than I had anticipated," said Walter.

"What do we do?" Eric glanced over his shoulder at the older zombie man.

"What we came here to do. This changes nothing."

Sam pulled her pistol.

They pushed for the radio tower. Many of the guards had headed inwards towards the city. In just a few minutes the gunfire had moved to their position. Tires were screeching and screams now joined the fray. The sounds grew more chaotic as if more and more people were converging here.

They had one street to cross. All five of them had their backs against a concrete wall of an old building. There wasn't much to see, which was bad. How many were out there and whose side were they on?

Bullets ricocheted against the building. Small pieces flew off. Sam held her pistol up, the barrel next to her face. Jance swung the strap of his rifle over his shoulder, readjusted, and trained the barrel forward. Eric had a pistol ready. She had nothing. Clenching her fists, she leaned her head back against the wall. Her heart pounded, half with fear and half with rage. She didn't want a weapon before. She'd never fired a gun and wouldn't have any idea how to use one. Despite that, she regretted her decision now.

They killed them. How... How could they just kill them?

"Stay down!" Eric shouted.

A sudden barrage of bullets rained down in their direction. There was a loud boom like an explosion nearby. It felt like seconds had passed, yet somehow it was enough time for forces to make their way right to their feet. She ducked with each sound. Twitching. Jerking. The ground rocked. She felt unsteady.

Eric ducked low with Sam covering above him. They opened counter fire at the guards across the street.

"Can't you do something?" Sam screamed. "Aren't these your people?"

"Not anymore." Eric pulled the trigger, blasting off several rounds. The shells ejected to the ground, silent against the roar of gunfire.

Moving as a group, Yanika found herself in the middle of them.

They were pushed back into the alley. So close but so far. Brick walls on either sides, with only a couple dumpsters for cover.

Guards closed in from every direction. Gunfire erupting around her as Eric and Sam were on the ends, emptying their magazines. Jance backed into her, knocking her against a wall and putting himself in front.

He popped off three rounds before a stary bullet split his head. The cold rush of terror hit Yanika like an ice bucket. The bullet went in one side and blew out the other. Like smashed watermelon. Blood splattered across the ground and at Eric's heels.

"Jance!" Eric spun towards his friend, only to jerk forward. A bullet shredded through his shoulder. He collapsed down to his knees. His gun dropped to the side, the metal clattering against the concrete.

"We've got reinforcements coming to help!" said Walter. "Get—"

Another stray round found its target as it shredded through Sam's chest. Walter spun and caught her before she fell. He jerked as rounds pelted his body.

Yanika dove to the ground and grabbed Eric. A line of rounds pitted the building where she had just stood.

"Run," Eric choked. He breathed, choked, and then threw up blood. Swallowed hardThe hot liquid hit her arm and sloshed over the ground.

"I'm not leaving you."

She looked up as a guard approached, but abruptly turned. People from both sides swarmed them. Jumping unnaturally high into the air and coming down on the military force. They were getting shot, but that didn't seem to stop them.

Walter pulled Sam against the wall. The other side of the alley filled with more of these people. Some were attacking the guards and others were forming a protective wall.

"Zombies..." she muttered.

"Liatris's forces are already here," said Walter. "I commanded them to give us cover."

Eric sucked a gargled breath. His body went limp in her arms.

"Can you do anything? Please!"

"Like what?" Walter snapped.

Sam was limp in his arms as well. Eyes closed.

"Damn everything!" he yelled.

"Can you turn them? Will that save them?"

Walter snarled. "They'd be mutated monsters. Third turned." He gargled as he spoke and then spit on the ground.

"We can't let them die!"

His eyes were on Sam. He wasn't even paying attention to her anymore. His brows were furrowed, but it didn't look like sadness. The way his face twitched it seemed more like anger with indecision. *What is he waiting on? What is he thinking?*

Bullets sprayed the building over her head making bits and pieces of brick rain down on her.

"They're going to die if we don't do something!"

"I know! Fuck don't you think I realize this?" Walter reached into an inside vest pocket and pulled out two syringes. One had a pinkish liquid in it and the other was blue. Walter ground his teeth, holding both vials up to the light. "This isn't how I wanted to test this."

"Test what?"

Walter popped the caps off both syringes and injected himself in the leg with both. "If this goes badly, you might want to run," he said through clenched teeth.

She used her leg to push herself back against the wall, trying to drag Eric with her. She didn't even know if he was alive still. If Sam was still alive.

Jance... there was no questioning that.

Walter was hunched over Sam, panting which turned into growls. He slammed one fist into the wall next to him. Spit dribbled from his open mouth. His teeth elongated into fangs like a rattle snake. Lurching forward he bit down on Sam's shoulder.

Yanika kicked, shoving herself hard against the wall. Walter shook a little, like a rabid animal. Like a zombie. She clutched Eric. The cold shattering like ice and fear setting back in. Every muscle in her body stiffened. Her stomach turned. Bile burned her throat.

Walter shifted, releasing Sam's limp body to the ground. He turned to Yanika. His eyes had turned red. His skin paler. He pushed himself up, but staggered a moment. In an unnatural motion he cocked his head from one side to the other. Bones cracked.

He stepped towards her. She was pinned. Nowhere to go. No escape. The narrow space was easy for him to cover. There was hunger in his eyes.

He dropped down on one knee. "Let me try to save him."

His voice was a dull growl. For what she could tell, Eric was dead. This could be the only thing that could bring him back.

"Tr—try..." she managed to stammer.

Walter moved fast, his motion a blur. He sunk his fanged teeth into

Eric's shoulder. There was a disgusting sucking sound. She heaved. Gunshots were more distant, making her pounding heart much more noticeable.

Walter wasn't long at Eric's body before he let loose and stepped back. Blood dripped from his mouth down onto his shirt. "Disgusting," he mumbled. He pulled a handkerchief from his pocket, but when he turned to Sam, he dropped it. He knelt at her side and scooped her body into his arms.

"What now?" asked Yanika. Her voice cracked.

"We wait."

"For what?"

"To see if they turn and what they turn into."

She swallowed hard. Her parched throat grated against itself. It'd been hours since she'd had anything to eat or drink. She had a little this morning, and was glad how little she ate as she almost threw up again.

The sounds of war were fading, but the blockade of zombies around them remained. They blocked both entrances to the alley. She ran a shaking finger across Eric's bloody cheek.

A cool breeze passed through bringing with it a foul stench. Metallic and burnt. Gunpower and blood, she guessed. She never thought the world would end to zombies. Even less thought she'd get caught up in a war. Now the impossible, she was here wishing that Eric would become a zombie.

She shook her head. *How is this possible? How did I get here?* Her hands were covered in blood. There was blood splatter down her shirt too. On the concrete. On the wall. It surrounded her.

"Sam!"

Walter's voice startled her. She jerked. Her eyes locked on the pair in front of her. She heard a soft grunt and quickly realized it wasn't coming from Walter.

Walter pulled her tightly to him, his focus centered on this one person. There was desperation she hadn't seen before. From their interaction she guessed they were close. This just conformed it. He acted a lot like Eric did towards her.

It made her chest tight. Her stomach squirmed. Sam was moving. There was a chance that what Walter did would work. Almost like Walter, she no longer cared about anything around her and turned all her attention to Eric.

He was cold and pale. Her stomach sunk hard enough it made her heave. He'd stopped bleeding. He looked dead. How could anything change that? One arm was wrapped around his shoulder to cradle him. Her other hand rested on his arm. She gripped him tightly.

There were more sounds coming from Sam. Sounds like she was waking up. Like Walter might have really revived her.

Eric twitched. Yanika gasped. Before she could say anything, stray bullets pitted the alley. There were screeches. The zombies blocking the alley scrambled. *More forces? A sneak attack? Why... why do I hurt?*

Yanika looked down to see blood pouring from her chest. A rush of panic hit her and in that instance everything went black.

HECTOR'S JOURNAL

March 16th, 2025

   Lisa and I have traveled a while with
spot. This alone time has been precious.
She is very kind, yet stronger than I
expected. We have acquired an RV which
provides safer travel since I am no longer
traveling alone. Recently we have come
across new members. I never thought I
would travel with other humans. So many
feared me.

   We rescued Flint from the side of the
road. He is feral, to put it nicely, but good
at heart. He was not afraid of me and
desired to travel with us. His presence has
been an incredible help as we now have
someone else to drive the RV and help
with renovations.

   Addendum:

   I deeply mourn Flint's loss. He was
family to me, like a son. He helped this
family so much.

Chapter 32

"Run! This way!" Lisa screamed. They had followed Liatris to the city to find it deep within a massacre. This nightmare was carnage like she had never seen. Hector tried to pull her away. To shield her from it. But there was no use.

The few buildings here with covered in bullet holes and things that looked like they could have once been small shopping stalls were in broken heaps of wood and tarps in the mud.

The guards of this place were leveling the people who lived here. Not all the guards. She spotted a few who tried to fight back and died. But most were in the middle of a mass execution.

She kept pushing the people who lived here out and away from the military force as they continued pushing towards the capitol. After a while they had to decide to stay or continue to the capitol with Liatris.

"Unless we can get all the forces to stop, there's nothing we can do," said Hector. His speech was rushed, and voice strained.

As much as it hurt, he was right. Flint would have said it fucking sucked. The thought made her sick. They followed Liatris's forces into the countryside, getting a brief break. Haven spanned many small towns, designed to encapsulate the hydroelectric dam and wind turbines. The walk, knowing people were currently dying everywhere, was grueling, as was Liatris's pace.

Lisa held her pistol in her sweaty hands jogging beside Hector. She could tell he was holding back to keep them all together. Jim was one pace beside and behind. He had slung his rifle over his shoulder. Mariah and Bruno were right behind them. Bruno had a pistol of his own now, but hadn't fired it once.

Lisa glanced back. Bruno still looked sickly pale. Mariah had taken a rifle and now looked like a military doctor. Her white coat bloodstained. The look in her eyes dark and fierce. Spot trailed them, guarding the rear. Good dog.

There were all sorts of vehicles that came their way. All appeared to be the military. Liatris's forces were stopping each one, pulling out the guards, killing them on the road and then taking the vehicles.

Liatris paused as he went to jump into a red truck. He glanced their way. There was a pause before he hopped off and went went to a blue jeep. They were a distance away, but she thought she heard Hector's name. They caught up as a group of zombies sped out towards the city.

Hector pointed at the truck. "Jim, you drive." He hopped in the truck bed.

Lisa grabbed the side and flung herself over. Mariah took shotgun, and Bruno and Spot joined them in the back. Jim pulled into the convoy, and they covered the last of the run on wheels. It was a peaceful five minutes, before they started running into other vehicles.

It was bumper cars left and right.

Hector grabbed Lisa and Bruno. Jim swayed in and out of wreckage. The truck bucked the deep ruts and slid as he went into the tall grass to avoid collisions. The sharp jerks back and forth threw her side to side, only staying in the bed of the truck thanks to Hector.

"Keep on Liatris!" Hector shouted.

The truck sped up. Jim got it back on the road and continued after the blue Jeep . They sped past crop fields, through the thick timber, and over the dam. Finally, a city came into view.

Lisa grabbed onto Hector's arm to steady herself. "Is that it?"

"I believe so." Hector muttered, his voice was barely heard over the engine.

There was a barricade out front. It looked like they were expecting forces to push back. Jim slowed, letting other vehicles go first. There was a recklessness the zombie army had. They crashed their vehicles into others just to push their way through.

Gunfire erupted. Bullets zinged off the concrete. Bang. Zing. Bang. Zing.

"Get down!" Hector shouted.

She ducked.

Bruno slid in next to her. "Are we going to die?"

The question took her off guard and she felt the instant rush of heat hit her body followed by pulsating anger. "Not a chance." *We're not losing anyone else.*

The majority of the zombie caravan blew past the blockage and into the city. There were troops everywhere. This was most likely the most heavily guarded part of Haven. The people here were expecting the push back. It reinforced the carnage she saw earlier. This was a planned attack on their own people.

The city was small. They came into what looked like a well-kept town square. Buildings were old with decorative facing. Streets were clean as was the grass in a central park. It looked like a normal city. Untouched by death. Untouched by carnage.

Her anger deepened. This place was stashed away only for important people. It was the politics of the old days, still clinging to their ways. The world changed, but that didn't. Greed didn't. She clenched and unclenched a fist before placing the hand back on her gun.

Jim pulled to the side, tucking the truck into an alley. The other zombies were putting their vehicles all over the square and getting out.

"Stay close," said Hector.

They hopped off and got into a tight group.

"Where are we going?" asked Lisa.

Hector groaned. He was more than tense. His body visibly shook. "Liatris knows. Let's stay close to his forces."

They edged along the alley and peered out at the streets. There was a large structure of white columns out in the central park. Guards were up the steps, firing down on the zombies. The Guards were in ramshackle gear. Some tactical, some hunter camouflage. Their weapons varied from rifles to revolvers.

It wasn't the precision group she had seen before. This looked like last ditch effort troops sent to defend the city. Zombies were getting slammed with volleys of gun fire. Bodies sent back and landing contorted in a heap, only to rise again and fight back.

Even from here, the horror on the guards' faces was evident. They, most likely, didn't know what they were sent to do. Or what they would encounter. The paved streets, one spot at a time, were getting splattered in blood.

The zombies moved fast. Some more than others. A few with multiple arms like Liatris grabbed guards and hurled them like they were in a wrestling match.

They spotted a large group of zombies moving down the street.

Hector pointed towards them. "There. We need to follow them."

They slid out onto the street, taking a stealthy approach. The careless way the zombies attacked made a good distraction. Their small group had to move fast to keep up. And they seemed to have a way to travel. Another two cars rolled out. Both police cars.

The mob around Liatris split and rushed them. Flashing her back to memories of mindless zombies rushing their food. She shivered. Hector and Jim kept themselves between Lisa, Mariah, and Bruno and the buildings. Spot now stood guard at her feet.

There were still lamp posts and little planters with flowers on the sidewalks as if this place had never been touched by the destruction seen outside its walls. Using what little they had for cover, they were able to follow in Liatris's wake. Bullets hit the buildings overhead, sending small pieces of brick and stone raining down.

They pushed across the street towards an intersection. The building looming before them was large, brick, with a tower attached to the side. Guards surrounded it like human walls. Cars were parked as a barricade.

The forces met head-to-head. Gunfire everywhere. Zombies ripping people to pieces. War. Out in the open, she felt every muscle tense. Jim flung the rifle from his shoulder. The zombies pushed in, but more guards were surrounding them.

Lisa pulled up her pistol and fired at the nearest guard. Mariah let loose a barrage of bullets. They hugged the right of the road. The brick building beside them had broken windows. Potshot with bullets. Liatris's forces pushed through. Taking bullet after bullet. Falling. Getting up again. Fighting back.

Blood. So much blood.

Another group of guards pushed towards them. Two zombies launched themselves at them, cutting the group in half. Four guards staggered, waving guns around. They were surprised. Uncoordinated, unlike the zombie forces.

As one Guard trained his gun on Lisa, she emptied her magazine. Hitting his tactical vest twice, shoulder, leg, and back to his chest. The man fell with one behind him to take his place. She pulled the trigger, hearing the click of an empty magazine. A split-second later Jim was by her side and a loud bang revibrated by her ear.

The rifle round struck the next man down. Her ears rang, muffling everything. Another round rang behind her. She turned in time to see Bruno jerk back from the recoil of his gun.

Spot lurched forward, sinking his teeth into the neck of a guard. The man fired into air as he went down. The five of them moved back to back, staying on the edge of the street. Liatris was nowhere to be found in the carnage now.

More and more of his forces pulled away to combat the guards. A never-ending siege. She patted her pockets, pulling out her last magazine. Something, out of the corner of her eye, flew through the sky. Lisa racked a round and trained the barrel on it. A man landed on the concrete.

It didn't make sense until she spotted Liatris, sending another guard flying.

"He's there!" she screamed.

Hector dove at a pair of guards with their back to them. He grabbed their heads and smashed the pair together. They felt limp into a pile.

"Stay close!" said Jim.

"I can't do this!" Bruno screamed.

"Yes, you can," said Jim.

Lisa sucked air. Her heart pounded. She couldn't catch her breath. The shots around her made her vibrate. Shake. Disoriented her. She turned. Spun. Popping rounds into anything that neared them. One. Two. Five. Emptying round after round. Hot shells ejected towards her face. Each chunk of metal stung as it hit.

They tried to close in towards Liatris. They couldn't afford to be separate now. Not when the army here were lumping the six of them with all the others. There wasn't enough of them. Not enough weapons. Not enough ammo. They had to rely on Liatris's forces to survive.

As the guards pushed to surround them, Liatris pushed to flank from the side. Zombies were hurling themselves over vehicles to get behind enemy lines. They were taking heavy fire. Bodies getting shredded, but still trying to move. The guards were changing from a brutal force to a scattered group of terrified men.

Hector rushed a guard in front of him. The man fired. Barrel flash lit Hector as he slung a punch at the man's face. The impact sent the guard to the ground.

Lisa's heart lurched up to her throat. "Hector!" she screamed, her voice a cracked screech.

"Get back towards the building!" he shouted.

Lisa spotted the gun of the guard Hector just downed. She sprayed her last few rounds at the barricade and then dove for the rifle. Desperately, she tried yanking it free from the man's limp arms. "Are— are you okay?"

"Get back!" Hector grabbed her shoulder and threw her back towards the sidewalk.

Gunfire pitted the walls behind them. Hector jerked and fell to a knee.

"No!" Lisa screamed.

Jim slid in front of her and popped off more rounds, hitting their attackers with precision. A group of six or so guards were trained on them.

A zombie grabbed one from the back and pulled him down. Leaving five. She scrambled for the rifle that landed by the curb. Mariah and Bruno moved to flank her, spraying bullets with no real precision.

Lisa dropped to one knee to get the gun and started firing.

"I'm out!" Bruno shouted.

Spot bounded forward between Lisa and Hector, taking a round right to the shoulder that was aimed at Lisa. The large beast was knocked back against her.

"Get behind Liatris's troops," said Hector.

Bruno's arms wrapped under her armpits, and he hauled her to her feet.

The zombie army moved in between them, giving temporary cover. Liatris was making a push to get into the building, but the forces there were equally pushing back.

Lisa spotted Liatris, the four-armed man, behind a wall of his forces. The gunfire raining down was pushing them back down the street. Hector, Jim, and Spot put themselves on the outside, pushing Lisa, Mariah, and Bruno towards the building.

The rapid bang of bullets was shifting. She could hear it moving around behind them. They were well behind enemy lines now. Liatris glanced their way. There was no way he didn't see them.

With the push behind them, they were forced into the street with the rest of them. Zombies were going down. Maybe dead for real. They laid in piles across the ground. Guards laid in puddles of blood. The car barricade was bullet riddled. Glass broke in every window.

Something zinged by her feet. A bullet ricocheted. Hector was leaving a trail of blood. Another round cracked against the street. And another. Spot let out a loud yelp.

Bruno darted to the side and bent to help Spot forward. "Come on. You're a good boy. You can do it."

"Get back here!" Jim shouted.

Hector turned towards them. He was holding his side. Blood coated his poncho. "Stay together. We retreat inside the— buildings." His voice was gargled. Broken.

They moved in together with the other zombies, all retreating to the buildings across the street. It faced the south side of the structure they were converging on. The front was a diagonal slanted front window, all shot out. The zombies inside were turning tables and throwing them to the doors for cover.

Mariah grabbed Bruno's arm. "Move."

Lisa was out of ammo. Jim gave her cover with his rife for four more shots until his weapon made the tell-tell click as well. He was out. Bruno was out. Mariah a few rounds left, but with no aim. The bullets sprayed high above the guards.

Zombies were running towards the building. A moving wall between them. They had near immortality, but the guards had the artillery.

The troops moved around towards them. They were surrounded. Choked. Too many trying to get in all at once.

"Go!" Hector screamed.

Jim got behind Lisa, pushing her. Mariah and Bruno in front. Spot staggering along. The zombies split, giving them a clear path to the building. It was their only out. All the forces pushed them to this one point. There was no other choice. Hector was a few feet out, just behind them.

"Grenade!"

She turned and then the street blew. An orange flash preceded the impact on her chest. She flew back. Shrapnel tearing skin. The hard impact knocked the air from her.

Her arms and legs burned. Ears rang. There were bodies around her, laying over rubble. Pieces of ceiling down on the ground. Dust. Sparking electrical cables. The floor seemed to be swaying back and forth. In and out of focus.

Breathing hurt. Moving hurt. She turned, trying to find everyone. Liatris was to her right, getting up from the rubble. Bruno was over by a support beam. She could see him coughing even though all she could hear was the ringing. Mariah was crouched at his feet. Alive. Spot on the ground not moving.

Several zombies in the cramped space were bloodied. Jim was on her left, standing up from within a pile of collapsed drywall. His body coated with a dusty white layer.

Where is Hector? The sudden rush of panic straightened the world. The building had taken a hard hit and electrical wires were sparking in the ceiling. It wouldn't be hard for this to go up in flames. Liatris had a group around him. Lisa staggered forward. He wasn't by Bruno or Jim.

"Hector?" Her voiced cracked.

Jim pushed away the final piece of drywall and staggered out into the room. "Hector?"

The pair stumbled towards the front. Dust clouds obscured the world beyond the door. Lisa spotted him. Hector. Laying in a bloody pile at the doorway.

"No!" she shrieked.

She bolted with Jim right beside her. Hector was face down, back badly shredded from shrapnel. His poncho torn to bits. Blood soaking into the dust around him.

"What is it?" asked Mariah.

Lisa dropped to Hector's side. The pain in her chest was immense. Heart crushed. The fear pulsating through her, driving hot tears to her eyes. The sensation of every nerve on fire.

"We need to get him inside," said Jim.

Lisa tried to take a breath, but instead gasped. She grabbed Hector's shoulder. Jim got his arm around Hector's torso. As they hefted Mariah came up to them and several other zombies, each taking part of his weight and helping her move him inside.

They turned him, laying him on his back. He was bloodied from the explosion and several bullet wounds. His hat was gone. Goggles broken.

Lisa was able to brush away what was left of his goggles. "No, no, no. You can't die. Hector? Hector!" She put a hand on his cheek.

Jim looked up to Mariah. "Is there anything you can do?"

She was pale and shaking. "I... I don't know. Zombies aren't like us."

Hector wasn't moving and since zombies didn't have a heartbeat or need to breath there was no way of knowing if he would pull out of this. He didn't look like it. There were so many injuries. So much blood. Tears ran down her cheeks. Her bottom lip quivered.

"I don't know what to do," said Mariah.

Liatris moved closer. The tall man with four arms looked over Hector's body.

"Please!" Lisa turned to him. "Please, you have to save him."

Gunfire erupted again. The bullets pitting the building.

"We need to move back and regroup," said Liatris to his troops.

"Please!" Lisa screamed again. "There has to be something you can do."

Liatris's gaze went back to her and then towards Hector's motionless body. He looked around. Tense.

"We need to run!" said Bruno.

Spot hadn't moved either. Blood trailed down Mariah's face from a forehead laceration.

"I can't..." Lisa leaned over Hector. He was her best friend. Her lover. He was an honest and amazing person. He was the kindest man she ever knew. "I can't lose him..." she muttered.

Liatris groaned. "Is there a back room?" he barked.

"There's a large storeroom back here," said a woman with a long tail curled around her body. She was standing by the back next to the restroom doors.

Liatris looked back to Hector. A snarl pulled at his lips. "Fine!" he snapped. "Get him to the back now!"

"What?" Without any explanation the zombies moved in around her and lifted Hector's limp body.

There was still gunfire and explosions outside. Jim grabbed her and pushed her behind the zombies carrying Hector, only stopping to grab Mariah and Bruno.

They all crammed into the storage room. A few of the zombies were tearing down shelves and pitching them in the corner to make more space.

They laid Hector down gently on the floor. There was a trail of his blood leading up to this spot. He was dead. He looked... He looked like there was no hope in bringing him back. She bent forward. A scream pushed at her insides, fighting to be free. She fought her tears. Fought herself for some control. Each breath she took was cut off by a silent sob. It was only a second or two, but it felt like minutes. Hours. Eternity.

Liatris burst into the room after them and crouched by Hector's body. He put one hand on Hector's chest and then a brief grin pulled at hips lips. "Stupid man. You're damn hard to take down."

"He's alive?" Lisa blurted, rising halfway up.

"In a sense." Liatris had a bag strapped to his leg. It had a hard plastic insert like a cooler. He fished around it for a minute before pulling out a large syringe filled with a pinkish liquid.

"What's that?"

"It's an amplified form of the serum I've been using to reduce the mutation changes in zombies. This just might bring him back."

"Wait!" Lisa leaned forward, putting her body over Hector's and between him and Liatris. "If that makes him more human, won't he bleed out and die?"

"I'm not a fool." Liatris grabbed Lisa's shoulder and pushed her back. "Humans can have rapid mutations from high enough exposure from non-lethal radiation. So, we can surmise that this could be reversed engineered. This should reverse some of his mutation and heal some of the damage by targeting what little human DNA he has."

"That sounds very risky," said Mariah. She came up behind them, her voice hushed.

"It's either that or just let him die," Liatris snapped. "Now what do you want?"

He looked like he was getting angry. Like he might just leave them at any moment. Lisa reached out and grabbed his arm. "I don't care. Just help him."

Liatris groaned again. He shoved a torn piece of Hector's poncho to the side and stabbed the needle directly over his heart. The glass syringe drained the pinkish liquid into Hector. "I've only got one left," Liatris mumbled. "I can't waste it." He yanked the empty syringe back. "This counter mutation will be intense and painful. He might live, but he's going to go through hell if he does."

He stood and pulled away from them. Jim filled his spot as did Bruno and Mariah. Another explosion rocked the building. The vibration made ceiling tiles come loose and crash to the floor.

"This building is no longer safe. We need to move," said Liatris. His troops began to gather and quickly the back room was empty.

Lisa sucked in a quick breath. "You all need to go with him."

Mariah shook her head. "We're not leaving you."

She balled up her fists. Yes, she was thinking of Flint, thinking of Hector, but she still had good reasons for feeling the way she did. "Just listen to me. We have to get this fight to stop, and we can't do that from back here. We'll just be crushed under the rubble. We need to stop the attack at least on this building until Hector comes to. I'll stay here, but..." She sucked in an unsteady breath. "I need your help."

Jim knelt beside her and pulled her to his chest. "Hector will kill me if he knows I abandoned you."

"You're not. If Liatris is right, Hector will come back." She rubbed her cheek against him. He stunk of sweat and dirt. But he was close. He was comfort.

"I hate this idea."

Another explosion came from outside. Bruno jerked and took quickened steps to the door of the back room to look out. "The army is leaving us." He spun to face the others. "What should we do?"

"You'll be the safest mixed in with Liatris's forces, said Lisa"

Jim gripped her arm. "If we leave you here, you'll be a sitting duck. I can't do that."

"Close up the door then."

"You're being foolish," said Mariah. "We can't just leave you."

The building rocked again. Lisa put her hand on Hector's shoulder. She wasn't going to leave him. Not if there was a chance, even a slim chance, that he might make it. But this building was taking heavy damage. It collapsing was a valid concern. Which made getting them out all the more important.

Lisa looked to Jim, pleading with her eyes. She loved him too and didn't want to see him die down here with her. The struggle hurt deep inside. Tension started at her spine and spread around her chest like large hands wrapping around her and squeezing. The pressure felt so tight she couldn't breathe.

Jim kept his eyes locked with hers. His brow furrowed. The longer time spanned out between them the more tense he got. His clenched his jaw several times. Over and over. His gaze searching her.

Finally, Jim lowered his head. "I'll do it. For you."

"Thank you," Lisa breathed.

"What?" Mariah looked between the pair. "What is going on?"

Jim stood and took Mariah's arm, pulling her towards the door. "We're leaving."

"You have to—"

"We are leaving," said Jim. His tone dropped and he enunciated each word. "All of us just standing here will not help anything. We need to get the guards away from this building."

"We can't leave her," said Bruno.

Lisa turned to him. The look in his large eyes. The paleness of his face. A little brother. That's what he was to her. Flint was a brother to her. Mariah was like the mother of them all. This was her family. This was what she had to protect.

"We are going," said Jim. "We'll pull fire away from here and try to stop this war." He strode to the door and placed his hand on Bruno's shoulder. He spoke to Lisa, without turning. "Promise me that when Hector is back on his feet you both will get out of here."

"Promise."

The others protested, but Jim pushed them from the room. She didn't hear Spot anymore. She wasn't even sure if he survived.

The room grew silent, but the roar outside remained. It sounded like a monster, moving and slithering away only to return moments later. She scooted closer to Hector. His motionless body. She clung to the hope that Liatris was right. That somehow some magic medicine could bring him back.

Tears rolled down her cheeks. She sniffed. "I can't live without you. I don't want to."

Several minutes passed. She closed her eyes and sobbed silently in the small storeroom. Only one door and one tiny window. No good way out. Shelves were smashed and stacked behind her with piles of boxes. Straws were strewn over the floor and a box of spilt silverware was near her. The window let a small beam of light in, but otherwise the corners of the room were dark.

With her eyes closed she thought she felt him twitch. She jerked, leaning closer. Her eyes shot open. She watched for signs of life... or undeath. Anything.

His arm jerked to the side. She scooted away. A leg kicked. His foot scattered a broken piece of shelving away. The metal scraping on the broken tiled floor. He started to shake. His mouth opened. He gargled like a drowning animal.

"Hector!" She grabbed his shoulders.

With all his injuries he didn't look like he could move, but he still thrashed upwards and knocked her back. His whole body now jerking like he was having a seizure. Each motion made him shriek. Blood smeared across the floor around him. Like a gruesome snow angel.

He bucked again, cracking his elbow on the floor. Shrieks gargled, like he was drowning. His eyes opened and closed several times. Each time wide but unfocused. Glossed over, more undead than he had ever looked before.

She slid an arm under his shoulder and pulled him tight. He was much stronger, smashing up against her. The sharpest convulsion sending his head back. He cracked her right on her nose. The snap registered after the waves of hot pain raked across her face.

She almost regained her senses when he threw an elbow back. He hit her right to the ribs. The old injuries, not fully healed, felt like he split her open.

Lisa screamed. She lost her grip and fell back to the floor.

Hector bucked more. His dark skin paling. Bones cracked like they were breaking one by one in his body.

"No..." She reached for him, tears blurring her vision. "Hector..."

He clawed his face. Wailing. The sound echoing through the building. Bouncing in the small room, igniting the ringing in her ears again.

She crawled closer, but again caught a flying hand. He struck her arm, knocking her hard enough to roll her away. His swings were so strong. Instantly she felt bruised. Pain meshed together like different streams of water all pooling together.

Her body shook.

He rolled to his side and back before folding backwards almost in half. Arched up on his heels and shoulders.

She pressed her face to the cold floor. Everything in her wanted to quit. Wanted it to end. There was so much pain. In an instant she felt the same she did years ago as she laid in the snow up in the mountain. Ready to give up. Give in. No fight left. Only pain that she wished to escape.

I... I can't... I can't give up. Hector saved her. He didn't have to. He didn't have to let her stay with him. But he did. "It's... my turn to save you." She pushed off the floor.

He thrashed again. His body cracking and contorting.

Lisa got on one knee and had just enough force to wrestle her arms around him. "It's okay. I'm here."

His arm jerked up, just missing her jaw.

"I'm not leaving you." She sucked in a breath which felt like knives in her sides. Pressing her eyes tightly closed, she pulled him tighter to her.

Hector's screams quieted and his breathing slowed. Actual breathing, like a real living creature. Lisa held him close to her in her arms. The new bruises stung. Blood ran from her nose and tainted her lips with a metallic taste.

Hector's skin held a more human color. He was still bald, but his face had more features, most notably a nose and ears. He was still tall and lanky like before, but his body less contorted. His hands looked more normal.

Lisa cradled him in her arm. Pulled close to her chest. His eyes slowly opened. They were dark, almost black, flecked with silver. The color unnatural, but the shape human.

"Li...sa..."

"Shhh." She rested her head on him. "I... I'm so glad you're alive."

"What... happened..." His voice was gravely and broken. Each word strained.

"Liatris used one of his serums to save you. He..." She shook her head. "He said that reversing the mutation would... or might heal your wounds."

"Huh. Healing by causing... rapid mutation of a certain... aspect."

She gripped him tightly. "I thought I lost you!"

"I think you did... for a while."

For the first time she had a glimpse of the man he was before becoming the creature she knew and loved. It didn't change how she felt. It didn't change anything. The weight lifted and the fear of losing him gone created such a euphoria that she bawled. Tears ran down her cheeks, dripping on Hector's face. She gasped for air. Her shoulder shook.

"I don't... I don't know what I would have done without you."

A soft smiled twitched on the side of his mouth. He had lips now. Real human-like lips. "You are strong. You would have made it."

"But I wouldn't have wanted to!" she screamed.

He didn't flinch. He didn't even bat an eye. Instead, he reached up and brushed his fingers against her cheek. "I... I can feel."

"What do you mean?"

"It feels like my own hands. My own... real..." He closed his eyes, taking a long-labored breath.

"You're hurt bad. Take it easy." Lisa pulled the poncho shreds away. There were deep gashes where bullet wounds used to be. He had healed mostly. *Where did the bullets go?*

He ran his hand across his chest and down to his stomach. He had on his old pants that were now too tight on his waist, no shoes, and his poncho was in tatters over his bare chest.

"Does it hurt?" Her voice cracked.

"Yes."

Lisa lowered her head. The tears kept coming. She couldn't stop them. The salt and blood taste mixing as the fluids ran together across her lips.

"You're hurt," he muttered.

"I'll live."

He pulled his hand back and examined his bloody knuckles. "Did I hurt you."

"No! You... things were happening. You didn't do anything."

"I'm so sorry."

The creases across his face deepened. Lisa looked down at this man. More a man now than the creature she fell in love with. He had the features of a man in his forties. Smooth skin, but sunken at the jaw. Before it blended with his mutation, but now it looked out of place. Sickly.

"Don't be. I'm just so..." A sob broke her voice. "I'm so glad you're alive."

"Funny... I feel alive now." He paused, his gaze distant. "Do... Do I dare ask what happened to the others?"

"They're alive. They followed Liatris to... to try and distract those people outside."

"That is a relief. That last thing I remember is... An explosion?"

Lisa nodded. "A grenade."

"But everyone got to cover safely."

"Thanks to you. You protected all of us. You idiot."

He put an arm down and started to push himself up.

"No. You're—"

He raised his free hand, and she went silent. Terrified that she could still lose him, the simple action gave her a little ease. It was more of the normal Hector.

"We can't stay here. It won't be safe for long."

Instead of fighting him Lisa pushed herself up. Every tiny movement caused so much pain she screamed in her head, but didn't dare let out a sound. She couldn't seem weak now. She had to protect him. Protect her family.

On her feet, her head spun. She staggered, but caught herself before she thought he noticed.

He was breathing heavily. Breathing at all. Before the only time he breathed it sounded like habit, but then he could go hours without taking a single breath. He was wheezing now.

Lisa stepped in, wrapping an arm around his waist and helping him to his feet. "You need to be careful. We don't know what all that serum did."

He turned to her, and she went speechless. She looked into human eyes. Looked into a human face. His tall lean body with all the shapes and curves of any normal man. The second wave of shock hit as she took in his features. The creases around his eyes. His bedroom gaze. The kindness and warmth. He had eyebrows now that were grayed. Lips that were pale and thin. He indeed looked injured, even sickly, but also very handsome.

"I take it my appearance has..." He touched his face and trailed his fingers back to his ears. "It seems Liatris was correct when he said he could reverse mutations."

"I didn't really believe him, but... I had to do something to save you."

"You saved me a long time ago."

"What?"

"Every day with you renewed my hope that I could do something to make amends. You gave me something to live for."

Heat washed across her face.

"You look so badly hurt." His brows dropped.

His expression was every bit what she imaged before he had features.

He ran a finger lightly from her forehead down to her nose. "You're in pain."

"Me! You are covered in blood."

"I'm accustomed to pain. You, on the other hand, should have never had to experience this."

"I'm fine... Wait? What do you mean? Accustomed to pain?"

He lowered his gaze and blinked. Shaking his head, he blinked again. "I'm not used to having eyelids," he muttered. He cleared his throat. "I was not immune to the hunger zombies are known for. It... physically hurt to keep control over it. It was another reason I was so afraid of getting close to you. But... But that changed when I thought I lost you."

"There's been a lot of that going on." She put her hand over her ribs and then slowly turned towards they door. "We need to regroup with the others. But there's a chance those guards will be out there."

"I will go first then." He took a step forward and swayed.

Lisa grabbed him, pulling him steady. "No! Not this time. You have to stop using yourself like a meat shield."

"I'm not going to let them hurt—"

"Shut up!"

He stiffened.

"I'm not going to let you keep shielding me and almost getting killed. We go out there, we do this together. But this time you are following me."

"But your—"

As soon as she saw his gaze travel back to her injuries, she cut him off. "I didn't just die. I'm leading. Liatris was trying to get into that main building across the street. That's where we need to go."

He went silent. She didn't press it, but she did stand her ground. When the zombies first came, she didn't have any close family left alive. A few relatives in different states that she hadn't spoken to in years, but no one she cared about. She left and hid in the mountains. She didn't feel the loss the others did. She hid from it. She fought to save herself, failed, and then failed several times again with Hector.

Each time he was the one saving her. No matter how hard she tried, he still ended up having to be her hero. That was one of the things she loved about him and hated about herself.

It was time for the tides to change. She had a family to protect, and they were all still in danger. *I'm going to get us all out of here safely. We're going to stop this and make a change. Make things better. I'm not losing anyone again. I'm not losing a home again.*

The cycle broke here.

HECTOR'S JOURNAL

July 9th, 2025

We have continued to modify the RV
to have more storage, better beds, and
solar power. Lisa is very handy, yet
too determined at times. She frequently
overworks herself.

We also have a new addition. While
stopping at a hospital for supplies we
found one survivor, Mariah. The poor
woman was traumatized as she watched all
her coworkers die. I can understand that.
She has started to settle in. The woman
is a marvelous doctor, and sensitive and
protective of the group.

We also added Bruno to our group. The
poor boy is terrified. For reasons I cannot
understand, he has bonded with Spot.
Despite this, he helps as he can.

Chapter 33

Yanika blinked a few times, pulling the bloodstained concrete into view. She didn't hurt and oddly enough everything felt still. She rolled to her back slowly making out the bullet riddled concrete of the building next to her. The sky had cleared and now was blue and sunny.

She didn't dare move, unsure if this was real or not. If she was dead and this was the way to the beyond. Worse, if she was alive and was slowly dying.

Someone coughed beside her. The higher pitched sound was familiar. A couple moans also joined the mix.

I... I don't think I'm dead. She took a breath and let it out, feeling no desire to take another one.

"What... what have you done?"

Eric? She turned her head to the side. Eric was on his stomach trying to push onto his elbows.

Walter was standing over them. His eyes were glowing blue, almost like backlit glass. Sam was in his arms. She was alive, but her eyes, too, glowed that prismarine blue.

"Yanika? Yanika, can you hear me?"

"Huh?" She blinked, pulling Eric more in focus. His eyes were blue as well, but deeper, with flecks of gold across them.

"Your... your eye..."

"What?" She rolled to her side and pushed up on her elbow. "What about it?"

"It's blue..."

Her brow furrowed. "So are yours."

"Funny thing, augmenting genetics," said Walter.

She got a better look at him. He seemed very similar, but with fangs and glowing eyes. He had injected himself with something before he turned them. She remembered that. But also remembered pain before darkness.

Yanika got up on her knees and stretched out a hand. She looked the same, but her body felt different.

"What did you do?" Eric stood up and reached for Walter.

"Stop!"

Eric froze at the command. She couldn't see his face, but his body was shaking.

"What have you done?" Eric growled.

"I tested a hypothesis with delightful results."

"What did you do to us?"

Walter's head cocked to the side. "Saved your pathetic lives." He raised a brow and pointed at Yanika. "At her request."

Eric turned, his mouth a gape. "You... you did what?"

Shaking her head, she stood. She didn't feel fatigued anymore. She stretched, testing each motion that used to cause her pain. "I asked Walter to save you."

"I'm... You made him make me a zombie?"

"Oh, shut up," said Walter. "I made you far beyond a zombie. And I saved your life."

Eric raised a finger like he wanted Walter to stop a moment while he grabbed his own head with his other hand. "How... How did you just stop me a second ago? Am... Am I one of your slaves now?"

Walter shrugged. "You are one of my subjects now. Be happy you're alive."

Yanika ran her hand across her face and flicked her sharpened canines with her thumb. "Fangs?"

"From what I can tell, you will be able to infect and turn anyone you bite. For the most part," said Walter.

"I don't understand," said Eric. "I..." He looked at his own arms and patted himself down. "I don't feel that different."

Walter loosened his grip on Sam, seemingly uninterested in the conversation now. "How are you feeling?"

"I... I feel fine. But... I thought that fucker shot me." Sam ran a hand from her shoulder across her chest.

Walter nodded. "He did. Eric and Yanika as well. I couldn't save that one." He glanced at Jance's bloodied motionless body.

I was shot too... That darkness... I was dying.

"No..." Eric's arms fell to the side. "He... The kid..."

"Even an undead cannot function without some sort of brain," said Walter. "He was too far gone. You almost were as well."

The guards that had shot at them were all strewn out across the street in pools of blood. The zombies that had been there were all gone.

"What... happened to everyone?" asked Yanika.

"It seems the changes in mutation from combining both serums have rendered my abilities to command the zombies null."

"You had two vials," said Yanika. "What were they?"

"It was a combination of the vial of Liatris's serum he used to treat the zombies, and Hector's trial at curing all aspects of zombie-ism."

"You were trying to be human?" asked Eric.

Walter rolled his eyes. "Far from it. You cannot revive the dead. This was the most optimal achievment. Can you not feel the power coursing through you?"

Yanika stretched again. She didn't breathe. Didn't feel a heartbeat. "Nothing hurts."

"Now you're catching on." Walter's eyes narrowed. He helped Sam stand, steadying her as she swayed. "It seems war has cleaned these streets out. We need to hurry to the radio tower."

"Now?" Eric was speaking, but mostly it seemed like panicked and confused muttering.

Yanika's shoulders sank. He was such a sweet man. He never had any idea things would end like this. That his friend would be murdered. That he'd be in a war.

She reached out and took his hand. He jerked back, looked stunned, and then slid his hand back into hers.

"We have a mission," said Yanika. "We could be completely dead now, but we're not. Let's get some justice for the ones we can't bring back."

The fear and panic faded from his face, replaced with dark shadows. "You're right."

"Bout time," Walter muttered. "Let's move." He took long hurried strides out into the street.

Sam grabbed the bag of papers and flash drives from Jance's body and followed.

Yanika bolted to follow. Finding her short legs were carrying her faster than before. Her muscles pulsated. Like she could leap buildings. She was quickly at their side with Eric keeping pace beside her.

They ran into the streets, joining the war. Bullets flew through the air, aimed somewhere in the distance. The guards quickly spotted them and turned to target the four of them.

Sam quickened pace, moving at unhuman speeds. She leapt up, easily making it six feet or more in the air before she came down on a group of three guards clad in Kevlar. The impact was so intense that the three men were all knocked in different directions.

That gained them more attention. The street met at a crossroads. An old gas station across the way. There was a group of guards there, ducked behind a large jeep. Their sudden appearance and attack brought upon them volleys of gunfire.

Walter cut straight down the middle. Yanika flanked right and Eric left. One, two, three bullets hit her. It stung a little, but only fueled her rage. They surrounded the group quickly.

Yanika shoved one man back, sending him flying several feet. As another turned, she caught his rifle and jerked it to the left, causing the panicked man to fire on his own teammate. She counted five still standing. The four right in front of her and one running into the gas station through the large, shattered windows.

Eric came sailing over the top of the jeep and down into one of the men. The impact made a loud crack that sounded like several bones shattering. The man dropped to the ground.

They cleared obstacles like they were fighting children. She felt her strength increase tenfold. Her speed tripled that of before. Endurance endless. Pain minimal. Healing rapidly, as each bullet hole closed shut and spit the crumbled pieces of lead back out.

The radio tower building was off the main square, allowing them to dodge most of the battle. It was brick, made to look like a small windmill with a large metal antenna at the top.

"That's it," said Walter. He was still in the lead, and not slowing pace.

He and Sam sent the two guards out front sailing against the building before busting the wooden door down.

Yanika heard someone scream as they entered. She barged in third, spotting a man in the corner of a small room. He was ducked behind a desk, poking only his eyes over it.

"We'll be quick." She waved at the man as she sped around the corner. There were several doors into offices and sound rooms. This place also had electricity. She had heard the capital still had modern amenities, but had never seen it until now.

They busted in the first two doors before finding a sound station all lit up and it looked like it could work for what they needed.

Walter stood by the door, waving them in. "Hurry. I'll stand guard."

Eric pushed around her and sat at what looked like a main control panel. Yanika and Sam stood behind him, pulling piles upon piles of the evidence they found from their bags and even their pockets.

"You know how to work this?" asked Yanika.

"Only a guess. I used some of their equipment in training," said Eric. "What should I say?"

"Read the reports," said Walter. "Ramble. Anything, just make it sound good. We need everyone to turn on this government."

"This is becoming a civil war," Eric muttered as he flipped some switches.

"It already was," said Yanika. "They were killing us long before now. We just weren't dying fast enough for them I guess."

The mic let out a harsh reverb sound. Yanika cringed.

Fumbling through the papers, he gave a broken announcement over the air. Any radio that was receiving would hear it. There wasn't much for radio at the Outer Rim, but the main thing was that it reached the residents of the capitol and some of the forces.

"I know you don't know me," he finished. "But if you believe anything, believe what is happening right now is wrong. Innocent people are getting slaughtered. The government is no longer your friend. But there are those out there who are. Your neighbors. Your family. A group of us have infiltrated to help, but it won't be enough until everyone... everyone realizes what's going on." Eric turned off the mic, sighed, and then shook his head. "That sounded terrible."

Yanika placed a hand on his shoulder. "You did the best you could do."

"Is it going to be enough though?"

"Who cares," said Sam. "We can't mope around about it now. Let's get out there and do something."

Yanika turned towards her, a bit surprised. "What are you suggesting?"

"We get out there and knock a few more heads together. Didn't you see us?" She patted her chest. "I got shot at least five times and didn't die."

Walter slipped into the room and placed a hand on her shoulder. "Don't push it. We are far more powerful than the basics of zombies. But there is no true immortality."

"We still are better at taking on those idiots than anyone else."

Walter sighed. "That is true. If you are insistent, I will have your back."

Eric looked up at Yanika.

She nodded. "I'm in."

There was a divide from the women to the men. Sam and Yanika were decided, but it seemed Eric was hesitant, and Walter was nearly reluctant. It seemed the only reason he agreed was because that's what Sam wanted to do.

They piled out of the room and headed out of the building. The man she passed earlier was still behind the desk, and eyed them as they left. He didn't say anything, and she didn't stop, unsure what she'd say if she did.

It was easy to find the fight, as all they had to do was follow the gunfire. The once perfect untouched streets were caked in blood and bodies. Guards. Civilians. Zombies. The four of them worked as a team, and they started sweeping away the corruption, watching as one by one, more forces joined their side.

HECTOR'S JOURNAL

January 8th, 2026

I never thought I would be comfortable being around people again, but I now have renewed hope. Purpose. Lisa is a kind soul. I feel warmth when she's around and her presence comforts.

Mariah and Bruno have settled in. Having medical assistance and an extra set of hands has been a great benefit. Mariah feels like a protective aunt or mother, even to me. Bruno feels like a son to me. Like the youngest of a family. Flint is, without a doubt, the wild older child of this group, yet very beneficial. He has an eye for finding supplies. He takes risks I wish he wouldn't, but every time it has paid off.

Chapter 34

Getting across to the capitol building wasn't hard as Liatris's forces had cleared a pretty wide path. Lisa kept Hector at her back. He almost died before and he looked frailer now that he had. She didn't know if he could take another injury.

Their path was one of pure carnage. Human bodies torn to shreds, but none of them were turning. The capitol building was large, but the entry was crowded by corpses of both kinds.

She recognized Liatris's forces as they turned towards them. She got some curious glances before everyone's attention was changed towards the upstairs where a volley of gunfire exploded. There were long staircases upwards, decorated with carved marble that was now riddled with bullet holes.

Doors from the main lobby area on this floor were either broken open or laying smashed on the floor. Many of them had piles of bodies around them. Lights were flickering from the chandeliers above.

In the mix there were sounds of static broken by a familiar voice. "I know you don't know me. But if you believe anything, believe what is happening right now is wrong."

Hector came up behind her. "They did it," he muttered.

"That's Eric?" asked Lisa.

"Yes. I recognize the inflection of his voice."

Another wave of gunfire made them both jolt. It sounded like ten maybe twenty or more guns all being shot at once from one of the floors above.

"We better move," said Hector.

Lisa put a hand on his chest, putting herself in front. Somehow, she could feel his disklike for this plan. It was like she knew how he looked, and it made her tense. Maybe she was imagining things.

She quickly dropped to a body near the stairs and pulled the rifle off of him. The magazine was nearly empty, but it had to do. There was pressure weighing down on her. The need to be armed and ready immediately. She didn't even bother finding another magazine. It seemed too risky.

"Upstairs," she said aloud, mostly to herself. She listened to make sure Hector was following, but paused when she heard more footsteps.

Turning, she spotted a few zombies also heading in the same direction. Hector moved close, just one step behind her. She hurried on, returning focus to the sound upstairs. They wove up the staircases, the incline enough to make her pant. Her ribs burned. The stabbing pain wrapped around her.

She took the last step and rounded the staircase to the large open spot. A stray bullet flew overhead. She ducked, pulling up the rifle. "Hector, stay back!"

There was sudden movement all around her. Jim, Bruno, and Mariah in a corner being guarded by a meat wall of zombies. Jim looked at her, shocked, but the expression quickly fled. His shoulders dropped.

She kept alert, not looking at them long. Liatris was here dead center. He cast a quick glance their way. His forces, much fewer in numbers than before, were all around him, pushing to one central door. From the piles of bodies this seemed to be the place. This was their goal. She pushed forward, crouched and keeping low.

Liatris looked from her to Hector, following behind. "I see you survived."

"Yes. Thank you, Liatris."

Liatris grunted.

Jim broke free from the group, rushing to her side. "Lisa, you're alright."

"What's going on here?" Lisa ducked again. This room was huge, and they were easily twenty feet or more from the door with a wall of military there with riot shields.

There wasn't time for an answer. Bullets collied with the zombies in front as they made the final push. She got lower, as did Hector and Jim. They backed away, ducking behind the zombies for cover.

Bullets hit the wall behind them. Dust flying from drywall. Bits of stone getting thrown into the air. More of the guards were falling. One. Two. Three. More bodies. Blood. A bullet struck the floor next to her.

The sound of bullets grew quieter and quieter until there was just one left— A gargled scream cut it off.

"Move in!" Liatris shouted.

Lisa stood in time to see the door go down. They moved into the room. Liatris had six zombies still standing. Lisa, Hector, and Jim quickly followed. Mariah and Bruno hot on their heels.

Loud shouts erupted as they entered a room of eight people. Two women and six men. Two of those men were elderly gentlemen in fine suits, one was a tanned skin man that looked a lot like Bruno. The last was a man well decorated with medals all over his uniform.

"Hammer!" Liatris screamed.

"How dare—"

Liatris leapt the expanse of the room, grabbed Hammer by his jacket using all four arms and hoisting him off the ground. "Finally. After all this time."

"You're... that scientist," Hammer growled.

"Dad!" Bruno screamed.

The man that looked like him turned their way. There was a look of recognition in his eyes.

Bruno burst from the back of the group and threw himself between this man and the zombies. "Don't hurt him. He's my papa."

"B— Bruno?"

There was chaos. Too much to follow. The zombies moved away from Bruno and backed all the rest of these well-dressed people into the corner. One pulled a revolver, leading to instant death as a zombie swung, ripping the man's throat out.

"How does it look?" Liatris screamed. "How do you like your creations now?"

"You wouldn't have existed without me."

"I would have been alive!" Liatris threw the man back.

Hammer's body collied with a coffee table and shattered it.

She heard another scream. One of the other officials fell. Mariah backed towards Bruno. The pair pushed Bruno's father into the corner, furthest away from the fight.

Jim came up and flanked Hector with her. Both armed. Both targeting the last few in the room. A woman in a long dress tried to run. A zombie grabbed her and threw her back. She hit the wall with enough force her body cracked and she fell in a heap.

One by one the officials fell, leaving Bruno's father safely tucked away, and Hammer.

"I made a new world. A better one," Hammer screamed.

"Fuck you!" Liatris lifted him again and threw him to the side.

This time Hammer's body collided with the wall. He let out a wet gargled sound. Without missing a beat, as he fell, he drew a pistol and fired.

Liatris was moving towards him at the same time. The bullet

struck with Liatris's temple. The four-armed hulk was knocked back. Stumbling.

Lisa didn't wait so see what would happen next. She pulled the rifle up and let loose three rounds until the mag ran out. Two shots hit the wall, the recoil knocking her off balance. The last connected right to the gut.

"No!" Liatris staggered. "He's mine."

"Don't get yourself killed!" Hector shouted. "You have something to live for now!"

Liatris froze. Hammer raised his gun again. Another bang rang out in the space. Not from Lisa. Not from Jim. She turned. Bruno's father was standing, smoking gun in hand.

Lisa whipped back around. The bullet had connected. Right to the chest. Hammer was limp.

"How— how dare you!" Liatris screamed.

All the zombies turned towards the trio in the corner.

"Don't hurt them!" Bruno shouted.

Hector walked forward, casually. His steps even. He strode to Liatris's side. "It's over old friend. You completed your goal."

"I... I..." All of Liatris's hands shook.

"Doesn't matter who got the kill shot. You were the one who made this happen." He emphasized you.

There was a tense moment in the room. Silent. So silent. No gunfire around them. No screams. Just them. Alive. Her body warmed and tingled, despite the aches and pain. There was a little rush that went from her toes to her head. It wasn't just a fight. It was to end a war that started. To free the humans. To give them a better life. By doing that she opened herself up to that. A better life.

Jim came up behind her and wrapped his arms around her. "I'm so glad you're alive."

"Is that really you, Bruno?"

Lisa lifted her head, glancing at Bruno and his father.

Bruno nodded. "Yeah. Yeah, it's me."

"But how? How did you survive?"

Bruno pointed out the rest of them. Mariah, Lisa, Jim, and Hector. "I've been with them. They've kept me safe."

There was shock on his father's face. He was drenched in sweat. Splattered in blood.

"I've dreamed of this moment my whole life since that day," Liatris mumbled.

"And this is that day," said Hector. "You instigated this. And... You were right."

Liatris jerked his head up, looking Hector dead in the eye.

Hector just nodded to him and then returned to Lisa's side. "How are you doing?"

"Just fine with a few days of uninterrupted rest. Do... Do you think that will be possible?"

"I think so," said Hector. "I think there's a good chance that we can all finally rest."

HECTOR'S JOURNAL

December 16th, 2052

We have begun rebuilding, repairing, and recovering. It did not get past me that the fear of zombies for many people has been alleviated due to their encounter with the full force of what corrupt human officials were capable of. I have also been made aware of the trust they have put into Liatris and I, and our ability to control the undead.

Chapter 35

Five weeks later since the war of Haven and things were finally getting put back together. Liatris's zombies were helping families rebuild, but there was much to discuss.

The first meeting of the Council of Haven had just finished. Officials elected. Positions were offered to a few people, some declined, others accepted. The final council was made up of Ernando Migel, Bruno's father, Hector, Lisa, and Jim. There would be elections for more later.

The group adjourned to a patio outside of the Capitol building. Bullet holes and broken windows remained to remind them of what happened. Otherwise, the bodies and blood had been cleaned and a nice seating area was made out here.

There were five round metal tables with chairs around them on this red brick patio. Three large flowerpots had been brought here and planted. The flowers were wilted, but still lovely. The crisp air of fall nipped at Lisa's skin. She had time to rest. Time to heal. No longer did every breath bring waves of pain.

The sky above was clear and blue, and the rays of sun warm on her face. She wore a soft long sleeved shirt today that was clean. Real clean with detergent that made it smell like lavender. She had a hot cup of tea steaming in front of her that Hector had made.

Jim sat across from her wearing a green polo. It was tight across his muscled body. He was clean shaven, with a new haircut. Mariah sat between them in a new white doctor's coat.

"Why do you look so nervous?" Lisa asked Mariah.

"I'm not sure I'm ready for this task," said Mariah.

"You're the perfect person for it," said Jim.

It was decided that Mariah would be the director of medicine in charge of getting a hospital up and running in Haven with the plan to expand and have clinics throughout Haven. Liatris's forces had all gathered here and they were working on getting her staff. The zombies would easily be able to get all the medical supplies out of the city safely.

"I've never had this much responsibility," said Mariah.

Lisa took a sip of her tea and then smiled. "Like Jim said, you're the perfect person for this."

"I get it," said Jim. "I'm not ready for this either."

Jim was elected head of construction. It was a working title. He had originally helped build this place, now he was back, tasked with repairs and building it better. Making an infrastructure happy and safe for the inhabitants, outside refugees, and for coming generations. He too would be getting his workforce from Liatris.

Ernando Migel headed their way with Bruno at his side.

Jim waved them over. "Pull up a chair."

"Thank you," said Ernando. He pulled up next to Jim and Bruno stuck a chair in beside him. "And thank you all for protecting my son."

Bruno was cleaned up, his hair trimmed, but still long. He looked healthier and happier. There was still an air of hesitance about him. Nervousness.

"What are you going to do?" asked Lisa.

Bruno glanced at his dad a moment. "Well... I'm going to learn how to be an official."

Ernando smiled. "But we'll take our time. It's been years and... I'm looking forward to catching up. Oh." He turned to Lisa. "I heard you are going to live in the blue cottage on the edge of town."

Lisa felt her whole body relax and the warmth of the sun take her. "Yeah. It's a nice place."

"I'm very glad."

There was a shadow over it all. The reason houses were available was because of all the corrupt officials that died. The mass loss of life was more than she could fathom, but she was looking forward now, not back. It would be a terrible moment in everyone's history, but she knew it was opening the way for a great future. One that she never could have imagined.

Lisa was simply a council member. One who would help make decisions for the better of Haven, but that was all. She didn't want any more responsibility that that. She would be a planner. Decision maker. A guide, one could say, for the future. Jim and Mariah would have a lot more on their plates. But there wasn't anyone else more fitting for the jobs.

"We're getting a dog," Bruno blurted out.

"Really?" asked Lisa.

Ernando reached out and clapped Bruno on the shoulder. "It'll take a little to find one. Even harder to tame it. But it'll be a good responsibility. I'm... I'm just sorry it took until now. I should have gotten you a dog many years ago."

"I wasn't ready then," said Bruno. He chuckled. "Shit, I'm getting to be an old man myself and I'm still not sure I'm ready."

The group laughed.

Mariah reached across the table and patted his hand. "Sweetie, you're ready. It's time you get a chance to live your life. It's never too late."

"Thanks, Mariah. I'm going to name him Spot."

Lisa smiled. "I think that's a perfect name."

They talked a while longer like a family gathered at the dinner table. When Hector finally joined them there were some pleasantries before they all departed.

Lisa, Jim, and Hector all walked to the edge of the city together to their new home. It was a two-story cottage style with blue siding and white shutters. It needed repair, but Jim had already fixed up so much. The concrete driveway was turned into a large patio. Jim had already built them a gazebo.

Hector had spent some of his time going into the cities. Despite having mutated back to almost totally human, he still had control over the lesser zombies. To distinguish things further, those lesser creatures were now being called parasites as many people now thought of zombies as friends. It differentiated the two.

Hector had gathered a lot of things for their new home. They had a patio set and flowerpots around ready for her to plant them.

Hector held the door open for them. She entered a warm homey space. They had furniture, plumbing, and electricity. It wasn't perfect, but it was a mansion compared to the places they lived.

She had decorations now. A bookcase. Before a brick hearth they had a table set up for card games. This was hers. This was her home.

Jim came up behind her and wrapped his arms around her. "You know how sexy you are?"

She blushed.

Hector moved towards her. It was shocking to see a man's emotive face where his blank expression used to be. The twinkle in his eyes was now highlighted by lashes and the creases around his eyes. He reached up, placing a hand on her cheek. He felt warm. His hands were normal. Fingers a little longer than Jim's but his skin was a pink color. His fingernails were nicely rounded.

He didn't wait, stepping in and claiming a kiss. It felt passionate.

Desperate like always. In a way it felt like the kiss of a man who was worried this may be the last kiss he experiences in his life.

She placed her hand on top of Jim's and with her other she reached up and laced it though Hector's hair. It was silver and short as he had slowly been growing it. Liatris's serum caused a significant reversal in Hector's mutation.

Despite the change in his physical appearance, he remained as strong as before. He breathed more. Now and then she heard the flicker of a heartbeat. But in the end, he was still an immortal Zombie Lord. He could still command any of the later turned.

As his lips tangled with hers, she felt Jim's hot breath on her neck before his lips met her skin. Chills ran down her body as she felt each muscle from head to toe unwind and relax. She hadn't had back pain in days. Her ribs felt fully healed.

Hector broke contact, pulling back just enough they could look into each other's eyes. "I love you," he whispered.

"I love you too."

Jim moved to the base of her neck. "Don't forget me," he breathed.

"Never."

Hector caressed her face again. "I never thought this day would come. Not like this."

"Humph." Jim paused. "Me too." He ran his tongue up the base of her neck. "What do you want to do?" he growled.

"Can..." She blushed and looked away from the pair. Asking for what she really wanted was embarrassing, and she didn't know why. They had been intimate in every way already. "Can you... take me from behind again?" She slowly glanced up at Hector.

He smiled, this time the emotion spreading to his whole face. Instead of guessing his expression, it was there, right in front of her. Fiery with deep passion. Possessive and fierce. "Any way you want, my love."

"I'll take you from the front," Jim growled. He was dominating. But she felt as if she had the power to say no at any time. Like he was in charge, but she was in control. It was an intoxicating mix of feeling safe in these boundaries and being totally turned on by them.

It hadn't been long, but they both became dominating males, working together as a pair, sharing power and her.

Jim gripped the bottom of her shirt and pulled it up over her head. She felt Hector's hands behind her, unhooking her bra. They had her sandwiched. Like two different but overwhelming elements. Hot and cold. Night and day.

Hector took her pants. She'd seen him fumble a little before, adjusting to the new size of his hands. This time he was like a master seamster and worked her pants clean off before she had time to react.

Jim laced a finger in her panties on one side as Hector did the other. They pulled them down, each running their hands down her legs in the process. She shivered. Not that it mattered before, but since having a home she was able to shave, which made her feel sexier. More sensual. Somehow, this made it even more pleasurable.

Jim turned her to face him and pulled her over to the couch. His disrobing was quick, but she noticed he took extra time to flex and roll his shoulders as he did so. He sat on the couch, length hard, erect, and ready.

He waved his hands towards it. "Have a seat," he growled.

For a moment she froze. Her insides getting hot. Moisture growing from that low, primal sound he made. The warm light of the setting sun shone in through the windows. It cast a shadow on his grin.

He patted the couch on either side of his lap. "Put your knees here." He waved to his length. "And I want the rest of you here."

She blushed more, this time feeling the heat wrap around her and travel down her body. Lisa stepped closer, trying to figure out how she was supposed to position herself. Jim didn't need her to figure it out as he took her and guided her step by step until one knee was on the couch, her other above there, and her hot wet center making a sheath for his length.

Hector slid up behind her. He had undressed as well, and his length brushed up against her.

Jim supported her again and kept direct eye contact the whole time. "Relax."

Lisa took a breath as Jim started to lower her. His tip slowly slid into her. Hector pressed against the tighter space, fighting more to make entry. She breathed again. It was the mix of apprehension and carnal desire that made each breath shaky.

Hector pushed in. Just the tip. The feeling of getting stuffed full from the inside began. The slight burning. Her body taking them inch by inch. Hector's length hadn't changed.

They continued to lower her, making her take more and more of them. She held onto Jim's shoulder. Breathing. Eyes closed. Even after being together multiple times, still wondering if she could really take them both.

Jim continued until he reached her core. The pair stopped at that point. Hector ran his hands across her back and to her shoulders. A silent reminder to relax and relish in the sensation.

They started moving, but this time opposite. When Jim would raise her, Hector would push in. Then the opposite. Finding a way to make a whole new sensation. She gasped, and then tried to hush herself.

"We're home," Hector whispered. "There's no need to be silent."

Jim pushed in and she let out a loud gasp.

"Good girl."

Her whole body heated. He growled as he spoke. It was deep. Sexy. Commanding. So many things that turned her insides to liquid.

She didn't hold back. Moaning with every stroke. Jim would growl. He kept a tight gasp on her hips. Even when her body felt like a noodle, he kept her in rhythm with them.

Hector moaned. His hands wrapped around her shoulders.

They continued, moving faster and faster. She started sputtering as she moaned. Eyes open. Eyes closed. Spots dancing in front of her. Her core getting tighter. Hotter. Wetter. Their lengths completely filling her. Stuffing her. Over and over. In and out. Rubbing against her insides.

She twitched. Spasmed. Getting tighter and tighter. Making her feel over full. Too full. Like there wasn't enough room for them both inside of her. Yet it drove her wild.

They were getting larger inside of her. Throbbing. It was overwhelming. They thrust harder. Faster. Burying themselves deeper.

"I'm... I'm..."

"Cum for me baby," Jim growled. He slammed her down on him.

Hector thrust inwards. They both filled her. She screamed. Exploding. Pulsating. Chills and shivers jolting over every nerve ending.

The pair let loose, exploding inside of her. The final stretch of the small space. Wet. Thick. She gasped and stopped breathing. Everything too tight. So pleasurable. Her body was rigid. Her insides continued to tense. Pulse. Grip and relax. All the liquids stirred together and dripping from her. Down her leg. Hot and sticky.

"Breath," said Hector. He whispered in her ear. Cradled her body.

Jim reached up and pulled her to his chest. Hector's hands remained on her. The pair cradled her until her body went limp with a loud gasp.

She quaked in their grasp, continuing to twitch. They remained inside of her. On occasion one or the other would throb and it made her spasm again.

"Want to go again?" asked Jim.

There was a split second of panic before Hector's voice chimed in.

"No. We need to have supper and get cleaned up. We all need to be up early tomorrow."

Jim sighed. "I suppose you're right. I'll take care of Lisa if you want to start on dinner."

"I'll start on a bath first." He leaned in closer and whispered in her ear. "You got us all dirty."

She spasmed again and their lengths throbbed in response.

Jim giggled.

Hector slowly pulled free of her. She gasped as the pressure lessened. Jim kept holding her. All the while she listened as Hector moved around the house and then she heard the water running in the bathroom.

"You going to be okay?" asked Jim.

She nodded against his chest. For a while she relished in this. Finally, she felt she could relax. They were safe. This home wasn't going to be taken away. Her friends were safe. She had a family. In reality, she now had more than she did before the zombie outbreak. She had what she didn't realize was what she truly wanted all along.

HECTOR'S JOURNAL

February 14th, 2053

    As everything falls into place, I find myself awestruck. I spent the greater part of my younger years as a scientist. My mutated years I continued to do the same. Now, I'm a governor for Haven. I have a family. I have a home. This brings me more of a sense of accomplishment than any research breakthrough ever has.

    I plan to take my duties very seriously, but I want to dote on Lisa as well. I've made a few trips to the city for things she would like. I'm hoping to surprise her for her birthday. Jim, Mariah, and Bruno are also involved. This should be a great party.

Chapter 36

Emily stretched. She slept in a plush bed overnight. They had to push two king beds together in what was a living room to fit both her and Liatris. She rolled over facing the large man.

His eyes were just cracking open in response to the rising sun. He glanced at her and smiled. "How is my queen this morning?"

"Wonderful." She propped herself up on an elbow and ran a finger down his chest.

Liatris reached over and ran a hand across her arm. His touch no longer felt cold because she too was cold now. A pair of undead. But that didn't lessen the sensation. Chills still tickled across her skin.

He leaned in, placing a soft kiss on her lips. As he pulled away there was a moment she remained still, relishing in it, before taking his head and pulling him back to her. Their lips tangled together. It wasn't the unsure kiss of a new couple they had before. This was passion. Love. The comfort of having each other and knowing that nothing would break them apart.

"Make love to me," Emily moaned.

Liatris rolled on top of her. His length again going all the way up along her abdomen. "Are you sure?"

"I took you just fine last time."

She grinned which prompted Liatris to smile. He backed away, scooting down so he could position his tip. Emily felt hot and damp already. This hulk of a man was attractive, handsome, and alluring. His body. His eyes. Her body tingled from his touch.

His length flared at the tip. He pushed into her hot center. His tip stretching her until it popped inside.

Emily threw her head back and moaned. Liatris paused a moment, not saying a word, before he pushed onwards. One inch. Two inches. Deeper inside of her.

Her body took him. Something about the mutation made her perfect for his length. Her thin frame made it easy to see just where he was in her body as it made a soft bulge in her belly.

He stroked in and out of her, taking each inch gently. Slowly.

Relishing each moment. Like he was savoring her. It drove her wild. She wanted it fast. Hard. But his motions drew out each moment, making it more intense. It made her want to beg.

She arched her back, trying to get him to push deeper. The concern on his face faded away, replaced by a soft twinkle in his eyes and a grin. He quickened his pace, making her moan and whimper. She let him have command this time. Although she loved being dominant, she also liked this. Liked having him take control. Liked to just lay there and relish in the pleasure he invoked.

He moved faster and faster. His length flossing her insides. Pleasure popped and pulsed inside of her. Tingles in her hands. Toes. Legs. Breasts. She arched her back again, letting him in as deep as he could. Letting her changed body take him. Knowing she was the only being that could do this even more intimately.

They rocked together. Bodies meshed. Both making soft sounds of pleasure. Being a new creature, she noticed she didn't tire. She didn't sweat. She had the endurance to keep going. So did he. And he was using it.

Minutes gave way to nearly an hour of him making love to her. Edging her. Pushing her almost to orgasm before slowing again, only to rebuild the tension. Over and over. Her insides were ruined. Her core spasming, but not able to fully finish.

He had control. With it he waited. Made her beg. Made her plead for release. Finally, with a grin, he thrust harder and faster, keeping a rhythm that made her scream. She grabbed his back, pulling him down to her. She thrashed and then suddenly they exploded. His seed spilled into her as she screamed again. Her insides pulsed. Her body shook. Electrical sparks danced across her body. It rendered her to putty, laying in bed, unable to move, but able to feel every pleasurable jolt in her body.

They laid there together a while, but if they stayed any longer, they would be late.

After getting dressed they headed out to meet Hector at the Capitol building. She opted for a lacy red dress. Liatris had several altered shirts made to accommodate his arms. They fit him nicely. Emily sucked in the smell of the fresh air, forgetting to exhale. She was becoming accustomed to being undead. Every day she woke up without pain. Without fatigue no matter how little or much sleep she got. Some nights they just stayed up watching the stars.

The city was cleaned up nicely and the stroll across the central park and over the red brick paths were pleasant. They met them at what was becoming their most common meeting place. The large patio outside the capitol building had cast iron chairs and tables and now a few planters with small wild flowers in them that hung on the metal fence surrounding most of it.

Jim looked up from Lisa and smiled. "Emily, you're looking good." He spoke in a soft way. He was happy for her, and his tone reflected it.

"You too," she said with a smile. "You all look good. Even you Lisa. You look healthier."

"Thank you," said Lisa. "Rest has made a big difference."

Hector walked up to Liatris, and they shook hands. "It's like old times," said Hector.

"New times," Liatris corrected.

Hector waved to the seating outside the building. "I have tea made. Would you like some?"

Liatris held up a hand. "No, but thank you. I wanted to talk to you about your proposal."

The council offered Liatris a position to be the head of a group designed to produce his serum with Hector in order to continue to turn the parasites to zombies.

"What have you decided?" asked Hector.

"I decline," said Liatris as he slid down onto a chair.

Hector pulled back. "But why? Your research is needed."

"I know, but I have a counter proposal. We've thought a lot about this." Liatris waved a hand towards Emily.

She placed her hand in his and elegantly slid into the chair next to them.

Lisa glanced at Hector and Jim. There was a look of confusion among them, but it was peaceful. Emily remembered the first time she met Hector. There was so much negative energy then. Now it was just friends.

"I want to put Elric up for election."

"Elric, really? Do you think he has what it takes?" Hector sat down and took a cup of tea Lisa had poured for him.

Liatris nodded. "He has been producing my serum for years. At this point he knows it better than I. In addition, I have something else I want to do."

"What would that be?"

Liatris laced his fingers together. "An academy, but not just a learning school. I've thought hard on this." He glanced at Emily and smiled.

It warmed her. There was no ceremony, but she considered him her husband. They were a mated pair. King and Queen as he put it.

Hector took another sip of tea. "Interesting. Please, elaborate."

"I want to train up a... task force you could say. There are resources we could use all over the world. I would like to train troops to be able to handle things like recovery missions. A..." He growled. "I hate this word. A military force that could keep the parasites at bay. Maybe even eliminate them eventually." He hung his head.

Emily tensed, knowing where he was going next. They talked about it several times. One of his deepest worries. A valid one.

"You and I have researched the mutations of this virus for years now," said Liatris. "I'm worried about further mutation."

Hector pulled back. He paused a moment before setting his cup down. "I hate to think of such thing but... it is probable."

"My thoughts exactly. We're rebuilding a sanctuary here, but the forces here are gone. I have my troops, but with what we're planning my forces are far too scattered. Really, there's nothing set up in case the parasites rush this place."

Out of the corner of her eye Emily caught Lisa shiver.

A military force?" asked Jim. "Are we sure after everything that's happened, we want to implement something that extreme now?"

"It won't just be military," said Liatris. "It would be a... college of sorts. Military, yes. But also, sciences to teach a new generation about the zombie mutations." He looked directly at Hector. "Two or three people cannot keep up with demand. I was constantly out of my serum. It just takes too long to produce." His gaze traveled over to Jim. "Trades would also be good. We have a wind farm and hydroelectric dam to maintain. I can take an educated guess that there's few that know anything about these."

Hector ran a knuckle across his chin. "Valid point. Even classes on animal management and crops would be good. We need to create an efficient sustainable food source if we are to survive."

"Exactly. I think an academy would accomplish this. I'm..." He rolled his eyes and sighed. "I'm trying to learn to think to the future and outside of my own goals."

Hector grinned. "I think you have a good idea. What if we propose having you and Emily elected as our heads of education?"

Emily shook her head. "No thanks. Liatris can have that title. I'll be a principal or something."

Jim laughed.

Huffing, Emily crossed her arms. "What's your problem."

"I'm just imaging you trying to be a principal of a bunch of college kids. You hate kids."

Emily rolled her eyes. "They're basically adults. Fine. Maybe I'll do security."

There was laughter around them. Emily spent so much time alone. A loner. Hungry. Lost. Dying inside. She didn't know at the time this is what she wanted. Friends. Family. Peace. At first, getting doted on by Liatris was what she thought she wanted. Living as a queen with all her needs met. But this... This was the final thing she needed. Community.

They chatted longer, but it was decided. Liatris was going to start an academy. They were going to usher the new generation into this new world.

HECTOR'S JOURNAL

June 23rd, 2053

I am excited once again to record good news into this journal. Mariah has gotten a hospital up and running along with the beginning processes of getting clinics set up around Haven. She has named it Flint Hospital. I feel it's a wonderful tribute.

In addition, Lisa has been getting sick every morning now for the past three weeks. I have my suspicions what this could be, but we're waiting to find out for sure. I'm both incredibly excited and terrified.

Chapter 37

Lisa was out at dusk walking with Jim, Hector, Liatris, and Emily. Walter had called on them and they were to meet at dusk. Lisa was confused, but not afraid. She was confident in herself and in those around her.

They all met at the gates of Haven. She hadn't seen the four of them since before the final war. Hector had, but hadn't said much about it except they were doing well.

Lisa stopped when the four turned to greet them. They were pale, even Yanika. All four of them had blue glowing eyes, but Sam's was the most pronounced of the group.

Liatris spoke first. "Walter, it has been some time." The large man stiffened.

There was more tension here than she expected.

"I see the serums you stole have worked well for you."

"Stole?" said Lisa.

Hector turned and whispered to her. "Walter stole a serum from me and Liatris and injected himself with both."

Lisa shivered.

"We wanted to say our goodbyes," said Yanika.

Despite being pale and still having her eye patch she looked stronger somehow.

"You're not going to stay?" asked Hector.

Walter raised his head. Nothing had changed with him. He was still standing as he was looking down on all of them. Like they were lesser. "We do not fit in here. We plan to travel and find a place to call our own."

"There is plenty of room here," said Jim. "You guys don't have to leave." He addressed all of them, but was more focused on Yanika.

"Jim," Yanika said sweetly, "Walter is right. We are not human anymore nor are we zombies. And the light... well... there's too much of it here."

"If you're not zombies then what are you?" asked Liatris. His tone was harsh.

Walter flashed his teeth, showing off his fangs. "I think the age old term vampire would be more fitting."

Sam glanced at him and flashed a pair of fangs of her own.

Liatris gave them a sharp nod. "Then I think parting ways would be best for all of is."

"What about your Lady Victoria?" asked Hector.

"She is no longer my Lady." He waved a hand in the air. "She's already moved on. Looking, I guess, for the same thing. A place of her own."

Hector nodded. "Then this is goodbye."

Lisa blinked a few times, processing. There were four factions now. Humans, Zombies, Parasites, and now Vampires.

HECTOR'S JOURNAL

April 16th, 2066

    With new information I have new fears for the future of Haven and humanity. Liatris Academy is behind schedule and there are reports coming in of new mutations. The very thing we all feared the most.

    There has been some stirring in the north. Rumors of ravenous vampires are spreading. No one has been able to reach Walter in some time. Walter has created his own following of masters under him, calling him their Vampire Lord.

    Victoria is passive out in Vegas, but is interested in sending her daughter to Liatris Academy. I'm not sure how others will react. There are many uncertainties coming and I'm not sure we're ready to handle them.

www.ingramcontent.com/pod-product-compliance
Lightning Source LLC
Chambersburg PA
CBHW071646260626
47170CB00001B/256